Also by Virginia DeBerry and Donna Grant

What Doesn't Kill You

Gotta Keep on Tryin'

Better Than I Know Myself

Far from the Tree

Tryin' to Sleep in the Bed You Made

Exposures

UPTOWN

Virginia DeBerry and Donna Grant

A Touchstone Book
Published by Simon & Schuster
New York London Toronto Sydney

TOUCHSTONE
A Division of Simon & Schuster, Inc.
1230 Avenue of the Americas
New York, NY 10020

This book is a work of fiction. Names, characters, places, and incidents either are products of the author's imagination or are used fictitiously. Any resemblance to actual events or locales or persons, living or dead, is entirely coincidental.

First Touchstone trade paperback edition March 2010

For information about special discounts for bulk purchases, please contact Simon & Schuster Special Sales at 1-866-506-1949 or business@simonandschuster.com.

The Simon & Schuster Speakers Bureau can bring authors to your live event. For more information or to book an event contact the Simon & Schuster Speakers Bureau at 1-866-248-3049 or visit our website at www.simonspeakers.com.

Designed by Aline Pace

Manufactured in the United States of America

10 9 8 7 6 5 4 3 2 1

Library of Congress Cataloging-in-Publication Data

DeBerry, Virginia.
Uptown / by Virginia DeBerry and Donna Grant.
p. cm.
"A Touchstone Book."
Summary: Uptown dives into the high-rolling world of Manhattan real estate. When money, power, and respect are at stake, a Harlem family's bonds are strained to the breaking point.
1. Harlem (New York, N.Y.)—Fiction. 2. Real estate development—New York (State)—New York—Fiction. 3. African Americans—Fiction. 4. Domestic fiction. I. Grant, Donna. II. Title.
PS3554.E17615U68 2010
813'.54—dc22 2009051122

ISBN 978-1-4391-3776-5
ISBN 978-1-4391-4932-4 (ebook)

For all those who need to
open the box again

Acknowledgments

We gratefully acknowledge:

Hiram L. Bell III, thank you, always and forever.—DG

Gloria Hammond Frye, Juanita Cameron DeBerry, and the late John L. DeBerry II for the right stuff.

Alexis, Lauren, and Jordan, in the years I have done this, you all have gone from training wheels to driver's licenses, nursery school to college, allowances to pay checks. I am proud of you and proud to be your Auntie VA.—VDB

Brian, Christine, and Arielle, the future—which becomes more present with every book.—DG

John L. DeBerry III and Valerie DeBerry, my brother and sister, for their unconditional love and support as I meander along the road less traveled.—VDB

"Seamus" you know all the reasons.—VDB

The good Dr. V for being here, there and everywhere. —VDB

JK for presence and possibility. For laughs and encouragement when the going got rough.—VDB

Our ART (Advance Reading Team): Gloria Frye, Juanita DeBerry, Keryl McCord, Valerie DeBerry, and Liz Opacity for making time in your lives to read and give us thoughtful and helpful feedback and keeping us mindful of why we do this.

Tyrha Lindsey, Tracey Kemble, and Cheryl Jenkins for keeping 4 Colored Girls Productions moving forward when we disappear into the writing cave.

Our Host With the Most—your friendship and unfailing generosity is constant and unmatched. Outstanding!

Vendetta Swain and Dorian Swain of inViting Solutions, and your Hospitality Team—your creativity and flair help make our parties so memorable.

Stuart Smith for knowing we were hungry and delivering doro wat and special tibs when the deadline loomed large and we couldn't make it to Makeda for gomen therapy.

Victoria Sanders, our agent, for her helpful, hopeful, and wise guidance, her positive energy, steadfast support—above and beyond the call of duty. You are advocate, ally, and friend. Thank you.

Our editor and champion, Sulay Hernandez, who uplifted and cheered us on throughout the writing process, and waited patiently for us to reach the finish line. Your praise humbles us.

And all of our friends and family members—you are too numerous to name individually—whose continued love and support is surely the grace of the Creator at work.

Prologue

. . . quite a coup for the family business—
turning Baltic Avenue into Park Place

Mid-2000s,
NEW YORK, NEW YORK

"We all ready to do this?" Dwight Dixon rubbed his palms together, already savoring how sweet this day would be. All the meetings and maneuvering, wooing the participants, dodging interference, glad-handing and greasing the wheels—it took him years to get here, and this was just the beginning, his initiation into a rarefied society. Glorious sunshine spilled over the morning and through the windows of The Dixon Group's midtown offices. Now it was 10:58 a.m., and he planned for his press conference to start precisely on time and run according to schedule like everything else about the project.

"No. We're sitting here waiting for lightning to strike." King Dixon sprawled in his son's desk chair, overwhelming it with his wide load, a silver-suited walrus at a glass-topped desk.

Everyone laughed, including Dwight, but not with his eyes.

"The lightning struck a few years back." Grace Kidder patted King's arm and stood in her red-soled skyscraper pumps. "And brought us all here together." She flipped her duckling-blond hair behind her shoulders, lips pursed in the insipid wince that passed for a smile. Dwight thought it made her look like a simple bitch, but he knew the only thing simple about her was her business instinct, simple like a killer shark.

On cue, Dwight's assistant, Madeline, whose high, wide forehead and overtweezed brows made her look perpetually stunned, opened the door and ushered the assembled participants toward the conference room. Dwight lagged behind, offered an arm to his aunt Forestina.

"Your mother would just be over the moon." Delicate and frothy, his mother's sister still maintained a party girl's good-hearted charm, pretty much the opposite of Dwight's mother, her battering ram of an older sister, at least the way Dwight remembered her. Whenever he needed a dose of unconditional gushing, Auntie Tina filled the bill. And since her late husband, Dr. Braithwaite, had been King's original real estate partner, she knew how far they had come and what it had taken to get to this moment. "I spoke to Avery yesterday . . . from Japan. I told her all about this."

Dwight let that bit of bubbling float over him, patted his aunt's hand. He and Avery had grown up right down the block—always together, hanging buddies and confidants, more like big brother and little sister than cousins. But there was no time to dwell on the past with his future blossoming before him. He left Forestina next to King, shook hands with his buildings manager, Eric Wallace, who looked awkward in his new blue suit, bought specially for the occasion, and took his place at the front of the parade where Madeline had saved his spot. Chivalry be damned, this was business. No way he was letting Grace enter that room ahead of him.

Through the glass door he checked out the rows of seated journalists, photographers, and the video cameras positioned along the wall. The room was SRO, just as he'd imagined in his wet dream. *Let's see King flap his lips about this.* As an infant, shortly after he had mastered *Dada,* Dwight learned to call his father *King,* just like everybody else. Harlemites, who knew King as a hustler, a businessman, a landlord, an associate, or a rival, still called Dwight *King Junior*, some out of respect, others meaning that he was a lightweight knockoff. Dwight despised the *Junior* thing. But his father's old cronies had been useful. Besides, they were dwindling fast—time keeps on slippin' slippin' slippin' into the future . . .

Dwight leveled his yellow paisley bow tie, walked briskly into the room, up to the front, like a man with no time to kill. Once flanked by his associates, including district representatives, Chamber of Commerce officials, and an influential pastor—he had hoped for the mayor, but got the no-go on this round—Dwight stepped to the mike.

"Today is a great day in Harlem." Ironic, since they were not actually in Harlem, but sixty blocks south, squarely midtown.

"Amen." "Long time comin'." "Speak, brother." Exclamations and applause erupted from community members peppered among the professional journalists. Dwight's wife, Renee, and daughter, Dominique, beamed in the first row. Renee looked sharp today. He had picked out the simple but elegant black, pin-dot suit so she looked the part of a Manhattan developer's wife, not like the weekend anchor on the *Boonie-ville News.*

"As a lifelong resident of this historic and proud community, I, along with my family, have continually sought opportunities to highlight and serve this precious Manhattan jewel. At its roots, I guess you can call this a family affair." Pinstripe suit tailored to skim his physique, gym-slim and hard without felon bulk, Dwight looked like one of *those* guys, either the power or the broker. The guy who makes things happen, works the room, gets results. He cultivated the image, knew people envied what they thought they saw, and the swag that came with the package. They just didn't know all the BS that accompanied the position, not that he was giving it up anytime soon. He'd been raised to be on top, his father never let him forget it. What else would he do?

"Today, The Dixon Group, is proud to announce a historic partnership, a Harlem Trust if you will, dedicated to bringing the luster back to an oft-neglected and maligned part of this city." One by one, Dwight highlighted the principals.

From their first meeting, years ago at an Ailey reception in D.C., he had courted Grace Kidder, daughter of Vance Kidder, founder of Kidder, Theismann, and the clown prince of Manhattan real estate until a stroke sidelined him. Grace was the understudy, waiting in the wings, and word on the street was that she was making a bid to step into Daddy's big shoes. So Dwight put his time and energy into wooing her to his project, appealing to her ego and ambition. He never brought up that they were on the same journey—to find their own place in the sun and outshine Big Daddys who cast giant shadows. All in all, it had taken less than a year to get Grace onboard—Vance, who was still chairman of the board, had been another story. In the beginning, he wanted nothing to do with a project without his name on it—the giant KT logo out front for everyone to see. Grace, who had by then been given her chance at running the company when it became clear to Vance that while the show must go on, he would never again be ringmaster, was on a singular quest. To replace the *heiress,* which always appeared after her name, with *mogul, tycoon, magnate*—she didn't care which.

And this was exactly the project she needed to make that happen. Always Daddy's girl, and a good student, Grace used many of the skills she had learned at her father's knee and made him see the wisdom of labeling such a speculative venture well above the traditional Ninety-sixth Street DMZ for a *native.* The prime location, bordering the fourth and final facet of New York's emerald, Central Park, and available at a significant discount to comparable acreage elsewhere on the island, was worth the gamble. On the upside, they would be the best, set the standard, and make gigabytes of money to boot. At worst, a failure would not tarnish the Kidder, Theismann brand.

St. John Talliwell, pronounced *sin gin,* like what you may do after too many Hendrick's martinis, represented Talliwell Hospitality International, the boutique hotelier, whose latest project, T^2-Abu Dhabi, had been dubbed one of the ten most soigné hotels in the world. T^2-Haarlem—they preferred the Dutch spelling—would be their first U.S. property. St. John had explained to Dwight in a stiff-lipped British accent that almost required subtitles that he favored exotic locales, and that Harlem, however it was spelled, was the only spot left in Manhattan at the crossroads of urbane sophistication and unbridled naturalism. Jolly good.

Bringing on the architect Cobb Rowan lent instant prestige to the project. He had been quoted publicly as saying he would never again work in New York, where developers were only interested in who could build the biggest phallus in the smallest space. Rowan, who always dressed in dazzling white, from his pearly, oval-rimmed glasses, to his white crocodile, T-strap shoes, required suitable vistas for people to appreciate his "environments." But this project had the lure of one of the world's most famous front lawns. He had to take the bait.

The intros made Dwight positively giddy. For decades King had pontificated about how 110th Street should be more than Manhattan's back alley, the place to stash the undesirables—a gas station, a correctional facility, folks with slim finances, few choices, and basic needs. But King became a skilled bottom-feeder, sucking up the properties that were no more than headaches, red ink, and liabilities for those who didn't have the patience to wait for a turnaround, or the stomach to start one, in what had, since the turn of the twentieth century, been strictly Brown Town. But even King didn't foresee $2 million penthouses rising in the footprint of the buildings he'd acquired. It took Dwight to make this more than Monopoly. He was on the verge of quite a coup for the family business—turning Baltic Avenue into Park Place.

Finally, Dwight moved beside the velvet-sheathed mystery that hovered on a Lucite base beside the podium. "Envisioned as the gateway to a revitalized uptown, Dixon Plaza will create thousands of much needed construction and permanent jobs and foster the climate of prosperity, dignity, and luxury that will ensure Harlem will assume it's place as the crown at the top of Manhattan." With a flourish, he revealed the big-wow architectural model. Cue the oohs, aahs, camera flashes, and applause. It had made him laugh when five-year-old Dominique told her friends about her daddy's new dollhouse. Quite the digs for corporate-counsel Barbie or hedge-fund Ken. For Dwight the complex was already real, actually surreal. Looking at it, he envisioned Maybachs and Bentleys pulling into the circular drive, leaving the well-heeled at the hotel and residential towers, or to browse the boutiques that would provide the toniest new commercial address in the city. The south side of the park had Bergdorf's and the Plaza. The revitalized Central Park North would have the thirty-five-story, limestone tri-towers of Dixon Plaza, the gleaming exclamation points at the apex of the park.

Press packets included elaborate renderings of Rowan's postmodern design, "Where a retro deco homage will enhance the relaxed glamour of the Twenty-first Century." Nine hundred thousand square feet of luxury surrounding the sanctuary of an inner court. Terraced setbacks would maximize exposure to the priceless work of human-engineered natural art, the dazzling park view. And there was the $1.3 billion budget, huge for any developer, record breaking for an African-American. Oh, yeah, Dwight liked to be on top.

There was no way to get through the program without including his father, so after the unveiling, Dwight brought King to the podium. For as much of a loudmouth as he was in private, King was not much for public speaking. Or did he just not like to be quoted? In any case he was content to sign the ceremonial hundred-year first lease for commercial space, the new home of The Dixon Group.

Dwight had barely finished the last syllable of *Now we'd be happy to take your questions* when Jasper Christmas lobbed the first one in his direction.

"Do you have a comment on Pastor Phillip Ewing's statement that . . ." Christmas flipped through his notes. "And I quote, Dixon Plaza is not about building up. It's about tearing down. This is not renewal. It's removal." Pen poised, Christmas waited for the answer.

When Dwight had opened the floor for questions, he was planning to call on the *Journal.* His perfect plan for the day did not include an inquiry from Jasper Christmas of the *New York Spectator,* but he had fast lips and a loud voice.

Dwight took a deep breath, felt for his you-can-pass-go card, because Pastor Phil was a pro. He'd been at the table for a long time and usually played with a full deck, and a few hidden up his sleeve. Dwight did not intend to provoke him.

Grace gave the this-is-your-territory, you-handle-it look. He gripped the podium. "With all due respect, I have not spoken with Pastor Ewing about this project, or its impact on the community."

Jasper shot back, "The pastor is right downstairs. I'm sure we can get a clarification."

Whatever was in Dwight's stomach curdled. He made his way to the window, but not before his father, who growled. "Thought you had sense enough to take care of this."

A hundred or so demonstrators circled in front of the building carrying signs that read OUR HOMES ARE NOT FOR SALE and MIGHT DON'T MAKE RIGHT. Pastor Phil, wearing his signature denim shirt and clerical collar, and shoulder-sweeping dreadlocks, chanted into a bullhorn. Above the sudden silence in the room the voices rose up from the street: "We shall not, we shall not be moved. We shall not, we shall not be moved . . ."

Not the theme song Dwight had anticipated. *What kind of fresh hell is this?*

ONE
Time costs nothing if it's not your money

Five years later,
NEW YORK, NEW YORK

"I have bent over backwards till my head touches my ass, Gordon." Dwight sat forward and the old wooden chair squeaked, announcing his movement.

"Look, I'm giving it to you straight. Without the additional public space, I can guarantee Dixon Plaza won't pass the Council." Chester Gordon sat back, his foot propped on the open bottom drawer of the desk in the stuffed cubbyhole of an office. His earnest likeness watched over the meeting from the campaign poster taped to the wall. Pictures of his smiling twins, Chester IV and Rachel, looked on from the desk.

"That's not the guarantee I'm looking for." It was always strange for Dwight to be sitting on the petitioner's side of this desk. It was the same one he'd worked at years ago, at the beginning of the public-service portion of his career, his time on the Council. He'd converted the former liquor store in one of his father's buildings into his office. "There's 843 acres of public space across the damn street."

"Bottom line, either you take ten stories off each tower . . ."

"Another ten stories." Early in the process the buildings had shrunk to twenty-five stories, a compromise to make their scale more in keeping with the surroundings.

"Or we need more areas available to the public."

"And what will that guarantee me? Because at this point I need some assurances." The hyperbole of that bright morning of the press conference had smacked up against the reality of getting a project off the ground in a city where interests collide and the balance is always in flux. While Dixon Plaza hadn't exactly descended into fresh hell, the project had been detained in purgatory, punctuated with plenty of hellish episodes. The original time line called for the buildings to be nearing completion, and although he'd been living, breathing, and dreaming DP-CPN, they still didn't have shovels in the ground.

Chester paused, choosing his words deliberately. "I can, with a high degree of probability, say that if you make these adjustments, we should have the votes to get you through."

Dwight felt as if he'd spent the last five years testifying before somebody's committee, awaiting the results of impact studies, making concessions, modifications, and reassessments. The Economic Development Council, the Environmental Protection Agency, the Budget Office, the Citizens Advisory Committee, the offices of the mayor, the governor, the council president, the state legislature—all had to be stroked and massaged, sometimes simultaneously in different directions. Dwight stood up. "I'm sure you understand how important this is to the continued viability of the project and the continued revitalization of the district." That was code for get-it-the-hell-done.

"You know I've been a consistent champion of your efforts."

Particularly after Dwight had made numerous campaign contributions and offered to create a scholarship to Dominique's school that would facilitate outreach and help create a more "diverse" student body and had it awarded to the son of one of Chester's aides. Dwight didn't have to say, "You owe me." He was sure Chester was aware of that.

"Anything on fire?" Dwight barked at Madeline through his ever-present Bluetooth earpiece as he hustled out of the building and into the waiting car. The next meeting was at his office with his architect, and he wasn't looking forward to it.

"Your wife called."

"Call her back. Tell her to have my aunt come for dinner tonight." Figured he might as well get this over with.

Whether it was the Council or the Community Board, each meeting with Dixon Plaza business on the agenda had brought out a loose coalition of foot-stomping, noisemaking, banner-waving activists, whose stated mission was to save Harlem. That always made Dwight want to laugh and ask them from what, each other? They had the nerve to try to dictate how the Dixon Group could, should, and would use their property, acquired at fire-sale prices in the sixties, seventies, and bad old eighties, when crack and AIDS had swept through the neighborhood out of control, and falling asleep to the pop of gunfire was as routine as the *Tonight* show. Their raucous indignation at these meeting always reminded him of when he was nine and he'd spent the day with King, threatening deadbeat tenants, finding local winos for day labor, backslapping political flunkies—a usual day in the neighborhood. King always went armed with a roll of small bills and a stubby .22. Dwight hated those dismal buildings with graffiti-tagged hallways that smelled like beer piss, roach powder, and fish fried in old grease.

That evening Dwight and King showered and took the bus down Broadway to Lincoln Center. With lights aglow, and elegant patrons milling about the Philharmonic, the Met, and the New York State Theater, Dwight thought it was magical—it was still one of his favorite vistas in the city. King bought him a lemonade, sat him by the dancing fountain, and with all the reverence due a Bible story told him how Robert Moses, the man who reshaped New York City, led the Rockefellers and other moneyed men of influence to bulldoze acres of loathsome, teeming San Juan Hill tenements and build the lustrous shrine of the arts. When Dwight asked what had happened to all the people who lived there, King cackled, "Every rat can find another hole." Only now the "rats" had pro bono counsel and advocacy groups.

But a new contingent of homeowners also knew that aside from forty blocks or so, the brownstones that went for $2 million on West Seventy-fifth Street were the same as the ones on 123rd Street for $200,000. Even with a half million in renovation they were way ahead of the game. These concerned citizens were firmly and vocally interested in further renewal in the neighborhood.

Dwight walked a high wire between camps, trying not to look down. Trying to keep Grace and the financing in place. The hotel was the first casualty. After two years of delays and the scale-back in size, St. John Talliwell pulled out, said Dixon Plaza had missed the cutting edge of the trend. Shortly thereafter, Talliwell Hospitality International announced T^2-Williamsburgh—they preferred the original English spelling—in the latest Brooklyn hipster enclave. To be built as part of the redevelopment of a historic sugar plant, the project boasted a riverfront address and sweeping views of lower Manhattan and the East River bridges, in what they labeled the bohemian vitality of a community that blended the old-world German, Polish, Hasidic, and Italian communities with Nuyorican intensity and new-millenneum artistic expression. To Dwight it sounded more like a colossal load of crap than it did when the hotelier was on their team.

After St. John's departure, Grace had done her best to rip Dwight a new one. Said he had to get his people in line. If he didn't need her connections, at least this first time, he'd have had a whole lot more to say. But he took one for the team. The delays reinforced his determination to bring the project to fruition.

Dwight strode into the office, his office, nodded at a few "Hi, Mr. Dixon's." King didn't bother to keep an office here anymore. He'd relinquished day-to-day duties, preferred to do his sideline quarterbacking from the comfort of home. Dwight passed the Dixon Plaza model, let his eyes linger. Seeing it was his booster shot, gave him strength to keep up the fight, even though it had been taken down a few pegs from it's to-scale glory. Sometimes, when he needed more, he'd take the silver ceremonial scissors from the top shelf of the closet in his office. All they needed was the opening date engraved on the blade, and he'd imagine how outstanding it was going to be to cut that red ribbon on opening day. But that wasn't now.

"Need to talk to you, Mr. Dixon." Eric Wallace, clipboard under his arm, appeared at Dwight's side.

"Is it on fire?" Eric managed the physical maintenance of The Dixon Group holdings, the bolts and screws and leaking roofs of the buildings.

"No, but it's smoking." Eric was two-thirds torso and one-third leg, so even though he was slim, his shirttails were usually in some stage of escaping his pants. His blue Dockers were cinched with a tooled-leather belt with a silver longhorn buckle.

"I've got an appointment, catch me up after."

Dwight drummed his fingers on Madeline's desk on the way by.

"Mr. Rowan is waiting for you."

Back to reality. When Chester gave Dwight news of the necessary changes, his architect was among the first people Dwight wanted to get in gear.

"This . . . this . . . is, is, is, is, is, is, is . . . It is a fiasco." Cobb Rowan stood with such force he tipped the slim leather-and-steel chair. It thunked on the rug. "This . . . this is not even the same project. These buildings will be nothing but . . . stumps." In his white turtleneck and trousers, face glowing crimson, he paced Dwight's office, looking like a giant match, ready for striking, although he was actually already inflamed. Cobb's assistant, dressed noir to Cobb's blanc, sat on the sofa, taking notes on a minilaptop.

"Cobb, I assure you—"

"You can assure me of nothing."

He had a point, but Dwight still had a tremendous advantage, although he'd never intended to use it. He planted his hands firmly on his desk, as much to appear calm as to keep from wrapping them around Rowan's neck. "We have access to additional property—"

"Where will you get it? From the moon?"

"We are likely to be able to acquire an additional ten thousand square feet from an adjacent property on 111th Street."

"Likely, possibly, maybe . . . it is all Swiss cheese."

"Fortunately, the building belongs to a relative." Or unfortunately. His aunt Forestina inherited it when her husband died, owned it jointly with her daughter, Avery. It was one of the first King and Doc B had acquired, back when they were partners. "That means we can accommodate the added public space and maintain the integrity and intent of your original design." Dwight took a breath, prepared for some ego stroking, with extra cheese. "These buildings will be iconic. No one can conceptualize space in the innovative way you do—"

"Do not patronize me. This will take a complete reimagination. I'm sick of builders patting me on the head—'Now go work your miracle,' as if I can move the pieces around like . . . like chessmen."

But you will, and we'll be suitably impressed. And you'll keep sending me the damn bill. Millions of dollars' worth and they weren't done yet. Dwight shot the architect one of his *Lean on Me* looks. "I'd like to think that after this many years in the trenches, you know me, Cobb. And you know the Dixon Group has nothing but the highest regard—"

"Please." Cobb waved away Dwight's declaration. "I'm sick of you builders smearing my plans in excrement." Cobb headed toward the door, his assistant already in front, hand on the knob. "I don't know what I'm going to do about this."

Annoy the piss out of me, make the damn changes, and cash the shitty checks. Rowan would bemoan the artistic travesty awhile longer, then revise the blueprints and pronounce it "a staggering synthesis of vertical habitability and horizontal visibility," or some other crazy dictum Dwight was sure Rowan coined while admiring himself in the mirror. Dwight wondered if the big name was worth the aggravation, but it wasn't the first time he'd found first class looked better from the outside than it felt on the inside.

Before he could call her, Madeline walked in. "Your favorite, Jasper Christmas, has called three times."

Dwight scowled. "Give him the PR firm. That's what we pay them for." Dwight resented Jasper's questioning, the way it seemed to imply wrongdoing. From that first press conference Dwight had the feeling Jasper Christmas was looking for the gotcha. A scoop to raise his profile at Dwight's expense.

"He says he'd like your perspective." Madeline laid the message on Dwight's desk, gave him the been-there, take-your-medicine eye. "It's always worse when you don't call them back. You hate it when the article says, 'Dixon Group president Dwight Dixon declined . . .' "

"I'll get to him when I'm ready. Everything he needs to know is a matter of public record."

Madeline handed Dwight a baseball cap and worked to keep her lips from poking out. "Sean is waiting downstairs. Will you be back?"

"Depends. I'll check in."

"Got a minute." Eric popped his head in the door.

"Thirty seconds." Dwight pulled his bow tie loose, unbuttoned the neck of his shirt.

"It's the furnace at 547 again."

"Can it be patched?" Dwight got up.

"Yeah, but it's older than my granddaddy, converted from coal. We're at the point of diminishing returns. I've done some research on replacements. Long term the increased fuel efficiency will save—"

"Let's deal with short term for now." Dwight grabbed his cap, came from around the desk. "If you can keep it going, let's do that. Anything else?"

"I'm heading over to 24 to look at the elevator."

"Good man." Dwight popped his earpiece in.

Each address came with an inventory of broken-down, patched, and reconditioned fixtures and utilities. Some of the buildings were more than one hundred years old. They don't make 'em like that anymore—often for a reason. Having to provide additional affordable housing in order to proceed with their luxury conversion had not been on their list of projected expenses, but to move on with Dixon Plaza it had to be done. And the money had to come from somewhere. Dwight arranged loans against some of their other properties, which squeezed their cash flow, in the short term. But his sights were set on the blue horizon. No pain, no gain. He would make it work. He was willing to make sacrifices to get there. And their tenants would have to as well.

Dwight headed around the corner to the usual pickup spot, in the NO STANDING ANYTIME zone, right behind the stinky souvlaki lunch truck. It was a good afternoon to talk to some kids, smile for a few photos. He ducked into the beat-up Crown Vic, rolled down the window. It felt as if Sean Booker had documented every handshake and backslap of Dwight's last fifteen years, but a good photo op was worth all the words nobody was going to read anyhow. "When you gonna wash this tub of shit." Dwight massaged his cap brim, shaping it.

"Urban camouflage." Maps, parking tickets, french-fry containers, and coffee cups littered the backseat. "Gets me where I want to go, under the radar." Sean's scraggly beard, baggy jeans, and double XXL Rocawear T-shirt complimented the decor. But his camera bag and photo vest were always organized. He'd been a kid, stocking shelves at C-Town, when Dwight first started seeing him hustling photos at rallies, community meetings, block parties—wherever people gathered and wanted to document the occasion. Dwight threw him a few bones, found out he delivered on time and the pictures were good, so he'd been calling ever since.

"Oh, come on!" Dwight reached across and mashed the car horn at the minivan waiting to make a left. "You drive like an old man."

"You fly, you die. Chill. We'll be on time."

To keep from losing his mind in stalled traffic, Dwight pulled out his phone. Checked some e-mail—yes, Dixon Group would buy a table for the Conservancy benefit. That would make Renee happy. More shopping, even though it always looked as if she bought the same gown—modest, appropriate, boring. He answered texts from Madeline—*Christmas again.*

Dwight didn't see Dancer and Blitzen—*Tell him later.*

—Tee Time Sat 10AM.

—OK. Tell Renee.

She had left him a voice mail too, probably about dinner, but he didn't have the head for it now. Vance Kidder had put together this foursome at the last minute. Even before his stroke he was the worst golfer ever to pick up a Big Bertha, but the outings seemed to do him good. Dwight wasn't fond of the sport—too slow—but he'd developed a passable game for the socializing, and when the old boy called, Dwight went. You never knew who would round out the party. Last time it was a recently retired pro quarterback, who spent eighteen holes wondering if maybe he really had another season in him. And Dwight had developed a budding acquaintanceship with the hedge-fund director in the group. He'd have to apologize to Dominique for missing the matinee they had planned as a family outing. Renee wouldn't be thrilled either. *She'll get over it.*

"So when is the other building coming down?" Sean maneuvered around a double-parked truck, stopped as the light turned yellow.

"You could have taken that." Dwight huffed, settled back in his seat. "It would be dust tomorrow if I could arrange it." Two years ago they'd started demolition. It was one of Dwight's shining moments. A rendering of the completed project graced the sidewalk shed surrounding the site. King was quiet, strangely melancholy that morning watching his building come down, floor by floor, but Dwight was effervescent. He'd stood there in his yellow construction helmet, and each blow to the facade, each dump truck full of rubble, felt like a victory. They had completed one teardown before they were hit with an injunction. Dwight had been scrambling ever since.

"It's gonna look kinda strange . . . skyscrapers on 110th Street. Rich people living in 'em."

"Doesn't look strange on Central Park South. Why should it on Central Park North?"

Sean shrugged. "It's never been like that."

"Everything changes. You'll forget the way it was so fast you'll think it was a dream."

The air-conditioned coaches were already parked out front when Dwight and Sean arrived. Hudson Common, the two buildings The Dixon Group had rehabbed in the West 120s—both bought as boarded-up shells at city auction—sat back-to-back with a shared play area—basketball court, swings, slides, benches. It was a private, secure park—not Central Park, but Dwight felt it was an admirable consolation prize, a more than adequate warehouse for the people he needed to displace.

After a great deal of posturing and negotiations, he was able to get Pastor Phil to see it that way too and stop the demonstrations, which had escalated and moved to include the Kidder, Theismann headquarters. That made for unfortunate footage on the local news—babies in strollers with protest signs on top, Dwight's brusque "No comment." Jasper Christmas had done a series of interviews with longtime tenants, who had no idea where they would go if they had to move. That's when Dwight knew it was time to change strategy.

Unlike other developers who promised affordable housing, The Dixon Group had actually delivered. The renovated properties had been occupied for two years. King told him he was a jackass, but Dwight had a heart or at least recognized a PR advantage in showing some, like by sponsoring two busloads of kids to go up to the Bronx for a ball game this afternoon.

"How's it goin', Mr. D?" The uniformed security guard shook Dwight's hand, ushered them inside.

"How they hangin', Buster?" Dwight clapped him on the back. A short, dark man with biceps like cannonballs, Buster had been a tenant in one of the CPN buildings. When the renovation was complete, he was one of the first to move in. It was a strategy Dwight learned from King. If you employ your tenants, you know they can pay the rent. It also gives you extra eyes and ears on the place, so you know what's really going on.

"Hangin' high. Keepin' it that way."

Laughter and squeals came from the community room and the playground. During the school year the Hope House Foundation—a not-for-profit generously funded by The Dixon Group through the Dixon Plaza financing, and overseen by Pastor Phil—ran an after-school, homework-help center, and a day camp in the summer.

"Oh, Mr. D," Buster called after him. "Crawford said he wants to talk to you. Think he's in the basement."

Dwight left Sean setting up, grabbed the elevator down, found his chief superintendent bagging recyclables in the compactor room.

"Just the man I want to see." Crawford wiped his hands on his coveralls over his protruding belly.

Dwight hoped it was quick. The aroma of fermenting garbage laced the air, and it was hard to have a conversation while holding his breath.

"Upper cabinets in another couple of units pulled away from the wall."

"You tell them not to do chin-ups from the handles?" Dwight had heard it all—a three-foot alligator in the bathtub, a sink stained purple after being used to stomp grapes for homemade wine, pipes that burst when a tenant snuck off in the middle of the night and left the windows wide-open in twelve-degree weather. At this point, nothing surprised him.

"Not this time. When I took a look, seemed like they weren't installed to the studs."

"You talk to Eric?" Dwight wanted to bring this to a conclusion.

"Yep. And I got 'em secure. Reinforced 'em with mollies. Better than new."

"That's why you are the man, Crawford." Dwight skipped the handshake, bounded up the stairs to get away from the smell. It lingered in his nostrils.

Upstairs, Dwight took off his suit jacket, rolled up his sleeves, and put on his baseball cap. Counselors and parent chaperones—including a larger than usual number of men for a trip in the middle of the day—had rounded up the young people, got them outside to the buses.

"Fine day for some baseball, Brother Dixon." Pastor Phil, whose locks now extended halfway down his back with a carefully hidden bald spot in the middle, clasped Dwight in a handshake.

Dwight could skip the brother bit. There had not been any fellowshipping when they'd sat across a table from each other at Phil's church and worked out how they would each get what he wanted. "I can make your life miserable and make you personally look like an uncaring, moneygrubbing son of Satan for as long as you want. And don't think your folks downtown won't ditch you if it gets too hot." The housing development, the center, and an anonymous donation to the church's building fund brought about the kumbaya moment.

But the afternoon was meant for fun and sport, so the builder and the preacher stood side by side amid a sea of bright shining faces and blue-and-gold PROJECT HOPE T-shirts—H-arlem O-pportunity to P-ursue E-xcellence—and smiled for

Sean's camera. The pictures would make the Hudson Common Hope House newsletter, distributed among the tenants here, and back in the old block, so they'd know how their former neighbors were doing. There was a website too, for those on the techno edge and for The Dixon Group's PR agency to distribute as necessary, to highlight their corporate caring.

With the buses off to the game, Dwight tossed his cap in Sean's backseat. "Can you drop me at 34th Street? Need to pick up something for the wife."

"How is Mrs. Dixon?"

Dwight gave his standard answer: "Great and getting better. I'll tell her you asked."

At the corner of Seventh Avenue Dwight got out by the world's largest department store, waved as he headed through the revolving doors. He stood inside by the retro pay phones, called Madeline on his cell. "Anything on fire?"

"No smoke."

"I'm going to do a little shopping for the Mrs. See you in the morning."

Dwight headed through men's, fingered a few bow ties—nothing special, but this wasn't his regular stomping ground. He wandered into the perfume mezzanine, picked up a bottle of his favorite fragrance—a little musk, a little citrus, funky and fresh. Petite shopping bag in hand, he made another call. "I'll be on the 4:28. Pick me up at the airport. Terminal A."

Dwight left the store, made his way across the street to Penn Station, and bought a New Jersey Transit ticket. He didn't bother sitting on the train, stood by the doors, drumming his fingers, staring at the marsh grass in the Meadowlands. *It's all coming together.* He'd lived with this project longer than he'd lived with his child. When he closed his eyes at night, he saw those towers, gleaming hot in the afternoon sun. He just had to raise them up.

At the Newark Airport stop he bolted, took the monorail

to the terminal. Not long after he walked outside, a gray Suburban stopped. He hopped in. They took off.

"A present? You shouldn't have." Mitch Branigan's meaty hands made the steering wheel look like a toy. The sleeves of his blue oxford-cloth shirt were rolled to below the elbow, revealing sun-baked, furry arms.

"Yeah. Let me spray some behind your ears." Dwight dropped the flowery bag on the floor. Dun-Right Construction had handled many projects for The Dixon Group, including Hudson Common. Dwight and Mitch had developed a working understanding. Dwight told him what he wanted. Mitch found a way to make it happen, on time and on budget. "Change of plan. Looks like DP is about to expand. For part of the structure, we're going through to 111th Street."

Mitch maneuvered past airport shuttle buses, triple-parked cars, and confused travelers cruising for the right door for Air Antarctica or wherever they were going. "Halle-frickin'-lujah. Where'd you get the property? Pull it outta your ass?"

"Exactly. I told you my shit was golden." In Manhattan that was always the multimillion-dollar question. If you wanted it bad enough, it was likely to cost you a fortune. But once again, King's omnivorous appetite for real estate would put them in good stead. Dwight just wished he'd kept 111th Street, but it was all going to work out. It had to.

Mitch headed along an access road, pulled into the post office parking lot.

"So what's with the cloak-and-dagger bit." Mitch had called that morning, said he needed to talk—out of the office. Not that Dwight minded. He wasn't big on Dun-Right's headquarters, down a desolate road, somewhere below the Pulaski Skyway.

Mitch reached over, turned on the radio—bottom of the second, play-by-play.

"This is a heads-up . . . probably nothing, but there could be problems with some of the drywall that went up at Hudson Common." The blue light in his ear blinked, keeping time.

"What the hell kind of problems?" Dwight had enough of those. He was interested in solutions.

Mitch slid his hands over his thicket of black hair, cupped them behind his head. "Some of the product might be defective."

"Defective how? We got some loose uppers in a couple of kitchens. That have anything to do with it?" Dwight felt his phone vibrate in his pocket, pushed to ignore the call.

Mitch dropped his hands to the steering wheel. "Naw. The cabinets are in the margin of error. That drywall came from China though. They're saying it might leach some chemicals, cause a bad smell. I don't really see—"

"Might cause?" Hudson Common was already a check mark on his to-do list. Dwight wasn't interested in a do-over. "How much of it did you use? Are we talking ten percent? Fifty percent?"

Mitch shrugged. "Can't tell you."

Dwight reached out, pressed his hands against the dashboard. "You put defective drywall in my buildings and you can't tell me how much?"

"You didn't ask me all that when you liked the bid."

Dwight looked straight ahead at the woman walking behind her two kids, who made a game of pushing a shopping cart with a box the size of a big-screen TV toward the building. "What are we supposed to do?"

"You could replace it."

"You *might* have used *some* and I'm supposed to replace all the damn drywall in two buildings?" And relocate the tenants. And put up with the fallout. And risk more delays on Dixon Plaza. And keep shelling out cash. Time costs nothing if it's not your money, but Dixon Group had been footing the bill for the delays. "Next option."

"Wait. Could be nothing."

They were silent through the bases-loaded walk that brought in a run.

"I'm going with Plan B." Dwight hadn't heard anything about bad smells, and he wasn't going looking for a solution in search of a problem. "Look. Just be ready to start up the rest of the 110th Street demo as soon as we get the Council approval. And as soon as we have title to 111th, I need you to move on it. Before another damn injunction hits my desk."

They were back at the terminal by the top of the fourth inning, two outs. Dwight hopped out.

"Don't forget your bag." Mitch held it with two fingertips, pinkie in the air.

Dwight snatched it. "Funny." He'd have tossed the bag and put the box in his pocket, but he knew Renee liked all the fluff stuff. It would earn him some points or at least keep the status quo. He checked the missed called—Renee, like he thought. Somehow her vibrations felt different, higher pitched, more annoying. He figured she had some words for him about bailing on their family theater outing. It could wait till he got home. Dwight's personal life interrupted his work flow, so whenever possible he kept a firewall between them. In the end, it was to their benefit to leave him alone. He was taking care of his family.

Before calling home, he voice-dialed another number while he walked back to the train. "Any cancellations tonight?" Dwight was hoping to make use of his free time. "May I have seven forty-five tomorrow morning? . . . No. I won't be late. . . . Thank you."

TWO

. . . another day, another round in the fight, ducking and weaving, trying not to get knocked out

The call home had not gone so smoothly. Dinner with Dwight's aunt was fine. She'd be there at seven. But his daughter had been confronted by one of her schoolmates about the Dixon Plaza buildings making people homeless. Fifth-grade political rhetoric was not what he had planned for the evening, but Renee made it sound as crucial as a presidential debate.

When he arrived, Renee met him at the door, exchanged a sensible kiss for his goody bag—she had more pressing matters on the agenda. "None of this would happen if we moved to Chappaqua or Greenwich—"

"They get news there too, Renee." He was not opening the house-in-the-suburbs discussion right now. Renee had wanted to pull up stakes and move to the land of lawns, country clubs, and E320 wagons from the time Dominique was born, but something kept him there, in that house. Something he hadn't yet finished. He removed his earpiece, turned his phone off—he didn't need something else to argue about.

"But it wouldn't be in her face every day, for the next how many years? It's not just your battle, Dwight." Renee plucked the dish towel from the waist of her apron and wiped her hands.

"So I'm the bad guy?" Something about her plainness had actually appealed to him. Basic, unfrilly, pleasant, sweet. And the way her chestnut-colored hair dangled in her eyes, when she didn't style it into submission. He hadn't seen that side in a while. Not since she gave birth and became Robo-Mom, devoting all of the energy that had gone to her career as a CPA to molding the ultimate offspring.

"That's not what I mean."

"Sounds like it, and I really don't need—"

"Fine. You go explain it to her."

No back rub, no "How was your day?" Just another turn of the screw.

Dwight trudged up the stairs, draped his jacket on the bedroom doorknob, and continued on. By day he controlled millions of dollars' worth of Manhattan real estate, employed people who called him Mr. Dixon and made every effort to please him, even when he wasn't nice. His efforts made the economy go round. But at home, he was reduced to absentee father and "Make it better, Daddy" duty. Like his experience growing up equipped him to do more than pay the bills.

Peering in the door, Dwight watched his child, who looked so much like him paternity was obvious, even to the casual observer. They shared the same bronze complexion, broad, flat forehead, pointed chin, and keenly arching brows. Already tall for her age, she was also lean—reminded him of Avery at that age. Renee found their close resemblance a personal hardship. Since they hadn't been able to have another, she'd have to do.

"Hey, pumpkin."

"Daddy!" Dominique leapt off her canopied bed, hugged him in a way he would be embarrassed to admit was like the way he used to greet his father, a long time ago, or try to. King put a stop to his filial shows of affection, or, as he put it, "Stop actin' like a little faggot."

"What's the word, baby bird?"

"Emily said you take advantage of people."

Dwight sat on the bed next to Dominique. "I think Emily doesn't know me the way you do."

"But she said black people have always lived in Harlem." Worried furrows creased her young forehead.

"And now black people can live wherever we want." If he was presenting his argument the way he usually did, Dwight would have added, anywhere they can afford, just like everybody else, but he opted to skip the economics lesson. "Don't you think that's better?"

Dominique twirled her ponytail around her finger.

"Why don't you invite Emily to the theater with you on Saturday." It was never too early for Dominique to learn to cozy up to her detractors.

"But, Daddy, I want you to go with us." She scooted next to him.

"Me too." It wasn't so much a lie as a favorable interpretation of the facts, which wouldn't significantly change the outcome. "But you can't always do what you want. Sometimes you've got to do what you've got to do." He gave two tugs to her ponytail. Case closed.

Voices filtered up from the parlor and Dominique hopped off the bed. "Auntie Tina's here!" She galloped downstairs. Dwight wanted to close the door and hide, but his work wasn't done. In fact, this next conversation might be the most significant of the day. Then he heard his father's growl. *Damn.* Time with King required more prior notice, mental preparation. They didn't share Father's Day–card fishing and golf moments—never had. The quick buffer was a stiff double vodka on the rocks.

Dwight came to Renee in the kitchen first, lowered his voice to a scratchy whisper. "You didn't tell me he was coming too."

"They were going to the market so he came along." Renee slid past him, opened the fridge. "They picked up one of those fruit tarts you like."

Like that would make his day complete. But the new gourmet market, nestled under the Henry Hudson Parkway at 125th Street, a mirror of the flagship store on the Upper West Side, had been yet another sign to Dwight that Harlem was ripe for development.

"You know I need some warning when he's going to be here." Dwight didn't even know why his father had come other than to give him grief and bellyache about Renee's cooking. And to hear what Chester had to say—King didn't do cell phones, sending or receiving. "I'm not talkin' to you on some Martian-looking headphone while I'm walkin' in the street." But he worried the hell out of Dwight's.

So Dwight prepared a vodka appetizer from the kitchen-cupboard stash, ignoring his wife's disapproving eye. At least he'd be prepared for the duel.

There were just the five of them, but they sat at the formal table, King and Dwight at opposite ends, the others sprinkled between with the platter of pork chops with braised apples, undercooked string beans, and overcooked rice to connect them. When Dwight had asked Renee to marry him, he'd presented her with his mother's engagement ring—the second potential Mrs. Dixon to be so honored. He didn't ask her if she could cook. After the wedding they'd moved into the old homestead, and aside from paint and new throw pillows, it looked pretty much the same as it always did. Meals included—Wilhelmina had had little interest in the kitchen and even fewer skills.

"Dwight, your father examined every single grape and strawberry." As usual, Forestina kept the conversation flowing. "And, oh my, the tomatoes, I swear he squeezed all of them."

Dwight still found it miraculous that his father had become such a produce aficionado, regularly tagging along when his sister-in-law drove to the out-of-the-way market to shop. Years ago, after Dwight's mother died, groceries had become the housekeeper's domain.

King took a bite of pork chop. "Same as everything else, they cheat you if you don't pay attention." But it was the sweet scent, the juicy taste of luscious, fresh blueberries, strawberries, tomatoes, that prompted his shopping excursions. It reminded him of being a barefoot boy with dirt under his nails, playing hide-and-seek in the fields of his family's Bordentown, New Jersey, truck farm, although you'd never hear that from his lips. He hadn't been back since he sold the place after his father died—King figured the mean finally ran out or killed him. The old man would say, "The world don't give no breaks. Why in the devil should I?"

That spread was King's first real estate transaction. He sure as hell didn't want to be a farmer. His brothers didn't either. The property didn't bring as much as he thought it should have—his first lesson in land valuation. The price depends on who's selling and who's buying. But it was his stake. The brothers split the proceeds and headed off in different directions. King caught the bus to New York, landed on 125th Street, right in front of the Hotel Theresa, the grandest building he'd ever seen, and he'd hardly ever crossed the George Washington Bridge since.

As Renee cleared the dishes, Dominique seized the floor. "My piano teacher says I have naturally perfect timing."

King snorted. "They think all God's chillun got—"

"She's been practicing faithfully." Dwight cut his father off at the discouraging word. He'd lived through enough of them.

"I always wished Avery had studied an instrument—she never would sit still long enough." Forestina sounded wistful. "But, boy oh boy, she was a gifted runner, wasn't she, Dwight?"

"Yep, she was that."

Forestina shook her head. "You two used to race up and down this block like something was chasing you."

"Until she could even beat you, Daddy. Right?" Dominique chimed in. "Auntie showed me her medals and trophies."

"Yep, she was definitely faster." And smarter, with a confidence that was obvious as soon as she could walk. Dwight's cousin had been his coconspirator and confidant, but other than at his wedding, in the last twenty years he hadn't seen more than the lopsided photographs Forestina had brought back from her visits to see her daughter.

"Wish I could meet her."

"You will, sweetie. Even if I have to hide you in my suitcase and take you with me."

"You could take me to Paris with you next week." Palms together, Dominique pleaded, "I won't take up much space."

"Not until school is out, missy." Renee came back from the kitchen, placed the dessert in the center of the table.

"What'd your man Gordon have to say? You gonna get the site cleared this time so we can build something and stop talking about it?" King wiped his lips, tossed his napkin on the table. "Or haven't we kissed enough—"

"I believe we have a way to clear the Council impasse." Dwight wished he had time to re-vodka his glass, but he plowed ahead. "And actually, it involves you, Aunt Tina."

"You know I'll do whatever you need. Just tell me."

Dwight explained the situation, and how his aunt's property would make it possible for the project to move forward. "I think we can come to a fair price. The building has appreciated a great deal since it was purchased."

"My goodness, I imagine it has." Forestina picked a plump strawberry off her tart with her fingers and bit it, to Dominique's delight. "I suppose you should have just lumped my property with the others in the first place." It was the second building King and Doc B had bought together. Back before the four of them were all married. Back when King had street sense and hustle money, and the good doctor had a busy neighborhood medical practice, and skin pale enough to go into a bank and expect decent terms. The two were partners for years, the quiet physician and the brash fast-talker. They even married sisters. But down the line they had run into some technical difficulties. Besides, King wanted to run his own show—no questions, no second guesses—and bought out his partner, except for 111th Street, although The Dixon Group continued to manage the six-story walk-up, adjacent to the CPN properties, charging appropriate fees. "At this point I can't imagine Avery will have an objection. I used to think maybe she'd want it when she came home, but . . ." Forestina looked off, rolled a blueberry around her plate.

Dwight wasn't sure Avery would see it that way, but it was his best gambit. She was precisely the reason he didn't buy his aunt out years ago. Forestina had kept the property for her, said it was better than insurance. But with his deal in a bind, Dwight had no choice but to appeal to his aunt's family spirit. Not having to further reduce the size of the project was worth it to him.

"I'll talk to her about it while we're in Paris." Forestina patted his hand. "I'm sure it will be fine. Unless you want to call her yourself. You two haven't spoken in so long."

"I'll leave it to you." Dwight knew he was the last person who could convince Avery to do anything. "But the quicker we turn this around, the better."

"I'd be pretty happy if somebody was gonna write me a great big check for a building I never saw." King pushed away from the table. "Shoulda been like this from the beginning." King tried to cross one chubby leg over the other. His feet slipped back to the floor. "Now you're gonna have a whole nother building full of niggas—"

"Leave it outside, King." Dwight eyed his father sharply. He'd grown up with King's foul mouth and blunt remarks, but tried to rein him in when Dominique was present.

"The girl's heard it before if she got ears."

"She doesn't need to hear it here." Nor did she need a primer on how her grandfather would clear a building. Dwight was familiar with his father's methods—the exterminator never shows, the super makes himself scarce, repairs don't get made, and in a pinch he'd subsidize a few units for lowlifes who threw loud parties for their scary friends and, in general, made the atmosphere inhospitable.

"I told you, it doesn't work that way anymore." The current crop of thugs was more entrepreneurial. They'd end up holding the building hostage and forcing the owner to pay ransom. Dwight wanted this as clinical as he could arrange. "I'm handling it."

"So you say. If I moved this slow, I'd still be in coveralls, snaking out shitty toilets . . ." King caught himself. "Just get it done." He sucked his teeth and stood up.

After his father and aunt had gone, Dwight showered, a long time, to rinse away the day, drown out the nonstop loop of events that played in his head. He reached through the steam for his towel, pulled on his white terry robe, yanked the hood over his head, and delivered three quick jabs to an imaginary heavy bag—another day, another round in the fight, ducking and weaving, trying not to get knocked out.

Watch set for 6 a.m., Dwight flopped into bed and was almost asleep when he felt Renee creep in beside him, rub her hand up his thigh, over his belly. Then he smelled her, funky and fresh.

"Your hand is cold." He moved it aside.

"But the rest of me's nice and warm." She nestled up close, rested her head on his shoulder.

Dwight felt the heat of her skin radiate through her silky gown. He kissed her forehead. "I've got an early morning." He rolled over. He could not perform one more function today.

Renee sat up in a huff, her back against the mahogany headboard.

He had almost drifted off when she turned on the ceiling light. "Damn it, Renee? I was almost—"

"Are you seeing someone?" She had put on her robe. Stood across the room, arms folded. "Because if you are . . ."

"Are you seriously asking me this?" He shielded his eyes, squinted to look at her.

"You never want to—"

"I have too much on my mind, too much pressure to think about sex with you or anybody else. When this project is done . . ."

"All right." She clicked off the light. "I'm sorry."

"Come to bed."

She got under the covers and he held her for a respectable time, then turned back over and went to sleep.

➢ ➢ ➢

"Sit wherever you want, Mom. Okay?" *Just make up your mind.* Avery Lyons traipsed around the boat pond behind her mother, carrying a white paper bag in one hand, a take-out cup of café crème in the other, and trying not to sound the way she really felt—over it after five days of togetherness.

"The daffodils, the tulips . . . so beautiful. This weather is such a gift." Butter-cream sunlight dappled the Tuileries Gardens. "And this is just the most delicious spot for breakfast." Forestina finally selected one of the black wrought-iron benches near the water and they sat down. "And it's even better because I'm here with you." A smile brightened her already cheery face. She held up her cup. "*À votre santé.*"

Does she have to make a toast with everything we drink? But Avery obliged and tapped paper cups. "To your health." Then she tore into the bag, passed her mother the croissant, and bit into the *pain au chocolat.* Still warm, the dark chocolate oozed out of the flaky pastry and onto the corner of her mouth.

"You would find a way to have dessert for breakfast." Forestina handed her a napkin, brushed at the crumbs on Avery's black skirt.

"Lunch and dinner too." Nobody ever guessed she was a sweet freak since she was still built lean, like the runner she was in the alternative reality called her youth. Not doughy, like the sedentary policy-pusher she'd become. Avery took a swig of coffee. She never cared for the coffee in France—too bitter, but the milk helped some and the caffeine was essential.

"Are you all packed for your move?" Forestina pulled her delicate pastry apart, nibbled on ladylike pieces.

Avery rolled her eyes. "Haven't had time to think about it yet." Her State Department career had taken her all over the world—consulates, embassies, missions—Bern, Barbados, a few years in Paris. She would be leaving her post in Osaka, Japan, and heading for Wellington, New Zealand, in a few weeks, and she hadn't had a Mom visit in a while—her mother reminded her of that. So she cooked up this rendezvous as a stopgap.

"I don't know how you do it, moving all the time. I would be frantic."

"You get used to it." Avery actually preferred it. By the time the place became routine and the people had become familiar enough to be annoying, she moved on.

"I don't suppose anything has opened up in New York."

Another bite of bread. "No. So many people want assignments there, it's hard to get one." And she had no interest in applying. The closest she'd been in years was D.C., because they had to come in every few years. That was pushing it. She preferred being in a different time zone from her family—better yet, a different hemisphere, a world away.

Her mother reached up, held Avery's chin in her hand. "Well, I miss you."

How can she not know? Open your mouth and ask her. Each time they were together, Avery swore to herself she would bring it up, get it out. She looked over at her mother. In spite of whatever sags and wrinkles time induced, she still resembled the lovely young woman little Avery used to marvel at in the mirror as her mother curled her hair or put on lipstick. Sometimes, after she'd blotted her lips together, she'd say she had put on too much and kiss off the extra on Avery's cheek. She used to love that. "Miss you too." It's not what she wanted to say, but it's all that would come out. And she did miss that, miss what it used to be. She washed the words down with a glug of coffee.

"And you let your hair grow longer. It looks nice."

"I'm overdue for a haircut. Haven't had time." Avery combed a hand through her pageboy.

Forestina sighed. "And I guess this is as good a time as any to talk about this." Forestina crossed her legs and swiveled so they faced each other.

"About what?" It was as if her mother had been in her head, reading her thoughts, knew something needed to be said.

"I hate discussing business when we have so little time together. You know the apartment building on 111th Street . . . the one your father bought a long time ago?"

"I guess." Not the topic Avery had in mind.

"Well, Dwight needs to buy it."

"He *needs* to buy it." *And the world must stop until Dwight gets what he needs.* Avery left the tranquil morning, retreated inside herself.

"Well, the company does."

Avery watched a toy boat with pink sails glide on the water as her mother explained the whos and whys of the current Dixon Plaza dilemma, but Avery wasn't listening. She never did.

"It's quite impressive really." Forestina followed her daughter's eyes, recognized the glazed look. "I told them I'd ask you."

"About what?"

"If you'd mind if I sell it."

"What difference would it make to me?"

"I've been holding that property for you. Your name is on the deed along with mine."

"Do what you want, Mom." Avery was not about to get bogged down in Dwight and King's affairs. That was like standing in front of stampeding cattle and expecting them to run around you.

"All right." They were quiet for a moment, side by side, miles apart—same as usual. "Dwight will have papers for you to execute. Such an awful way to put that. You'll have to sign them. And we'll have to discuss the best way to handle the money. It'll be quite a cushion for you. Maybe you'd like a little pied-à-terre in the city, so you can pop in and out. Not that you can't always stay at home, but you might like your own place. . . ."

"I'm not planning to come home anytime soon."

"Well . . . we'll figure out how to handle the money."

Avery gathered their trash and stood up. "Let's get to the d'Orsay before it's crowded."

"Is something wrong, dear?" Forestina looked up at her daughter, absentmindedly smoothed Avery's blouse collar so it lay flat against her suit lapel.

It's always got to look perfect. "I'm fine, Mom." *What's the point?* And so she was fine, or at least appeared to be. "Come on. It's the last day. There's still a lot on your to-do list."

They returned to the business at hand. Avery kept her mother on the go—at the museum, the impressionists took up the rest of their morning, and that barely scratched the surface. They lunched alfresco at a brasserie, sharing a bucket of *moules frites,* letting the parade of pedestrians entertain them.

"They dress so much better here. Like people used to when your aunt Wilhelmina and I were young. Heels, hose, hats, and gloves. I miss that. And dancing in someone's arms. Your father was an excellent dancer—mambo, fox-trot."

Where'd that come from? The man Avery knew, the good doctor, was far too serious for dancing, and her mom didn't do much strolling down memory lane.

"Do you and your young man go dancing?"

"Van? Hardly." Her mother had been trying to get tidbits about Avery's man of the moment, but there wasn't a lot to tell. "And we're not planning to elope, if that's what you're worried about." She'd done that once—no more drama. She didn't ache for anybody that much anymore.

"As long as he makes you happy."

Happy? She never thought of her parents as a happy couple. Responsible. Reliable. Sure. But Avery never received the happy memo—or saw the video.

They window-shopped the quaint galleries and gilded antique stores along the rue de Rivoli, neither one inclined to test out the big bankroll their real estate sale would provide. But they stopped in more modest boutiques, eyed the antique purses and costume jewelry.

"I must have him." Nose nearly to the display case, Forestina pointed out a brooch, the bust of a blackamoor with ebony skin and a gold-leafed turban.

Avery conducted the negotiation, what there was of it. Despite all her shopping in far-flung markets, she'd never got the hang of bargaining. She just wanted to know the price so she could pay it.

"He'd look lovely on your suit." Forestina held the pin to Avery's jacket.

"No. I think he's your man." Avery pinned him on her mother's green knit dress. "Perfect."

"Nothing ever is, Avery. Nothing ever is."

THREE

. . . any deal can be golden with the right players

Three weeks later,
ABOVE CENTRAL PENNSYLVANIA

"No. Thank you. Really. I'm just not hungry." Avery managed a weak smile to dismiss the overzealous flight attendant. *How many times do I have to say it before you leave me alone?* Snack-cart clatter had jostled Avery from sleep, and she was definitely not interested in being awake or fed. But at least they'd be landing in an hour, news that was delivered by the chirpy snack-pusher in lieu of pretzels or chocolate-chip cookies. Avery felt for her already fastened seat belt—just checking, although right about now nothing would make her feel safe and secure. She mashed the crusty kernels from the corners of her eyes and flicked on the light. Sleep was her escape of last resort—a way to check out whenever inescapable confinement with her own thoughts made her want to chew glass or people's heads off. Out of habit she smoothed the wrinkles in the lap of her navy sheath, the one with the de rigueur red, white, and blue flag pin attached to the lapel of the matching jacket. *Still presentable. Mom will like that.* The outfit looked surprisingly fresh considering she'd been wearing it since the embassy welcome reception two days ago. Hard to believe it could take that long to get anywhere on the planet anymore, and it felt as if she'd been flying for a week, but it took a solid twenty-three hours in the air to go from her new post in Wellington, New Zealand, to New York. Under normal circumstances, just about long enough for her to prepare for family reentry, but normal was on a leave of absence. Even Avery couldn't prepare.

She fluffed the back of her freshly trimmed hair, laid two breath strips on her tongue, and reapplied lip-colored lipstick, all without looking, without thinking. Like it actually mattered. Avery had picked at her meals, elegantly served on moderne china in business class. Even left the mascarpone and raspberry-ripple ice cream with berry compote until it was pink slush. Normally she'd have been all over it, skipped the entrée and asked for a second dessert. But, in spite of the coaxing of her overzealous flight attendant, she declined warm nuts, countless snacks, wine, coffee, and drank only enough water to keep her throat from feeling like sandpaper. Right now she just couldn't choke down any more.

To make some use of this unplanned family leave, make the time seem more regular, Avery had isolated herself in her passenger pod and attempted to read work she'd downloaded to her laptop—embassy participation in Waitangi Day, office-kitchen protocol—you are getting sleepy. Wellington wasn't exactly a hotbed of political controversy, and her predecessor had left things in order, but as the new embassy counselor for public affairs she needed to get up to speed. Although the documents were in English, the letters wriggled on the screen like ants in a pile of sugar, which is how she used to feel about reading Japanese until she mastered it. Usually Avery could press on through distraction, boredom, temptation, and pain. Suck it up and drive on—her father taught her that when she was a little girl and reinforced it regularly.

But this time, in the hushed hum of the cabin, she had succumbed to a four-suit spider-solitaire trance—316 games had numbed her beyond worry and across the Pacific. She only won once, not that it mattered—much. Occasionally she'd stare at the movie pantomime on her personal in-flight entertainment center. A guy slogging through the jungle wearing camouflage and blackface made as much sense without the sound as it would have with headphones. Besides, she didn't care what the flick was about because the bigger problem was that the real world didn't make sense either, not since that phone call.

Fortunately her new assistant—she wasn't even sure she liked him yet because he'd been late two of her first five days—had had sense enough to read her glazed expression, arrange transportation, and point Avery in the right direction. She had only arrived from Osaka the week before—her bags were still splayed on her bedroom floor, the better to grab and go.

Usually Avery liked flying—heading someplace new once her surroundings got too familiar. She'd stare out the window, taking in the world from the safety of thirty-five thousand feet. But this time she kept her shade shut, preferring not to know what was going on out there, as if it didn't exist. She had inhaled twenty-two hours' worth of recycled, pressurized air—or at least as much as the shallow little pants that passed for breathing would allow. With the light back off, her hands folded in her lap, the closer they got to JFK, the more Avery wanted to reach up and pull the oxygen mask down over her nose and mouth because she felt woozy. Especially when she let herself think about what she might have to deal with at the hospital. *Wait for the facts. Don't overreact.*

NEW YORK, NEW YORK

She'll pull through. We'll work it out. Dwight passed the elevator and reached the end of the nondescript corridor in three long strides, his mantra moving him forward. It was better when his mind was blank after his session, but too much was going on for that. He shoved open the fire door, bounded down the stairs, two at a time. Usually, he rode the elevator up to the third floor, but by the time he had finished his appointment, the stairs beckoned. He always felt more centered, recharged, lighter, so with the energy that came after unburdening himself, his dash was a small reassurance that even when the world was doing its best to chew him up, he could at least handle what was on his plate. And they were so close. He couldn't believe Avery had agreed to the property sale without making it some kind of war game. Maybe it was the money. He didn't know or care, but their lawyers had the paperwork. The money was in place. Then the week went to hell and he needed to keep his feet out of the fire. This wasn't his regular appointment so he was grateful to be worked in. Except the timing jammed his already overbooked schedule. *Make it work.* He'd come too far. That was the only option.

Bursting onto West Nineteenth Street, Dwight sucked the prickly April air into his lungs. His black gabardine raincoat flapped in the wind—it cooled the layer of sweat beneath his Egyptian-cotton shirt. Nothing in the damp, frosty night promised a change of season. The weather, like pretty much everything else in his life, felt like a threat. *I'm a man. I can handle it.* But he for damn sure wished it were different.

Wish—the way a kid wishes for a blizzard on the day of a test he didn't study for, firmly believing it's possible. Until he opens his eyes the next morning, doesn't see flake one, and knows he's doomed. He'd done that enough times as a kid to learn to make alternative arrangements for when the wish thing fell through. The way Dwight figured, he got his wishes more often than most people because plan B kept him ahead. So while he wished for the magic BlackBerry—the one without a dozen snarling messages from King, an insipid reminder from his wife to stop for flowers, like that was the most important thing in his world, or another condescending bulletin from Grace Kidder like he wasn't busting his hump to get it done. Dwight had worked like a demon so they could finally begin phase one. It only took two seconds, a slick street, and a highway trestle to screw it up. Correction—delay the proceedings. Over the blueberries on sale his father had to have. It would be hilarious if it weren't tragic. And inconvenient. So he wished for the magic phone—as if it could happen. *And I could fall and break my damn neck.*

Dwight scanned the cars double-parked along the block, spotted the Town Car with the MILES AHEAD logo and the faint white plume of exhaust. It was parked near the corner of Tenth Avenue, by the scaffolding surrounding the luxury-condo construction site. *Luxury my ass. What a lazy excuse for design.* But at this point West Nineteenth Street—smack in the middle of the trendy Chelsea art district—sold itself. The neighborhood had no residential history—no community groups clamoring for their share of something they didn't own. He knew the bones of this building wouldn't be much different from public housing, but they'd slap on granite countertops, add stainless-steel appliances, and, bingo, even in a recession somebody would pay for a hip new address. What took vision was following the artists priced out of SoHo to their new studio space in dilapidated West Side waterfront warehouses. Eureka! A neighborhood is born. And now there was the Highline right down the block. Only in New York would somebody envision abandoned elevated freight-train tracks as a great site for a park and actually make it happen. Translation—in the 22.7 square miles of Manhattan, any deal can be golden given the right players. He still believed in the alchemy of his deal, but clearly he didn't know the magic word—he had run into challenges around every corner.

Ordinarily Dwight didn't hitch a ride with Sean or use the limo service when he had an appointment. On his calendar the hour was noted as "lunch" or "dentist," and Madeline never questioned his whereabouts. King already acted like Dwight was company property, so he worked to keep his personal business private, quite a challenge in the era of security cams, cell phones, E-ZPass, and GPS. But this once it was easier to break his own rule and have a car waiting than to face his wife's sulking, or his daughter's disappointment, if he missed her recital, even with an emergency on his hands. For weeks Dominique had dutifully practiced her polonaise on the baby grand at home, loving when her father sat beside her on the bench, turning the pages. It had been his mother's piano, but Dwight had no sentimental attachment to the instrument or to the legacy of his daughter's playing it. And although Dominique had heard stories about her grandmother from time to time, Wilhelmina Manning Dixon was no more real to her than the stern portrait that hung in the music room. Piano lessons were solely Renee's doing. She wanted Dominique exposed to as many of the "right" activities as a nine-year-old's stamina allowed. He ducked into the car, settled in the seat.

"Where to congressman?"

That bit of nostalgia always felt like a shank between the ribs, though he'd learned not to flinch. So much for anonymity.

"Been out of politics awhile now"—he leaned forward—"Tariq," grabbing the name from the driver's ID on the dashboard. Fifteen years to be exact. After a semisuccessful career in the City Council, he marshaled all his favors, spent beaucoup family bucks, and engineered a congressional victory in a burn-your-bridges mud-fest. But it was one term in the House and done, Dwight's greatest embarrassment. Just barely ahead of being left at the altar in front of four hundred of his nearest and dearest. Right after the fall from office, announced with the headline "Voters Dump Dixon," King officially took possession of Dwight's nuts.

"I voted for you."

And if everybody who said that actually did, the race would at least have been close.

"Appreciate your support." Dwight fastened his seat belt. *Now shut up and drive.*

OVER NYC

Tray tables up, flaps down, the landing was routine, and Avery shot up when the FASTEN SEAT BELT light went off, darted as far down the aisle as she could before she hit the logjam of passengers shuffling to the door. *Pigs.* She eyed the blankets, peanut shells, newspapers, and other assorted debris covering the floor in one of the rows she passed, wondering why people couldn't keep their crap to themselves—knowing countries couldn't do it either. Otherwise she'd be a career diplomat out of a job.

Trudging through the terminal, she could have been anywhere—Helsinki, Jakarta—none of it looked familiar, but how long was it since she'd been . . . home? That's what people usually called the place where they were born and raised, so New York in general and Harlem in particular was home. But Avery was over the wishbone-after-Thanksgiving-dinner, faded-Polaroids, click-your-heels-together, no-place-like-home feeling. There were already enough people to wake up in the city that never sleeps. She'd just as soon reside elsewhere. She didn't make it home for Dwight's first wedding—the one where the bride had an epiphany and walked back up the aisle and out the big doors without him—scandalously embarrassing, but Avery always wished she'd known what her cousin had done to cause bride number one to bail. Then there was the command appearance for the second, face-saving, rebound, need-a-wife-to-run-for-Congress nuptials. Bride number two—was her name Renee?—looked as desperately loyal as a golden retriever. As if she would have rolled over and begged to hear Dwight say, "I do." To Avery the whole thing seemed as fake as pink flamingos on an AstroTurf lawn. Fake as Dwight's Chiclets smile when he said he was sorry she wasn't one of the bridesmaids. He was smart enough to do that in front of her mother, knowing he'd get a polite reply. At the moment, what difference did any of it make, especially since she still had to clear customs?

➢ ➢ ➢

Dwight relaxed a moment as the car sailed up Broadway. He spotted a deli with a bountiful sidewalk flower stand, had Tariq pull to the curb by the hydrant for the three minutes it took him to select and pay for a dozen white roses. Renee would have preferred pink or yellow, or one of those awful mixed bouquets that come flecked with sparkles. But Dwight was fond of the simple beauty of white roses—always appropriate, and tasteful, they were exactly what his daughter, Dominique, should want, whether she did or not.

As the car continued north, Dwight finally checked his messages. No surprises, no last-minute stays of execution. The ones from his father he deleted unheard. That simple act gave him great pleasure. They were some version of the same harangue King had been on since they'd removed the tube from his throat. IV morphine tempered the pain in King's shattered leg, broken clavicle, and cracked ribs. It did nothing to take the edge off his temper. But then, Scotch made him ornery too, always had.

➢ ➢ ➢

As long as there was luggage to claim, forms to fill out, lines to stand in, Avery could keep her mind from filling in the hazy details with the worst-case scenario. During her LAX layover she'd checked out the headlines—"Harlem RE King in Fight of His Life." Her uncle King was always fighting about something, and Avery figured if it was between him and the devil, the odds were even. Her mother wasn't mentioned by name until the third paragraph, a footnote to King's headline, as usual. They were both listed as critical but stable—exactly what she'd been told by the hospital when they'd reached her at the reception. One moment Avery had been sipping tea and chatting with staff and local officials gathered at the ambassador's residence, the next she was on the phone, struggling to make sense of the words, simple words, no translation required. She'd grabbed a napkin to take notes, but afterward could hardly read the words staggering down the paper. *Critical but stable*—she added that one to her doublespeak list—sounds reassuring, but means exactly what? Something more unpleasant than you actually want to say. Almost twenty years in diplomatic service had taught her to recognize officialese immediately and calmly respond in kind. But did the social worker really care what Avery said, other than she'd be there as soon as possible? Define care—real concern, or it's off my desk for now?

➢ ➢ ➢

A few blocks from the Strivers' Row house Dwight had lived in his entire life—aside from his years at Brown—he felt

Uptown

for the bow tie dangling open around his neck. Eyes closed, he buttoned his collar, fingered the burgundy-and-gold strip of silk—cross over, flip through. The tie was the last step in donning his armor, preparing his public face. He pulled at the loops, felt the symmetry, felt himself straighten, just as they stopped in front of the blond-brick town house. He opened his eyes in time to see Renee disappear from the parlor window. Right on time, as always. As if she were late she wouldn't get to go and would never be asked again. That suited Dwight fine. He'd never bothered to ask her why, assumed her obsession was the result of some childhood incident, and he knew imprints from childhood were nearly impossible to unlearn without years of therapy—and maybe not even then.

In a few seconds she was outside locking up. Dwight got out to open the car door.

Renee smiled as she walked down the limestone steps. Pleasant. Sturdy. Dependable. Eager to please. And as usual, overdressed—the only trait, besides her culinary acumen, Dwight felt she shared with his late mother. Not a Christmas tree on the Fourth of July—just too matronly in a casually chic world. Dads like himself, in subtly custom-tailored suits, swooping in after extricating themselves from some moneymaking pit in the bowels of Manhattan—that was always in style. Even the career women in the crowd would be more expensively unpremeditated. But Renee's St. John suits and pearls looked so staid amid the Prada jackets and True Religion jeans worn by the other stay-at-home moms who would be there. The evening was a command performance for parents who, like the Dixons, came to cheer on their musical prodigies and shore up any social or business connections that might prove useful down the line.

"You know I don't like red lipstick."

"I thought it looked nice with—never mind." Renee took out a tissue, wiped her mouth. "Better?" She gave him a cursory kiss, then filled him in on the day's minutiae while she redid her lips in her usual coral shade.

Dwight heard a third of it. Once they'd settled in the auditorium and the lights dimmed, he could stop pretending to listen, try to tune in to the musical entertainment. First up, a painfully flat violin rendition of something laughably called "My Little Star" according to the program. The redheaded boy with the Beatle bangs stood only feet from the curtain, as if he knew his solo wasn't very good and he could escape at any moment. Dwight escaped into his thoughts.

By all rights it should have been King still in the ICU. He instigated their 8 p.m. fruit run. Not to be mercenary, but the deal could go on without King present. Dwight had a springing power of attorney for his father, who wasted no sentiment and called his son every kind of stupid bastard for not having one on file for Forestina.

Renee's elbow in his side let him know Dominique had taken her position at the piano.

Not Juilliard material. He expected Dominique would fill out in the usual places soon enough and move more surely into the area of the unknowable, which is pretty much the way he felt about the rest of her gender. As far as women were concerned, he only understood what was expected of him, liked it laid out in explicit terms—questions he could answer, tasks he could accomplish, items he could buy. Dwight had hoped for a son. Not to carry on the family name, although King reminded him he'd failed on that front too. Dwight had hoped he could identify with a male child, at least enough to prove he was a better father than his own.

But they had a girl, so Dwight vowed to "first do no harm," which translated into benign neglect. He mostly left her to her mother, except occasionally to give her the kind of polish he knew Renee didn't have.

Tilting his head toward the music, Dwight listened attentively as Dominique played the solo he knew by heart—so unlike Renee, he actually noticed when Dominique lost her place and repeated the section she had just played. Still, as was the custom, he jumped to his feet as she took her bow, and presented her with the bouquet. The whole thing was done in under two hours.

So Dwight had Tariq drop mother, daughter, and bouquet at home, then continue on to the hospital. King and his tirade would have to wait until tomorrow, but he could check on his aunt, see if she had made any progress or was at least holding her own. He opened the window, drew another deep, biting breath, let the cold air brace him for whatever the hospital would bring. Not exactly navy SEAL training, but survival was survival, and Dwight worked with what he had.

➢ ➢ ➢

Baggage cleared, passport stamped, Avery left the holding pen and followed the international symbols to the taxi line. She walked through the automatic doors—

—and smack into a frosty gust of welcome back that whipped through her lightweight raincoat and chilled her until she shivered. Her cabdriver turned the heat up full blast, but Avery couldn't stop her teeth from chattering. Couldn't imagine seeing her mother . . . like that. *Suck it up.*

The good thing about the ICU—it's open 24-7, no pesky time constraints when your loved one is hanging on by a thread. After hours, hospital corridors have the same dim hush as the inside of an airplane, which eased Avery's entry. In the halls, the smell of canned string beans and cold gravy lingered. The RN logging charts at the nurses' station had tailored black scrubs piped in pink, and auburn hair pulled tight into a ballerina topknot that raised her eyes at the corners. Avery let herself be comforted by the concern in the woman's Texas twang, followed her quick steps to the window looking in on Forestina's room.

First thing Avery noticed was her hair. No matter the season or time of day, her mother's hair was carefully arranged—dignified. Now the flossy, blondish cotton candy stood all over her head like tumbleweed, except for the patch above her left ear that was shaved, revealing impossibly pink scalp. A cast was on her leg. It looked as if it weighed a ton. She looked so still—mouth open, face slack, breath so slow. Avery always thought of her mother in motion—chirping, cajoling, making everyone feel welcome. It's how she had been in Paris, only weeks before.

Avery sort of knew the nurse was talking—about a small subdural hematoma, cracked ribs, a broken femur that had required a rod and pins, what time doctors did rounds, going to admissions to complete forms. Hands clasped behind her at parade rest, Avery nodded like she understood. She knew she was supposed to have questions, but the best she could do was to keep herself standing. No need to bother a total stranger with an unseemly breakdown. *Open your eyes.* Avery wanted to see the sparkle in them. That's when she noticed the wrist restraints. The nurse noticed her notice them too.

"She pulled her IVs out twice. We had to keep her sedated so she's a little out of it. It's normal." The nurse said it like an apology. "I'll leave you alone. You can go on in."

No, she couldn't. Avery could handle the scene as a movie—a spectacle she could observe from a safe distance, no interaction, please. Opening the door meant it was really her mother in that bed, attached to monitors. What was she supposed to do with that? Her father had never been in the hospital. Avery was three years into her first post, in Belize. Her mother called, all in a flummox, said he was fine when she left for church that morning—in his robe and pajamas, sitting in the breakfast nook with apple juice, a peanut-butter, bacon, and jelly sandwich, and the crossword puzzle, as usual. By the time Forestina got home, he was on the floor, cold. End of story. It was hard for Avery to feel anything for the man in the mahogany box. The essence of her father wasn't in there, which was good—she was still furious at him, but she was enough his daughter to carry on, greet those who came to pay respects, sit through the endless tributes, secret ceremonies, and be the dutiful daughter.

She watched from outside for a long time. Finally, her mother stirred, and Avery counted down, four, three, two . . . and launched herself inside. The light was so bright—like standing inside a fluorescent bulb. Somehow she expected her mother to take over, tell her what a surprise this was, how she didn't have to come all this way, how good she looked. Instead, her mother rocked side to side, tugged at her restraints, kicked the covers, hurled a slurred stream of gibberish, jumbled like in an angry dream.

"Mom, are you in pain? Should I get the nurse?" Avery bent down to eye level, cupped her mother's hand, so cold. For a startling moment she didn't know if her mother recognized her. "Mom, it's me." Couldn't imagine how that could be. "Avery."

Forestina quieted, so still, dull eyes locked on her daughter as Avery smoothed the storm of hair. She hadn't noticed it was so sparse—like a baby's. Then one tear bubbled in the corner of her mother's eye, quivered there, rolled down her cheek. Avery wiped it away with her fingertips, kissed her forehead. In a moment her mother's eyes fluttered closed, but Avery felt known.

She dimmed the glare in the room to twilight, moved the stack of sheets from the chair to the counter by the sink. She dragged the chair next to the bed, sat down, and gingerly lowered one side of the cage. It was just the two of them—so quiet. Avery wished for something to do, but for now there was just the hush, the waiting, the anxious flutter. She rested her head next to her mother's hand, thought how much they had to talk about. *As soon as she's better.* For real this time—

—when she first woke up, she thought she was back on the plane, until she felt the fingers resting on her cheek. She wanted it to be comforting, but they gave her goose bumps. Avery slid herself clear, sat up. Her mother was still asleep, or drugged, something other than conscious. As soon as Avery blinked her eyes in focus, she was startled by the shadowy figure standing at the window, watching. Then their eyes met, and she knew it was him. She gathered herself a moment—it had been so long. Finally, she stood, walked to the door.

For Dwight, it was all taking care of business until now—handling the press, getting the best doctors, assuring partners and contractors that the accident wouldn't affect progress on Dixon Plaza—just the facts, nothing personal. Seeing Avery sitting there, seeing the two of them, made his aunt's condition feel like more than information to spin. It gave him a bright pain in a place that hadn't been touched in a while—sharp and surprising, like ice cream on the wrong tooth. Their family—it was so small. Not many people to share the memories, and when he had seen his aunt that first night—honestly he was sure she was gone, but the old ones were tough. Renee had been hovering, waiting for him to crack. Well, she could use all that pent-up mothering on Dominique, who was worried about her beloved aunt, and about Kinger, as she called her grandfather—the only unauthorized nickname he dignified with a response. For Dwight, sharing anything with King read weak—he'd get it rammed down his throat. But with Avery . . . Dwight moved in closer, wanting to connect, at least for a moment.

"It's the middle of the night. What are you doing here?" Arms folded tight across her chest, Avery spoke like she was asking about the weather. It was frosty. When they were young, she was his shadow, followed everywhere he'd let her.

Dwight felt the chill. "I stop in—on both of them." Arms glued to his sides, he looked past Avery, at his aunt. They'd raced slot cars. They'd raced home from school. "She talk to you?"

Avery shook her head. Didn't look at him. "King?"

"Hasn't shut up." Dwight decided this wasn't a time to be silent either. "There's no good time to bring this up." He paused until she looked at him. "Do you have a power of attorney for your . . ."

"No. Why?" Avery didn't know where this was going, but official documents were not up for discussion.

Damn. "No. Nothing. There just might be some decisions you need to make . . . about her treatment, those kinds of issues. It might have made things easier." It would have for him, but easy was in short supply.

"I'm her daughter. There's just me." Avery could feel her voice creeping louder. She shifted back to neutral. "What else do they need?"

The words that passed between them sucked the air out of the room.

"Really, it'll be okay. I'm sure." But Dwight was going to have to come up with a plan in a hurry. He needed to know about 111th Street.

"Look, I'm going back inside." Without her mother to prod or King to instigate, there wasn't anything else she wanted to say to him.

Dwight could tell she'd already turned him off. "Yep. Okay." *It wasn't my fault.* But he said nothing. No point wasting his breath on a losing argument.

FOUR

. . . home to Harlem

"Here okay?"

As if the driver actually gave Avery a chance to answer before depositing her bag in a puddle in front of the house. Even had the nerve to smile like he'd done a good deed while he shifted side to side, waiting in the predawn darkness to get paid.

Big, loud, juicy drops pelted Avery, pounded the pavement, syncopating her agitation—as if she needed accompaniment. She was just grateful to be free of the overheated, fake-jasmine fog in the backseat of the yellow cab. Free of her mother's room, at least long enough to grab a shower, get her head straight, gather a few personal items. Having her own hairbrush and underwear would definitely make her mother feel better when she woke up and was herself again.

Avery peeled bills from the stash of U.S. cash she kept

with her wherever she was posted, handed them to the driver. It was too much—better than too little, like her dad. She just wanted to be alone, wanted to stop rerunning the conversation with Dwight in her head. He still got to her, and she hated that, hated that she wasn't more prepared to deal with him—mad that it mattered. In her usual orbit, Dwight had ceased to exist, left the galaxy. But there was no way to get through this and avoid him completely. She had sat, paced, worried, prayed for hours—long enough to decide it wouldn't change anything, at least right away. So she decided to leave and go home, regroup for the next day.

She lugged her bag up the stairs of the blond-brick row house. It was identical to its conjoined cousins, with a sturdy, stately wrought-iron fence and balconet—pricey, artisan-crafted replicas of the originals, which had been stolen. A lovely facade, like some Hollywood-backlot Huxtable world—looks real, if you don't look too close.

Welcome home, kiddo.

Even though no one was there, the golden glow from deliberately aged sconces beside the door greeted her. *He's still running her life.* As far back as memory would carry her—sometimes a good trip, sometimes not—the oning and offing of house lights had taken place at regularly scheduled intervals, determined ages ago by her father, Dr. Braithwaite, or as everyone called him, Doc B. Creating a lived-in appearance became his obsession after the house was robbed during the bad old days, when some of the gracious homes on the block had become not-so-genteel rooming houses, and Harlem was a code word for a scary, lawless place. He devised elaborate programs to make lamps and chandeliers brighten and dim, so it looked as if a houseful of people bustled about. Her mother tried to convince him it was common neighborhood knowledge that only the three of them lived there. "We won't be burgled by our kind, Forestina. It's the outsiders." Avery was never sure how far beyond the back-to-back blocks that made up Strivers' Row *our kind* ended, and outsiders began. But the bright setting looked as welcoming and cozy as a Norman Rockwell print. Good old Norm had, in fact, grown up only a few blocks away. The Rockwells didn't live there anymore, although from what she'd heard, it seemed "their kind" might be moving home to Harlem.

Avery dug in her pocket for her keys. It was ages since she'd actually opened the door with them, but the locks hadn't changed, and the keys were in the same order her father had put them. He had organized all of their key rings exactly the same way on their matching key chains—hers had an *A*, her mother's an *F*, like they couldn't be trusted to recognize them without a label.

A plastic bag scuttled along the curb, snatched Avery's breath. She whipped around, checked the street for marauders lurking in the shadows. Nothing. Just too much of her father's paranoia racing through her system. The offending bag continued along the sidewalk, toward King's house.

She'd managed not to look that way until now. It was the first place she'd ever gone by herself. That day she strolled down the block in her new yellow-and-green shorts set. She held her head high, like a big girl, held her breath, determined not to look back at her mother, watching from the stoop. When she arrived a full sixty seconds later, Dwight was sitting on the steps with her reward—a grape Popsicle, her favorite flavor—and she finally exhaled. She was five, Dwight was eight. The house was his now, or at least he lived in it. King had long ago abandoned Harlem—his grand "kiss my ass," since old-timers on the Row had always looked down their refined noses at him, whispered about the "tainted" money that had bought the house and all his others. Payback is a better address. He'd finagled his way into a tony Fifth Avenue co-op that regularly rejected folks with longer pedigrees and fancier résumés, leaving the heir apparent in residence in the hood. Avery hoped her little clash with Dwight had made him feel bad, wondered if he even gave it a second thought. Or was he nestled all snug in his bed. *Enough.* It was hard to stay in the present when home dredged up so much past.

In one smooth motion, Avery poked the key in the lock, opened the heavy oak door, stepped into the vestibule, and went immediately to the keypad. Her fingers recalled the security code—her birthday in reverse. She could hear her father explaining how it would make them safer—her and her mother, like scary strangers had been the problem. Nice try.

So, now she was in the box and she felt like Pandora.

Just inside the entry hall, she choked back a giant, heaving sob that almost overwhelmed her. *Smells the same.* Avery had lived all over the world, and each place had a distinct aroma that could bring her there, even with her eyes closed. Mornings in Paris had a dewy musk, like dying flowers, that conjured up grand passion—or what she imagined it would be—and great loss. Dakar was honey and cloves and dust—tranquil, solitary, the way her home might smell, if she ever chose to have one. And the stuff she grew up on—dried lavender, lemon oil, Lysol, and Youth-Dew—assaulted her now. It lived in the wainscoting and the faded gold flocked wallpaper as surely as Avery had lived there once. Every breath was mingled with memories—roast chicken, string beans, and rice for solemn Sunday dinners right after church. Her mother's club meetings, with tall, sweaty glasses of iced tea, hors d'oeuvres arranged on the three-tiered lazy Susan—the gossip Avery wasn't supposed to hear floated to her perch on the upstairs landing. The scent of Scotch accompanied cordial innuendo lobbed between her parents, and just enough antiseptic to keep it all clean. Just a whiff took her back to this house. But this wasn't a memory. She was in the mother ship.

Avery shook herself from the trance, tossed her coat over the newel post, and blamed the chill that settled over her like a net on the preprogrammed thermostat—a lot easier than unraveling her tangled emotions. In only a few hours she had to be back at the hospital, and she was already exhausted. She wasn't about to be cold too. So, defiant, as if her father were still there to lecture her about wasting heat on an empty house, she marched into the parlor, upped the heat from sixty to a toasty seventy-four degrees. Back when she was a child, green was just a color, not a movement. To Avery, her father was not a man ahead of his time, conserving resources to save the planet. He was annoying, embarrassing, and cheap.

But her mother was obviously still following Father's *Little Instruction Book*—correction, books. Doc B cataloged everything from gas-meter readings to which shirts he sent to the laundry. He wrote down the details of each expenditure of money, without exception, including Avery's allowance, and her mother's. He was especially vigilant about the particulars of keeping the house shipshape. He noted when appliances were bought, the cost, the length of warranties, who to call during the service contract, and who to contact after it expired. There were color chips and wallpaper swatches for each room, along with who was responsible for the painting or hanging. He had notes about every contractor and handyman who had worked on the house—whether they were prompt, late, or no-shows which were starred in red. Then he listed the amount paid for their services, and whether they were worth it. He kept decades' worth of these diaries, along with similar ones for the apartment building they owned, on the shelf above the desk in his *study*—not his *office,* which, he was quick to point out, was where he saw patients. At home, it was his study. When she was six, Avery had surprised him and drawn a butterfly sitting on a daisy in one of his diaries. When he found it, he lectured her about respecting other people's property, then, ignoring her tears, carefully removed the offending page, balled it up, and threw it away.

As Avery got older, her father would regularly extol the virtues of keeping careful notes, ridiculing her mother, who couldn't ever find her Christmas-card list from one year to the next. "Write it down, Avery. You'll never regret it." She used to wonder if his endless record keeping was a by-product of his medical training. Maybe it was his army service—like his meticulously arranged closet and spit-shined shoes. Or was he just an obsessive-compulsive nutcase? The last time he brought it up, she was fifteen. Avery answered, "Why should I write stuff down? So you can read it?" He never mentioned it again. She used to get furious at her mother for just going along with the program. Her answer? A laugh, a pat on the hand. "You know how your father is." Like that made it OK.

Avery wrapped her arms around herself, wandered into the front room. Her dad had been gone sixteen years, and nothing had changed. He could have been sitting in the roll-armed leather chair, *his* chair—it didn't go with the damask and chintz, but he didn't care. Avery used to hate the old-timey hodgepodge of "good pieces"—mahogany and cherry tables with graceful curved limbs and little brass feet, dark Oriental rugs over shiny parquet floors, heavy silk drapery with fussy tassels and swags. It was like living in a museum nobody wanted to visit. Her mother had promised they would last a lifetime, as if that were something to look forward to.

But there was no time for remembering, much less time for a nap, so Avery dragged her bag into the dining room, zipped it open—she didn't have energy to carry the thing another step further. Besides, who was there to complain about her mess? She dug a turtleneck, some jeans, and fresh underwear out of her suitcase and headed upstairs.

The third step from the top still creaked. That slow, low

groan made it clear how loud the quiet was. As a teenager she'd gotten good at avoiding the booby trap when she snuck in past curfew, but the house always had other sounds as distraction. The minute hand of the mantel clock on the second floor clicked back before it moved ahead, like it was reluctant to let go of the moment. The old refrigerator in the study hummed nonstop. Then there was the snoring coming from her parents' separate bedrooms—their own nocturnal call-and-response, which was about as close as they got to communicating.

What happened to that clock?

The door to Avery's room stood open. She hesitated, flicked on the light. There it was, her early life—trophies dusted, pillows fluffed, as if she'd slept there the night before. At thirteen her mother let her redecorate. Good-bye four-poster rice bed and all the traditional trimmings. Her room became a vision in curvilinear, ivory Formica, with pink wall-to-wall carpeting, nothing like the rest of the house. She loved it—until a semester in France introduced her to the casual glamour of living with heirlooms. She fell for the bohemian romance of it all, but couldn't quite figure out how to ask her mom for a do-over. One morning, over Frosted Flakes, Avery mentioned, as offhandedly as a seventeen-year-old could manage, that since she would soon be away at college and would then move into her own place, probably in San Francisco, it was okay if her mother wanted to put the old furniture back—make it more like a guest room. Next semester, when Avery returned from a weekend visiting Dwight at Brown, her room had been transformed into a chic retreat featuring a sophisticated arrangement of her very own heirlooms. Her mother was so tickled with the surprise. Avery played along as best she could, as she had sworn to her father she would, but no place felt like home after that weekend.

A twist of her guts forced the teeniest, airless whimper.

Must be hunger. Seemed logical. But then she felt the water level rising, blinked furiously to hold back the flash flood that threatened the levees she had built so painstakingly over the years. *Nope. Not going to happen.* Right there in the hall, she stripped off her suit, heels, and hose, like she was in the locker room after a track meet. She left them in a heap in the doorway and darted, butt naked, into the bathroom. She used to hate to be the first one to shower in the morning. The water spat and sputtered through the old pipes to the third floor, finally emerging in a frigid spray. Her father fussed if she let the water run until it was at least warm, but this time Avery just stepped in. The icy cascade stung like needles, chased her tears, gave her focus. By the time it was close to warm, she had soaped up, rinsed clean, and stepped out, shivering, but dry-eyed. Once toweled off, she fished her clean clothes from under the pile on the floor, dressed without looking.

She marched downstairs and into her mother's room without hesitation, rummaged through the closet for some kind of bag. First she unearthed a wad of shopping bags so old, most of the stores had gone out of business. *Why does she still have these?* She dropped them on the floor. Clearly her mom needed help moving into the twenty-first century—a productive project for Avery's stint in New York. She emptied the umbrella and black patent pumps from an Estée Lauder gift-with-purchase tote, found an old shopping list inside—salt, raisins, deodorant. She hadn't looked at her mother's delicate, loopy handwriting in a while. *How can penmanship be cheerful?*

The answering machine on the bedside table had twelve messages. *Later.* Next, the dresser. *Which is the underwear drawer? The top one?* No—jewelry, scarves, hankies—and white gloves? *Really?* The second held the treasure and saved Avery from further invasion of her mother's privacy. Except choosing panties felt like trespassing. Avery wasn't surprised to find neatly arranged stacks of regulation beige and black drawers and no-nonsense brassieres, but in the back there were matching sets of bras and panties in lollipop colors, tropical flowers, zebra stripes. *Mom?* That was a shocker, unless your mother is Tina Turner, and she didn't picture good old Forestina rollin' on anybody's river. Avery snatched a few of the unremarkable undergarments, shoved the drawer closed, grabbed her mother's comb, brush, toothbrush, and lotion out of the bathroom, and went in search of coffee.

A solitary boneless chicken breast languished in a freezer bag in the sink. Her mother had left home for an afternoon meeting fully intending to be back in time for her five o'clock manhattan on the rocks, the evening news, *Wheel of Fortune,* and supper. That was three days ago. Avery ditched the chicken, made a mental note to take out the trash.

The hint of daylight through yellow-check curtains made Avery feel more normal—like the woman she was used to showing the world. Over oatmeal cookies and coffee—who knew they still made freeze-dried crystals, but it would have to do—Avery jotted her action plan on her PDA. Go by the hospital early, in time for morning rounds, so she could talk with her mother's doctors, help her with breakfast. It would give her some sustenance to counteract all that pain medication that Avery decided was clouding her mind. Coffee and a croissant at the Tuileries on the morning her mother had called a "gift" fluttered into Avery's mind. She waved the thought away, made a note to stop by the hospital business office to do paperwork. After that she needed to track down the police report for the accident, find out where the car had been towed, see if the insurance company had been notified. She set a reminder to call her office at 5 p.m. It would be nine the next morning there, which meant her assistant should be in—if he'd managed to show up on time. She could check in, let them know she would be stateside for at least two weeks. She figured she'd have her mother pretty much squared away by then, probably at a rehab facility first, then with a home attendant—that would be a battle. Aside from Jessie, who attended the same church and had been the Braithwaites' cleaning lady since before Avery left for college, Forestina did not like strange people poking around her house. *She'll have to deal with it.* Maneuvering up narrow stairs with that cast was out. They could bring the double bed from the guest room to the downstairs parlor. A kitchen and a bathroom were on that floor.

She considered calling Van in Sapporo. He had offered to meet her in New York, but she told him it would be okay. She'd keep him up-to-date. In the two years they'd been seeing each other, she'd learned to enjoy time they spent together. But Avery was also happy when she was alone. As chief technology officer for a leading worldwide software developer, Van traveled a lot, and they kept in touch by e-mail and Skype. At times she wanted to miss him more than she actually did. Before she left for Wellington, they talked about the separation and decided that since even when they were in the same city, they were never together all the time anyway, living five thousand miles apart wouldn't be that different. At least for now.

Game plan in place, Avery headed out the door, figured she could snag a gypsy cab on Adam Clayton Powell—and not have to pass Dwight's house. She wasn't feeling another encounter yet.

Without the wind it felt warmer than the night before. A siren in the distance let her know she was back in New York. But the youngish white woman in sweats jogging toward her, greyhound trotting at her side, was definitely a new highlight of the scenery. So was the Mickey D's diagonally across the boulevard. Storefronts had stylish new awnings, and the gypsy cab she waved down was a black Lincoln, not a beat-up junker with no shocks. Avery had heard a lot had changed in her old stomping ground. She just hadn't pictured it.

At the hospital gift shop, she picked up two papers, one for news, one for the juicy tidbits her mother swore she didn't read. *Wonder if she has an iPod? Probably not. I'll pick one up*. She snaked her way to the correct elevator bank, held the door for a security guard with his bushy hair parted down the middle.

Avery rounded the corner toward the room, hoped to see her mother sitting up. She was always an early riser. But when she got to the window, a chill, colder than that of the shower, oozed through Avery's veins. The bed was empty. The room looked ransacked. Dwight stood by the window, starring into space.

"Where is she?" *Wait for the facts*. Her voice came out whispery, stricken.

"I called, but you didn't—"

"The phone never rang." Shrill panic—she tried to push it down, to keep the walls from collapsing. "Did they take her for tests?"

Dwight wanted to move closer, decided that wouldn't go well. Hell, he wanted to cry, but what good would that do? "She had a heart attack, Avery." The call woke him straight out of a dead sleep. He barely knew where he was when he picked up the phone, then put on clothes by remote control, left Renee and Dominique huddled together. For a moment he'd thought about going down the block, ringing the bell. But in spite of the lights he figured she'd be asleep, decided to let her rest. She'd at least be fresh when she got the news.

"Where is she now? Or will they bring her back here?"

"They couldn't bring her back." Dwight had rehearsed the words, but they still didn't come out right. Really, there was no right.

"From where?" Avery sat her bags in the chair, scrambled for a different meaning.

"Avery, your mom died."

The blood rushed to Avery's head. She could hear it pulse in her ears. Hand to her mouth, she could still feel her mother's forehead on her lips—warm and dry—from last night's kiss. The last kiss good-night? She didn't remember dropping to her knees, but there was Dwight standing over her, lifting her up.

"No." She pulled away, got to her feet. "Leave me."

"You can't do this by yourself."

"Myself is what I can count on, Dwight." She could hear the words, but couldn't feel them leave her mouth.

It would have been easier if she'd just hit him, pounded him. Instead, her words cut like a thousand razor gashes. He reached in his pocket, handed her his business card. "My cell is here. I'm going to tell King."

Avery shoved it in her pocket, glared him out of the room, turned to the bed, like this had all been some evil magic and her mother would suddenly reappear from behind the curtain. Shazam. Months, sometimes years, went by when they didn't see each other, but whatever remained unsettled between them, knowing her mother was at home, rolling her hair on pink sponge curlers, clipping coupons she never remembered to redeem, that made the planet all right. Except that spirit was gone, and the atmosphere had already changed. It wasn't supposed to happen. Not now.

Avery stayed in the room a long while. It was the last place she had seen her mother, felt her. The resident and last night's nurse stopped by, offered condolences. The windows overlooked the river's early-morning sparkle. Cars crept along the drive, carrying people whose day would be completely ordinary. But Avery knew that as soon as she walked into the corridor, she would officially be in the new world, the one without her mother in it.

FIVE

Life is more than solitaire

"Oh, Lord." It's all King could say as Dwight told him the news. King felt like he'd stepped in a sinkhole and it sucked him down, covered him over.

There had been the four of them—young, each with dreams bigger than the world they lived in. Now King was the only one left. He told Dwight he was tired, wanted to be by himself. His son had never seen him cry. No point starting now.

King never spent much time looking back—"If that's where I wanted to be, I'da stayed there." But he lay with his eyes closed, seeing them all the way they used to be.

When he arrived in Harlem, King was lean, eager, and always talking, always in motion, fit in like it was where he belonged. He was only sixty-five miles from the farm, but he may as well have landed on Mars. He found a room, shared a bath in the hall—he didn't need much. He was always out in the street, "seeing" he called it. Early in the morning until late at night he was checking out the action, finding out how things got done and who did them, looking at all those buildings, one right up next to the other as if the space were too precious to waste. He figured they must be worth something if black folks lived in them, but white folks still owned most of them. And he wanted to own some too. His father had told him long ago, "If you own some land, you'll always have someplace to lay your head and make your bread."

King started out shining shoes, near the Theresa because he felt important looking at that big, impressive hotel and the swell people strolling in and out, like they owned the stars. He learned to pop that rag, make the shoes gleam, talk enough trash to keep the tips generous and encourage repeat business. By winter he'd finagled an arrangement with a barbershop down the block. He'd shine shoes, and for an extra cut he'd steer performers from nearby clubs to the shop, tell jokes, and in general keep the joint lively, which earned him his nickname. A man who was new to the place became annoyed with his antics and said, "Who are you, the court jester?" The reply: "Maybe so, but one day this fool's gonna be king." So that day he was crowned and he liked it. After a while folks who used to know his name forgot. The rest had never heard it, which was fine and dandy with him, because King Dixon never saw shining shoes as a long-term gig—he was not interested in staying on the ground at anybody's feet.

So he picked up a handyman job in a five-story walk-up. On the farm he'd learned to fix whatever was broken—the tractor, the furnace, the plumbing, the roof—or shame on you, you'd do without. The owner, a second-generation son of Polish immigrants who had long ago moved his family to Cedarhurst, Long Island, liked the way King took care of the property—like he owned it—including shaking up the occasional troublemaker or rent delinquent, for a bonus. King was not averse to busting heads in the name of order.

That's how he met Doc B. A few nights a week King would see this acutely serious-looking young guy, booking it down the block toward Seventh Avenue, head high, suit and tie, but not flashy. Early one bitter morning when even the stray cats had found some place to hunker down, King was setting garbage cans out by the curb when he heard a commotion up the block. He turned to see two thugs shove Mr. Serious up against a Pontiac Star Chief. King had learned the ways of the city well enough to know he should mind his own business, but he grabbed a metal trash-can lid and the switchblade in his pocket and went charging down the block, the Zulu warrior of 136th Street.

By the time King ran up on the hoodlums, they'd already sliced the man's coat pocket and pant leg, looking for his wallet. One of them wheeled around, thrust his knife at King. It glanced off his makeshift shield. Mr. Serious grabbed at the other man's coat. The slick parka slipped through his fingers, and the pair took off running, but not before a parting knife jab caught King in the side. He braced himself on the car.

"Man, you're crazy." Now rescuer, Mr. Serious hoisted King in his arms and went running.

"Bet you glad I am."

Turned out he was Dr. Serious, a resident at Harlem Hospital, just blocks away. He got King tended to—the knife nicked a rib, but all in all he was lucky.

Now dressed in scrubs and a white lab coat, the doctor came by King's bed to thank him, introduced himself as Dr. Uriah Braithwaite.

"Good thing you are a doctor, 'cause nobody but your mama should call you Uriah."

The men could not have been more opposite—Doc B, a

man of few, clipped words, was from a family held in high regard in the community. He'd followed in his father's footsteps, graduated from Howard Medical School. King could talk loud and long, make you think he was a fool, while he plotted his next move. The only standing he had in the world was on his two feet, but each man was determined in his way. King looked out for Doc B on his walks to the hospital. Doc B would check out King's various aches and complaints at the office he shared with his father without money passing between them. The doctor would meet him out on occasion for a few shots, of the nonhypodermic kind, in a place where nobody's life was in his hands. For as much as King talked, the doctor was the only person King told about his real estate schemes. Doc B said to keep him in mind.

Soon King had more buildings to maintain—now with a gun as his sidekick. The additional properties gave him a wider territorial reach, perfect for his side hustle, running some numbers. He didn't tolerate drugs or whores in his buildings, but a little gambling didn't hurt—everybody likes to win sometimes and he required more than a super's salary. He always had a variety of vacant apartments at his disposal, and he'd charge the numbers bankers to use them for the evening tally. Whatever he could do to make a buck.

When he wasn't slinging a mop, King liked to cut a distinguished figure around town—kept his suits pressed, let his hair grow long enough to get that wave the ladies liked, but he was steady saving his money, getting ready for the day when he could make his move. By digging around and by word of mouth King found an eight-unit building just east of Morningside Park—rodents were rampant and nobody had lifted a hammer or a paintbrush since Prohibition, but he was determined to make it his first stake. Except even with his gray flannel suit and his down payment, he couldn't find a bank that would give him the mortgage. So he went to Doc B, showed him the building.

Initially the doctor was not impressed. "Place looks like a barn and the park looks like a jungle. What can you make out of this?"

"Give me enough time, I can make it into gold."

Doc B had sterling credentials. He gave the enterprise the financials to pass bank scrutiny and was able to bring the deal to a close, so Dixon and Braithwaite became partners, King managing the properties as well as those of other owners and scouting new ones.

They had three buildings by the time they met the Manning sisters, Wilhelmina and Forestina, the daughters of Doc B's med-school mentor. He called when they were coming to New York to spend the summer with their aunt, an eccentric spinster who'd been living in the swank building on Edgecombe Avenue since the days Duke Ellington, Paul Robeson, and Joe Louis called it home. He asked his former student to take them out, show them around. Out and about was definitely King's area of expertise, so Doc B invited him along to meet the young ladies. King said he'd do a favor, but couldn't promise a whole summer of tagging along.

When the two men arrived, they found the gold-leaf ceiling in the once grand marble lobby was peeling, but Aunt Vashti's apartment was a Harlem Renaissance time capsule. She met them at the door, caftan flowing, silver turban encircling her head, her cigarette secured in a foot-long, black-lacquer holder, and welcomed them to her salon, full of tasseled red upholstery with white crocheted antimacassars, milk-glass lamps, and crystal chandeliers. The mirrored bar was set with silver martini shaker at the ready. They followed her past a wall covered in artwork—oils, pastels, and etchings, some of them racy nudes, and the many photos of Vashti in her Cotton Club showgirl glory, and with the outstanding artists, writers, and jazzmen of the time. King and Doc B exchanged wary glances, wondering what kind of strange the afternoon would be. But then they caught sight of her Petersburg, Virginia, nieces, perched on the sofa drinking sweet tea, like a fresh breeze gracing a summer afternoon. The men's eyes lit up like searchlights.

Wilhelmina, the older by all of eleven months, wore her hair a little longer than was fashionable and held herself with a quiet reserve, befitting a conservatory-trained pianist. She was dignified, formal, not loud or common like the women King found in his circle. Forestina was light and frothy like butterfly wings or meringue on lemon pie, perfect for Miss Tina, the just graduated, aspiring first-grade teacher. The usually reserved Doc B blossomed in the light of her attentions, especially her tinkling laughter.

At Tina's urging, that first day they took the train all the way to Coney Island, strolled the boardwalk, sampling bags of hot roasted peanuts, which the gentlemen chivalrously shelled, paper boats filled with fried clams, and crinkly fries they ate with what Forestina said looked like little wooden pitchforks. She and Doc B rode the climbs and dives of the Cyclone—she screamed the entire minute and fifty seconds of the run and held his arm so tight, she almost tore the sleeve out of his shirt. King and Wilhelmina took a trip through the Tunnel of Love, where she allowed him to put his arm around her shoulder. She returned to her ladylike rectitude before they emerged, and King was left to imagine more.

That summer they went to the Palladium Ballroom—where Doc and Tina dared step on the floor and mamboed with dance royalty, while King and Willie sat in the candlelight, listened to hot horns and throbbing congas play intoxicating Latin rhythms, and held hands. King asked Doc B where he learned his moves. "You pick up a lot as a soldier on R and R in Seoul."

They fed llamas at the Bronx Zoo, took a boat ride up the Hudson to West Point and back. By summer's end the two couples were firmly locked in courtship.

King made long-distance calls to Willie on Sunday afternoons. Tina wrote long, chatty letters to Doc and he'd dash back a reply.

By Christmas the ladies were back in the city, this time accompanied by their father, Dr. Manning, who wished to know Doc B's and King's intentions. Dr. Daddy was happy to encourage his protégé's affections toward Forestina, especially since he'd joined his father's practice. But King's entrepreneurial energy, and big land plans for the future, did not earn him any points as a potential son-in-law. Which made King twice as determined to prove he was good enough for Wilhelmina.

By the following summer Tina had hatched a plan—it was imperative that Willie come to New York to further her musical studies. Tina would selflessly accompany her, to help her sister manage in the big city. Aunt Vashti lent her apartment and her seal of approval to the plan.

That summer, King was absent from his usual haunts, spent his free time away from the nightlife, on Aunt Vashti's couch, wooing Willie with a 1,001 tales of making his way from the farm to the Big Apple. She played him nocturnes and fantasies on the upright in the parlor. He was rough, decisive, more unpredictable than the milquetoasts her father paraded as suitable partners. By the end of the season, King proudly shopped for a delicate diamond ring, asked Willie to marry him. Defying her father, who demanded she come home immediately, she jumped at the offer.

Doc B felt the pressure—from Forestina, from her family and his. When it became clear that Forestina and her dazzling demeanor would disappear from his life if he didn't step up, he bought the ring, asked the question. Tina bubbled over, like it had been his idea all along, and said yes.

They had a small, tasteful double wedding, with matching brides in satin dresses. Tina and Willie were escorted, arm in arm in arm, down the aisle by their reluctant father. Afterward, as the happy couples posed by their two-tier cake, Tina couldn't help but gush, "This is just perfect."

➢ ➢ ➢

I can't do this. But Avery kept moving through the morning, trying to fight the looming fog of confusion and sadness. She finished the hospital paperwork by rote, filling in the blanks, signing by the *X*'s. Not until the social worker mentioned having her funeral director claim the body did it hit Avery that plans needed to be made and she was alone to make them. She felt Dwight's card in her pocket, crumpled it in her fist. Thought of calling Van. What could he do from the other side of the world?

The day was sunny when she walked outside, but she ached for darkness, wanted to go back to the house and sleep so she wouldn't know or feel what was going on until it was over. *It will never be over.* The thought stopped her, as if she'd forgotten how to walk. She stood there, staring, eyes unfocused so the steady stream of cars and taxis became a swirl of color. She had no idea how long she'd been frozen when the bushy-haired guard came over, asked if she was all right. The answer was no, but he couldn't help her. So she thanked him, got into a vacant cab. Asked him to take her to St. Nicholas, to the funeral home that had handled her father. It was a place to start, before she lost the nerve.

Everyone from the receptionist on up knew of her mother and seemed to express sincere sadness for her loss. Avery wondered how they did it—remain professionally sorrowful forty hours a week. LaNeisha, her funeral director, a petite woman with chin-length braids and an eye just lazy enough so you noticed, looked only college-aged—like she should be wearing jeans and a T-shirt, not a somber black suit, but despite her apparent youth she skillfully led Avery through the preliminary planning.

It simplified matters once LaNeisha checked the records and found that Doc B had prepaid arrangements, for both himself and Forestina, well before his passing—even picked out matching bronze caskets. "Your father must have been a thoughtful man." Not exactly how Avery would have put it, but it wasn't surprising. Just as it hadn't surprised her that he'd chosen to spend eternity in a mausoleum—sealed in a file drawer, shielded from bugs and the elements—neat and tidy. Avery said yes to the same number of limos they had for Doc B's funeral. She'd have to figure out later who would fill them. She said yes to the flowers LaNeisha suggested. Yes, twenty copies of the death certificate should be enough, as if Avery knew what she'd need them for or could even imagine such a document with her mother's name on it. She took notes about what she had to bring them, then headed home because there was no way to avoid it.

Entering the house, she was overwhelmed with the reality that no one lived there anymore. *I have to let people know.* That would mean she'd have to say it out loud, over and over, like an awful punishment. There weren't really any old friends in New York she wanted to contact. Once she'd left, she'd pretty much shed her attachments—it was a little painful back then, but the scars were neater that way. But her mother knew so many people and Avery didn't know where to begin to find them.

Sitting in the parlor, she tried to get her mind to stop racing in circles. She stared at the phone a long time before she willed herself to pick it up, call information, get the number for the family church. Last time she'd been there was for Dwight's wedding.

The pastor was out, but even speaking to his secretary helped Avery find her voice. Then she went back to the answering machine, listened to the messages she'd seen when she arrived. Some were before—appointment reminders, charity solicitations, friends checking in, a reporter named Jasper Christmas from the *New York Spectator.* He wanted her mother's comment regarding something about the property on 111th Street. *Why does it matter so much?* Avery had made a point of staying clear of the family real estate holdings. Buying and selling people's homes, deciding how much rent to charge, whom to evict, how much heat to send up. Way too personal, too messy. It wasn't for her.

And there were the after messages—shaken, hesitant voices, looking for answers. It was all unreal, even when she phoned her office to tell them the news. Her assistant answered, bright and on time, said he would alert the ambassador. When she caught up with Van, he was at the airport, on his way to Munich. He offered to come to New York after his meetings. Avery told him she would be all right. It would be easier by herself—less to explain.

Then she began returning calls. She had switched into her diplomatic spokesperson mode, but by the afternoon she wished for a recorded announcement. Dealing with everyone's shock and grief was exhausting. She knew the word would spread, like ripples on a pond, that the phone would start ringing, that she'd have to keep talking.

After that she wandered from room to room, searching for an address book, some way to reach the important people in her mother's life, sad she no longer knew who they were. Her heart skipped the first time the phone rang. It was a different sound than the one she remembered in that house. The choir director—he called as soon as he heard. She walked into what had been her father's bedroom as she spoke, was startled to see that the bed, dressers, and somber decor had been exorcized, replaced by a ruffled confection of blue and white stripes and a mass of florals with flowing, sheer drapes at the windows—like a beachfront sunroom. Her mother's checkbook and a stack of bills lay on the white wicker-and-glass coffee table, next to a yellow coffee cup with a swallow left in it, and a plate with a half-eaten piece of toast with strawberry preserves. *Breakfast.* The room was so . . . happy, not how she usually thought of the house.

Avery perched on the love seat, realized her hands were trembling. *If I can just rest a few minutes.* When she got off the phone, she curled up, pulled the crocheted throw over her. It smelled like baby powder and lavender. One quiet tear dripped on the polished cotton, slipped over the edge of the cushion—

—Avery wasn't sure how long the doorbell had been ringing before she realized the chimes weren't part of her dream. She bounced up, trotted downstairs.

The woman looked familiar enough that Avery opened the door, even though she couldn't place her right away.

"I would have invited you over for lunch, but Dwight said you'd probably be tired, so I brought you a little something. You must be starving. That is, if you can even eat at a time like this."

Renee. Great. Did he send her here? Avery had only seen a few pictures since the wedding. Most of them right after their daughter was born. She remembered thinking Renee looked so serious. More like his mother than his wife. *Still does.*

"I'll leave you alone. I just can't imagine . . ." Renee's already reddened eyes brimmed with tears. She turned her head, brushed them away, then handed Avery a foil-wrapped plate.

I can't take this. "No. Please, come in." She wasn't even

sure why she said it. Avery wasn't exactly ready for open house, but bringing food was a nice gesture. "Thank you for this." She led her inside, put the plate on the dining room table.

"We've had so many lovely meals here. Dominique . . . our daughter . . . she's just devastated. Auntie Tina was like a grandmother to her."

That's what Dwight always called her. "I can't wait to meet her." Which is what Avery knew she was supposed to say about her cousin's child.

"You must have a hundred things to do. I'd be happy to help you. Not happy . . . I mean . . . I can do whatever you'd like, run errands, make phone calls." Renee smoothed a hand over the satiny table runner. "Tina just knew so many people, and they all just love her. She's just the best."

Avery could tell the faucet was about to spring a leak. "That's very kind, but you must be on your way out." Renee's raincoat topped a burgundy pantsuit, and her hair was arranged with beauty-shop perfection.

"No. I freed up my afternoon . . . just in case you need a hand. I mean, it's so difficult when you're . . . alone."

It's not a social disease. Normally Avery would launch into her defense of being unmarried, but not right now. "I really need to find Mom's address book."

"She keeps it in the junk drawer." Renee shrugged off her coat, led the way to the kitchen. The drawer overflowed with all manner of stuff that needed someplace to be—string, hotel pens, thumbtacks, matchbooks, duck-sauce packets, and the red leather book Avery remembered from childhood, held together with a fat rubber band. Erasures marked moves, feuds, or changes of status. Extra pages had been added to the *S*'s, *T*'s, and *B*'s. In some places the faint pencil strokes were nearly illegible.

Avery didn't know where to begin. "Well, if you've got some time . . ."

Renee was perfect for the assignment. She set up shop in the sunroom—"Aunt Tina's favorite place in the house"—seemed to know exactly who to call and was tireless in repeating the sad story with the proper degree of solemnity. Her patter became the background for Avery's wandering.

She found her mother's cell phone, still charging in the powder room. *Must have forgotten it before* . . . Avery put it in her pocket. It would be good to have a local number. She made more coffee, brought Renee a Fresca, put the ham-and-cheese on a roll and macaroni salad in the fridge for dinner, complimented the peach cobbler she'd brought, even though it had too much cinnamon. Then Avery made herself go back to Forestina's bedroom. She'd promised to bring clothes for her mother to the funeral home in the morning. Avery considered shopping for something new, but that seemed impersonal. At least the clothes her mother owned were presumably things she liked. Not that it exactly mattered now.

Avery went to the dresser, reached in the lingerie drawer, and picked out a lacy peach bra and panty instead of the bloomers she'd put in the tote. She grabbed two packages of pale taupe panty hose, then headed for the closet before she lost the momentum.

Staring at the riot of clothes, Avery didn't know where to begin. So much of it looked unfamiliar.

"She looked so pretty in that white suit with the rosebud appliqués."

Avery nearly jumped out of her shoes. Renee apologized profusely, but continued the guided tour of Forestina's closet, pulling out suits and dresses, laying them across the bed. Like Avery needed to be told what her mother liked, where she bought it and wore it.

"Thanks so much for your help, Renee. I think I can take it from here."

"There I go. I'm sorry." Renee retreated toward the doorway. "Dwight says I don't know when to stop."

"No. I really appreciate all you've done." *What nerve telling her that. And she takes it?* "I just need to get my thoughts together and make up my mind."

The green knit dress her mother had worn that last day in Paris—that's the outfit Avery chose. They'd had a nice time together that day, the way it used to be. Avery had come so close to asking, but didn't want to spoil things. Now she searched drawers and jewelry boxes until she found the blackamoor brooch her mother bought that afternoon, attached it to her own sweater. Then she curled up on her mother's bed, next to the piles of clothes, and fell asleep.

The next day Avery finalized plans—the wake Thursday evening, the funeral at church Friday morning. Dwight was courteous enough to stay out of her way—Renee became a convenient intermediary.

The hardest part was the shock of seeing her mother that first time. LaNeisha asked if she was satisfied, like she'd just had the car detailed—good as new—but that wasn't possible. It wasn't even that she looked as if she were sleeping, like at the hospital. Now Avery knew that in spite of the clothes, and the hair, fluffed in her usual style, her mother was completely gone, like a wax figure framed by frothy white satin. Avery touched the blackamoor brooch at the shoulder of her sheath. She had worn it since she took it from her mother's jewelry box.

When Dwight and family arrived, Avery was unprepared for how much Dominique looked like she did as a child, from her wide eyes to her bony knees. She came directly to Avery, looked up. "I love your mommy so much." She just barely got it out before she burst into tears.

That reminded her of herself at that age too. Avery nearly came unhinged. She knelt and Dominique's arms went around her neck and the girl sobbed.

Dwight came over. "I can take her."

Avery shook her head, mouthed, "It's all right," held Dominique till the heaving stopped, took the handkerchief Dwight offered to wipe her tears. "I'm happy Mom had you right down the block, so she could see you all the time. That made her happy." They'd never talked about it, but Avery was sure it did.

Dominique went to her mother. Dwight reached out his hand to help Avery up. She stood without his assistance, handed him the handkerchief. He shoved the square back in his pocket. "I don't know what to say. This is a tragedy."

Avery didn't have words, none she would use at that moment. She nodded her head, turned away.

Dwight lowered his voice. "I'm sorry."

She faced him, looked directly in his eyes. He looked back at her, until he couldn't anymore. She spoke low and slow. "Yes. You are."

The rest of the wake she spent faced away from the casket, or letting the mass of wreathes, gladiolas, and chrysanthemum crosses block her view. Clearly the "in lieu of flowers" request had been ignored, so the room resembled the aisles at Macy's annual flower show. Every year her mother would drag her there and coo and ooh over phalaenopsis and jacarandas. *Where'd that come from?* She was surprised the names of the flowers floated so easily to the top.

So she talked, hugged, comforted. The reception in New Zealand had been easier. She felt at ease in a crowd of people she'd never met. These folks, who were entwined in the life she'd left behind, made her feel alien. There was a constant flow, so many people she hadn't seen or thought about in ages. People who still called her Avery Braithwaite. It sounded so strange, like somebody she hardly remembered, but there had been no big hoopdedoo wedding like Dwight's. The esteemed Denis Lyons, Ph.D., whom she'd met and married during an early post in romantic Rome, was already exed and re-ensconced in his dusty tower at the University of Edinburgh, working on the next volume in his series of texts on the ancient Etruscans, before anyone, including her mother, had met him. Besides, it only lasted a few months—that certainly didn't count for more than a young woman's poor judgment.

So in addition to expressions of affection for Forestina, and words of comfort for Avery, there was lots of polite quizzing and commentary about the state of her life. The choir's reigning coloratura, a bosomy woman with enough hair for three people on her head and a black velvet cape that swept the floor, kissed her on both cheeks, then said, "I'm so sorry about your mother. Such a shame she didn't live to see her grandchildren." Avery wanted to ask where they were coming from because she certainly had no plans, but she let it go. As she did the overheard whispers about which funeral home does a better job, why were there no laminated prayer cards, and why didn't she look more upset.

As soon as Reginald Bishop shuffled up, Avery remembered him. He was one of her parents' set, and she and Dwight used to call him and his wife Mr. and Mrs. Sprat because he was so skinny and she was so round. Complications from diabetes took Mrs. Sprat some time ago, but he was still so slim his double-breasted suit seemed to button almost at the side seam. A precise, three-pointed handkerchief decorated his pocket. Clearly her mother and Reginald had remained friends. He held Avery's hand tight. "Your mother was a fine lady. Yes, she was." He could hardly get the words out.

Then there was the official contingent—government officials and those doing business with The Dixon Group—both the councilman from Dwight's old district, and the congressman sent representatives. A steady stream of contractors and vendors paid respects. Avery took up residence on one side of the room, Dwight on the other, the official hosts. At moments she'd look over at him and want to share a hug, crack a joke. He was the only other person who remembered what it was like when they were growing up. But they weren't sharing memories these days.

About six thirty Grace Kidder sliced a path through the crowd. She seemed surprised when she had to introduce herself to Avery.

"I've been out of the country many years." Avery had met all kinds of people, but none like Grace. She seemed to attract more light, and like a diamond it made her sparkle. Even with achingly high-heeled shoes Grace was small, slight. Avery towered over her, but Grace seemed substantial too. Not weighty, but like someone who could not be overlooked.

"Forestina was a sweetheart. It was a pleasure to know her." Grace patted Avery's hand. "She always spoke so glowingly of you."

As Grace walked toward Dwight, Avery couldn't imagine what her mother would say about her to a woman like Grace.

"How's it going, Av?"

Avery spun around. "LiLi." She and Alicia had grown up together, run track together in high school, hadn't seen each other since college and circumstances sent them down separate paths. It was the first hug that really felt like home—too much for comfort. Avery pulled away slowly to examine her. "How did you know?"

"I saw the news about the accident. Dwight's wife called me."

"Mom had your number?" Alicia looked good, but then, Avery would have expected that. Alicia used to wear makeup to track practice, and her nails were always done. A little rounder than in her running days, but she wore it well, and those dimples still made her look like the cutest doll in the toy store.

"I kinda kept up with her. Even when I lived in L.A. Been back in the city a few months—long story." Alicia rolled her eyes. "Anyway, we had brunch, maybe six weeks ago. She was so, I don't know, frisky, good."

"Mom, frisky?"

"It's a compliment."

"Yeah. I know. I'm just trying to picture it." Avery smiled. She hadn't used those muscles in days.

Alicia stepped toward the casket, bowed her head, closed her eyes. In a few moments she came back to Avery. "Whatever you need me to do."

"I'm good."

"Tell that to somebody else."

"I'm dealing."

"Well, don't deal alone. Life is more than solitaire."

A gruff laugh erupted from the hall and they both looked up, knew who it was. King's arrival caused the sea of people to part, making way for his wheelchair, but making waves was pretty much the way he always rolled. He shook hands and received sympathies as his attendant pushed him down the aisle, among his people, his companion, Barbara, dealing with the overflow.

Avery awaited her audience. She hadn't been by his apartment since he was released from the hospital. She figured this was soon enough for their reunion. Really, she hadn't seen him since she'd left home. Always a big man, now he looked more ponderous than imposing to her. During his convalescence, and separation from the coloring comb, his waves of jet-black hair had sprouted white roots.

Barbara was still tied up in conversation when the attendant wheeled him to Avery and stepped aside to give them privacy. She didn't know what to say to him. *It's good you're not dead too* didn't seem the way to go, but the usual chatter seemed beside the point.

King took her hand, pulled her more to his level. "Glad you could join us for your mother's funeral."

It was as if someone had rung a giant bell with her inside. The words were deafening. They left her quivering.

Alicia leaned in, like she was going to kiss him, spoke only loud enough for him to hear. "Don't mess with her, Mr. Dixon." Even when they were kids, Alicia wouldn't call him King to his face—"King of what?"—preferring to find ways not to have to say his name at all. She straightened, smiled, and patted his shoulder. For once, King had nothing to say. He grumbled at his attendant and moved on.

"Alicia Jackson." Dwight swooped in from across the room. The three of them had not been together since Avery's and Alicia's freshman year of college, Dwight's junior. "Good to see you."

Avery doubted it. They didn't kiss. She didn't tell him Alicia wasn't Jackson anymore because she wasn't sure what her name was now.

"Don't waste any of your oily charm on me, Dwight," Alicia hissed through a smile.

He didn't linger. It was awkward, the three of them together again. Time hadn't changed that.

Then Alicia put her arm through Avery's. "Walk me outside."

Once they were in the lobby, Alicia stopped. "Av, I'm supposed to catch the train to D.C. tonight, but I'll cancel if . . ."

"No. Really. I can do this. I appreciate your—"

Alicia waved her off. "Hey, your mom was my girl." Her voice almost broke, but she sped past it, took Avery's hand. "Do not let them walk on you." Alicia smirked. "Oops, guess King won't be doing that right now, will he?"

Avery cracked a smile.

"Seriously. I will stomp them. It's the only thing they understand."

"Avery?" Renee poked her head out of the chapel. "They'd like to start the service . . . if you're ready."

"Uh, sure." It seemed right to introduce the two women, although Avery couldn't imagine them having a latte, but too many worlds were already colliding. "Be right in." Once Renee was gone, Avery added, "Dwight's wife."

"I know, seen pictures. They have a lovely daughter. I'll leave it at that." Alicia kissed Avery's cheek. "My digits are in your mom's book, under Prentiss . . . part of that long story. Use 'em, okay? Before you fly off."

Avery couldn't keep her mind from wandering during the service that night, or the next day at the funeral. To her, none of the ceremony and spectacle had the remotest connection to her mother's being gone. She drifted in and out of the tributes from her mother's sorority and other organizations, lost in her own recollections, aching in her regrets, until some phrase in the obituary, the minister's admonition to rejoice because Sister Forestina had gone home, or the coloratura's hypervibrato rendition of "A City Called Heaven," yanked her back. It was easier once the coffin was closed and she could conjure up her mom in her mind's eye, until it struck her that she'd never actually see her again. It knocked the air from her. She had to grip her purse as hard as she could to stay composed as Dominique sobbed in the pew next to her. On the ride to the cemetery, she on one side of the limo, Dwight on the other, with Renee and Dominique the buffer zone, she stared out the window, her head throbbing. Perhaps her father was right about the mausoleum. It was so spare, so antiseptic, like a brand-new airport terminal. No mossy headstones or shovels full of earth. Those last roses, usually placed atop the coffin as each mourner said good-bye, were instead deposited in a bronze vase. By the time Avery inserted the last one, it was a huge arrangement.

One of the churchwomen fixed Avery a plate at the repast back at church, but she didn't eat more than a forkful, knowing the day was not over, that people would stop by the house. More to eat, more to drink, more stories to tell. It was part of the ritual and there was no way to say that what she wanted more than anything else was to be alone. She'd been away all this time, the least she could do was give them what they expected this day. She had stopped counting the fruit baskets that had arrived, or how many times she'd opened the door for friends of her mother's bringing trays of macaroni and cheese, ham, chicken, cakes, as if she were hosting a party, only sadder. Renee recommended two ladies who would lay out the buffet and clean up after. "They're good. They're honest, very reasonable. We use them regularly."

By the time they carried the trash out back and left, Avery was barefoot and spent. She found two extrastrength somethings in the powder room, chased them with a glass of merlot. She stretched out on the chaise in the parlor, closed her eyes to let her head stop pounding—

—the phone jolted her awake. She was startled by the sunlight peeking through the shutter slats, grabbed the phone out of instinct.

"Hello. My name is Jasper Christmas, from the *New York Spectator*—"

"What?" Avery squinted at her watch, couldn't believe it was 12:37 p.m. the next day.

"Jasper Christmas. I'm researching a piece on the Central Park North Dixon Plaza development."

"Then you are talking to the wrong person." Avery recalled his phone message. "I don't know anything. I don't want to know anything." She swung her feet to the floor, winced at the crick in her neck.

"May I ask your name? I've spoken with Forestina Dixon."

"Well, I guess you know you won't be doing that anymore." It came out of her mouth before she could find a more mannerly response.

"Yes, I was sad to hear—"

"Look, really, I can't tell you anything and I don't want to talk about this now. Good-bye." It was all she could do not to scream. She hung up, couldn't wait to be done with the stuff, the business of her mother's life, so she could get back to her own.

SIX

. . . a pipe dream spun around a big hole in the ground

"What the hell are you waiting for?" King bellowed like a bull elephant, his gray silk robe enhancing the resemblance. "Somebody else to die so we can see how much more screwed we can be?" He was newly enthroned on his state-of-the-art, mid-wheel drive, power-tilt wheelchair. King's orthopedist had recommended a postdischarge rehab center, but King wanted to go home, and home he went, confined either to his superchair or the hospital bed that had been squeezed into his room—next to the king-size one he insisted remain where it was. "Or we can wait for Christmas to keep digging until he finds something to hang us with." Although well on his way to pre-accident health, King's skin, normally a rich rusty brown, still had an ashy tinge. Decades-old smoky circles had dug themselves deeper under his heavy-lidded eyes.

"Aunt Tina has only been in the ground a day. And as you know, Avery is not exactly happy to see me." Dwight stayed seated, out of his father's path. "What was I supposed to do, drop by the house for some pound cake, say, 'Sorry about your mom. You look good in black. Sign right here. The check is in the mail'?"

For reasons Dwight never deciphered, pleasing his father had never been an available option. He'd attended one of the three Ivy Leagues where he'd been accepted, graduated with honors, been elected to the City Council and the U.S. Congress, and steered the family real estate business to the yard where the big dogs play. But for his father it was never enough. Harvard, Yale, and Princeton didn't accept Dwight even though Columbia, Brown, and Cornell did. His two terms on the City Council and one in the House didn't lead to the governor's mansion, the White House, or the chairmanship of a Fortune 100 company. "Who ever heard of a one-term congressman? Even my dog could get elected twice" had been King's summation of his son's political career. And there was that pesky grandson problem. Dwight hadn't given him one. He always fell short. He was used to it. This snafu was just another check in his minus column.

"We've been flushing money down a goddamn sewer long enough. I'd like to see this happen in my lifetime!"

It wasn't like Dwight was happy with the turn of events. Aunt Tina had been one of his favorite people—a very short list. Yes, the project was behind schedule, but he couldn't force Avery's hand now. He had to figure out a strategy to get her to sign on the dotted line. "I said I'd take care of it."

"Blugh!" King issued one of his frequent grunts of displeasure.

Dwight watched his father fidget with the chair controls, but knew better than to offer assistance. King's me-centric tantrums were only surpassed by those of a truculent two-year-old, and he didn't take kindly to reminders of how many decades had passed since he was legitimately a brat. Dwight guessed King was in the vicinity of eighty, but his father's driver's license and birth certificate each listed different years for Abraham Dixon's arrival on the planet. A while back Dwight asked for clarification. King announced, "My age is none of your damn business." So a guesstimate had to suffice.

"I don't care *how* you get it done, Junior." King mashed the controls and the royal wheels lurched forward, then veered hard to the left like a bumper car steered by a nine-year-old.

Dwight wanted to chuckle, but didn't because that would have been another distraction. He didn't react to "Junior," either. That was bait and he didn't take it.

"Just don't let this little girl fuck up everything I worked for."

You worked for? Dwight bristled, but let it slide. *You can't bully me anymore, fat man.*

Well before the public announcement of Dixon Plaza, Dwight had been massaging this idea into reality. Yes, in the early years King had acquired the land, given voice to the dream, but DP-CPN would never have been more than a pipe dream spun around a big hole in the ground without the right financing partners. That's what Dwight had brought to the table. Even if King didn't give him credit, for better or worse Dwight was a Dixon and this was his legacy too.

"She's not a little girl. Avery is as grown as I am." Dwight shoved his hands in his pockets. "And she doesn't care about the building—or anything here for that matter. But it's too soon to start grilling her about the disposition of her mother's estate."

"Hunnngh!" King looked at his son like he was ready to challenge the statement, but scratched his crotch instead. "I need some Scotch."

"Aren't you still taking pain medicine?" Dwight went

over to the bank of windows that looked out on Central Park, Fifth Avenue, and the majestic Metropolitan Museum, right down the block. "Do you think that's wise? Besides, it's the middle of the afternoon."

"Yes, I think Scotch is wise." King followed, his chair whining and whirring as it carted his considerable bulk across the terrazzo floor. He jerked too hard on his joystick and his chair shot into reverse, barely missing a glass table. Twenty years ago, he had declared, "I own enough of Harlem not to have to live here," deeded the Strivers' Row house to Dwight, and moved into the Fifth Avenue building he now called home. It wasn't that he forgot where he came from, or where he got rich. Quite the contrary, he had embraced his own personal mantra—he could have whatever was haveable, all of which he would remind you of, whether you asked him or not, especially after a couple of Scotches. For King, his move wasn't denying his Africanness, it was embracing his Americanness. He was movin' on up—living his own Jeffersonian dream—even if it was George, not Thomas.

"And I know exactly what goddamn time it is." King eased up on the throttle, corrected his direction, and headed across the room. In keeping with the image he had cultivated so deliberately, the apartment was an ode to early-twentieth-century modern—deco curves in silvery gray, chalky white, and black lacquer, open, airy space punctuated with long, low leather sofas, ottomans, and sleek sculpted chairs with stainless-steel arms and legs that even four score and seven pounds ago, King could no more get into or out of than he could scale the outside of the building. The decor suited the location and the vision King had of himself, the one he'd concocted from old movies. Not long after he settled in, he'd been happy to be photographed in his new digs for a feature in *Ebony* magazine, "The King Has a New Castle." He didn't own a television network, run a publishing empire, or chair a multinational corporation, but for a kid from Bordentown, New Jersey, who barely got his high school diploma, who had created himself one day, one decision, one deal, at a time, he'd done all right.

King continued to maneuver the wheelchair until he pulled up alongside the liquor cabinet, which allowed him to access the door. "Javier and whoever the hell that is on nights smother me like I'm a damn baby. Not that they give a crap about *me*. They just don't want me to croak on their watch. But believe me, it'll take more than a little Scotch and Percocet to kill me."

Because you're too fat or too mean? "Suit yourself."

King poured himself two fingers—which would have been three on a less meaty hand. "Barbara is just as bad. Watches me like a hawk. Told her she was already in the will so she could relax." He stopped to laugh, remembering his joke. "That got her riled up. Told me I wasn't funny." He took a slow first sip. Eyes closed, he savored his drink. "Women."

Barbara Sandiford had been King's "companion" for ages. After Wilhelmina died, there had been a rotating slate of ladies, all willing to do whatever it took to become the King's consort. They knitted him scarves, baked him pies, and offered all manner of additional accommodations—including a willingness to "share him," should King so desire, as long as they could have first position. But after about ten years, Barbara slid into what had become a permanent place at his side, and no one but King knew how or why. A good thirty years his junior, she was definitely closer to Dwight's generation than his father's. She was effervescent, attractive, charming, accommodating, possibly even intelligent. But that she'd put up with King's rudeness, bullying, and general bad humor by choice for so long made Dwight seriously question how bright she actually was. King and Barbara didn't live together—she maintained her own apartment, a three-bedroom high-floor in a prewar building on the West Side, with a camera-ready view of Riverside Park, the

New Jersey Palisades, and the Hudson River. Her occupation, as far as the IRS was concerned, was "consultant," though Dwight wasn't sure whom she consulted about what.

But Dwight liked Barbara. They got along well enough, and she had been right by King's side since the accident—put up with everything from his foul mouth to diarrhea. The situation showed Dwight a different side of her—the one with the backbone. Not quite up to the bar set by iron-spined Wilhelmina, but somehow Barbara got the doctors to heel. They showed up when they said they would and gave explanations in terms a normal person could understand. She made King treat the nurses as if they had both sense and feelings. She took total charge of the home-care arrangements, including ordering the special-needs equipment, supervising its delivery, and requesting the service send male caregivers only. She had invested too many years in King to chance having it usurped by some flirty Nurse Betty with boobs and booty to spare, enough larceny in her loins to realize the old boy had enough life and ego in him to believe he could handle it, and enough money to make it worth her while. Dwight was pretty certain Barbara would stop King from having his Lagavulin and pain meds, even if she had to pour it down the sink. And she would be there before too long—after all she had an investment to protect, so King needed to get his drink on before she arrived.

Dwight didn't know she had it in her, but he was relieved—he had enough to do. As far as he was concerned, Barbara had paid her dues, and without her to take up some of King's time and energy, Dwight couldn't imagine how much more miserable his life would have been all these years.

"Why couldn't the crash happen *after* we bought the damn building?" King knocked back the remaining Scotch and held out the empty to Dwight. "That'll hold me."

Dwight took the glass, headed to the kitchen, ignoring the crass statement. It was typical. His father had never been known to mix sentiment with business. Dwight rinsed and dried the tumbler quickly. The single malt smelled like camphor and peat moss—definitely an acquired taste, and he hadn't. In fact, since his mother—also a Scotch drinker—had passed, he could stomach neither the smell nor taste. He returned the glass to the tray on the bar cart just as Javier came in the door. *Finally.*

"Hey there, Mr. Dixon!" The nurse came over and shook Dwight's hand. "Nice to see you. Your pops is doing pretty good, in spite of himself. Retaining a little too much water, but these should help." He shook a bag from the pharmacy and the pills inside rattled.

King grunted, tried to redirect himself, and bumped into a chair. "Just what I've been sitting here hoping for, something to make me pee in that damn plastic bottle more often."

"We're both just grateful it's not the other end." Javier laughed. "Right, King?!"

Javier looked as if he could bench-press the sofa without breaking a sweat, so getting King on and off a bedpan wasn't as big a challenge as it would be for most folks. All of it was an image Dwight didn't want to conjure up. He snatched his trench from the mirrored coat-tree in the hall. "You're going to have to let me handle Avery my way. I'll take care of it, but right now I have a meeting with Grace."

"I don't like that bitch."

Because she reminds you of yourself, or Mother? Dwight opened the door. "Thanks, Javier. Call you later, King." And he was gone.

One down. His head was tight, like a balloon just before it explodes. If he could just make it through the day. *I can take it.*

Dwight selected two stools at the end of the mostly deserted bar. He draped his coat over the back of one, sat on the other, ordered a club soda. She would keep him waiting. He knew this. It never mattered how late he was for a meeting, she was always at least five minutes later. But he knew the drill. Grace thrived on social intercourse—"I already know what's going on in my office"—so they frequently met outside at a place of her choosing, and the range of spots was as wide and as varied as the city itself. A quirky saloon on the Lower East Side displaying enough dead-mammal taxidermy to warrant a PETA protest. A hip-hop mogul's midtown sports bar and lounge. A rustic *enoteca,* not two blocks from Times Square, that looked as if you'd stepped into Florence. A paneled Wall Street citadel where the most buzz-worthy sale, merger, or acquisition of the next fiscal cycle was being negotiated in one of the tufted-leather booths. The underground cave maze in Alphabet City that Dwight couldn't find again if his life depended on it. Grace knew the newest, most exclusive, and most expensive. Even though they never met in the same place more than once, Grace had always been there before. They knew her—Charlie, Beau, Anika, Thor—owners, managers, servers, chefs, bartenders—and she knew them. Grace never picked up a tab when it was just the two of them. But if it was a group, she always arranged with the maître d' to pay without the bill ever being presented. When others at the table, usually men, tried to catch the waiter's eye, she would just smile her Grace-ous smile and say, "I've taken care of it."

Grace always had a car waiting—not from a service. The plate read KIDDCAR. And she always wore something red—the soles of her shoes, a handbag, shirt, scarf, rubies the size of nickels—and if he couldn't see red, Dwight still presumed it was there, somewhere. He thought it might satisfy her taste for blood and keep her from feeding on the living.

Dwight sipped his club soda, which came with lime he didn't ask for, and wondered if all the drinks came adorned with a hint of the color. Today's rendezvous spot was the lounge of a new boutique hotel called Green—which spoke to both the Greene Street location and their philosophy of sustainable luxury. The decor was entirely eco-friendly, renewable, recycled, repurposed materials in a salad palette that ranged from deep wilted spinach to the palest iceberg. At four o'clock, the room was mostly deserted, but Dwight knew in another hour a trendy, thirsty, but environmentally responsible crowd who separated glass, paper, and cardboard and wrote checks to the Wildlife Fund would be ready for end-of-the-workday libations. He shifted on the hemp-and-bamboo barstool, trying to find a comfortable way to sit. It wasn't designed with anyone over six feet in mind. Not something Grace would have to consider—or maybe that was the point?

Not much had been going his way, like this time was different from any other. His entire life had been fits and starts, a few miles of peaceful scenery, then—wham! The life equivalent of a flat tire, a busted hose, an overheated radiator, or a head-on collision. The kid that broke his arm in third grade because Dwight had a straight-A report card and talked "white," his mother's choking death at his thirteenth birthday party, Jewell abandoning him at the altar—literally. He was accustomed to the partnership of bitter and sweet. It had become a familiar flavor, although not one he craved, so his aunt Tina's accident and untimely demise, while sad, was just another bump in his pothole-gouged road. But nothing was going to stop Dixon Plaza from happening—including Avery.

When Grace called the day after the funeral, he knew it wasn't to express more sympathy. He was getting no special dispensation for bereavement. She had flipped when she found out 111th Street wasn't deeded to Dixon Group yet. "Do you know how many ways we can get screwed over this?" Dwight assured her it was in the family. She wasn't reassured. "My family are some of the craziest sons of bitches I know." So he'd just have to convince her this was only a temporary setback—like the dozens of others they had endured—zoning ordinances, easements, permits, injunctions, protests, squatters. They'd weathered them all. They'd get through this too. And unlike his father, she would at least be reasonable—in the end, after all, she wanted this too. The new Kidder, Theismann president did not like to appear wrong.

After fifteen minutes, a conversation with the bartender about the governor's uphill election battle, two calls from King—ignored—and three-quarters of his club soda, Grace arrived in a flurry of "So good to see you's" that started as soon as the doorman ushered her into the lobby. From all the commotion she generated, Dwight would have sworn there was a packed house if he didn't know better. But that was Grace, who firmly believed that wherever she was, that was the most vital and exceptional place to be and weren't you lucky to be included.

Dwight refused to turn around, but if he had glanced over his shoulder, he would have seen most of the commotion was made by staff, who came out of the woodwork to greet Ms. Kidder. What he could not have known was that prior to Grace's arrival anywhere, someone on her staff, under the pretext of some urgent need, always called the establishment, alerting them to Grace's imminent entrance. If the management was smart, that triggered a fawning welcome committee. Grace Kidder in your restaurant was good for business whether she ever ate a bite or not. Chances were better than even a boldface item would show up in one of the pseudonews gossip-pages newspaper readers thrived on, which translated into booked reservations and lines to get in. Grace Kidder was what Paris Hilton should want to be if she ever grows up.

Grace's suit was scarlet—no mistaking the power was all hers, and today she wanted to make sure no one missed the message, especially Dwight, who stood, like the gentleman he was, at her approach.

"Dwight." Grace slid onto her stool without the slightest squirm, no kiss, no hug, no handshake. Over the years they hadn't zeroed in on a comfortable place for physical contact in their relationship. They had tried them all. The double-miss social air kiss felt plain stupid—a lot like it looked. A kiss on one cheek felt too familiar—they weren't friends, more cordial associates, although sometimes the veneer was thin. A handshake seemed too contrived and conventional. The convivial pat on the back felt too much like one of the old boys, and Grace was not trying to be anybody's buddy. So by mutual but unspoken agreement, they let that part of doing business go by the wayside. Dwight was pretty certain there would be nothing left unspoken today.

"I'm sure you're having a hell of a time with all this."

Grace sounded almost sympathetic, but Dwight didn't let his guard down. He knew Grace used her voice, smoky, earthy, sensual, to lure you in. He'd listened to her do it. Dwight thought that if the sun-warmed sand under your feet had a voice—the fine snowy kind like on the beach at Panama City where he'd gone once on spring break—it would sound like Grace Kidder's.

"And at this point in our relationship, I know we understand each other." The bartender delivered a martini that Dwight never saw Grace order. She took a sip, then she rolled the clear plastic saber that held three ginormous olives around the rim of her glass, creating gentle, concentric waves.

"That we do. So you are fully aware that my commitment to the project is—"

"Good. Then let's not drag this out, shall we?"

But just under that lovely soft sand, you'll hit the cold, rough, damp layer that conceals hermit crabs, razor-shell clams, other things that will hurt you if you're not careful. It's the coarse, grainy sand you build castles with.

"We're on the same page with this, Grace. And I know time is of the essence." Dwight's collar felt tight, his club soda tasted bitter, but he kept his voice low, his tone even.

"I realize your hands are tied. Though we both also know that a little foresight would have prevented this in the first place—which can be said about so much of this venture." She plopped the olives back in the glass, took another sip. "But at the moment, that's irrelevant. We have to commit to the added public space because shrinking the buildings further does not make financial sense. Now, as you've explained it to me, you had reached agreeable terms with your aunt and your cousin to sell DP the property on 111th Street."

"Yes, and our attorney—"

"Good. And I'm going to presume that your cousin will move forward with the deal as it was negotiated."

"Yes." Dwight knew there was no point in longer answers. Grace didn't come to listen.

"Excellent." She fixed the bottom olive in her teeth, skinned her lips back so it didn't smudge her lipstick, pulled it into her mouth, and chewed. "It will still take at least ninety days to get through all the attendant legal bits. So for good measure, we will give you another thirty days because—well, just because. That gives you one hundred and twenty days from today to make this all nice and tidy."

It was the first time Grace had invoked a drop-dead date. Dwight laid his hands flat on the recycled-glass bar—steady. "I'm excited. This is the moment we've been working toward. When all the pieces come together and our vision for the—"

"Superb." Right there, the voice changed, the sand got cold and hard. "But that's it, Dwight. Not one day more. As you know, we need to be under construction by the end of the year, otherwise we lose millions in tax incentives. That can't happen. And I have been a busy girl. Dubai is lining up nicely—contracts are with lawyers and will be sorted out by next month. And we have approval for the Macao project."

The heat started between his shoulder blades and expanded. Last time she'd mentioned those deals, the land wasn't even secured. Unless. *Grace lied.* Which is what it was called when someone else bent the truth beyond its natural boundaries. "Those projects were still in the planning stages." At least the sweat ran down his back so she couldn't see it.

"It seems that the scope of the Dixon undertaking and my vision in terms of Kidder involvement was enough of a buy-in. Our associates in Asia and the Emirates are confident that I can spearhead those projects." Grace gave him her thin, watery smile. "Bottom line, where there's oil, there's money. And thanks to you, we have Cobb on board for the Macao build. He was so excited about doing green and sustainable in China. You should see the drawings, the model. Breathtaking. I'll send you the video." She took another sip. "So the deadline is firm. You'll be receiving the papers. Four months. Or we pull the plug and divert the funds over there. Which is amusing in its own way, don't you think? Since that's where the money is from anyway." Grace smiled, pulled another olive off the little plastic sword with her teeth.

Dwight didn't find any part of what Grace had said amusing. As long as Kidder was in the game, there was a game. If they pulled out—game over. He had been able to keep the project looking as if it were moving along despite all the setbacks because it had the KT stamp of approval. Delays were normal—to be expected. A project of this size was never completed on time. Just look at how far they were behind with the new Trade Center. The four months wasn't the issue—he'd been prepared for three, but Grace had played him.

"Can't stay." She slipped off the stool, smoothed the skirt of her suit, picked up her Birkin, ran her hand through her downy hair.

Dwight got up again, on what had become rubbery, Gumby legs. He was feeling green too, in a bilious, I'm-going-to-hurl-all-over-the-bamboo-floor way.

"I have another appointment. But let me know if you need anything. You know how to find me." The echo of Grace's scarlet-soled stilettos faded into the distance.

His father was a blowhard and a bully and as impossible to please as he had always been, but dealing with him earlier had only been an annoyance—not cause for Dwight to break a sweat. He'd been handling King his whole life. But he had just been reminded, you didn't handle a Kidder.

The six Kedarefschenkos who'd arrived at the Emigrant Landing Depot at Castle Garden in New York Harbor disappeared with the stroke of a pen from an intake clerk who didn't even attempt to say or spell the name. "You gotta be kidding." He joked with a fellow clerk, and thinking he was quite clever, as if he himself had been born a Smith or a Davis, wrote the name Kidder instead. For five generations they had been Kidders. The other trappings of the family's Russian past—kerchiefs, prayer shawls, accents—were dispatched in two generations, as quickly as they could say Yankee-Doodle. With that second generation born in America, those relics became ancient history, disposable by-products of assimilation. The cart from which Kidder and his sons had sold trinkets as treasures became a store. They bought the building where the store and their apartment had been. Then the one next door. This is where the new family history and the Kidder corporate history began.

By the third generation the Kidders became Episcopalian, moved to Park Avenue, purchased a winter home in Palm Beach. Mrs. Kidder joined the Colony Club, Mr. Kidder the

Metropolitan, where he met and befriended Mr. Theismann, a banker and financier. Mr. Kidder joined forces with Mr. Theismann and formed a real estate development company. They planned to put up houses, hospitals, factories, and office buildings from coast to coast.

But in 1929 the stock market crashed. Mr. Theismann lost 80 percent of his net worth in one day. Mr. Kidder was never keen on the market. His money was in gold and land because as he used to say, "You can print gibberish on paper. Land and gold will always have value." He was certain the economy would right itself, eventually. That's how the cycle goes. When he failed to bring Mr. Theismann around to his way of thinking, Mr. Kidder shrugged and said, "Then you may as well jump out a window like the rest of the schmucks." Mr. Theismann took his advice.

Mr. Kidder was right of course. He held on, quietly continued to acquire land and gobble up properties whose owners were unable to withstand the hard times, and when the Depression ended, Kidder, Theismann was solid—at the top of the real estate heap with holdings in New York, Philadelphia, Baltimore, Chicago, Boston, Pittsburgh, and Detroit. Top was the only place Grace had ever known. For her, Dixon Plaza was disposable, plug and play—or not.

Dwight was aware *partner* wasn't an accurate assessment of their relationship. They might be *your* partner, but you were never *theirs*. Ever. And when Dwight signed on, he knew, as did most of the Kidder "partners," that the playing field wasn't level, that he wasn't an equal. But it would take him twenty years to make a project like Dixon Plaza happen without the Kidder clout—not to mention their billions. He knew his risk would be greater, his loss bigger if the project didn't work out. Failure would be only a flesh wound for Grace, probably wouldn't even require a bandage, while for him it might prove fatal. But Dwight didn't care. He wanted in because a win like this would show everyone what he could do—who he was. Kidder. Trump. Dixon. He'd be up there with the kings.

Everything costs something.

In a trance, Dwight paid the tab, overtipped the bartender. On his way out, he returned the Bluetooth to it's rightful place, pushed to talk, gave a voice-dial command, glanced at his watch. A woman in pewter-colored parachute pants and a faded denim jacket got out of a cab and Dwight got in before the door closed. "Nineteenth and Tenth."

He had to get this off his chest. And he was willing to pay.

➢ ➢ ➢

"May I come in?" Dwight could barely hold his head up when he arrived—too much swirling around in it. Shirt collar open, his tie hanging limp around his neck.

"You don't deserve to enter." Cold, dismissive, her voice came through the door.

"Please . . . I'm begging." His forehead rested on the metal door between them. Without this outlet he would never have survived.

He could feel the snap and rattle of the locks and chains. It made him tingle. He was almost inside.

She snatched the door open so suddenly he stumbled. She pushed him to his knees with the tip of her black braided-leather riding crop. "That wasn't begging, you weak, pathetic excuse for a man."

"I can take it, Mistress Delilah." Dwight said her name in a hush. The small black and white tiles in the entryway dug into his knees, but he said nothing. Stayed still at her feet. Stiletto ankle boots left a sliver of tawny skin before the shiny black cat suit that clung to her body like paint. He wanted to reach out his finger, trace that skin along her ankle, but he was strong. He could resist.

"Look at you . . . groveling like the worm that you are." With the tip of her crop she raised his head to look at her. Wild hair danced around her face. She wore no makeup aside from the full red lips he never touched. "You are a stupid, miserable miscreant. Get up off your knees. You know what to do."

"Thank you, Mistress Delilah." Dim sconces lit the way down the hall to a small dressing room. All the walls were charcoal gray with slashes, like purple lightning. Blackout drapes at the windows meant there was no daylight. He thought of it as the cave.

Dwight entered the small room, furnished with only a wooden chair. He removed each item of clothing as if it were a ritual, folded it neatly, placed it on the seat, until he was down to his socks. Carefully he knotted his blue-and-white-striped bow tie around his bare neck, pulled and arranged it until it was even. Then he stood at the threshold. "May I come out?"

No answer.

"Mistress Delilah, please let me come out and sit at your feet."

"Don't keep me waiting, you worthless, spineless slug."

Dwight could feel himself growing stronger with every insult she hurled. He hurried to the front room where Delilah stood beside a glass desk, arms folded, tapping her foot impatiently. She looked him up and down, turned her head in disgust. Without a word she pointed under the desk with her crop.

Dutifully, he crawled beneath it, lay on his back looking up through the glass. He felt calm in the small space, focused. Then Mistress Delilah sat in the desk chair, her feet on his chest, sometimes ignoring him, sometimes unleashing a string of humiliation. Dwight looked at her red lips as she snarled at him. *I'm a man. I'm strong. I can handle it.*

He knew they all thought Dixon Plaza was too much for him—King, Grace, Renee, even Dominique had her questions. The papers second-guessed his every move, called the design a second-rate rehash, questioned the wisdom of such a lavish undertaking. He googled himself three times a day to see what else had been heaped on him. But he'd learned when he was young, never let them smell the fear. Never let them know that every day he woke up and longed to be somebody else. To disappear into the ether, with another name, in another town, where nobody would find him. And he'd get some simple job where he wouldn't need a suit, and nobody pressured him to do the impossible in half the time required, with a chorus of naysayers hounding him.

What Delilah said, she said to his face. It gave him pleasure to be able to take it. And nothing much else gave him pleasure anymore.

SEVEN

. . . the first, best night of their grown-up lives

I have to get up. Avery stretched, pushed the blanket aside, and strained to see her watch hands without turning on the light. *Looks like 12:27.* Last night she'd slept on the sofa in her father's study. Since the return she'd sacked out in a different room each night—none of them hers—trying to find one where she didn't feel like a trespasser. *Why did I tell Alicia she could come by this afternoon?* She'd wanted to say no, but couldn't. Not to her. Unconsciously, she stroked the cushion beside her. The brown leather had grown slack. Worn spots and cracks marred the cowhide she recalled as supple and shiny.

When her father was out, she used to sneak into his study, curl up under this same itchy Navajo blanket and read, or listen to her Walkman—precisely because she wasn't supposed to be here. "There's a whole house for you to play in." Her mother would always find her, make her leave, then refold the blanket just so—as if it had never been disturbed. "This room is off-limits." Avery shoved that memory back wherever it came from, got up, and defying rules no one would ever enforce again, walked away, leaving the balled-up blanket and the sunken spot where she'd slept.

Avery had lived in countries where people thought nothing of serving sautéed puppy or routinely slaughtered baby daughters because they were not sons. In those places, she had expected to feel alien, cautious about what she said and to whom. But this was home, where the heart is, but here she felt more adrift than grounded. Like she didn't belong. Here? Where the good Dr. and Mrs. Braithwaite were no more. Where everybody knew her. Where nobody did. This was the strangest place of all.

In the four days since the funeral, she had been paralyzed. There was so much to be done, the kinds of tasks at which she usually excelled—making calls, securing documents, sorting, delegating, dispensing, disposing. Goodness, Avery Lyons was known for doing what needed to be done so balls stayed in the air, feathers remained unruffled, and the beat went on. This was her stock-in-trade and a most excellent quality in her chosen line of work. But since the last visitor had departed, and she'd thanked her mother's cleaning lady, Jessie, for helping her through the day—keeping glasses filled, calling people by name so Avery would know who they were—she had done exactly nothing. Everything was a priority, so nothing was.

She hadn't even showered, much less left the house, hadn't picked up the phone, and only answered the door because florists' vans continued to bring plants and baskets from those who couldn't make the funeral, those in other cities who had just heard. At first deliverymen left them on the steps when she didn't answer the bell, but that brought well-meaning neighbors, like Rachel and Louis, the couple from across the street, to see if she was all right. It was easier to just go to the door.

When her father died, this had been her mother's turf. All Avery had to do was show up. Smiling. Dutiful. Five days later she was back on a plane to Switzerland. Currently she was in uncharted territory.

At the stairs, she stopped at the intersection of up and down, unable to make a choice. Up—shower and get dressed, or down to the kitchen for fortification. Lots of things had been bubbling to the surface—names, places, feelings—long-forgotten bits of the past that had been buried, sometimes on purpose, under the growing pile of ever-present now.

She headed up, where the baskets were not. She could at least be clean and clothed for her guest.

Alicia arrived ten minutes early—loaded with shopping bags. "Still can't resist a sale!" She left her booty from Barneys and Tracy Reese by the front door. "But I guess you wouldn't know that, would you? There wasn't a lot of shopping going on back then."

"T-shirts and running shoes." Avery gave her a reserved we-used-to-be-close-but-I-don't-know-what-we-are-now hug.

"I made up for all those high school years of trying to accessorize that bo-ring uniform." Alicia dropped her leather jacket on top of the bags, fluffed her hair. "It's hard to believe your mom's not coming down the stairs, or up from the kitchen chirping about some committee or luncheon." Alicia wore a black silk sweater, a caramel pencil skirt that matched her jacket, and tall, black patent boots. "I just saw her—before I went back to L.A. I'd take her to lunch, or we'd meet for 'smart cocktails,' as she called them. I mean it wasn't so frequent when I was living in London or out West—I've been something of a globe-trotter myself, not nearly as exotic as you, but . . . you know what I mean."

No. Actually I don't. Avery had pushed Alicia away from her life—and had done a pretty good job of keeping her out there—some far-off space where distance was measured in time, not miles. "Thanks for staying in touch with her. It wasn't always easy for me to get back . . ."—*home* got caught in Avery's throat—". . . back to the States, as much as I might have liked. Come on. Let's sit in here." Avery started for the living room.

"How 'bout the kitchen? I'm starving."

Like always. Avery smirked.

"What? You said not to bring anything."

"I wouldn't have a place to put it if you did." Avery led the way downstairs, thinking about how Alicia made herself at home wherever she was—no hesitation. Avery used to wish she could be like that. Alicia had a knack for fitting in, without becoming somebody else in the process. Whether she just met you or had known you her whole life, she slipped into the groove like she belonged, and mostly others accepted that she did.

Alicia was scholarshipped into Avery's school, a posh institution where Avery, far from hard up, was one of the lesser-advantaged students. The girl from West 113th Street, whose father was a subway mechanic and whose mother worked part-time in a beauty parlor, was exactly the kind who usually became dog meat. The subject of ridicule followed by fake apologies, because the "it" girls used manners like the cat-eyed half masks they wore on Halloween. Only sort of a disguise—you could always tell who was behind it. But Alicia got a pass on the hazing. She was so real, so smart, so brave, and so much fun that even upper-class girls befriended her. After six years, she was voted most popular girl, hands down, and elected senior-class president. And she was Avery Braithwaite's bestest friend. Avery and Alicia, the double AA's—"like the batteries, not the bra size," as Alicia put it. But Av and LiLi had run out of juice a while back.

"This house was so beautiful . . . is. Not like my old apartment, with the tacky, layaway furniture, and mismatched dishes—plastic at that. And we won't even go into my dad's string-art collection. But your folks were so classy, so . . . well . . . you know. An-y-way."

The first time Avery heard Alicia say *an-y-way,* in that singsongy voice, was shortly after they met in sixth grade. By high school, it annoyed the crap out of her, but she dealt with it—just one of LiLi's things. Apparently she'd been an-y-way-ing through her life. Hey, it seemed to be working for her. Avery shook her head, smiled to herself. She had forgotten that little bit of silliness. "There's enough here for a block party."

"You still eat like a teenaged boy? You used to chow down, like my brother, and never gain an ounce. Drove me nuts. I can still put on five pounds from standing too close to a French fry." Alicia patted her firm but rounded butt. "Like I actually care. But in LaLa Land, life was all about five pounds. Two pounds really!" Alicia laughed. "It's so good to see you, Av. The circumstances suck. Believe me, I know. Lost both my folks . . . six and seven years ago. Colon cancer took Mom, and I don't think Daddy wanted to live in a world where she wasn't. Eleven months later he had a stroke—didn't last long after that."

"I'm sorry. I didn't know." Avery tried to remember if her mother had mentioned it, which meant it had been filed in the "Too Complicated" folder and forgotten.

Alicia shrugged. "Life begins and it ends. It's what you do in between that matters."

Avery wasn't sure where this philosophical bent came from and had no interest in straying near the deep end, so she steered the conversation back to shallow waters. "You name it, it's here. We've got your kosher, your vegan, your ham, greens, and potato salad." Avery actually laughed for the first time in days. "And desserts . . . from Sacher torte to bean pies. I counted five pound cakes and dozens of brownies. What am I going to do with all this food? I wish they had given it to a shelter or something in Mom's name."

"You could donate it. Sad truth is most churches up here have soup kitchens—I mean it's good, but unfortunate we need so many." Alicia went directly to the cabinet where the dishes were kept, grabbed one of the everyday Lenox plates, not the Sunday Haviland—real-special-occasion Meissen was on display in the china cabinet upstairs. "And there's that program for teen girls . . . where your mom volunteered. Bet the brownies would be a big hit."

"What program?" Avery almost didn't ask. It was irritating, all the things people had to tell her about her mother that she didn't know.

"Think it's called Ladies First. Don't know a whole lot about it, but she seemed to spend a lot of time there. At least she talked about it whenever I saw her. Ty Washington—he's a music producer I know through Guy—has a label called Big Bang. Ty's a major player *and* one of the good guys, not a slime dog like my ex. An-y-way, he's on the board. Lives up here too. He was doing Harlem before it got nouveau."

Avery had a flash of the man in the black suit with the gap-toothed smile. *He gave me a card. Must be in my pocket. Somewhere.*

Alicia plunked a hunk of cold macaroni and cheese on top of a thick slice of ham, right next to smoked salmon and country pâté.

"Do you want to microwave that? You don't still like cold mac and cheese, do you?"

"Love it." Alicia picked up the wedge in her French-manicured fingertips and bit into it. "Thank God we're not in L.A. There was always someone with a phone cam ready to snap a picture of Guy Harvey's wife eating again."

"Are you serious?"

"I'm glad you don't know. Sometimes it felt like the world was in my business." Alicia found some stoned-wheat crackers in the pantry to go with her pâté. "After three seasons of *Make Me Platinum,* we had no personal life. If I ate an Oreo on my patio, the headline was 'Alicia Lets It All Hang Out.' "

"*Make Me* what?" Avery lifted a corner of cling wrap and got two peanut-butter cookies from the plate.

"You are too cute." Alicia pulled up a seat at the kitchen table and explained she was fresh off her latest divorce—"Strike three. I am oh so out." Avery hadn't met numbers one and two either, but neither had been high profile enough for anyone but those involved to know or care about the divorces. But Alicia's newest former hubby, Guy Harvey, had spent twenty years behind the scenes in the music business. "It was hard enough dealing with the starry-eyed, no-talent, wack jobs who would stand on my head if it meant they could get close enough to give him their demo. But then he became a judge on *Make Me Platinum,* and, bang, there were people hiding in the hedges and digging in our Dumpster. You have no idea what it's like to go to the supermarket and see a picture of yourself looking like hell-a-rina . . . in the privacy of my own house mind you . . . staring back at you under the headline 'Who Could Blame Him for Cheating.' "

"Sounds awful." Avery poured two glasses of OJ.

"It was horrifying. But he swore it was all lies and innuendo. And you know, I actually believed him. Until I went back to the supermarket and there they were, butt naked in a swimming pool. 'Platinum Guy in Love Nest with Teen Temptress Protégée.' I think the heifer sent the pictures herself, but ultimately I guess she did me a favor. What do you expect from a man I met at a car wash in Vegas? Should have left him before the hot wax dried."

Avery snorted juice up her nose. "I didn't mean . . . That's not funny."

"Like hell it's not. I've been laughing too . . . since the settlement."

Alicia raised her glass, they clinked. Reminded Avery of her mother in Paris. *Stop.*

"What was that look?"

"Nothing." Avery didn't mean for it to show. "So, are you here visiting?"

Alicia put some salmon on a cracker. "Needed a change of venue. And as long as I don't marry Jay-Z or the billionaire mayor, nobody cares who I am or what I eat. Speaking of, is that all you're having?"

"Not much appetite."

"I get it. It made me eat more." Alicia took a napkin from the stack on the table, wiped her fingers. "An-y-way . . . I'm planning to stay in New York, at least for a few years. My brother's still here, and his kids are growing up. I'd like to know them better . . . be more than Auntie Alicia who sends fab presents and fat checks. I'm in a sublet now—month-to-month lease—but as soon as I zero in on the right spot, I'm there. And . . . drum roll please." She paused for more dramatic effect. "I'm going to open a boutique. Up here. Everybody's downtown—we could use some more hot shopping uptown . . . hip, chic, trendy clothes—you know, like Jeffrey or Yigal in the Meatpacking District."

Avery nodded, although Jeffrey and Yigal could have been the next Siegfried and Roy for all she knew. The last time she lived in New York, the Meatpacking District was a smelly, scary place filled with butchers and slaughterhouses, not designer boutiques, cool people, and four-star eateries.

Alicia toyed with her pendant—a black Tahitian pearl the size of Avery's first thumb joint that dangled from a braided platinum chain. "Besides, buying for my own store might keep me out of other people's."

Avery remembered that laugh, raucous and full out, as if Alicia had heard the best dirty joke, and if she liked you, she'd share it. They had shared many laughs.

"Hey, I can hope, can't I?" Alicia sighed, then winked. "Enough about me. How are you? I know this isn't a great time to be playing catch-up. But you don't write . . . you don't call." Alicia laughed again. This time it was short, static, and Avery knew she was only half-joking.

Avery had assumed the conversation would go there eventually—it had to. Considering Alicia's usual bluntness, she had actually taken her time getting around to the subject. "I know you tried to be my friend. . . . You were the best, LiLi. You were looking out for me."

"Never mind." Alicia pushed her plate away. "I promised myself I wouldn't bring this up. So let's not beat a sleeping horse, an old dead horse, however it goes. Okay? New subject." She swigged the last of her juice. "It's early in all of this, but you've got an awful lot to handle. Have you thought about what you're going to do? I mean, I had help—my brother and my sister-in-law, who is really great, and we still had a mountain to climb."

Avery shook her head. "I came because Mom had an accident. I never expected it would . . . I didn't think . . ." *This is where I'm supposed to choke up, fill with tears, have a lump in my throat. Something.* But, like at the funeral, it didn't come. Not even with Alicia. Avery cried at movies and in books when the hero died. She cried at seeing the inconceivable, horrible conditions people in so many parts of the world dealt with in their everyday lives. She cried when she was nine and her turtle, whom she had never even liked enough to name, died. But so far she'd only found that one tear, a match for the one her mother had shed in the hospital—even steven. So she hesitated, looked down, then away, like she had at the cemetery, hoped it allowed whoever was watching to translate her actions into what they expected as bereavement.

"I know you're hurting." Alicia patted Avery's hand. "I know what this feels like."

No you don't. You had a real family. "I'll get it together. I have to." Avery cleared her throat—another special effect. "I have a job to go back to."

"And your life?"

That threw her for a moment. "Of course." Avery considered telling her about Van, didn't have the energy to make that dreamy. "I got extended leave because of the distance. But I don't know if even that'll be enough. I mean, I have to put the house on the market. I'm just glad she sold the Oak Bluffs cottage. She kept asking if I wanted her to keep it—for me. I haven't summered there since we were kids." Avery swept crumbs from the table into her palm, sprinkled them on Alicia's empty plate. "We never had one of those talks . . . about last wishes . . ." Avery trailed off. *Any wishes.*

"My folks had it with us long before we needed to know—they were still in their forties. Then every couple of years, they'd give us updates. I hated it. But in the end, it was great not to have to comb through all of that blind."

They stayed in the kitchen, the way they used to, as though being surrounded by food and a place to cook it triggered some genetic predisposition to gather around the fire and share stories.

And they talked—about the present or the recent past. Not much venturing back to the old days, the ones that had frayed their friendship till it gave way. They shared safe, inconsequential anecdotes, like Alicia's surprise at finding a box of naughty videos under her parents' bed. And she offered to introduce Avery to the broker who was helping her find an apartment—when she was ready for that step.

They relaxed enough with each other to conjure the feeling of being together back when they used to stay up all night looking out Avery's bedroom window—breathing life into their hopes and plotting their dreams in the moonlight. Avery wanted to be a doctor—not because her father was, but because that's what Dwight wanted to be. She'd specialize in sports medicine. *Yeah, well.* And Alicia, torn between being an existential playwright and a jewelry designer, concluded on one of their window wish nights that she could do both. *Did you design that necklace, LiLi?* The knot of diamonds at the top of the pearl was certainly unique—but Avery left the question unasked.

"What am I gonna do? Four floors and nearly fifty years. Do you know how much stuff there is here? Where do I even start?" Avery sounded more anxious than she meant to.

"Pick a room, a drawer, a closet. I'll help if you want. I've got plenty of time these days." Alicia winked. "But I'm not thinking you're going to find the Braithwaite X-rated pictures collection. And I'm also guessing you're on your own with this since dear old cousin Dwight has to still be on your shit list. I personally would sooner eat a bowl of spiders than be friendly with DD." A smile lit up Alicia's face. "Your mom told me about the actress who dumped him. I loved that story. Not the part about how she died not long after. That was sad, but how she just said, 'No, Dwight. I don't want to marry you.' Left his ring on the altar and walked out of the church! I would have given anything to see that." Alicia looked directly at Avery. "Believe me, it took all my restraint not to call the papers and tell them exactly the kind of man he is when he ran for Congress. But that would have involved more than just him."

"Thank you for your restraint. I know how hard that is for you." Avery laughed. "And, no, Dwight won't be helping me out. But you know, in his own Dwighty way, I believe he loved Mom. They seemed to have their own thing. You know, when she died, the hospital called him, not me? He was her 'in case of emergency' contact. I haven't been able to say thank-you—yet."

"Must have been a cold slap for you." Alicia stood, started to clear the dishes. "I need to go, Av. Taking my niece to dinner. I'm going to do this Auntie Mame thing right."

"I'm sure you will. Don't worry about that—leave them. Dishes I can handle."

"That how you handle them?" Alicia nodded toward the pile already in the sink.

Avery laughed. "I'll get there. Let's get your stuff." Avery led the way back up to the hall. "Listen, Li." She turned, spoke over her shoulder. "I'm sorry about—I just couldn't do it your way. I knew you were right. But I didn't know how to fight them—so I didn't."

"You did what you had to do. I didn't agree." Alicia's smile was sad. "No apology required." She gathered her things from the hall. "If you want, call me after the lawyer tomorrow. I'll help you come up with a plan."

"Thanks for coming and for still being you."

They shared a quick hug—this one real enough to be sincere, but still not deep enough to qualify as a full reunion. "We couldn't get past it. But that was then. We don't have to go there. Okay?" And Alicia was out the door.

But sometimes Avery did go there, whether she wanted to or not.

➢ ➢ ➢

She'd been looking forward to that weekend since Dwight first came home mouthing about it when she was sixteen. For three years he tantalized her with stories about College Hill—dorm life, hanging out at Faunce Hall, Bears football, dancing till you could wring the sweat out of your shirt, frat parties and after parties—so cool she could hardly stand it. She'd made him promise she and Alicia could come to Brown for Spring Weekend once they finally got in college. But when it was time, he hedged—"It gets a little crazy up there." Her parents' okay hinged on Dwight's participation, so Avery was relentless—"I'm the same age as you when you first went. You survived."

When Avery hit her teens, Dwight seemed to struggle with her evolution from little cousin to young woman, especially after he left for college. Their relationship shifted—more to accommodate him than her. They were still tight, although Avery spent more time with school friends and less with him. But now she wasn't a high school kid anymore. She was a coed.

So Dwight gave in. "But you can't run home and tell every little thing you see." He arranged the details—a girlfriend's place where they could crash, a weekend full of parties and dances. Best of all, because Avery had begged—"What's the matter? You think we're losers or something?"—and finally threatened to tell all his friends he was deathly afraid of pigeons, he gave in and rounded up dates for them for the Friday-night concert. It didn't even matter who was playing.

That Friday morning Alicia, a student at Hunter—"Decent education. No student loans,"—left New York and picked Avery up from Smith in her thirdhand, cherry red Chevelle—the car she'd proudly bought with money she saved from two years of part-time and summer jobs. She didn't care that it was ancient, it was wheels of her own, and, most important, it was a convertible, the car of her dreams. It had its share of dings and scratches, but her father made sure it purred, and he signed off on their adventure.

Avery drove the next leg of the journey, from her campus in Northampton east to Providence—top down, heater on high, they sang, giggled, and felt totally grown about their big weekend. Smith's campus was less than two hours away, but the life of a freshman at a women's college, even one considered progressive, didn't do much to encourage or accommodate weekend junkets to neighboring campuses. So Avery was psyched to be venturing out.

Dwight met them in town and delivered them to his girlfriend, Jackie—a blonde from Prairie du Chien, Wisconsin, who had sizable breasts with no visible means of support. Her floor was their designated crash pad. They had showered and changed outfits three times before he returned an hour later with their escorts for the evening, Trey Gordon and Luke Ford, new pledgee Dwight's frat brothers.

Avery didn't know if the guys had flipped a coin or drawn straws—and honestly it didn't matter how they'd worked out the matchup. Both contestants in this dating game were highly cute. Av and LiLi tried to be cool and not go bug-eyed and squeal as Luke grabbed Alicia's hand, and Trey took Avery gently by the arm.

The couples exchanged particulars as they headed out. Avery absorbed Trey's every word so she could embellish them when she got back to campus. Trey was a poli sci major with golden skin, dancing eyes, a lean, athletic build—used to run hurdles—and a hint of swagger to his lope. His father was a prominent jurist whose name was bandied about whenever there was talk of potential High Court vacancies. Trey was slated for Harvard Law in the fall. "Trumps my old man." Avery couldn't believe her luck, couldn't wait to tell Dwight it was good looking out. He'd have some kind of ribbing in store for her, but that was a small price she was totally willing to pay.

The streets became a sea of rambunctious revelers. Their sextet met up with some other students, and the group, about a dozen strong, headed for Meehan Auditorium. On the way, pint bottles of rum, the traditional beverage of the celebration, appeared—an oblique homage to the school's rum-trading and slave-trading origins—and it got laced into half-filled cups of Coke and passed around. Avery declined. They cracked up when Alicia said, "I'm naturally high."

The biggest surprise came when Dwight pulled two fat reefers out of his shirt pocket, put them both to his lips, lit up, took a stereo toke, and passed them around to a chorus of "Aright. My man came through," "You all right, D." Avery nearly fell over. She caught his eye. He shrugged. Luke offered to show Alicia how to inhale. "I don't think so." Trey offered Avery. She smiled. "No thanks." He pinched the joint, eyes squinted as he took a drag, held the smoke, and finally blew it out. "Suit yourself."

The concert was too perfect—seats down front, so close Avery could see beads of spotlight-illuminated sweat glistening on the musicians' bodies. So close the music rippled through her as she and Trey and the thousands in attendance danced at their seats to rock, blues, jazz, folk, played by indie bands and renowned headliners. Some of the music she knew well enough to sing along, but new melodies and rhythms opened her up wide, eyes closed in the darkness, her hand in Trey's. It was big, and hot, and she didn't dare move so he wouldn't take it away.

Even more amazing, after the show they hung by the stage, like they belonged, while Dwight, Luke, and Trey talked to some of the techies, even a few musicians. When they filtered out into the night, Avery watched as Jackie and the other coeds in their group drank from Styrofoam cups Avery knew contained more rum than Coke. They took easy drags every time the joint came around. She and Alicia kept each other in sight, arched eyebrows, rolled eyes, and mouthed asides behind a back, over a shoulder, couldn't wait for the chance to recap details, eager for what the next day could bring to top this. But the night wasn't over yet. The lighting guy gave them the address for an after party. This was officially going to be the first, best night of their grown-up lives.

Another jay came around as they walked back toward Jackie's. This time when it came her way, Avery didn't say no. She and Dwight exchanged a look, but neither had anything to say. She took a deep hit, flipped off Alicia's questioning look. "Have to experience the moment." And even though she'd never had so much as a cigarette, Avery didn't cough or gag.

The six of them piled into Luke's chocolate brown Cordoba. Avery crouched on Trey's lap, waiting to feel different, wondering what the big deal was. On the ride to the party, she accepted another hit and a few sips from Trey's Styrofoam cup to prove her point.

Music and voices leaked from the open jalousies of the sunporch at the party house. Inside, it was cavern dark and close, with too many people flopped on sofas and chairs, stacked on the stairs, to actually see what the room looked like. If you'd asked her if she was high, Avery would have said no—not dizzy or woozy or out of control. Just lighter, freer, happy, but she was supposed to be. Music pulsed through the rooms like a heartbeat, and clusters, couples—suns and satellites—danced, talked, laughed, argued, drank—partaking in that time-honored ancient bacchanal of the secret off-campus party, ones Avery had heard about, after the fact, in Amherst. Nothing at all like the anemic gatherings they pieced together in Northampton with cheese and chips and a few bottles of purloined beer or wine. But exactly like ones Alicia had gone to in some fourth-floor walk-up on Amsterdam or 118th Street—thrown by students at City College or Columbia. And even though she claimed not to be that impressed—been-there, done-that New Yorker that she was, even for Alicia something was more edgy, more outside, about this dark, buzzing hive of energy and excess that smelled ripe—like fresh sweat and bad cologne and sweet smoke and eternal youth, and freedom. An off-campus party in a place where lines and boundaries were much more defined than in New York made crossing them feel bolder.

Avery held on to Trey's hand as he led the way through the room, caught snippets of conversations about GREs and MCATs, what married profs were screwing which students, who was getting engaged after graduation—all heady adult stuff to two rank freshmen. Alicia and Luke found a corner, Dwight and Jackie disappeared into the smoky pit of the basement. Trey said, "Let's find someplace quiet, so we can talk." Perfect.

The time between those words—her tingly anticipation of a deep conversation that would lead to a deep kiss, phone numbers, and tomorrow plans, and being trapped in that room—was a blink, a breath, a heartbeat. She'd been dreaming about whether the train or the bus would be best for their next weekend rendezvous. Then he slammed her against the door—his full weight pinning her, tongue cold and wet like a serpent in her mouth. And she couldn't scream. Her raw, rough growl grated her throat. Her giddy high morphed to disoriented panic. His leg pushed higher, harder, and through her gauzy yellow skirt, she felt the cold metal of the doorknob boring into her hip. In the seconds it took for her to realize her arms were free, his hand was already under her skirt, clawing at her panties, jagged-nailed fingers probing, insistent. Avery pounded him, writhed, but that didn't stop him. She tensed the muscles in her thighs, wanting a moment when he relaxed—just a second—took a breath, moved his leg. She was strong. Her legs had carried her across too many finish lines. They wouldn't fail her. For a flash she wished for Dwight or Alicia, but in that moment she was alone.

Then her hands were on Trey's face, pulling, pinching whatever skin she could grab—an ear, his cheek. She slapped and squeezed until she found a weak spot—jabbed her fingers into his eye. He grabbed his face. "Bitch!" He dropped his knee enough for her to bring hers up—hard, swift, with all the force she could muster. Trey let her go, bent over holding his crotch, but not long enough for her to get away. More angry that she'd got the best of him, that he was hurt, he recovered enough to punch Avery across the jaw and nose, then landed a full right to her gut. She went down, and the toes of his tasseled loafer slammed into her chest, her arms, her side. That's the last she remembered.

When Alicia found her, Avery was struggling to consciousness. In the din, Alicia's calls for help went unnoticed until she went out and started turning on lights wherever she found a switch, a lamp, staring into the crowd at faces until she saw Dwight. He used his spectacularly limited premed skills and insisted no one move Avery—asked if she knew who he was, her name, the day, who was president. He finally got around to asking who had assaulted her, and as soon as she told him, he decided that it would be best to move her after all. Alicia wanted to call an ambulance, the police, but Dwight explained that because of the drugs and underage drinking, it would probably be a bad idea to get the authorities involved. He said Avery looked like she'd be all right.

Alicia yelled up at him, "How would you know?"

By then the crowd was restless. Somebody turned the lights back off.

That's when Alicia ran outside, flagged down a cab that was about to pull off. They left Dwight, who'd gone to find Jackie.

Avery couldn't stop shivering, couldn't stop begging. "Please take me home. I want to go home."

➢ ➢ ➢

Avery locked the front door and set the alarm. Yes, at times she still went there. Some days a ragged corner of a random memory from that night would flash into her mind without warning and she'd be back there again—meeting Trey. The doorknob digging into her side. Standing around the stage after the concert. The cutting assault of Trey's jagged nails. Singing along with Janet Jackson in Alicia's car on the way to Providence. Trey sweet and gentle, holding her hand. Trey's hand over her mouth. It would be blinding and bright, but for only a few seconds, then it would fade, but not without leaving a haunting residue.

EIGHT

. . . she'd finally fallen off the edge of logic

"There are no surprises here, Avery. But I'm sure you weren't expecting any. Your mother put most of her assets in a living trust for you right after your dad passed away. Her bank accounts—at least the ones listed here—name you the sole beneficiary. You can claim the balances and transfer them to any other account you specify immediately." Walker Brown, who had been her parents' attorney her whole life, sat behind a massive oak desk, which only made him look more diminutive. With his sharp chin, large ears, and beak of a nose, Avery used to imagine that if there could ever be such a thing as a black leprechaun, he would look like Walker Brown. "We did this to avoid probate. Since you're the only heir, I thought it best to simplify things, not go through all the rigamarole."

To be discussing her mother's estate at all made Avery queasy. "Tell you the truth, Mr. Brown—"

"We can dispense with the *mister*. I'm still an old man to you, but you're not a little girl anymore." Now in his eighties, and as sharp as ever, his voice, a sonorous bass, was still surprising coming out of that little body. His eyes still twinkled with a hint of playful I-know-something-you-don't-know mischief. He used both attributes to great effect in disarming witnesses and captivating juries. "*Walker* will do just fine."

"Okay . . . Walker." She had a hard time getting it out of her mouth. "I didn't have any expectations. Maybe it's naive, or plain stupid, but I never considered the reality of this day."

"None of us want to. But your mother thought about it." Walker stopped, looked out the window. "I'll miss Forestina. I knew her—and your father of course, a very long time—since they were first married. They were friends you know, not just clients. And I want you to feel the same way. Besides, I might still need to consult with you on a couple of matters—since you're in town."

Avery smiled slowly. When she was little, she thought ATTORNEY AT LAW written in gold on the frosted-glass door sounded impressive. Whenever she was in the office with her mother, Mr. Brown shook her hand and spoke to her as if she were an adult. Before they left, he would come around the desk and ask for her advice about one of his cases. Arms folded across his chest, he'd look her squarely in the eye. "Do you think I should ask for a continuance on *Harris v. Oglethorpe* or just get on with it?" Of course, she had no idea what he was talking about, but she would pretend to deliberate her choices, then render her opinion. Until she was twelve, Avery wanted to be an attorney when she grew up. But by the time she was fourteen, she had discovered her running legs, and they were ready to carry her into another future. That's when Avery decided on med school and sports medicine. It hadn't hurt that Dwight wanted to be a doctor then too.

The office was still in the Empire State Building—clearly for the élan of the address, not for the fancy digs. A warren of narrow corridors and cramped cubicles overflowed with people, desks, files, in a space that was strictly utilitarian. Even though the practice had expanded into several adjoining offices, not much had changed—except for the building's new stringent security check, and the absence from the lobby of the Riverboat Restaurant, where she and her mom would stop for lunch when they left the lawyer, it all looked and felt the same.

"I can go through the formality of reading this." Walker held Forestina's will. "Or you can look it over when you're ready. It's pretty straightforward." Aside from a few bequests to charities—a small trust for her alma mater, the church, and one for Ladies First, a program for teen girls in Harlem—the rest of her mother's assets passed to Avery. "Barring some catastrophic occurrence, you should be quite comfortable for the foreseeable future."

Comfortable was not a way Avery thought of herself. Inheriting money wouldn't change that. "This is overwhelming. I'm living abroad. I don't know where to begin."

"I'll be happy to help you figure this out. I just wouldn't make any decisions about the disposition of the property too hastily. Certainly not before you consult an accountant."

Avery toyed with the strap of her purse. "I guess I need to start making lists then."

"Oh, yes—you should be aware that there is the property your mother was planning to sell to your uncle King. We'd already worked out terms—quite favorable I might add—all the paperwork was done, including documents for you, and the closing date was set but . . ." He cleared his throat.

"She mentioned it when I saw her in Paris." Avery brushed past that memory. "I told her I didn't care what she did with it. And I still don't."

"That building would have been taken out of the will, but since sale never closed, I never changed the schedule of assets. I presume you'll go through with the sale. There is a degree of urgency on the part of the buyers. But as I always advise my clients, you are under no obligation to feel pressured."

"If I already have a buyer, that's at least one thing off my plate." Avery smiled. "But you're right. There's a lot to digest and I'm sure I'll have plenty of questions." This wasn't like some long-lost relative who left her a fortune. This was her parents' estate, their legacy to her, and Avery couldn't have felt more ambivalent.

"Call me anytime. You have my home and my mobile. Use them. I mean that, Avery." Then he got up, came around to the front of his desk, folded his arms across his chest. "Now I want to ask your opinion about this negligence case we got handed last week."

"I think you should settle." Avery laughed, then slipped the envelope containing her mother's will into her purse, got up, kissed him on the cheek. "Thank you, Walker."

Outside, the morning clouds had broken, and the sun made Avery believe that spring might actually be coming after all. She couldn't remember the last time she had walked in Manhattan, so she turned up her collar, hiked her bag higher and tighter on her shoulder, and with the wind at her back headed up Fifth Avenue.

New York in all of its contradictory glory has a way of being familiar no matter how long you've been away—the changes may be subtle or monumental, sometimes for the better, sometimes not, but you still hold the city in your heart and your mind's eye—the way it was. Like looking at your spouse of forty years and still seeing who you saw when youth was your present, not your past. It's not in the least judgmental—you accept the inevitability of change and continue to cherish what you see. You just don't forget what was.

Avery walked a few blocks in the city that was always the same, but she took in the differences. What had been her mother's favorite store, B. Altman, now bustled with students heading for classes at the CUNY Graduate Center. The shoe store where she would pick out the styles she would buy if she were a grown-up lady, while her mother and the salesman bent over swatches of fabric, discussing whether the best match would be achieved on peau de soie or satin, was now a health-food café. Avery accepted a flyer from a girl in a white lab coat standing in front of a sleek day spa that had taken up residence in what used to be a furniture showroom. It struck her how much of the scenery reminded her of her mother. Memories she'd banished to a corner where she didn't go digging around.

She searched for the right walking rhythm—faster, then slower, but still felt out of sync. For a few blocks she upped her pace to match the natives who dashed and zigzagged, timing their progress to avoid losing precious seconds at red lights, as though there were a prize for covering the most sidewalk in the least amount of time. There seemed to be extra points for not making eye contact.

By Fortieth Street she dropped out of competition, downshifted to stroll, meandering, with stops and starts—some planned, others spontaneous—like a tourist. Her gaze wandered and a thought or memory carried her off course. A young couple in coordinated desert camouflage—her pants, his jacket—held hands and laughed as though they shared the secret to eternal happiness. It was a rude reminder that Avery had never been young and in love in New York. *Too late for that.* She passed an elderly gent in a topcoat and hat—she wouldn't know a bowler from a homburg, but it was a real hat. It looked as if he'd made an error in timing and stepped from a bygone decade smack into the twenty-first century. His posture and correctness made her think about her father. Not a warm or fuzzy memory, but those were pretty scarce where he was concerned. The only person who ever seemed to light up his eyes was her mother. After a while, Avery had stopped trying.

Watching a frazzled mom negotiate a two-seater stroller, containing a toddler and a five-year-old, onto a kneeling bus made her try to recall the story her mother told of taking Dwight and her to the Central Park Zoo. Had they been about that age? It had to do with feeding the lambs, but Avery couldn't summon the particulars, and of the other two people involved one was dead and the other may as well have been, and she didn't want to play that game anymore. She snapped herself out of that reverie in time to help the woman raise the stroller enough to navigate the lift.

At Forty-second Street, she passed Patience and Fortitude, the library lions—thinking she'd need plenty of both. Walking felt good, her legs solid—not running strong, but at least sturdy enough to carry her where she would have to go. She had a lot of territory to cover in the next couple of weeks.

The blocks between the library and Fifty-ninth Street provided a dazzling display of eye candy. Exclusive hair salons, jewelers, designer boutiques, many the same as on Bond Street in London or avenue Montaigne in Paris. *Just a month ago.* She let the thought pass without engaging it. The stores' New York posture seemed somehow more aggressive, but New York had teeth and a bite that let you know you shouldn't even think about sitting all afternoon in a café over one cup of coffee, or a glass of wine. In Paris or Florence it would never enter your head not to linger.

Tiffany & Co. still looked discreet and bank-vaultish. When she was fourteen, her mother brought her there to get her first strand of pearls—the ones around her neck now. She wore them when they walked across the way to have lunch at the Plaza, which looked the same too. Whatever they turned it into hadn't altered the hotel's facade.

By the time she got to the hulking ghost of what would forever be the GM Building—whether they'd gone bankrupt or not—Avery had a handful of postcards, brochures, and flyers from two cosmetic surgeons, a psychic, a sushi buffet, a secret sample sale, and at least a half dozen other businesses looking to snare new customers. She shoved them in her bag, headed east to Madison. The shops seemed equally pricey, but less flashy than on Fifth Avenue—in that reserved East Side manner. But the street looked flush with shoppers and their treasures. Black cars waited in front of tony restaurants and shops. *What recession?*

Another twenty blocks and Avery's feet were fried. Her pumps, though midheeled and sensible compared to, say, Grace Kidder's, were not meant for a pavement-pounding hike. But as long as the route hadn't changed, the bus up Madison was the best way for her to get home. So she tramped passed the designer emporiums of nouveau-American understated opulence and crossed Seventy-second Street. That's when it dawned on her the journey had taken her back in the neighborhood of her old school, to the stop where she and Alicia would wait for the pumpkin that would carry them away from the Upper East Side fairyland, chockablock with swank galleries, uniformed doormen, and prim nannies pushing navy blue prams, and back home to the world north of 110th Street where bodegas specializing in candy, *plantanos* chips, and loosies, storefront churches, liquor stores, and fried-chicken joints were abundant, and richly colored kente or *adinkra* and polyester track suits mixed with the denim and worsted. Avery's uniquely private enclave on the Row was an outpost, totally different from Alicia's 113th Street block, where owners were absentee, and some tenants did their best, while others did their worst. But both blocks were bordered by the same tough avenues, renamed Adam Clayton Powell, Frederick Douglass, and Malcolm X after past and present heroes of the community. It was a galaxy far far away from the East Seventies.

When she'd left the house, Avery hadn't intended to travel the flashback circuit. Or had she? Standing at the bus stop, she realized she didn't know the fare—a dollar last she remembered. That had to be wrong. Exact change? She dug in her purse, moving gingerly past the white envelope with the Walker Brown & Associates, LLC, return address, until her fingers found the small leather case that came with the rest of her mother's belongings from the car. She'd glanced at the MetroCard inside, dropped it in her purse, and not thought about it since. Once the bus arrived, she dipped it for her fare, following the others before her. "You look mighty good for the senior fare." The driver smiled. "Thank you." She smiled back and he let it ride. *Where did Mom go on the bus and the subway?*

Avery took a window seat on the bus up memory lane. As a kid she'd ridden this route hundreds of times, knew the drill. Now, as they traveled farther up Madison, it looked status quo. In the nineties the ritzy apartment towers gave way to boxier, utilitarian buildings, same as when she and Alicia had ridden home after school and track practice. Two chatterboxes full of the day's happenings, they used the time to catch up on their days. They had very different class schedules—Avery's heavy in the sciences, Alicia's in the arts and humanities. They timed their conversations by the landmarks they passed. Teacher and subject discussions needed to be winding up by the time they reached Sarabeth's Kitchen at Ninety-second Street. By Mt. Sinai Hospital they would be cramming to get in all the good gossip before Alicia's stop—the same overheated dilemmas and dreams that filled their window wish sessions. Such hot topics often had to be continued the moment Avery got home, twenty-five blocks later—because there was always more to be said.

Still is.

When she got to the redbrick, government-subsidized Lehman Houses, and the bus turned onto 110th, they were officially in the hood. At least that's what Avery expected. They passed the Schomburg Plaza towers, rounded the circle—when did the statue of Duke Ellington and his grand piano arrive? And across the great divide, Fifth Avenue, Avery started to see that things weren't what they used to be. First up, she looked around and noticed the bus hadn't completely emptied of people of a lighter hue. They were still sitting in their seats—texting, reading the *Times* or the *NY Spectator,* bopping their heads to whatever tunes snaked through the skinny, white wires plugged into their ears. On her rides home from school, they would have been clutching their belongings or frantically pressing the STOP REQUESTED bar because they had snoozed by their stop and needed to get back to Madison and Ninety-eighth, the outer limits.

She was stunned as the sparkling glass-and-steel high-rise appeared across from the north side of the park. It was so unexpected that Avery couldn't even remember what used to be on that corner, couldn't imagine who lived there now, but it was crystal clear that change had arrived. The sky had grayed again since her adventure began, but Avery was compelled to get off the bus and investigate at Alicia's old stop.

Avery had gone to the Jacksons' apartment many times—loved feeling swept up by a family who talked loud, laughed often, ate from big bowls that would always feed more, teased, argued, and loved without reservation or filters. A vibrant blizzard of artwork covered the walls, old concert posters—Stevie, Chaka, Smokey, Tito Puente—and movie posters: *The Defiant Ones, Shaft, Anna Lucasta, Nothing but a Man.* Photos of family members, Martin Luther King, Malcolm X, Nelson Mandela, an all-black version of the Last Supper, flanked by first-grade finger-painted masterpieces, Bearden, Lawrence, and Rivera reproductions, and signed eight-by-tens of Sammy Davis, Abbey Lincoln, André Watts, and Leontyne Price. The TV would be on, music blared, WBAI played in the kitchen. The apartment was messy and warm and happy, and Avery loved it. But Alicia adored Avery's house because it was orderly and quiet and Avery had her own room. Avery never thought her friend would have liked living there though.

Avery noticed that the churches, apartment buildings, SRO hotel, and stores on both sides of the avenue hadn't received the uptown makeover. A homeless couple minced across the street pushing a three-wheeled shopping cart, their possessions, covered by a daisy-print comforter, teeming over the top. She thought it probably doubled as their bed. *Wonder if the jail is still back there?* She forgot to look. She and Alicia thought it was hilarious that most folks who lived uptown, not to mention the ones south of the border, had no clue a crook motel was in their midst with a stunning view of the Harlem Meer. But as a general rule, New Yorkers don't look up. Otherwise they might have noticed the windows covered with metal or the rooftop terrace that looked more like a cage than a cool place to hang out with homeys and grill a few steaks.

Avery scanned the avenue. Not crowded at this time of day; a few folks dribbled out of the subway. Kids just dismissed from school bounced with energy. She could almost see Alicia in her gray blazer and burgundy skirt—she only wore the pants part of their uniform on the coldest days, so she could show off her legs. She'd sprint up the street, her backpack bobbing as she ran, and be at her corner ready to hang a left before the bus got halfway up the block.

But what used to be here?

She crossed the street to the park side, where she could have a better view, and not look as if she were doing surveillance. Hands in her pockets, she leaned against the stone wall, closed her eyes for a few moments, then opened them hoping to conjure an image. Nothing—like the glass monolith had blotted out all recollection of what had come before. *Why is this bugging me?* She watched for a while, curious about the occupants, but saw only package and flower deliveries going in and out of the service entrance.

A police car, lights flashing, siren screaming, interrupted Avery's reverie, so she marched back across the street. Her intention was to ask the doorman what used to be at this address. Except there wasn't one. The doors revolved automatically. But a lobby attendant was behind a spare, imposing counter. The moment she saw how young he was, she was sure he'd have no idea.

"May I help you?"

She'd been in her own head so long the words startled her. "Uh . . . do you have . . . um, any information on the building?" *Great question, Avery.*

"Certainly, ma'am." He handed her a brochure. "This is a general overview of the property, but if you'd like more, there's an office on the premises and I'd be happy to—"

"This will be fine for now." She smiled. "Thank you." *Either they get a lot of nosy people or he's delusional enough to think I look like I could buy a place here.* "It's a beautiful building," Avery said over her shoulder.

"Yes, it is. Thank you, ma'am," she heard as she entered the glass pinwheel.

I'm now a ma'am? *Thanks, sonny.*

Avery stuffed the brochure in her bag, continued down the street, concentrating on the pale green fuzz of leaves, just appearing on the trees across the way. Farther along she walked beneath a long run of the usual under-construction sidewalk shed, painted forest green. It was dank, smelled musty. Despite the stenciled POST NO BILLS it was covered with posters and flyers—for a poetry slam, an upcoming show at the Apollo, a prayer vigil for a teen slain in a drive-by, the latest CD from something called Big Bang. The array reminded her of Alicia's walls. She peered through the cracks to see what was on the other side. One huge lot had been reduced to rubble. It's neighboring building was still standing. A couple of small signs read DUN-RIGHT CONSTRUCTION, with a New Jersey address. Whatever it was would certainly be big.

Avery shrugged it off. She had more immediate concerns than what was going to become of a hole in the ground on Central Park North, as the street signs seemed to be calling this section of West 110th Street. *Like Cathedral Parkway.* Which is what the section of 110th that ran past St. John the Divine had been called for years. *How many names does one street need?*

Posh high-rise condos, fancy dogs, white people, trattorias, and wine bars? Avery didn't know what else was going on in Harlem, and at the moment she didn't want to. She'd had enough for one day. She wasn't sure if her feet were up to the walk, but in true New Yorker fashion, she kept her head down, her eyes ahead, and made it home without any further bends in her time-space continuum.

Until she started up the stairs.

"Excuse me, Mrs. Lyons?"

The voice came from a man exiting a car parked across the street. *Damn. Another nosy neighbor who wants to make nice. How about tomorrow? Or never?* The last thing she wanted to do was make small talk and help a stranger feel less bad about trying to make her feel less bad about her mother. Duck and cover had been her strategy—hoping to get in before the briefcase-laptop-shopping-bag-from-Sephora crowd flooded the block. *Mrs. Lyons?* Whoever he was, he must have read her name from the "Mrs. Braithwaite is survived by" part of the obit.

"Yes?" It was both an answer and another question. *I'm her and I know you're sorry. But do you have to share that at this very moment?* Out of instinct, because some things are in your DNA not your memory imprint, she hoisted her bag higher as the man approached. He wore jeans and a leather bomber jacket—one that had definitely seen combat somewhere, maybe just the subway. His hair was close-cropped, a few flecks of gray made him look old enough, but not too, and he was that new kind of bearded—more unshaven, neatly scruffy, than an actual beard. Avery realized she was mentally preparing a description—in case.

"Jasper Christmas . . . Jazz. I called a few days ago but you couldn't talk." He stayed on the sidewalk and she was on the top step, so she could only guess at his height, but definitely over six feet.

Avery tried to recall. The name was familiar. Certainly unusual enough for her to remember, although there had been so many names in the last week. But he continued before she placed him.

"I'm so very sorry about your mother." He paused. "My parents are gone as well—my mom just last year."

Not another one. Avery was sick of sympathy. And she was especially tired of people who had lost a parent, or two, the woe-is-me-late-in-life orphans, telling her they knew what she was going through. Because they didn't.

Jazz cleared his throat. "So I wanted to give you a little time. I know there's a lot to sort through—to reconcile."

Something she caught in his voice made Avery think maybe he did, or at least he thought he understood what she might be feeling—that her relationship with her mother could have been like his. "Yes . . . well, thank you." She didn't know exactly what to say.

"You don't remember . . . I'm with the *New York Spectator.*"

The lightbulb came on about a second before he announced his affiliation with the paper.

"I'd been speaking to your mother and I wanted to ask you a couple of—"

"Listen, Mr. Christmas. I have no idea what you're looking for. But like I already told you, I'm not the person to talk to. I don't live here and I have no involvement in my mother's business dealings—and certainly not the Dixons'. Now, if you'll excuse me." Avery opened her purse, had to remove the condo brochure, the rest of the paper-phernalia she'd been handed on her way home, and the envelope from the lawyer, to dig around for her keys.

"I understand that, Mrs. Lyons. I'm aware you haven't lived in New York for many years. But aren't your mother's business affairs yours now? I'm afraid you are or will be involved, whether you choose to or not. And I just have a few questions about the Central Park North project—Dixon Plaza."

"The what?" Of all the real estate projects on all the streets—

"More specifically about your building on 111th, which abuts the remaining building on the Dixon property."

The papers she was holding slipped out of one hand just as the other finally found the keys. *He can't mean the site I just passed. Can he?* But it didn't matter. Whatever his questions were about, Avery had no answers.

Jazz picked up the papers she had dropped. "I see you're at least getting familiar with the neighborhood." He held them out to her—the glossy, colorful condo brochure on top. "That's a good thing in a landlord."

"Huh?"

"Or are you planning to sell it to the Dixon Group too?"

Avery grabbed the stack from him. "Like I said, I can't help you, Mr. Christmas." She put her key in the lock. "If you'll excuse me."

"Here's my card. You might want to talk to me after you get a handle on what's going on. At any rate you'll definitely have questions. Maybe I'll have some answers for you."

"That's what attorneys are for, Mr. Christmas." Avery didn't exactly slam the door, but it was forceful enough to make her point.

Jazz slipped his card through the mail slot, making a point of his own.

➢ ➢ ➢

In keeping with Avery's new and ever-improving skill at putting off till tomorrow what you don't even want to think about today, she took a full twenty-four hours to sit down with the envelope containing her mother's will. Once again she had roamed from room to room, looking for the appropriate place. The kitchen was cozy, but felt too casual—not exactly reverent enough, especially since she hadn't done the dishes as she told Alicia she would. Her mom's bedroom smelled like she was still there—not the right place for Avery to be comfortable with the details of her last wishes. Then she tried out the new sunroom, but Avery wasn't sure if it was just more perky than she could stand, or if the room's total re-creation made her uncomfortable. All that yellow and blue look-on-the-bright-side wallpaper and furniture made it feel as out of place as Avery herself did. Not to mention much too cheery for such a somber undertaking.

By the next afternoon, she had finally settled on the dining room. It had the right amount of decorum, and she was surrounded by things her mother treasured in a space that had remained virtually unchanged. There was comfort in that. *There's the clock.* No longer ticking forward and back, it sat on the mantel unwound, frozen in time. She steeped Earl Grey in a cabbage-rose porcelain teapot and carried it upstairs on a tray, along with a matching cup and saucer, not the mug from the Harlem Y or the one with the three frogs sitting on a rainbow she had been using, rinsing out, and using again. Avery knew her mother would have been pleased.

She took a side chair in the middle of the table, which sat ten without the additional leaves. The head and foot had substantial armchairs—her folks had directed hundreds of dinners from those seats. Avery left them empty. Not until she sat there did she remember doing the same thing with her mother, the morning after her father's funeral. Her mother assured her they both had been well provided for, that Avery should have no worries on that front. Then Forestina had said, "He loved you, you know. He really did. In his own way." Which is exactly how Avery had explained Dwight's feelings about her mother to Alicia. Was that some kind of family creed? *We don't love you like we should. We don't love you like you ought to be loved. But we do love you, "in our own way."* Maybe they should get T-shirts? They wouldn't need many. The Manning-Braithwaite-Dixon clan was shriveling. None too soon if you asked Avery.

She sipped her tea, took a breath, opened the envelope.

Even with rereading a few paragraphs, it took less than fifteen minutes, beginning to end. No curveballs, no soap-opera illegitimate half sisters given up for adoption, or huge sums left to a home for mentally ill parakeets—nothing unexpected, except the amount. There was so much more than she expected, than she ever thought about. Avery knew her parents had done well, made sound, conservative investments meant to carry them through their golden years without alterations in their lifestyle. And they certainly never lived lavishly. Avery had been on her own so long and she did just fine. Her salary wasn't private-sector, corner-office cushy, but it was offset by a housing allowance, excellent benefits, and unequaled travel opportunities. And she had received additional income from a small trust and a few investments her parents had made for her when she was young and said she wanted to be a doctor. After Trey, it was all she could do to get through the four years of college. In senior year she spoke to the State Department recruiter on campus, lined up a job, and away she went, not looking back—as far away from family and medicine as she could get.

But more than that? Avery returned the will to the envelope, laid it back on the table, and clasped her hands on top—like she'd finished her test and was waiting to hand it in. Except it felt like the test was just beginning.

She looked around at the perfect, lovely room. Quiet, tasteful landscapes in gilt frames hung on the walls, which were covered in ruby red, embossed wallpaper. Plaster ceiling medallions, the brass-and-crystal chandelier, and mahogany wainscoting all spoke to permanence. Other than the wallpaper and the upholstery on the chair seats, nothing in this room, not the antique sideboard that held the sterling tea service and the embroidered table linens that used to belong to a great-great-aunt Avery had never met, or the sparkling beveled-glass doors to the china cabinet that showed off a store-worthy display of crystal, china, and silver flatware, had changed in Avery's lifetime.

But now this house, along with everything else, including the building Jasper Christmas kept badgering her about, belonged to her. Her house. To do with as she pleased. Live in it. Sell it. Love it. Despise it.

In that moment the enormity of it all crystallized. Avery rested her arms on the table, put her head down. Until then, she had been going through the motions, doing what had to be done, in a logical, rational, unemotional way. And as always, she had done a good job. But she'd finally fallen off the edge of logic. How could it be that two weeks ago she was celebrating her arrival in Wellington? Ten days ago, she was on a plane flying to New York because her mother had been in an accident . . . *Has it really only been ten days?*

Of course Avery knew that life could change in an instant. It happened each day, to people who were going about the business of their lives when suddenly their world was thrown off its axis. She knew what that was like. But even in the awful, indelible imprint of those moments in Providence, the entirety of her world hadn't changed—only the way she saw it. And home, the place where she grew up, that still existed. Whether she would ever feel the same about it, or the people in it, was not the point. It was still there—for her to go to, or run away from.

Which somehow meant she wasn't alone.

Yes, she was an only child with an extended family that could hold a reunion in a phone booth, and most of her adult life had been spent five or six time zones away from them. She had no husband or children, but even so, Avery never thought of herself as alone. She was a solo, not a solitary. It was choice. She could add other voices or companion travelers anytime she chose. And she mostly sang her own song since she hadn't had a lot of luck in the love department. When she was younger, she fell early and often, hoping she'd be caught or at least that her fall would be broken by someone who cared. But those relationships had crash-landed, ending with something broken—like her heart.

Denis Lyons, Ph.D., had been one of those dizzying, off-balance, early loves. Then she went through the poetic longing, unrequited period. She had more than one boss or embassy coworker who fit that bill. From there she entered the multi-man quantity, not quality, period. This was the time when finding the elusive perfect man didn't matter. She found traits she liked in each man, and when she put them all together, it seemed like enough. That phase was exhausting and short-lived. Then came Van. He neither wanted too much or gave too little. He made no demands and she made none of him. They didn't ask questions that went too deep, and if you broke down the amount of time they had actually spent together in the three years they had been seeing each other, it probably added up to about three months. Van was perfect. He was smart, but not bookish or an academic snob. He had wide-ranging interests beyond his work—reclaiming the rain forests, soccer and cycling, straight-ahead jazz. He had lived all over the world, and like her he had no siblings. He was an add-on when she wanted a duet, a willing partner when she wanted a view for two, and not offended when she'd had enough twosomeness, because he got it. Van was a kindred spirit. But alone? Avery had never felt alone, until now.

So she was startled when she realized her sleeve was wet. Avery sat up. No sound, no sobs, no wrenching ache came from deep inside where tears were supposed to come from. Just little rivers sliding down her cheeks. *This is crazy.* She wiped her eyes with her damp sleeve, but still a silent, slow trickle continued to leak. She cleared the table and headed back to the kitchen, where she snatched a paper towel from the roll, pressed it hard against her eyelids, hoping the pressure would stop the water.

Enough. She went into the pantry, where she knew her mother kept the Maker's Mark and vermouth, and made herself a manhattan on the rocks in a juice glass. She leaned against the sink, sipped her drink, and surveyed the mess in the kitchen. Not only had she not done the dishes, she hadn't taken out the garbage or looked into donating the excess food. She hadn't let Jessie know when she should come to clean. She hadn't opened the mail or returned at least twenty phone calls. Besides her trip to the lawyer's office, Avery had done exactly nothing.

Between the drink and the sobering mess in the kitchen, at least the crying stopped, but that wasn't enough. She had to get a grip, snap out of the funk. The clock was ticking and it was clear she couldn't do all that needed doing, even with the extra two weeks' leave. Could not. It wasn't a concept she embraced, not an admission she made easily, but there it was. She'd run smack into her limit and she wasn't sure what happened after that.

She checked her watch. Cocktail hour in New York meant first thing in the morning in New Zealand. *No time like now.* She got her purse, found one of her brand-new, never-been-handed-out business cards because she hadn't had her new phone number long enough to commit it to memory, and dialed.

NINE

That's when the light went out in her heart

"I told them I need a leave of absence. I could tell they weren't happy, but I'm entitled, so they pretended to be understanding and e-mailed me the paperwork." Avery and Alicia had once again found their way to the kitchen. "Would you believe my mother has wireless? I turned my laptop on and the little icon popped up asking me if I wanted to connect to the Internet. Boy, was I shocked. I was geared up to try and remember how to use dial-up. She must have a computer I haven't found yet."

"Your mom was actually a pretty hip chick, considering." Alicia smiled. "She tried to stay young, grow with the times. I think that's why she enjoyed her Ladies First girls."

"Just not the Mom I knew. But I filled it out, found a Staples on 125th, scanned it, and sent it back to them first thing this morning." Avery perched on the windowsill—the one her mother used to fuss at her for sitting on. "I needed to make the decision and act on it."

"It's a start." Alicia sat on a stool by the island. She knew Avery could use a friend and had hoped she would call, but whatever ties bound them to the past, she wasn't sure Avery was ready to reconnect in the present. So she was surprised, but happy, to hear from her. "And by giving yourself six months, you take the pressure down several notches. But what will you do about your things—the stuff you left in New Zealand?"

"There isn't much. You learn to live lean when you move every couple of years. My assistant—I guess he's my replacement's assistant now—will ship me what I never got around to unpacking anyway. I just don't hold on to things. Especially not clothes." Avery patted her thigh. "Present outfit excluded." She had on a pair of eighties-vintage, acid-washed Levi's and a sweater she'd found in the closet in her room—the room she still hadn't slept in.

Alicia laughed. "At least you still fit in your old clothes."

It wasn't her old clothes Avery was having trouble fitting into. It was her old life. "I'm always presentable, at least I think so. Besides, when you move from Senegal to Switzerland, you just have to start over again anyway." Avery laughed. "Sub-Saharan cotton just won't cut it in the Alps."

"I probably have enough clothes in storage to open the boutique. I've got five closets in this two-bedroom sublet—not enough. And I don't even have half my stuff. I told Toni, she's my broker, that closet space is more important than a kitchen. Hell, I can eat out!"

Avery looked at the fitted, navy suede shirt, supple as silk, embroidered with pink and purple lilies, dark indigo jeans—jeans that unlike Avery she hadn't owned since she was fifteen—fuchsia suede ankle boots, and took Alicia at her word.

"I guess she does need to know your priorities."

"Speaking of stuff you left behind . . . you haven't said anything, but is there a somebody? A boyfriend? Man friend? Some other kind of friend?" Alicia crossed her legs, bobbed her foot.

Avery laughed, folded her arms across her chest. "I have a special friend, yes. Van is from South Africa . . . Johannesburg, but he's been living in Osaka for a number of years."

"South Africa? And the ex, Dr. Lyons, was from Scotland? Working your way through *S* countries?"

"Ha-ha. Just the way my ball bounced, I guess. Anyway, the thing with Van became a long-distance relationship when I moved to Wellington, but we always gave each other plenty of room anyway. This isn't that much different."

"And you trust him?"

"Trust him?" Avery realized she hadn't given a lot of thought to what Van might be doing when they weren't together. "Sure. I guess so."

"Uh-huh." Alicia snorted. "I can tell you one thing . . . wouldn't be me."

Van checked in fairly regularly. Avery knew where he was on the planet, mostly—meeting in Cairo, conference in Buenos Aires, presentation in London. But who he had dinner with, or might have met, or what hotel he was staying in—and whether he was alone—had never been a concern. She assumed the same was true on his part. They spoke at odd hours, she only had his office and mobile numbers, but he didn't have a home phone—she had been there often enough to know. Overnights were more or less planned and they didn't exchange keys or have drawers at each other's place. You brought what you needed and took it when you left. They hadn't discussed exclusivity or commitment, and she hadn't made any assumptions about what that meant, one way or the other, except to believe he hadn't made any either. But Avery heard

Alicia and wondered why it was a question she had never asked herself.

"This just works for us."

"So—when is this Van from South Africa coming to see you? I promise to behave and not tell stories about when we were fourteen." Alicia got up off the stool.

"He has a meeting in New York in early July. So we're planning to see each other then."

"Goody. Something to look forward to!"

"Yes, it is." *I guess.*

"On to more immediate matters." Alicia put her hands on her hips. "Have you thought any more about whether you want to list the house right away or wait till you sort through things and decide if you want to sell it with the contents?"

"I think meeting with your broker—just to get an opinion—is a good first step. But the whole point of taking the extra leave is so I can take my time, figure out what I'm dealing with so I don't make stupid mistakes."

"It took three of us almost a month to get through the stuff in my parents' apartment and that was, I don't know, about a fifth of what's in this house. And we didn't need estimates from appraisers or antique dealers," Alicia said. "We did find a guy who collected black memorabilia, white guy no less, who bought all those old posters. You remember them?"

Avery nodded. "That stuff was great."

"Yeah, well, that made three of you. Four counting our buyer. We got a whole fifteen hundred bucks, which was a total surprise. But this?" Alicia swept her arm around. "You know there are services—bonded, licensed, whatever—that come in and take care of every detail of 'liquidating the estate,' but I didn't think that's the way you would want to go." Alicia looked at Avery a few seconds before she went on, "No matter what happened in the past."

"You're right. I need to do this myself."

"And I think the best we can do today is make a plan. Start to look at what's here and begin an inventory. You're gonna have lots of lists."

"Great. Something I'm skilled at." Avery gave herself a thumbs-up.

"After you called last night, I went ahead and ordered boxes and plastic bins. They should be here this afternoon."

"You didn't have to—"

"Relax, Av. I knew you wouldn't be thinking about that kind of stuff." Alicia smiled. "I've been home watching TV for four years—such was the life of this Beverly Hills wife. So I've seen plenty of those 'organize or else' shows. You know—throw away, keep, donate, sell. At least I think those are the categories. I got filing supplies too—folders, labels, blah, blah. I didn't know what was here and didn't want to chance not having what we needed."

"How did you find a place that delivers so fast?"

"We're in New York, Av. The city that really, truly never sleeps. Which I like so much better than L.A., which goes to bed when the streetlights come on." Alicia laughed. "An-y-way, nowadays you can get speedy deliveries, even up in these parts. Besides, I'm pretty good at this household-management thing. That was my j-o-b when I was married to Guy. So if you ever need to find 'people' to take care of . . . hmmm . . . hell, people to take care of anything that has to do with a house . . . I'm your girl. I kept seventy-two hundred square feet of tacky, overpriced, sprawling Mediterranean *casa* running like a Rolex. Now I don't imagine you're going to need a seismically stable pool house, but if you know someone who does . . ." Alicia shrugged.

Avery had a hard time imagining the feisty, independent, gonna-set-the-world-on-fire Alicia as the lady of the manor. But no harder than she did imagining herself in the same role. And here she was facing chatelaine duty. Avery got up, rested a hand on Alicia's shoulder. "Thanks for coming, LiLi."

"Enough thank-yous." She reached up, patted Avery's hand. "You're welcome. Besides, as long as I'm helping you, I'm not procrastinating about the boutique thing. I'm busy helping a friend with a project!" Alicia winked. "So let's get this party started!" She caught herself. "Sorry, Av. I know this isn't gonna be a good time. But you know me. Like always, I still get carried away and find my tootsies in my mouth so often, toe jam has become a familiar taste."

"No worries. I know what you meant. I'll start up in Mom's room . . . *rooms* I guess I should say. Anything that needs handling right away is probably there where she seems to have set up her own study. But knowing how scattered she was, I could be completely off base. And the mail . . . I've been avoiding it big-time. There have to be bills to be paid."

"Divide and conquer it is. I'll take the parlor floor—start inventorying what's there. I brought my handy-dandy digital camera, which will help when I can't figure out how to describe whatever it is!"

"You did think of everything, didn't you?" Avery grabbed a box of trash bags from under the sink.

"Hardly, but it's a beginning." They left the kitchen and headed upstairs. "And, Av, if you get overwhelmed, it's okay to take a break. You're probably going to find stuff that will stop you in your tracks and take you somewhere you weren't expecting to go . . ." Alicia's voice trailed off. "You know what I mean."

"It's been that way since I stepped off the plane." Avery sighed, grabbed the Bloomie's bag she'd been using to store the mail, and dragged it upstairs, leaving Alicia to her inventory.

"An-y-way—if you need me, holla!"

"It's been that way since I stepped off the plane, LiLi, so at least I've been practicing."

Avery had no idea what her mother called her expanded quarters, but the sunroom seemed right. Not because it got a lot of sun—like all row houses the windows were only in the front and back, so daylight in the room was limited to the oblique rays that came from the northern exposure in the back of the house. But her mother had made it so bright, so happy, so much the opposite of the way it was when it had been her father's room. Another question to add to those she'd never asked and wasn't going to get answered now: *Why don't you sleep together like married people are supposed to?* Did her father's snoring keep her mother awake? Was her mother a restless sleeper who disturbed the doc's rest? Did she catch him cheating? "Ha!" The thought made Avery laugh out loud. She could no more imagine her uptight, by-the-book father being caught in flagrante delicto than she could imagine him joining a nudist colony.

She settled herself on the love seat, a good spot for sorting, and went to work on the Big Brown Bag. Avery couldn't believe how much was just a waste of paper—her mail experience overseas hadn't prepared her for the glut of garbage. She divided it into toss or shred. The stack of sympathy cards quickly turned into towering bundles.

Avery had spent a morning with her mother's personal banker, arranging accounts so she could use them. Now she paid bills as she came across them. She was shocked by what it cost to heat the house. For a month? She made a list of magazine subscriptions to cancel—who even knew *Reader's Digest* was still around. And she hadn't seen a *Jet* in years—aside from hairstyles, it looked about the same as it did when she was a kid—chocolate eye-candy center pinup and all. She put letters that required a response to the side—she'd come back to them.

The more Avery opened, the more her mother remained the enigma she'd always been.

Theirs was not a like-mother, like-daughter relationship. Avery, athletic, opinionated, headstrong, adventurous, was the polar opposite of the ladylike, compromising, amenable, and cautious Forestina. But then Avery wasn't like her strait-laced, exacting father either. As a kid she used to look for similarities to connect her to these two people who made her, but she came up empty. Alicia asked if maybe she was adopted, but Avery had seen her birth certificate. And in one of those awful dressing-room moments when you get an eyeful of more than you bargained for, she saw her mother's cesarean scar. Not a neat, nearly invisible bikini cut. It was a Frankenstein-looking, puckered vertical line down the middle of her mother's pale belly, with clumsy stitch marks where they'd closed her up again. For weeks, haunted by evidence of what her mother had gone through for her, Avery set the table and took out the trash without being asked, got up on time for church, even wore her hair down and curled with bangs the way her mother liked, instead of in her standard ponytail. Her reparations didn't last long, but Avery had no doubt she was her parents' child.

Then in eighth grade biology she learned about recessive traits. She asked her teacher if that applied to personalities too, not just eye color. Her teacher didn't know, but allowed it might be possible, since some forms of mental illness were passed on that way. Right then Avery decided she was the result of both parents' recessive personality genes, and that was that.

As she opened boxes, drawers, and envelopes, Avery realized she didn't know much about what either of her parents liked—what they enjoyed. They were always busy—meetings, events, theater, committees—especially her mom. But they didn't seem to have hobbies or activities where they had fun—

either alone or together. Her mother seemed to like puttering in the garden when they had the house on the Vineyard, and she did love that flower show, but did that make her happy? Avery had no clue. *I don't even know what makes me happy.*

But so far so good, no more tears popping up unannounced. The flashes from the past came up clean—no messy feelings attached.

During Operation Sunroom, Avery discovered that her mother bought greeting cards and packs of felt-tip pens by the dozen, had issues of *Architectural Digest* and *House Beautiful* dating back to the seventies, and read tons of romances and legal thrillers. Avery even found a slim notebook computer under a pile of newspapers. *Mom?* Avery was definitely not ready to go poking around her mother's hard drive, so she added it to the "later pile."

And she found notes everywhere—an address in Boston on a faded Post-it in a December 1993 issue of *AD*. Twenty-three names, first names only, on stationery from the Drake Hotel in Chicago. Some notes had a clear purpose—*Dr. Webb, 3PM, October 14.* But reminders, phone numbers, addresses, amounts, directions, ingredients, and recipes were scribbled on church bulletins, flyers from African-braiding salons, yellow legal paper, pink and green scallop-edged notepaper, old phone bills, receipts from Duane Reade and Fairway. She also found a note or a list—Avery wasn't sure which it was—on the back of a bake-sale notice from a Seventh-Day Adventist church—*glue for show, left, knives later. Ranch rose.* Was it code known only to her mother or something else? Avery tossed the paper in the trash, retrieved it, then threw it away again.

There were also scads of her mother's rough-draft thank-you notes, works in progress she notoriously rewrote before committing the final version to one of the monogrammed vellum cards she'd ordered from Saks for as long as Avery could remember. "I ~~don't think~~ ~~can't remember,~~ don't believe I've ever ~~had,~~ ~~been to,~~ experienced a lovelier ~~time,~~ ~~lunch,~~ afternoon. Thank you for ~~inviting~~ including me . . ." She could hear her mother: "There is always the right word, Avery. It just takes time to find it."

While her mom wasn't as organized as her father might have liked, she was a stickler for the social graces. But Avery had done her best to dodge the "When I was a young lady coming up" decorum conversations. Wherever they were leading, Avery wasn't interested in hearing some long, drawn-out, irrelevant story that was supposed to foster self-improvement. *Please, thank you,* and *excuse me* got plenty of use in her vocabulary. What else did she need? In the beginning of Avery's friendship with Alicia, Forestina had made Avery write Mrs. Jackson a thank-you each time Avery spent the night or ate dinner at the Jacksons' house. When Alicia's mom told Avery she thought of her as family and that the formal thank-you notes made both her and Alicia feel awkward, Forestina finally relented and let Avery stop sending them.

Avery thought about how long she dawdled over a report or letter until she was satisfied it said exactly what she meant, and how often a colleague complimented the way she handled a situation that required an abundance of grace, patience, or charm, and felt a twinge of—she didn't know what for sure. *See, Mom, it wasn't all in vain. I learned a few graces whether I wanted to or not.*

She dropped a handful of the beta-version notes in the trash and continued her expedition, finding things she understood and plenty she couldn't make sense of, and yet she had to. Didn't she?

Reconcile. That's the word that reporter used. She thought about that term in conjunction with bank statements. She grabbed the dictionary on her mother's desk. The fourth definition struck a chord: "To bring into agreement or harmony;

make compatible or consistent . . ." *Yep. That's what this is all right. But what does Mr. Christmas know about it? And what kind of name is that anyway?*

When the third trash bag bulged to overflowing, Avery decided it was time to take the plunge—or at least dip her toes in murkier waters—and headed into the bedroom. She looked at the bureau and dresser—thought about the racy underwear she'd found and wasn't sure she was ready for what else those drawers might hold. Ditto for the closet, so Avery started with the tables on either side of the Queen Anne bed. She turned on the milk-glass lamp, opened the first drawer. Tissues, a tin of Altoids, several emery boards, a bottle of aspirin, a peacock blue silk scarf, several bobby pins, old-fashioned pin-curl clips, and a comb and brush. A small, heart-shaped, quilted box held a watch that wasn't working, a pair of amethyst clip-on earrings, and a tie bar. *Daddy never wore a tie bar.* But she convinced herself it didn't mean anything and moved to the other side of the bed.

In the other table she found an NLT Bible, as well as a King James Version, the birthday card Avery sent her mother in January, *Prevention* magazines with pages dog-eared for quick reference. Beneath those was a packet of envelopes tied with a red satin ribbon. Avery could see the one on top was addressed to her mother; the return-address corner was empty. She reached in to pick up the bundle, then stopped, looked over her shoulder the way she did when she used to sneak into her mother's closet looking for hidden Christmas presents. She shook away the memory, took a deep breath, and eased the packet out of the drawer—like she might detonate it if she wasn't careful.

While the whole house was full of questions she would likely never answer, and corners that would remain dim, Avery had a gut feeling that this room, with its distinct Forestina air—delicate lace curtains, intricately carved furniture—might be Pandora's box. The zebra underwear might only hint at what else there was to find. *But do I really want to know?* She was sure women didn't keep cards and letters hidden in a drawer, tied with a red bow, unless some pretty serious sentiment was attached. *Maybe they're from Dad.* Certainly not the Dad she knew. Or from when her mom was a girl? But the envelopes didn't look that old. Avery held them tight. *Where's that bomb-sniffing dog when you need him?*

Mom was a grown woman. Avery untied the bow. *A widow for sixteen years.* Lifted the flap on the first envelope and slipped the card out. It was covered with dark pink and red roses. Valentine's Day. *Open it? Don't?* She flipped it open. The wording was sweet, mushy Valentine's—nothing earth-shattering. But the handwritten note underneath: "Tina, I don't have to ask if you'll be mine. I know that you are, that you have been, whether you'll marry me or not. As ever, I am yours now and for all eternity. Love, Reggie."

Reggie? Reginald Bishop? She remembered Mr. Bishop at the wake and funeral and saw on his face the genuine sadness in his heart. *He looked so lost.* But—"As ever"? "All eternity"? Avery leafed through the stack—all the handwriting was the same. The postage changed. When she got to a twenty-cent stamp, she stopped looking. It was a long time since postage was that cheap. No need to do the math.

Avery tucked the card back in the envelope. Not much was sentimental between her parents. No displays of affection, public or otherwise, except on state occasions like birthdays and anniversaries, always civil and polite. She never heard them argue. Disagreements seemed minor and fizzled before they flamed. *Mom had a lover?* It didn't compute. She wasn't prepared to know. And right then, she couldn't read any more "Reggie *hearts* Tina" declarations of love. *What difference does it make, Avery?*

"How's it going?" Alicia called from the hall.

Avery slammed the drawer closed, on her thumb. "Dammit!"

"What?!" Alicia popped her head around the corner.

"Nothing!" Avery snapped. "Sorry. Just smashed my thumb."

"I made lunch."

"Thought you didn't cook." Avery blew on her thumb as if that would make it better.

"Even I can make a sandwich. Come on down, you can put some ice on that. The boxes and stuff just came."

"I didn't hear the bell." But Avery knew she was so distracted, she probably wouldn't have heard a Chinese gong.

"Never rang. I saw the truck pull up. Anything scandalous?"

Avery whipped her head around. "What do you mean?"

"Mean? I don't mean anything, Av. Just a little humor."

"Sorry. Guess I'm a little more frazzled than I expected." *Oh, yeah, that, and my mother's secret lover.* But the phone stopped Avery from responding to Alicia. Really, she didn't want to answer it, but that would be backsliding. Not in keeping with the attitude adjustment she was trying on for size. "I'll get that and be right down." She waved Alicia on and grabbed the extension in her father's study.

"Braithwaite residence." Avery still hadn't figured out how she should answer the phone. Plain old *hello* sounded as if she might be expecting the call, which meant she belonged there. It implied a proprietary position that she wasn't ready to claim—whatever Walker Brown and the will said.

"Avery? It's Renee."

Oh, goody.

"Sorry to bother you. I know you must have a million and one things to do without being interrupted by the phone, but I was wondering if Dwight called to let you know he was planning to stop by this afternoon?"

Avery felt a flush of heat up her back to the top of her head. *Why?* "Uh . . . no. I haven't spoken to him."

And as if Renee had heard her: "He's not always the best at letting other people know his plans, and I know you two have your little thing . . . whatever it is . . . but it seemed to me the last thing you need is unexpected company . . . even if it's family. Now I know I rang your doorbell from out of the blue, and I would never do that again without calling first. It's just the polite thing to do. But you'd just gotten here and I was worried about whether you had anything to eat or if you needed something. Now your cousin does things his own way—but I guess I don't have to tell you that."

"Thanks, Renee."

Renee rattled on. And on. "Oh, and I know he wants to talk to you about some building or other. You know we girls have to stick together, because men . . . they just don't think! And Dwight . . . he is so much more like his father than he'll ever admit."

"I appreciate the call."

"If you get overwhelmed with all you have to do, remember I'm just at the end of the block. Or maybe you'd like to go to lunch one day. There are some really lovely—"

"Okay. I'll remember. Thanks again for the heads-up." Avery rested the phone back in its cradle. *What does he want?*

They had just finished lunch, or at least Alicia had. The news of Dwight's impending arrival, and her mother's stash of secret missives, killed what little appetite Avery had. When the doorbell rang, Avery heard it this time. Alicia followed her to the door.

"Sorry to drop in like this, Avery, but—"

"Fortunately I had a warning."

"Pardon?"

"Never mind." Avery almost revealed the source of her

information, then thought better of it. "You're here. I'm busy. What do you want?"

"Can I come in?"

Avery realized he was still standing on the stoop. "Yeah. Sure."

"Oh, hello, Alicia." He jammed his hands in his coat pockets, not that there was any danger of an awkward handshake or a hug—from either side. "I know you have a lot going on, Avery, and I won't take up much of your time." He looked from his cousin to Alicia and back again. "Can we talk—uh—alone? It's family business."

"Uh. I don't think so. As far as I'm concerned, Alicia is pretty much all the family I have these days." Avery realized what she had just said was true and that she meant it. "So I'd like her to stay." She folded her arms across her chest. "Besides, Dwight, with you, somehow I feel like a witness might be a good idea." Avery went into the living room and sat on the couch. Alicia planted herself on the sofa arm right next to Avery, like a sentry.

Dwight followed, stood on the opposite side of the room.

"You can sit," Avery said.

"Thanks." He sat on the edge of the wingback chair across from them, leaned forward, the omnipresent blue light blinking steady on the side of his head. "Listen, I'm sorry about all this—the circumstances are about as bad as they get—and I don't want to stir up any of the old business between us. I really don't. But life goes on and I know Aunt Tina would understand." He took a breath. "I need to conclude some business I started with your mom. I know I'm far from your favorite person on the planet, and that the timing of this isn't optimal, but there's no way around this." Dwight stopped, but Avery didn't say anything, so he continued, "It's about the building on 111th Street. I understand that your mother spoke to you about our offer to purchase it, and that you had no objections." Dwight reached up, adjusted his red foulard bow tie. "But as you know, we weren't able to complete the transaction before . . ."

"Before Avery's mom died and screwed up your deal?" Alicia piped in.

"It's okay, Alicia. Yes, I told her I didn't care if she sold it, or to whom."

"Well, I'd really like to get this done as soon as possible. And of course we'll stick to the same terms we offered your mother, 3.1 million dollars. That's top dollar, better than market for a building we'll have to de-occupy."

"Fine," Avery said

"However much you're paying her, Dwight, I know there's more in it for you," Alicia said.

"Really, Alicia. I don't want the building. He does. This means I don't have to look for a buyer. What else is there to talk about? Unless you'd like to buy this house too?"

"I—uh—what? No, I don't think . . . Oh, I see, you're being facetious. Well, I'm glad you're in agreement and I'd like to schedule the closing as soon as possible. I'm certain it will be good to get this off your list of things to take care of."

"Fine . . . work out the details with Walker Brown's office." Avery got up. "Is that all?"

"Yes. And—thanks, Avery." Dwight stood too. "I know we'll probably never get past . . . well, the past. But I am here if you . . ."

"Need anything?" Alicia couldn't hold her tongue any longer. "Surely you weren't going to tell your cousin that you're available to *help* her if she needs it? Because we all know what a lying sack of sorry shit that would make you."

Dwight glared at Alicia but didn't say a word. Then he looked at Avery, who shrugged like the parent of a precocious nine-year-old who had just said something remarkably clever but totally inappropriate. He followed Avery to the front door. "Be in touch."

"Dwight?" Avery called as he headed down the stairs. "Tell Renee I said hi."

"So why is he going to pay you above market for that building?" Alicia asked as soon as Avery closed the door. "You know Dwight. Unless he's had a personality transplant, he's not doing anything for anyone that he's not getting something from. I don't buy it. And you are too nice to him. I wanted to yank that damn blue thing out of Dwight Vader's ear and shove it down his throat."

"I'm not nice to him. I just can't give Dwight any energy. I barely have enough to get me through the day, so there isn't any for me to waste on him." Avery sat on the stairs. "I know you're just the opposite—you get charged from the fight. You always did."

"You used to be that way too."

"Maybe so, but what's the point?" Nothing Avery had said that morning changed the tide once it had turned against her.

➢ ➢ ➢

Early 1980s

"I've got an office full of sick people. But I have to come home because all of a sudden you don't know how to conduct yourself."

That knocked the words out of Avery's mouth, took her breath away as violently as Trey's punch to her gut. Her world seemed fractured in kaleidoscopic pieces, and they wouldn't stop whirling. She'd begged Alicia to bring her home because that's where it was supposed to make sense. So her friend drove for hours in the middle of the night to get her back. Whatever would make it better.

"Where's Mom?"

"Hilton Head."

That's when Avery remembered her mom's getaway weekend with her college roommate. Her mom had been traveling a lot since Avery started freshman year, but keeping up with her parents' comings and goings wasn't high on Avery's priority list. Now her father stood in her room, anger carved on his face, acting as if she had no right to feel anything but ashamed.

"And it's a very good thing she's not here. This would be very upsetting to her."

A spanking would have been less painful to Avery.

But it just made Alicia flaming mad. "For her? I don't believe you. What about Avery? He had no business putting his hands on her."

"That's what men do when you go into bedrooms and shut the door." He wore his short white coat—glasses and two ballpoints in the breast pocket, like always. "At that point they're not interested in what you have to *say,* or didn't your mothers tell you that?"

His tone made Avery feel like an idiot.

When they got outside the party, Alicia had commandeered a taxi that had just dropped two guys in front of the house. The driver, reluctant to pick up any more wasted revelers, tried to ignore them and pull off, but Alicia ran into the street, stood in front of the cab, arms outstretched. "Run me over then, 'cause I'm not moving."

Avery rode with her head on Alicia's shoulder, trying to stop crying, to stop her teeth from chattering. Alicia patted her cheek, tried to convince her to go to the hospital, but all Avery wanted to do was get out of Providence and go home.

So Alicia popped the lock on Jackie's door, tossed stuff in their bags while Avery changed, washed her face. By the time they were loading up the Chevelle, Dwight and Jackie had made it back. He tried to get Avery to calm down and stay the rest of the weekend, which only upset her more and made Alicia mad.

"Got so much to say now. You didn't say jack to your boy."

Dwight saw the blinds upstairs separate at eye level. "Keep your voice down."

That made Alicia louder. "That's all you care about. Hiding your tracks. He hurt your cousin. Why don't you worry about that? They should throw his ass in jail!"

When they arrived, the Braithwaite house was empty. Avery trudged upstairs to her room, was stopped cold by the new decor. Since she'd been away for spring semester, her mother had redone it—just as Avery had suggested. It was supposed to be a surprise, for when she came home for the summer. It was a refined space, back to four-poster formality, with buttery gold walls, botanical prints to replace the neon posters—sophisticated, lovely, and alien. Her body ached, and it felt as if her eyes looked out of someone else's head because she couldn't keep her thoughts straight. Avery huddled under the new green-and-gold paisley duvet and kept reliving that slam against the door. That's the moment when the adventure soured.

Her father had her sit up, peppered her with questions as he examined her for fractures, contusions, other signs of physical harm. Was she drinking, smoking, taking pills, cocaine, he ran the laundry list of recreational substances. She shook or nodded, yea or nay, supremely aware of his mounting disapproval.

Before he concluded his exam, the doorbell rang and Alicia was dispatched to answer it. Avery could hear the sharp in Alicia's voice, the insistent rumble in reply. Moments later, she returned, a stormy look on her face. "It's Dwight and your uncle. They want to *talk*."

So the inquest moved downstairs, Alicia all the while asking if Avery was up to it.

"What difference does it make?" was Avery's answer.

King leaned against the mantel, fat thumbs hooked through suspenders that framed the expanse of his belly like green-and-brown-striped parentheses, as though his girth was only tangential. "Avery tell you who it is?"

"What's that supposed to mean? It wasn't her fault." Alicia could barely contain her rage.

Doc B stood on the opposite side of the room from his brother-in-law. "I'll thank you to mind your own business, Alicia. This is as much your fault as it is hers. What were you two thinking? As a matter of fact, I think you should go home, unless you'd like me to call your parents and fill them in on your escapade."

"No biggie. I'll tell them myself."

Avery slumped in a slipper chair, let her eyes fall on Dwight, looking for their accustomed connection. She wasn't even sure what she wanted—understanding, support from the one other person who knew her, maybe even better than Alicia did. Understood what it was like to grow up in their family.

"You can go, LiLi. It's all right."

"It's not all right!" Alicia was about to burst. "Dwight was there. It was his friend. He hasn't said boo." Alicia glared in his direction.

Avery knew when her family was closing ranks. She wanted to get her friend out of the way. But she would be fine. Dwight was still there to cover her back. "I appreciate all you did." She got up and stood by her friend.

"You'd have done the same. It could have been me." It was the first time Alicia was on a tearful edge.

"I'll call you tomorrow." Avery's voice was weary.

Alicia threw her arms around Avery and they hugged, long

and as tight as Avery's bruises would allow. Alicia squeezed her shoulder, whispered in her ear, "Keep your head up."

Dwight looked fresh, new clothes, new day. All she wanted was to lay her head on a pillow, close her eyes, let it all go away. But this was the chance to get the facts on the record.

"Trey said it was a misunderstanding."

"What?" Avery tried to look in Dwight's eyes, but he looked away, wouldn't engage. It was like he was talking about some other day in somebody else's life, except Dwight had seen her, how upset she was. What was there to misunderstand?

"He said he was just playing with you."

That's when the light went out in her heart. She gave up, wanted the inquest to be over. Wanted them all to shut up. She should have expected her father to be clinical. To keep the family image tidy, unimpeachable above all. King would go out of his way to protect Dwight from anybody, except himself. But Dwight lied and Avery knew he knew it. To make himself look better, to save face, for whatever reason, he lied. It hurt her so deeply she couldn't find the bottom.

And after King and her father had gone, Dwight kept standing there, like it was April Fools' Day, the joke was on her. But by then she couldn't see him, wouldn't, not anymore. As far as she was concerned, what he did was worse than what Trey did. She was supposed to be able to trust Dwight, but that was over.

She avoided her father in the house that evening—not hard to do. She wasn't hiding. He wasn't seeking. When her mother came home Sunday afternoon, her father explained that Avery had come home for the weekend, got drunk, and fallen down the stairs, giving Avery his chastising I'm-disappointed-but-you're-only-hurting-yourself look, the one reserved for patients who didn't follow instructions. Avery never told her mother the truth, but somehow expected her to know. That she would feel the disturbance in the air in Avery's bedroom, notice that her heart was heavier, her eyes lifeless. Wasn't that what mothers were supposed to do? But Forestina stepped into her accustomed role, chirping and chattering, trying to make nice. By Tuesday morning Avery couldn't take any more, made herself "well enough" to take the train back to Massachusetts. Her calls home became fewer and shorter and emptier. But the incident was handled, locked up in a box. And she'd locked herself up with it. She had sucked it up. It was tidy. And nobody seemed to care.

TEN
blow over. Or blow up

Dwight didn't know what to call the house down the block anymore. Aunt Tina's house? Avery's house? Whatever it was, he was floating like Snoopy in the Thanksgiving Day Parade when he left the place. He'd been awake the night before, worried about what Avery would say to his offer. At that point, it was all that mattered. He'd given up on any reconciliation long ago. She could have kicked him down the stairs and called him any name she could think of. He'd heard it before. He was prepared. He could take it. What he could offer in the way of apology was a decent payday, *vaya con Dios,* have a nice life. Was it enough? Dwight didn't even know what that meant, but it would have to do.

Since he was uptown, he stopped by home. Hadn't been there on a regular weekday afternoon since when? A long time. Vacations were spent away. Holidays had an agenda—

hang the lights, open the presents, baste the turkey. But he was feeling good, better than good. Maybe he could give Renee a little of what she'd been asking for. He was in the mood. She'd be happy and off his case for a while. "Hey, Renee." The house smelled sweet and buttery. In the kitchen he found her surrounded by trays and plates of snickerdoodles for the music-school bake sale.

"And?" Renee walked across the kitchen, fed him a cookie.

He deadpanned for a moment, finished chewing. "It's on."

She threw her arms around him. "I knew it would be fine."

"Glad you were sure." He reached for another cookie. They were warm and laced with cinnamon. Dwight's mother never baked. She practiced her dirges and sonatas, and Dwight wasn't to interrupt her. And she yelled at his father. That pretty much covered it.

"Want some milk?" Renee dunked one of the broken bits in a mug of cold coffee.

He did. But he couldn't say it. "No. I just stopped in. I'm heading back to the office." He did come closer for a hug, nuzzled her neck. She smelled like vanilla, familiar, comforting.

She fed him another cookie.

He unbuttoned her blouse.

She returned the favor, undid his tie, swept the jacket and shirt over his shoulders in one movement like a woman who knew what she wanted and where she could get it. Pulled the V-neck T down to kiss his chest. Stopped. "What happened here?" Her fingers rested beside the two red abrasions.

"This . . ." Dwight straightened, looked down like he was surprised. Because he was. "The gym. Opened the locker door and bam." He was always so careful.

"Ow. That must have hurt."

How did I forget? His separate lives were supposed to be

vacuum sealed, away from each other, never the twain shall meet. *Why did I forget?*

"We need to put something on it." Renee looked up at him.

So pretty, and plain, and loving. "No. It's all right." Dwight picked his shirt off the floor.

"Let me kiss it better."

Please stop. But he'd never be able to explain. He braced himself against the sink. And Renee's lips were so plush and warm as they caressed him, made him open his mouth to them, so they could crash into the Mistress Delilah, whose mouth was red and cruel, who was haughty and hard and made those wounds with her stilettos. She made him be strong, not like in Providence with Avery, when he'd been a lame-ass coward. So Dwight peeled himself away. Delilah was there, mocking him. He had to go. "I should get back downtown."

"Sure?"

"Yes." Before any more bits of his life smashed up together.

Renee turned back to the sink, buttoned her blouse.

Dwight righted his suit, picked his tie off the floor, pretended not to see the tears she brushed away. He needed to find something to say. "Avery sends you regards."

Renee sipped more of her coffee, sighed. "Dwight . . . what happened between you two?"

Oh, hell. You have got to be kidding me. Now? She asks me that now? "It was so long ago." Dwight didn't know what Avery had said during the years, but he'd never told another soul. He wasn't about to play true confessions today. "It was a misunderstanding. But she just won't let it go."

"Maybe if you talked about it now. Time heals all . . ."

"Not this one. The best I can do is leave it alone."

"That's so sad. I'm really sorry."

He was too, but it was too late to kiss and make up, so

Dwight escaped to his office, where he was in control. First thing he did was call Stanley, his lawyer, "One Hundred and Eleventh is good to go. Get the documents ready and get this done so we can move on."

All of Dwight's ducks would be in a row, well before Grace's deadline, and he looked forward to her simpering smile when there were finally no impediments—when the heavy equipment rolled in and the fun began. Then maybe he could stop doing the magic math that balanced The Dixon Group's books each month—income minus outgo equals close enough to positive numbers that he could continue to float the boat. He was grateful his personal balance sheet was so simple. The mortgage was paid before King deeded him the property, a story he lived through often enough, especially in the early days—"I gave you a damn house, bought and paid for." Dominique's tuition was their biggest expense. The business paid for bipartisan entertaining—the conservancy gala table, contributions to both parties to cover all bases so they could play no matter who held sway. But Dwight knew their finances weren't Manhattan-worthy. Their dollars and cents didn't keep up with inflation or the consumer luxury index. Yeah, the company owned real estate, but you can't spend that. It never made Dwight feel good to wonder whether in the current climate he could afford his own house. But that was all going to change.

When the time for the monthly Hudson Common Tenants' Association meeting rolled around, Dwight was ready for the pep rally. Those buildings had been a detour on the road to Dixon Plaza, but they had certainly been worth their weight in good news, providing upbeat photos and encouraging testimonials about The Dixon Group and its projects.

The souvlaki cart had gone by the time Dwight went down to meet Sean. The tub of a car was gone too, replaced by a shiny white, later-model sedan. Even the backseat was clear of junk.

"Business must be good."

"Can't complain."

Evening traffic crept up the West Side Highway, and Sean crept carefully with it. As they approached the Seventy-ninth Street Boat Basin, Dwight's cell rang.

"Buster here, Mr. D. There's a whole mess of people for the meeting, carrying signs and whatnot. Thought you should know."

Dwight would have preferred the warning sooner, like a week ago. So much for having eyes and ears on the inside.

Dwight reached Pastor Phil next. "What the hell's going on over there?"

"Said they're from your other properties. And let me tell you, brother, they are riled up. I'll send Buster and a couple of the others out to meet you."

Dwight detected a hint of glee in the minister's voice, and that ticked him off. Next he got on the horn with Baily, his publicist. "It sounds like a damn ambush. What am I supposed to do?"

Baily paused for what seemed like eternity to Dwight. "At this point, it'll be worse if you don't go in. We'll handle the fallout in the morning if there is any. This could all blow over."

Or blow up.

The car was about to round the corner into the block, but the green light turned yellow. They slowed to a stop, and Dwight had never been more grateful for Sean's poky driving, although he would have preferred more time than a traffic light. Time to get away, anywhere. His head was about to burst with anticipation, but he had to get hold of his thoughts, find out what was happening. "What the . . . ? "

"Whoa. There must be a hundred—"

"I can see." And as Sean slowed, Dwight read their signs: WE DESERVE RESPECT. DON'T BUILD DIXON PLAZA ON OUR BACKS. A girl of about eight wore a makeshift sandwich board, MAKE MY HOME SAFE.

Sean double-parked. Dwight wasn't ready to get out, but it was time to go. The crowd milled peacefully, but as soon as they saw him, the chanting started.

"Hey, hey. Ho, ho. Dixon Plaza's got to go."

Dwight worked to slow his pace, to look authoritative, unperturbed, instead of panicked, like he was surrounded by wolves while he had lamb chops in his pockets and a beef medallion pinned to his lapel, which was closer to how he felt. *I can take it.* He squeezed the keys in his pocket hard. Hard enough to make the jagged tips bite his palm, let the pain sharpen his awareness.

The official meeting agenda called for a discussion of plantings for the courtyard gardens, a personal-safety presentation by the community-affairs officer from the local precinct, and awards to essay-contest winners from the center. Dwight had talked Councilman Gordon into coming to do the essay honors.

When Dwight arrived, Chester was already there, puffed up like a blowfish. He hissed under his breath, "This wasn't supposed to be—"

"I'm as surprised as you are." Dwight slid into the chair beside him at the dais-cum-lunch-table. He knew it was a flimsy answer, but it was the only one he had. The room was full—all seats taken. Tables had become the bleacher seats, with overflow up against the wall.

Pastor Phil looked like the DJ had just put on his favorite song and he was ready to dance. "Gentlemen, it is an abundant blessing to have you both here this evening." He shook both their hands, one shake, the other hand cupped around—sincere or you are sincerely surrounded?

The Hudson Common Tenants' Association was brought to order by its president, Nedra Cortes, 6F, single mother of two sons. By an emphatic voice vote the motion carried to table the stated agenda in favor of more pressing matters—namely, the conditions at Dixon-owned properties.

Dwight felt like this was a roast, but it wasn't funny. He was about to be tied to the spit and hung over the fire.

Nedra's crinkly shirt in shades of blue looked calm, but she was decidedly not. "I'd like to welcome our neighbors and friends from Hudson Common, as well as other buildings owned by The Dixon Group."

Nedra received a rousing holler back.

"I believe I speak for many of us when I say we are weary. You fight for your kids, you fight for your job. When you get home, all you want is a little peace. Am I right?"

There was applause, shouts of agreement. Dwight remembered Nedra as a pudgy woman with a round laugh. When did she become the voice of Hudson Common?

"This is our lives, people. We're not playing bingo here."

Pastor Phil, brow furrowed, nodded in agreement.

Councilman Gordon looked down at the notes he was scribbling furiously on the back side of the jettisoned agenda.

Dwight struggled for an appropriate response, since he wasn't sure yet what was going to be thrown his way. But he didn't have long to wait.

"We live at different addresses, but we're here tonight to talk about our day-to-day challenges. When we came here, we hoped for the best. What else could we do? We were forced from our homes, with no place to go, until Pastor Phil took up our cause."

From the look on Phil's face, Dwight expected to see a halo.

"But it's been a struggle. Let me tell you my story." Nedra outlined how she had moved into her new two-bedroom apartment. "The first place I ever lived where nobody lived before me." Except little by little her sons got sick—"Colds, allergies, they were always coughing and sneezing, I don't know why." She talked about the smell in the apartment—"Like rotten eggs some days. I figured it was cheap paint. But nobody listened to me. Crawford said the boys just needed to go out and play. Except it's two years later, and my boys, they ain't better. It wasn't like this in the old building. The rich people who will live where we did . . . I bet they won't be like this."

Dwight could see the nods of agreement, tried not to squirm, because he couldn't have this problem. He wanted to talk about all he had done, how The Dixon Group had made life better for them. But it wasn't his turn.

And there were more complaints about Hudson Common—doors that wouldn't stay closed, loose cabinets, windows that didn't close flush. These were the new buildings. They weren't supposed to be a problem.

Next came the parade of tenants, doing their own version of *America's Worst Landlord,* each address with a different complaint—finicky furnaces, temperamental elevators, cranky plumbing, leaks, drafty windows.

"All I gotta say is, you bring your family and let them live in our apartment." The grandmother held her toddler granddaughter in her arms. "We're doing the best we can, but it's like nobody's there to meet us."

Dwight hated this part—dealing with the people and their families and their issues. Why did they expect him to solve their problems? He had not a soul in his life he could complain to and expect sudden satisfaction. You want it your way? Do it yourself. But that didn't stop the moaning.

"And where the jobs we supposed to get?" The man looked scrawny but powerful—all gristle, no fat. "All this buildin' goin' on. I can work construction. I was born to work, ready to work. Somebody's got my job, 'cause it sure ain't me."

Right about now Dwight wanted to feed Mitch to the pack. The jobs, the wallboard, the slipshod workmanship—those were his fault. Dwight hadn't come up with someone to blame for the mess in his other buildings—but he was working on it.

After the prosecution's case was laid out, the defense was allowed to speak.

Chester attempted to rouse them with his campaign spiel—"More money brought into the community means more money for all. I am dedicated to lifting the district because I want to raise us all up. And I will be looking into these allegations of substandard conditions. I will not tolerate negligence on the part of any landlord."

"Sellout!"

"Won't get my vote."

Angry outbursts electrified the room, but that was only the opening act. The crowd saved a special fervor for Dwight. He was horrified sitting there listening to the venom directed his way. He scrambled to find a comeback, words that would calm them down, win them over. "As a lifelong resident of this community, I am as disturbed as you are by what you're telling me." While he was speaking, he heard the song begin, from the back of the room, then get louder.

"Money, money, money, money. Money!"

"I am glad to be here with you, face-to-face. As the head of a company, you can get isolated from the people you serve. But tonight I hear you loud and clear."

Still the chorus grew. *"Some people got to have it. Some people really need it."*

Dwight spoke louder. "You have my pledge that I will find out what's wrong and fix it. Because you are the energy, the vitality, in this community, and that will never change." Which wasn't a lie. It was rhetoric. At that moment he would have said whatever was necessary to get this over with and get out of that room.

But the singing took over. *"Do things, do things, do bad things with it."*

They knew all the words and united into a loud chorus that forced Dwight to sit down and shut up. As he took his seat, he noticed Sean snapping away. Not pictures Dwight intended to feature in anything except the recycle bin.

Pastor Phil ended the evening by throwing another log on the fire. "You got to speak the truth wherever you find it. You got to speak the truth, even to those who don't want to hear it. It's not your truth. It's not my truth. It's not their truth. It's *the* truth. And when you speak the truth, you will be heard. The *truth* shall set you free!"

Dwight didn't remember discussing the truth when they came to this arrangement a few years ago. It was all about the dividends.

➢ ➢ ➢

Chester snubbed Dwight after the meeting, which made him furious. Not after all Dwight had done. He'd practically guaranteed Chester that seat and made it nice and cushy.

By the time Dwight got out of there, he was fried. He marched back toward the car with Sean, voices from the evening's events echoing in his head.

"Mr. Dixon . . ."

Dwight turned to find—*Jesus! Christmas*—the reporter at his side, the perfect ending for his awful evening.

"Any comment you care to make about the meeting?"

Dwight could not imagine how that scene in there would look in print, or what he could say to make it any better. He mustered the last of his energy. "I am disturbed by what I heard tonight, and I will be working tirelessly to rectify the situation."

"Did you have knowledge of the maintenance complaints about your properties?" Jasper's pad and pen were at the ready.

"Mr. Christmas, day-to-day maintenance issues are handled by my staff, but we will be reviewing each situation separately." Dwight opened the car door.

"So you did not have knowledge of these issues prior—"

"It's been a long day." Dwight hated being trapped into yes-or-no answers—so precise, no wiggle room. "Mr. Christmas." He nodded, ducked into the car, was immediately on the phone. "May I come now?"

"Sean, I need to make a stop before I go home. Can I get you to drop me on Nineteenth Street?"

"Yeah. Sure."

Dwight knew he shouldn't, but this was an emergency. No one he knew had ever seen him on that block, but he had to get control. It felt like he had a lot to handle and not enough hands. Delilah would get him through—make him man up.

First thing the next morning Dwight called Eric in from the field. They went elbow to elbow through the building inventory. Eric had maintenance records, careful notes about tenant complaints. While Eric talked about repairs and replacements, what Dwight heard was the rustling of dollars in the wind.

He'd already blown the Hudson Common budget. It was a gut rehab. There weren't supposed to be major maintenance issues for years. He'd been shuffling expenses on the other buildings for a long time. The rent rolls versus the cost of upkeep on those old behemoths did not make for an even equation. Once the Dixon Plaza funding came through, he'd have some leeway to take care of old problems with new money. In the meantime, he had to make it work.

"Eric, I need you to prioritize the repairs."

"That shouldn't take me long."

Not the right answer. "We'll discuss the list when you have it and we can start getting bids." Dwight needed to drag this out a while.

Unfortunately, when Christmas's article hit the paper, Dwight was no longer dragging it out in private.

"You look like an imbecile." King hit the roof when he read the *New York Spectator* headline—"Dixon Bldgs Plagued by Repair Woes." "How could you not know—"

"I'm not supposed to know every screw that needs replacing." Dwight had been summoned immediately to the co-op. It was better that way. At least he could walk out if necessary.

"You better. Nobody will ever look after your property the way you do."

"Right. And this is the part where you lecture me on how it was in the old days, when you, single-handedly, maintained every toilet, shoveled the walks, tarred the roofs—"

"It's got to be done, Junior. On a regular basis or they will fall down around your ears. Gluuumph . . ." King adjusted himself in his seat. "Then all you'll have is a cabbage patch, like that mess you got sitting up on 110th. Great big pigeon coops. I gave you more than that—"

"And I'm making it more than that." Dwight looked King squarely in the eye. "Just leave me the hell alone and let me do it."

ELEVEN

Wherever Negroes live uptown is called Harlem

"Uh-oh. I'm scared a you." Alicia sat at the dining room table, surrounded by the contents of the breakfront. "Avery has laced on her sneakers and is back on the run."

"Back on the walk is more like it." Avery unzipped her windbreaker, tried not to pant. "When did you get here?" She had given Alicia keys and the alarm code, figured someone else should have them—in case of emergency. And Alicia could let herself in when she had time, even if Avery was out. It had been ages since she'd come home and found someone waiting for her.

"'Bout half hour ago. If I had known you were going to do your fitness walk, I would have . . . Wait, let me not tell that lie."

"What possessed me to think I could run today?" It used to feel so good, her muscles warm, her body moving effortlessly. Today she felt awkward and knew what would ache tomorrow. Avery trotted upstairs, came back wiping sweat off her face with a hand towel. She couldn't believe she got winded from jogging a few lousy blocks. She knew she wasn't in running shape—hadn't been for ages. More often than not, her workdays were jammed and long, and in so many countries, predawn/postdusk solitary runs were not advised. Most of the embassies had gyms, but Avery had never felt one with the treadmill, so exercise slowly disappeared from her routine. But after all the sorting, counting, listing, junking, and praying not to find any more surprises, she realized she was at some kind of crossroads—and where it would lead was still unclear.

Every day she opened her eyes, she felt disoriented, not because she was still sleeping around the house—taking the gold velour blanket and a pillow she'd found in the guest room, and camping wherever the weary hit her—but with nowhere she *had* to go, and nothing she *had* to do. Avery found it hard to tell if she was moving ahead or drifting backward. Time had no markings or boundaries, and she needed some. So she decided on a morning walk—a routine to start each day, get in some exercise, and in the process reacquaint herself with a neighborhood which was far different from the one she remembered.

She hadn't intended to go far afield or work up a sweat. But on her first perambulation, Avery found herself in front of "her" building on 111th Street. Until then, the property had been only a concept, the subject or object of conversation—with her mother, Dwight, even Alicia—but it wasn't a real place.

From the outside, it didn't appear remarkable enough to warrant so much attention. Center entrance, light-colored brick, six stories, with just enough stone flourishes and ornamentation to give it a touch of distinction from its neighbors next door and across the street. She wasn't sure why, but Avery had now been by five times, each visit providing a different snapshot of the place: children bounding out the front door on their way to school, an elderly couple leaving and walking arm in arm up the block, a mom with an infant in a snuggly, a set of twins, and two grocery bags checking to make sure the door was locked behind her, a man in dark green work clothes with a broom and long-handled dustpan sweeping the sidewalk out front.

Avery sat next to Alicia. "I had been thinking about what you said."

"I say so much." Alicia examined a dinner plate.

"About why Dwight is willing to pay so much for the building?"

"Good. You should be thinking about it. 'Cause it's so not Dwight."

"I've been going by there almost every day."

"Stakeout? Or are you looking for the secret entrance to the buried treasure that must be inside?" Alicia squinted at the back of the dish, trying to make out the name of the china pattern.

"Funny ha-ha. It looks like a perfectly fine place. I haven't been inside, wasn't sure ringing somebody's buzzer and saying, 'Hi, I'm your new landlord, can I come in?' was the way to go. That even sounds bizarre, me a landlord."

Alicia held the plate out to Avery. "Can you read that?"

"It's called dragon something. I remember these." Avery traced her finger over the fierce beast in the center.

"They're quite beautiful—it's almost a shame to put food on them."

"When I was a kid, I used to play a game, in my own head of course. We'd be having Sunday dinner and I would eat around the dragon—couldn't eat what was on top of it until Dad said 'precisely' three times."

"What if he didn't say it?"

"Dwight asked the same thing." Avery crossed her leg, massaged her calf. "Believe me, I was never in danger of not getting to finish my dinner. I couldn't believe Dwight didn't realize how often my father used that word. Probably a hundred times a day."

"Self-absorbed even as a kid."

"I don't know. It was easy to zone out. We'd be the only kids at these dinners, and the seen-and-not-heard rule applied. He was better at it than I was."

"Well, as far as I'm concerned, Dwight is still in his own world. Maybe when your father's a King it comes naturally."

Avery shook her head. "I talked to my lawyer about the offer. He agreed it was generous, but said he just thought it was a family bonus. It was the same offer they made Mom, so he saw no reason to question it. We're supposed to close soon." Avery scooted her chair back. "But those people are living their lives, minding their own business—I wonder if they know they're going to have to move?"

"Knowing Dwight, probably not. Just make sure the check is good. I don't trust your cousin any more than I would, say, hmmmm . . . how about my ex-husband?!" Gingerly Alicia added the dragon plate to the stack on the table. "You sure you don't want to keep these? Maybe you could make up a new game. It's a perfect, complete service for twelve. No chips or missing gravy boats or sugar-bowl lids. And I don't know what these are, but there are a dozen of them too." She held up a small, shallow dish.

"Finger bowls." Avery started to laugh. "I kid you not."

Alicia cracked up. "I've seen them in restaurants, and old movies. But never in anybody's house!"

"There was so much ceremony. It worked for Dwight better than it did for me."

"Why do you keep bringing him up, Av?"

"This . . . this *stuff*." She gestured around her, looking for the words. "Everything that's happened since I got here . . . it's all about the past. I can't erase him from my memories, no matter what I do. He was part of my growing up." Avery paused. "Then he wasn't." She stood up. "And, no, I don't want the dishes. Not into antique china. Never was. I eat take-out from the container. I have never fed more than three other people at the same time, and I didn't cook then. And I was lucky to find four plates and forks. Maybe they matched, maybe not. For all I know, there are still people who talk about my lame attempts at entertaining. What does it matter in the grand scheme?"

"I've got a question for you." Alicia stopped for a second. "You've said that more times than I can count. So, what does matter, Av? Okay. It's not your mom's china. And I realize I may be pushing it here . . . but what do you care about? What makes you happy? What makes your life work? I don't know, but let's say for instance you were keeping the house, planning to live here. I know your mom's antiques and brocades aren't your cup of tea or java or whatever you prefer in your cup, but what would you do to it? How would you make it 'you'? I mean, I guess we're getting to know each other again, and while we can base this, uh, renewed friendship on the old one, some clues to the new you would be kinda helpful. I'm sure I've changed too, and I'm happy to share."

"That's quite a leap from finger bowls." Avery folded her arms across her chest.

"I didn't mean to—"

"Not your fault. I'm sorry, Li." Avery sighed, sat back down, and fiddled with a knife rest for a while. "I don't have an answer for you. I haven't had time to think about what makes me happy. I do my job. I'm good at it. I like traveling. I'm content. That's about it."

"Yeah. Okay." Alicia opened the door to the china cabinet. She knew that wasn't "about it." But she remembered that pushing back wasn't ever the way to get Avery to open up, so she left it alone. This time. "I should put these back. Toni will be here in about an hour."

"I'm going to throw myself in the shower—see you in a few." Avery stopped in the doorway, turned back to Alicia. "You're still you, Li. You haven't changed all that much. Sorry, I have."

➢ ➢ ➢

Toni was prompt, efficient, businesslike, and completely not what Avery expected. She was anticipating a high-style, high-heeled, high-maintenance Manhattan-mansion maven. The kind of real estate diva she figured the girls from her set would have become after they married their doctor, lawyer, investment banker, popped out a baby or two, which they handed over to the nanny, then needed to find themselves and develop their talents. Preferably this involved long lunches, required pricey wardrobes, assured they wouldn't have to deal with people who weren't at least as well-off as they were, and hopefully widened their social circle beyond Sag Harbor to include the Hamptons, while earning the occasional commission, which they would then spend on lipo, boobs, Botox, or the Canyon Ranch. But Toni Whittaker was not like that. She looked to be in her early sixties, though her face was unlined except for crinkles at the corners of her eyes and two deep creases on either side of her mouth. The rusty henna rinse was losing the battle against white fuzz that sprouted along the hairline of her press-and-curl do. Instead of the latest look from Bergdorf or Bendel, Toni wore a frowsy floral dress and boxy black jacket with hose that were at least two shades too light and flat, lace-up, ripple-soled shoes—an outfit that reminded Avery of her first-grade Sunday-school teacher.

They traipsed through every square foot indoors and out,

including the garage, Toni exclaiming, "Super," at each new original detail. When she wasn't measuring or making notes, she dispensed Harlem real estate factoids, which she seemed to have in endless supply.

"And Ty Washington . . . you know, the big-deal producer, former rapper Boney T?"

Although her rap knowledge was sketchy at best, Avery nodded, trying to imagine Toni pumping up a Boney T side in her Honda.

"He bought an abandoned theater, turned it into a youth center with apartments above. Really super. Says he plans to do a lot more."

"Good for Ty." Alicia brought up the rear. "I'll have to check him out. Didn't know he was into all that."

Avery actually remembered him from the funeral. "I guess that's where . . . what was the name of the group, Ladies First? My mother was a volunteer."

After the tour, Toni took a few minutes to do some calculations. "This isn't a firm number. . . . No inspections, no checking out HVAC, plumbing, and the like. But from what I see here, even in the current economy the house will net you somewhere in the neighborhood of a million six or seven. Could be more. Could be less. There are lots of variables. But that gives you something to go on." Toni accepted her well-worn trench coat from Avery, fished a business card from the pocket. "If you decide to sell, or rent, I hope you'll let me handle the listing."

"I can't thank you enough, Mrs. Whittaker."

"Happy I could help. Alicia's a friend—we've known each a long time."

"Toni helped me find my first apartment twenty years ago. Let's just say we've both done okay."

"I've got a couple of new listings for you to look at. Tomorrow afternoon good?"

Alicia pointed her thumb at Avery. "As long as my boss here gives me time off."

"Take as much time as you need—but you'll have to make it up!" Avery laughed. "Can I ask you a question, Toni? Not about the house, but it is about real estate."

"Shoot."

"Is there a reason someone would pay more for a piece of property than the valuation?"

"Could be emotion, could be prestige. Mostly, they expect to make it back—one way or another. You have a specific property in mind?"

"A building I own now, on 111th Street. My cousin wants it."

"Ah, yes. The Misters Dixon and their magic Kingdom on the Park." Toni shook her head, smiled. "Everyone knows about it. But you can't be in this business in New York and not have heard stories about Dixon Plaza. It's been picketed. It's been delayed, but what hasn't these days? Last I heard it was hung up in the Council. But the answer to your question is that whatever they want to pay you, it's probably worth double to them."

"I knew it." Alicia sounded triumphant.

"And they're not just another developer eating up more than their fair share of the Apple. They're the first blacks to get this far up the tree and actually have the fruit in reach. And Lord knows there's been enough fuss. Phil Ewing and Jasper Christmas have kept that pot stirred."

"The Christmas guy has called a couple of times—even came by here. Said he'd been talking to Mom."

"Well, this whole gentrification issue has been a burr under Jazz's saddle for years." Toni paused, then laughed. "I grew up in Texas—every now and again it slips out. Sorry. So your building, is it empty or occupied?"

"Occupied." Avery had actually been going over some of

the miles of documents Walker had been sending, "for your own records." "No vacant units. Most of the tenants seem to stay at least three years. Some have been there more than forty. I don't really know all the details, but it seems like Dwight and King have been managing the property for years anyway."

"Well, seems like a good time for you to find out as much as you can. The devil is in the details." Toni smiled, held out her hand. "Gotta run. I have another appointment. Hope to hear from you. I know I've got buyers who would eat this up."

After Alicia was gone, Avery walked past the table in the front hall where she had put Toni Whittaker's card six times, before she retrieved the one she had placed it on top of.

➢ ➢ ➢

"I'm meeting someone," Avery said to the young woman who stood next to a bowl of white roses on a rustic chest of drawers retrofitted as a hostess stand. But Jazz spotted Avery before she explained further. He stood, waved, and Avery made her way to the table.

She had passed Jewellzz Beanzz on one of her morning walks. She couldn't help but notice it. The crisp green-and-white awning stood out on a block where the exteriors were decidedly more somber, and a peek in the window revealed a quirky mix of modern, avant-garde, and antique that looked more like a club or lounge than a coffee shop, so it was definitely in step with this new Harlem that had sprung up in her absence. The logo—the name stenciled in green on an open sack of coffee beans—was all that gave it away as a place whose staff would consist of baristas instead of bartenders. So Avery was glad when he suggested it as a place to meet.

"Mrs. Lyons." Jazz offered his hand. "I got here a little early—sometimes it's hard to get a table." He pulled her chair out. "I'm glad you called, and I promise not to take up much of your time."

"Can we do Avery and Jasper? It's less cumbersome." Avery sat, wriggled out of her coat, smoothed her skirt. Her chair was upholstered in a purple, red, and green harlequin brocade and had an exaggeratedly high asymmetrical back that rose at least three feet above her head. In contrast to her chair's modern whimsy, his looked right out of the Middle Ages—straight-backed, gold velvet chair with nailheads, and lion paws for feet and at the end of the arms. The same battered leather jacket he had on the first time they met hung from one corner. Between them sat a red glass cube that was somewhere between standard and coffee-table height.

"Great—can we make that Jazz, then? I promise no glib anecdotes about how I got the nickname. It's just what most people call me." He scooted his chair back, crossed his leg over his knee. Today, instead of jeans, he had on black slacks, and a caramel-colored crew-neck sweater.

"Interesting place." Avery resisted the urge to smooth her skirt again. Her previous conversations with reporters were always in an official capacity. She'd have a prepared statement and the subject wasn't personal. Was polite small talk in order? Did the questions start right away? She didn't exactly know what she wanted out of this meeting, but she was pretty sure Jazz Christmas had clear objectives, which put her at a disadvantage she didn't much care for—a position that was becoming much too familiar.

"It's a favorite spot when I'm uptown. And they have the best mocha coconut cake." He leaned back, steepled his hands. "But I have to admit, I'm biased. It's owned by a friend—well, I was actually friends with her older brothers. Regina's done quite well for herself though. She's got six of these in the city now and I think at least that many in Jersey. And her dad's the baker. He used to do it as a hobby, but when he retired a few years ago, he started working for her. So if I'm not making my coffee at home, which doesn't happen too often anymore, I'd rather give her the business than a chain. It also meant you wouldn't have to go far, so this seemed the right choice."

"All in the family, huh? Sounds nice." The thought of even attempting to be in business with her father, with her as *his* boss, gave Avery a headache. "So, tell me how you think I can help you with whatever kind of story it is you're working on?"

Jazz's voice and rhythm were relaxed, easy, but controlled. Avery had spent years learning to read and interpret that which was not said, while at the same time absorbing all that was—another of her job skills. His fingers remained tip to tip—an unmistakable show of confidence, but the crossed leg was casual enough to keep him from appearing arrogant or negative. She could see how Jazz Christmas could put an interview subject at ease, just by his own demeanor, and end up getting all the information he was looking for, and them some. The difference here was that she didn't have any, but she was hoping he did.

A young woman dressed all in black, with hot-pink-tipped, blond dreadlocks neatly tied into a ponytail, introduced herself, smiled, revealing rainbow-colored braces, and took their order. Cardamom-flavored Ethiopian coffee for Avery, and a *cortado* with a piece of his favorite cake for Jazz.

"Basically, I'm doing background on Dixon Plaza."

"Then you know I haven't been involved. And I wouldn't be now if—"

"Yes, I understand. So this could be a very short interview."

"I'll make this easy. What I know is"—as soon as she started to speak, a narrow, spiral reporter's notebook emerged from his jacket pocket—"one, my cousin and my uncle are developing something they're calling Dixon Plaza. Two, they want to buy a building that my parents owned which is now unexpectedly mine. Three, my mother agreed to sell it to them, but not until after I assured her I had no interest in holding on to a piece of real estate in a city where I don't intend to live. That's it." Avery thought it was strange having someone write down whatever she said, as if it would be quotable someday.

"When did you first become aware The Dixon Group wanted to purchase your 111th Street building?"

"A couple of months ago."

"Can you be more specific?"

"Is that really important?" Avery shifted in her seat, wishing the back of her chair weren't so high. It made her sit ramrod straight, which made her feel like she was on the witness stand.

"I don't always know what's important until it is."

Avery remembered her PDA. It used to be like an annex to her brain, but she had hardly used it since she'd been home. She scrolled through, found the date. "Mom and I met for a few days in Paris before I moved to Wellington. That's when she told me about Dwight's offer. She was making sure I didn't want to keep it as income property—some kind of insurance policy for my future, unmarried, childless old age."

Jazz chuckled. "Parents are funny. They see your future through their past. I'm sure she just wanted to protect you."

"Spoken like a parent."

He nodded. "I have a son. Don't see him much, so I guess I understand your mom's position." He paused while the server delivered their coffee.

Avery hadn't anticipated any personal revelations and was anxious to steer the conversation away from the fringes of the familial wilderness. She preferred not to walk in that forest, especially with strangers. "At any rate, Paris is when I heard about it."

"And what is the amount of the offer?"

"Um, I'd rather not say." She wasn't sure why. She found this public-disclosure business unsettling.

"And do you have a closing date?"

"It's to be determined."

"Do you have any idea how long she had known Dixon wanted the property?"

"She didn't say anything about that—I don't think. But honestly, I don't remember. I just wanted to get off the subject."

"May I ask why?"

"I don't do conversation about, or with, my cousin, if I can avoid it. That's all."

"I've gathered the warm, fuzzy family deal isn't exactly your thing."

"Listen," Avery bristled. They were heading back to the woods again. "I'd rather not make this about my family."

Jazz held up both his hands. "Understood. I aim to present as full and fair a picture as I can, and that means asking questions of anybody I think may have answers. Your mother seemed willing, it just never got to happen."

To keep Jazz from slipping in another offhand comment that might lead to her saying more than she wanted about family, Avery got back on topic. "That's really all I know. But I do have a question for you." She paused. "Why would Dwight be willing to pay more than the going market rate for the building? And we both already know you can spare me the do-good, be-nice family angle."

"So you're saying the offer is above market rate?"

Walked right into that. "Yes."

"Why he's willing, I can't answer. I can say they've been stuck in the maze. They can see the exit but can't find their way out and break ground. They make some progress and the project stalls again. Which in and of itself isn't unusual. Atlantic Yards has been in development since 2003." Jazz read her puzzled look. "Long story, it's in Brooklyn. And I'll quote a community activist here. She feels the developer's motto is 'Never say die, even when you're dead.' " Jazz gave Avery a wry smile. "And the truth is, they're not—yet, but the project is absolutely different than the way it started. But there are lots of unusual elements to Dixon Plaza—"

"Other than it's the biggest project by a black developer and the largest non–Columbia University build uptown in the city's history?" Avery saw his surprise. Toni's factoids had come in handy.

"Yes, other than that." Jazz nodded. "So you've done some background of your own." He finished the last crumbs of his cake. "This is so good." And wiped his mouth. "Everything I'm telling you is on the record. It's information that's been in my stories before."

Avery sipped her coffee and devoured information, about the Kidder, Theismann financing, the defection of the hotel, about Pastor Phil, Hudson Common, the contraction of the buildings. All that info about Dwight and his undertakings should have made her proud. She was sad that it couldn't.

"So why didn't they try to buy it a year ago? Or at the beginning, when they started the project?" With so many pieces, she wasn't sure where hers fit.

"Can't speculate on that, and your cousin has not shared that information with me. But this morning the Council okayed a resolution that would allow them to keep the towers at twenty-five stories by including additional public space in the complex."

"People can't live in public space."

"The people in your building now are not the target occupants for the new structures. Those folks will be priced out. But the Dixons, like others who've come in and improved the housing stock in 'bad' neighborhoods—they drastically change the community culture as well."

Avery wasn't sure how much she wanted to know about drastic changes in community culture. Jazz clearly cared about his stories. His conviction was refreshing. But she wanted 111th Street to be officially out of her jurisdiction.

Christmas flipped back through his notes. "I would imagine the culture of Harlem might be of interest to you, since you're a native. I don't mean of the 110th Street area specifically. But, and I'm paraphrasing Ralph Ellison when I say, 'Wherever Negroes live uptown—' "

" '—is called Harlem.' Yes, I'm familiar with the quote." Her father dragged it out regularly when he felt that all black folks were being lumped together in the same barrel—one he usually thought unfair.

"Good. And I see from my notes that your work abroad seems to have had a particular focus on making sure U.S. missions in other countries do all they can to support and sustain local culture and tradition—within limits of course. Clearly I don't mean places where ignoring human rights and dignity is local custom."

"You have been doing your homework."

"That's all a reporter's job is really. There is no story without the research."

Avery folded her napkin, thought a moment. "And I guess what's happening here is the same as what I've watched in developing countries time and again. It's all about who has the land someone else wants. In Africa and Central America it's usually about natural resources. And they'll kill you while you sleep if need be." She refolded her napkin. "And since Manhattan isn't sitting on a mother lode of oil or bauxite or gold, I guess it's all about what can be put on the land, since that's the only way to get something out of it."

Jazz pushed his empty cup aside. "I just try to make sure we hear from all sides—the folks who have to pack up their lives and start over when the place where they live and put down roots becomes the hot spot, the people with enough money and clout to change the face of the city and the elected officials who are charged with representing each person equally."

"That's a lot of sides." She was sure there were. But Avery didn't really want to talk about how the people she had seen, people who were now real, would fit into Jazz Christmas's carol, the one where she and Dwight were Ebenezer Scrooge and everyone else was the Cratchit family.

"You take someone like Chester Gordon. He's the Council representative for the district that contains Dixon Plaza, and your 111th Street property. Some of his constituents are at or below the poverty line, but now there's an influx of people with money and different priorities, and he's supposed to advocate for all of them. He's been a strong Dixon supporter. Says the project brings jobs and revenue to the community. But I also know he was a classmate of Dwight Dixon's from Brown. His office is in one of the Dixon Group buildings. It was Dwight's old Council office when that was his seat. Does that change the balance? The only way to tell is to investigate."

Avery tried to look like she was still listening, but she couldn't hear Jazz above the sound of that name ping-ponging around in her head. *Gordon? At Brown together . . . Chester Gordon?*

"Have you ever been to your building?"

Avery stared at her watch—not to tell the time, but to focus on something she could understand. *It couldn't be the same person.* It kept clanging in her head and she needed to know she hadn't disconnected totally—that time still ticked forward, second by second, that this conversation was actually happening.

"Are you okay?" Jazz leaned forward.

He's still talking to me. "What?" *Focus, Avery.* "Uh—yes. Not inside—yet. But I've been by there." Avery tried to keep her cool, sound calm. But she had to ask. "Do you know when

Chester Gordon graduated from Brown? Or if he ever went by another name?"

"Not offhand. I'm sure it's in my notes, but we can find out in a second." Jazz dug his laptop out of the backpack on the floor by his chair. "Wireless." He glanced up at the hammered tin ceiling as if that's where the Internet fairies presided, then back at the computer, and a couple of minutes later informed her that Gordon graduated the year before Dwight. Then Jazz added, "And because Chester was a 'third' he was also called Trey, by close friends and family."

Breathe, Avery. Close friends and girls he tried to rape? Say something. "Oh. Okay . . . thank you." She took her wallet out of her purse, tried to keep her hands from shaking. "I . . . I lost track of the time. I need to be going." Avery wanted out of there. She needed air.

"No problem. I've taken up enough of your afternoon. I've got the check." Jazz smiled. "I'm the one who's been hounding you."

"Sorry I wasn't more helpful." Avery pushed her chair back, got to her feet. "Please, don't get up." *Dwight and Trey? How could he?*

"No can do." Jazz stood. "Not being sexist—just home training. Can't shake it, no matter how hard I try. Are you sure you're okay?"

Avery reached for her coat. "Yes. Really I'm fine." She tried to smile. "It's all been so much so fast. Some days I feel it—whether I want to or not."

Jazz helped with her jacket. "Thanks again for agreeing to talk to me." He started to extend his hand, then let it fall to his side. "I enjoyed it. And believe me, I don't always say that." When he smiled this time, she realized that under his nonbeard was a dimple, only on his right cheek. "And I know this isn't exactly professional, but since we're off the matter, would you like to have coffee, or something, another time?"

"Pardon?" Avery knew the question was straightforward, but she couldn't handle it with her brain seizing. She hadn't put what had happened behind her, but she had stored it in her lockbox. As long as she stayed away, didn't jostle it too hard, so did the memories—mostly. But now she was back and so were they.

"I'm asking you out. You know. Out."

Out? What is he talking about? I have to get out *of here.*

Jazz ran his first two fingers along the neck of his sweater. "Your collar is—may I?" He stepped closer.

Avery beat him to it, flipped her collar back on the outside of her coat, the way it was supposed to be. "Thanks. I've got it." She ran a hand over her hair, suddenly self-conscious about how she looked.

"Listen, I like talking to you. I think you're having a very interesting life. Not weird interesting, but really different and intriguing, and I'm insatiably curious. Or maybe I'm just plain nosy and that's why I became a reporter. But I thought we might be friends or at least friendly—while you're in New York, that is." He shifted his weight from one foot to the other, then back again. The first sign he had shown of being the least bit hesitant. "Nothing more."

"I really don't know." Avery put her hands in her coat pocket. "I have so much on my plate—I mean, thank you. I'm flattered." *Aren't I?* "But I'm not sure I'll have the time."

Jazz nodded. "Sure. I understand, no problem. But should you find yourself at loose ends, with an hour or two to spare, you have my number. And for the record, despite my profession, I'm a decent guy."

"I'm sure you are, Jazz." *And I know who isn't.* "I have to go."

TWELVE

Sentiment was a commodity that wasn't in his budget

"The vote went thirty-two to nineteen for approval." The only time Dwight regretted having a glass-top desk was when he wanted to rear back and put his feet up on it. He wished Grace were on the other side of the desk and not on the other side of the pond in London, so she could see him gloat, but a speakerphone would have to do.

"How soon can we be up and running?"

"I'll have a better idea in a few days." He wanted to slap her. As long and hard as he'd worked to get to this moment, he needed to bask in it, swim in it, rub it all over himself. Dwight wasn't a smoker, but it felt like he should be lounging in a cigar bar, puffing on a Diamond Crown Maximus Corona, backslapping and letting his associates toast his business acumen, not listening to Grace dismiss it. "I put in a call to

Cobb. Mitch can resume demo on building two while we work on emptying 111th Street." The Dixon Group attorneys were still prepping closing documents for that building, but Grace didn't need to know that. He would press them to get a date on the calendar. Dwight didn't know Avery's plans. Frankly, it would be better if the attorneys handled it all, transferred the funds—and neither of them had to be in the room—neat and bloodless. It was really unfortunate she got hurt all those years ago, but at least now she'd get paid.

"We need to get on this yesterday. The whole Bear Stearns debacle has people jumpy. Keep me posted. My car is here. Dashing."

Yes, it seemed like Moe, Larry, and Curly had caused such a prestigious, New York Stock Exchange–listed, big-bonus-paying bulwark of capitalism to melt, like chocolate coins in your mouth. King had said, "That's what happens when you start buying and selling shit that ain't real." Like real was any more than what you could dream and were willing to pay for. But Dwight knew Grace's tactics—he'd grown up with them. She and King were more alike then either of them would ever admit. The better he was doing, the less she had to say, so he figured he was so hot he must be ready to burst into flame. Property values in other places might ebb and flow, but location was still king, and the center of Manhattan, Central Park, trumped pretty much anywhere else on the planet even when the economic slope got slippery. Dwight was sure of it.

It had gotten ugly between Dwight and Chester before the Council vote—come down to an emergency meeting at the Flash Inn, where the red-jacketed waiter brought veal medallions and porterhouse steak, and angry words passed between gritted teeth. Chester reminded Dwight he had an election coming up in the next year. "I need to protect my seat. There are rumblings I'm in bed with the developers, and all the crap you got going on in your buildings is only making me look worse."

Dwight reminded him it was Dixon support that got him elected in the first place. "I'll take care of the buildings and I'll get you reelected. Just get me that vote. You owe me, Chester."

They both knew what he meant. Dwight reached way back for that one, but what good are chits if you never use them? Whatever he had on the table, it was time to let it ride. They skipped dessert, but each left knowing where he stood and what he had to do.

Madeline bounced into the office as soon as Dwight hung up. "I took a message from Crawford at Hudson Common. Something about kitchen cabinets." She handed him the pink sheet. "And lunch is here."

When Chester called midmorning and said, "Signed. Sealed. Delivered," Dwight practically levitated. He stood on two upside-down trash cans in the middle of the office to announce that Dixon Plaza was officially under development, and the staff of ten barked, Arsenio-style. He told Madeline to have lunch catered because he needed the celebration, needed to feel the release. And counter to his home/office divide, in a moment of exuberance he called Renee, asked her to join the festivities.

Trays of sandwiches, bowls of salads, bottles of sparkly wine, and diet soda—they lunched and shared the excited would-bes of the project that were yet to come. Renee brought a dozen black and white cupcakes. She looked happy to be part of the celebration. They took turns posing for Madeline's cell-phone cam, standing next to the building model. Renee pulled Dwight by her side, kissed his cheek at the snap of the flash.

During the cleanup, Dwight sat on the couch in reception,

drinking coffee to counter the champagne buzz as Renee prepared to leave.

"When it's done, I think we should have one of the penthouses." Renee picked up her purse.

"We'll see." But Dwight had already imagined them in a duplex, facing the park. The two-story living room, furnished in white and taupe with sleek midcentury modern furniture, was bathed in sunshine.

"Grace lives in one of the Kidder—"

The door banged open with such force it bounced against the wall and shook the room.

"You are disgusting." It didn't take Avery long to get downtown, but in that time, years of studied cool began to heat, microwave hot, burning from the inside out. "Did you think I would be so overwhelmed with grief—"

"Avery, let's go inside." Dwight moved toward her, tried to keep the tremor out of his voice. He wasn't sure what just erupted, but he was all about containment.

Renee had backed against the wall and looked on in mouth-open amazement. Madeline and Eric had run to investigate the commotion. Despite building security, occasional protesters who were still dead set against Dixon Plaza and the perceived theft of "their Harlem" sometimes made it upstairs and into the office, insisting on having their say. Now the staff watched like rubberneckers on the highway, unable to look away from the wreck.

But the only person Avery had in her sights was Dwight. "Don't you *dare* try to shut me up." She could hear him trying to hush her that night, whisk her away from anybody who might be a witness to what had really happened—not for her sake, but for his. "That's exactly what you did to me that night at the party. And I let you, but it will *never* happen again." Avery spewed molten words like lava. There was no stopping the fiery stream or the tears that burned down her face. She let them flow. "Mom dies and I'm supposed to be too overwrought to notice you've got Trey Gordon pushing for your project." Just saying that name made Avery flash hot, feel the anger she had iced for so long she had almost forgotten it was real. "Trey Gordon! How could you do that, Dwight? How could you do that to me?"

"You can all go back inside." Avery clearly wasn't going behind closed doors. It was time to dismiss the audience, try to control the damage. "Renee, I'll see you at home."

Dwight wished Avery hadn't mentioned that name, hoped that in the uproar it had slipped by them, unnoticed. Nobody had called him Trey since college, and the last thing Dwight wanted was to get Chester Gordon's name tied up in this.

"I don't care who hears me, Dwight. I will say this to your face, and to anybody who asks me. I think you're a despicable man. And under no circumstances will I sell you the building on 111th Street. Not today. Not next week. Not twenty years from now." It was not polite or diplomatic, but she spoke her mind. "Not for *any* amount of money. So before you start thinking that you can sweeten the pot and get me to change my mind, think again."

He heard the muffled gasps, felt the chill spread down his body like death.

"And I am done with you." Avery turned to go.

"We need to talk, Avery." Dwight's heart pounded in hard, slow beats he could hear in his ears.

"No. We don't." She walked out.

Dwight followed her into the hall. "Let's discuss this."

"Discussing it will change nothing." She dug in her purse for a tissue.

"Name your price. I need that lot, Avery."

"Didn't you hear what I just said?" Avery blew her nose. "I needed you to tell the truth. To stand up for me. So it looks like nobody will get what they need." She chuckled. "You don't even know when you're being insulting." Avery heard the elevator doors open down the hall. "Hold the elevator." She trotted off.

Leaving Dwight standing alone, feeling like he'd just stepped on a land mine. But it hadn't gone off yet, so he had to keep moving.

"Get Stan on the phone." He didn't look at Madeline as he charged past her desk. First step, talk to his lawyer. Weren't they like a bomb squad anyway—trained to diffuse explosive situations without blowing up everything in sight?

Dwight could barely repeat the part about not selling him 111th Street, as if giving it voice made it something other than impossible. "My cousin and I have a long-standing disagreement." In the pause Dwight could hear the attorney's congested nasal breathing; that meant he was organizing his strategy. Stan asked if he needed to know what the dispute was about. "Family decisions." Dwight would leave it at that.

The rest of the afternoon he spent with his door closed, taking no calls, no questions. He plopped down in his chair, laid his head on his folded arms. *This is not possible.* He did not come this far to end up further behind than he started.

Dwight rolled his chair out, slid to the floor, drawn down, oppressed by the weight of those towers, or even more, by their absence. He lay flat on the floor beneath his desk, where he deserved to be, and stared up at the ceiling through his glass cage. What if he'd brought the property years ago? It seemed that Avery wouldn't have stood in his way, like he'd thought she would. Seemed that she'd spent years successfully denying his existence. What if King had sold Dwight's uncle a different property? What if the sale was on mangoes, not blueberries? What if Fairway had never opened. What if the street had been dry? What if he hadn't been such a spineless weasel back when they were in college? Dwight tortured himself—he'd become good at it, but not as good as Delilah.

He waited till most of the staff had gone to make one last call. He had tried to be strong. Tried not to need it, but there was so much pressure—too much. And he'd never survive it without her.

"The number you have reached is not in service."

He disconnected quickly, like it never happened, dialed again, and got the same officious, artificial voice, the same nothing, and his pulse pounded in his ears. He'd been so good. Hadn't called in weeks, and now this, when he needed her desperately. She was testing him, punishing him. He deserved it.

So Dwight made his way home, knowing that too would be a test. That's why he usually kept personal and professional so far apart—fewer questions to answer.

Dominique was with Emily for the night—a pajama birthday party—so he wouldn't have her to shield him from awkward conversation. He found Renee sipping white zinfandel when he got home. She barely drank at all, never alone, so he knew this was a situation. She didn't get up when he opened the door, didn't wait for him to fix a drink before she started in.

"What was that, at the office?"

He still didn't have a good answer. "I'll be back in a minute." Went to the kitchen for vodka and a little more time to come up with something to tell her.

Dwight sat beside her on the couch, wrapped his arm around her shoulders so he didn't have to look directly in her eyes as he spoke. Other than the parties and the parents involved, he'd never told another soul what went on that weekend in Providence. But there was a lot about him his wife didn't know, couldn't know, wouldn't understand. Who would? But he didn't get married for understanding. He got married to fulfill his obligation to his constituents, and to King, although the lack of a son still called that into question. So he knew he had to fabricate a story of some kind to tell Renee.

"Avery and I had a misunderstanding, when we were in our teens."

"I argued with my brothers and sisters, but I don't think they're disgusting."

Dwight was touched by the way she sounded so hurt for him. "It was a long time ago. It all got out of hand. I'm sure we'll iron this out." Which was more hope than lie.

"But what was it about that would make her sound that way? I don't know her well, but she doesn't seem . . . crazy, barging into your office and yelling like that."

Dwight squirmed, needed to find a hole, just big enough to wriggle through. "Somebody I set her up with didn't work out and she took it the wrong way." Which was what happened—just not all of it.

"That doesn't make any sense."

"Exactly. It got blown out of—"

"And who is Trey Gordon? Is he related to Chester?"

The hole got smaller, with no way to get through it clean. "Not to my knowledge." He eased his arm from around her and got up. "I've got a few things to check on. Let me know when dinner's ready. I'll be in the office."

Dwight spent most of the evening alone with papers, his computer, doing his best imitation of busy long enough to outwait Renee's bedtime. But no matter what he did, he couldn't stop himself from replaying Avery: "I needed you to stand up for me."

It was still when he sat by himself with an old-fashioned glass of vodka poured over some ice cubes. It was getting to be routine, as regular as it had become for the past to slam into the present, for him to feel as desperate as he did that morning when he got home from Spring Weekend.

➢ ➢ ➢

"Why didn't you kick his ass and be done with it instead of runnin' home to me like a damn punk?" King was headed out on his Saturday-morning ramble—to pick up the papers, get a haircut, and see what was perking—when Dwight rolled in around seven thirty. "You a grown-ass man. I can't be fightin' your battles."

"I wasn't thinking straight." Dwight paced across the narrow parlor, looking like he'd been dug out of the Dumpster. "I mean, it was late and—"

"Doesn't take thinkin'. It takes doin'. Boy, stand still!" King roared, and Dwight stopped. "She's blood. You got to protect that. Can't let folks mess over you."

"You can't punch your way out of everything."

"From what you're tellin' me, it's a language he understands." King hauled off, pounded Dwight in the arm to punctuate his point.

Dwight backed up, put space between them. "Look, we were all a little . . . high . . ."

"You think I don't know that? Humph!" King hoisted his suspenders. "Come in here smelling like reefer and rotgut. I don't give a shit what you drink, smoke, or screw. You're old enough to figure that out for yourself."

"Well, if we went wrestling around on the lawn, somebody would have called the police, and getting arrested with Judge Gordon's son didn't seem like the best idea."

"Aw, hell." King tossed his keys. They jangled on the table. "It's just what they think. You can dress 'em up but you can't take the jungle out."

"Trey was doing me a favor by going in the first place. Then this happens." Dwight spoke in jumpy bursts, his voice creeping higher. "And Alicia is screaming about going to the hospital and calling the cops. And people are looking at me like 'Take your crazy friends and go.' " Dwight plopped on an ottoman, dropped his head in his hands. "Maybe I should have called the cops. I don't know. But I'd have been iced after that."

"If you sit there and cry, I will beat your ass myself."

Dwight wanted to kneel in King's chest, pummel him with his fists. Thought he could probably take him, but kept the fantasy to himself.

And King had moved into containment mode, lowered himself into a chair, grunting as he went. "How is your cousin? For the sake of your sorry ass I hope she's all right."

"I don't know . . . I guess so. Alicia was driving her here."

"You talk to Trey?"

"Not yet."

King sucked his teeth. "Go wash yourself."

Scalding shower, hot enough to feel cold—Dwight lathered, let the water stream over his head, down his body. He tried so hard to make things right, but he kept ending up almost, not quite. Or worse yet, not even close.

Dwight twirled his washcloth into a tight, wet rope. Jackie was mad at him, he wasn't sure exactly for what, but there was plenty to choose from—the busted lock, the fouled-up plans, his wishy-washy response. And who knew what Trey was saying up on campus, if anything. How was he supposed to know Trey liked it rough? Nobody passed the word around in confidential whispers. At least not the guys, and Dwight sure never asked the women. The weekend was supposed to be about kicking back, having some fun. Except he was tangled in a thorny mess and he wasn't sure how to get out.

"Stupid, stupid, stupid." He struck his legs again and again with his washcloth whip, until fat, red welts covered his thighs—the way he'd done since he was a little boy, when his mother and father yelled like they hated each other and he wanted desperately to make it stop. No one could see his tears in the shower. When they waited until he went to bed to battle, about King's continued carousing while she stayed home alone—"with your son"—Dwight would close his bedroom door, crawl under his desk, and wrap his pillow around his head until silence or the slammed front door meant the round was over. It was almost a relief when his mother died. At least the fighting stopped.

When he came down dressed, his father was sitting at the kitchen table, jingling his keys. "Call your buddy Trey. See what he has to say."

Dwight wasn't eager to make that connection. And Trey jumped all over him from a dead sleep. "How was I supposed to know the bitch would go ape shit. Some people get crazy when they smoke a little herb. What was that shit you brought?" Dwight heard the smug in Trey's voice, daring him to disagree. "Lucus will back me up. I know you understand, my brother."

The fraternal appeal was also not lost on Dwight. Nor was the threat. "Bet, but you owe me big, my man. If you want me to stop my father from calling yours, that is." It sounded like something King would have said. Take an advantage wherever you can make one. Dwight knew the men knew each other and that Trey would not be interested in the judge's opinion on the matter. That shifted the balance back in Dwight's direction. Yes, he should have fought back, defended Avery, but at that moment it was easier to be one of the boys. *It couldn't have been that bad.* Avery was strong. She'd get over it. Besides, she'd got him into this bind in the first place. He had tried to tell her she wasn't ready.

King was waiting when Dwight hung up. "You got it straight?"

It wasn't so much a question as a command. Dwight nodded.

"Come on. We're going up the street. Cut this thing off at the knees."

When she opened the door, Alicia looked like she'd just as soon spit on him as speak. She fussed with his father about Avery being in no condition to talk, but he insisted she tell Doc B they were there.

After Avery and her father came downstairs and Alicia left. Dwight could hardly look at Avery. It was as if she'd crumpled, folded in on herself. But she perked up when she looked at him.

"Trey said it was a misunderstanding." Dwight spewed out the words before he lost the nerve.

"What?"

Dwight could feel Avery's eyes, searing him like a brand. "He said he was just playing with you."

"He shoved me on the floor. He kicked me."

Dwight had never seen that expression on her face—some mix of pain and disbelief. He couldn't take it. He looked away.

"Maybe I should have let Alicia call the police."

"For what?" Doc B looked disgusted. "He said, she said, with two intoxicated, black college students?"

"That's a Friday-night special." King posed by the mantel.

Dwight wanted to shove his fist down King's throat, make him shut the hell up.

Avery looked like a fish on a hook, mouth working, straining for air, but losing the fight. "I have never done anything . . ."

"And I don't know how old this boy is, but I know you're underage. Do you want to embarrass yourself any more than you have?"

"Daddy."

To Dwight, Avery's pleading seemed so frail against the rising tide. *Do something.*

"She tell you it's Chet's son?" King chimed in.

"Chet Gordon?"

"What difference does it make? He was wrong."

"The judge didn't spend thirty years building a respected record to have it torn down over childish foolishness."

"What's this got to do with the judge?" Avery sank into the chair. "His son hurt me."

"Wouldn't they just love that mug shot for the papers. 'Son of Prominent Judge in Sex Attack.' We see enough thugs in the paper."

Dwight felt her voice getting thinner, smaller. "What if Trey apologized?" He didn't know how he'd arrange that or what else to say.

King's tone was ripe with ridicule. "You are too stupid to be my son."

The words landed hard and heavy.

"I'm trying to work this out and all you want to do is—"

"Can we bring this back to the business at hand?" Doc B broke in. "I'll talk to Chet."

"That won't be necessary. I took care of it with Trey." Dwight looked at his uncle and his father, like he was finally one of them. "He understands the seriousness of the matter."

"And what am I supposed to do?" Avery had curled herself tighter into the chair.

"Maybe you won't be so curious next time. And you'll count yourself lucky it wasn't worse than it is. If you want to see what that means, come to the hospital with me sometime." Doc B started to leave, turned back around. "I wouldn't think I'd need to say this, because I believe we raised you to have a modicum of self-respect." He fastened Avery in his sights. "But under no circumstances tell your mother. You want to be grown? Going places where you have no business being? Suck it up and handle yourself."

Doc B left for the office and King went off to start his morning as he intended. Dwight hung behind, now silently urging Avery to look at him, connect with him the way she always had. But she was in her own world, like he didn't exist.

"I didn't mean—"

"I don't care, Dwight."

She'd never turned him off before—always understood. They had each other's back, it had been unspoken, but that was their deal. "I'll do whatever—"

"Avery, I'm sorry. I didn't know."

"You didn't ask me. Not what I wanted. Not how I felt." She paused, like she was about to say something else, but stopped. "Just go."

"But I want to—"

"Get out!"

➢ ➢ ➢

Avery's dismissal still echoed in Dwight's ears. He tipped his head back, let the melted ice from his drink slide into his mouth, crunched the frozen remains. Those things happened a long time ago. Sentiment was a commodity that wasn't in his budget. He had to have 111th Street, or all his vision, all his foresight, wouldn't amount to more than a lottery quick pick—a stupid gamble that gave a moment's hope then ended up in the trash, worthless and ripped in two. Avery's backward glances were in his way.

He didn't know what time it was when Renee shook him awake on the couch and he went up to bed. It was the weekend, but the next morning he was up first, as usual—made French-roast coffee, hit the computer to check business news, politics, local headlines. He could hardly sleep, waiting to see if the Dixon Plaza approval had any coverage, wanting to find out the angles, check if he'd been quoted anywhere, whether he'd been painted as astute or greedy, so he'd know what was likely to hit him when he stepped in the office on Monday. He had to stay a step ahead. A small item was in both the *News* and the *Times*. They brought up the glass tower down the street, as usual—both how an $8 million condo had been sold, and how the street-level storefronts were still empty. *That's not news*. As if rehashing the past made it more profound. His mission was to give them a new story to tell. Dixon Plaza had broken too late to make the weekend real estate sections—maybe next week. He'd have to wait until Wednesday to see if Jasper Christmas had anything to add.

After that Dwight stayed busy—an attempt to keep his brain from feeding on itself. At the gym he did his usual spin class, slant-board sit-ups, free weights—ordinarily it was enough to keep his head clear, at least for a couple of hours, but his mental gymnastics swung from how he was going to convince Avery to let go of 111th Street, to what would happen to DP-CPN if she didn't. Then there was Delilah. He tried not to, but he called the number—again and again. Sometimes he'd sneak up on it, like the next time could be the charm. Then he had walked for blocks, his hand on the phone in his pocket, alternating between hitting redial and voice command, as though one would work if the other didn't, as if the answer would be different in the next second, and the next. He volunteered to pick up Dominique from her friend's house to keep himself from going to Nineteenth Street. What would he do there? Ring the bell? That was enough to get him banished for good. Or stand across the street, staring at the building like some kind of heartsick loser? He was stronger than that.

The next day they spent an old-fashioned rainy Sunday afternoon. Dwight plowed through the stacks of newspapers, half watching the final rounds of a golf tourney. Renee puttered in the kitchen, cooking a roast and whatever went with it. Dwight didn't ask—it would show up on his plate soon enough. Dominique had pulled the ottoman up to the coffee table, writing numbers, erasing them, deep in concentration to solve the Sunday sudoku. Occasionally she'd consult her father. All he could do was nod. He was having enough trouble getting the puzzle pieces of his life to add up.

Then his hands tightened on the pages, clenched into fists. He laid the paper facedown in his lap so it wouldn't rattle, sent Dominique to get him some cheese and crackers and a soda. He wasn't hungry, just couldn't even continue to read with her in the room. Once she'd gone, he flipped the paper over, looked at the headline again to make sure it was real. "Sting Yields Chelsea Madam—and Her Mistresses."

Dwight rifled the pages, tried to talk himself down off the ledge. *Chelsea is a whole section. It doesn't mean* . . . Except the bust was at several apartments in a building on Nineteenth Street. He felt hot and dizzy, as if he were going to faint. No names were given for the five women arrested—not that he would know her real name, and from the logical perspective of his living room sofa, he was certain her parents did not name her Delilah. Computers were confiscated. He thought of all the times he'd called, wondered if they had surveillance footage. Swore he would never see her again, never do that again, if he just escaped this time. It didn't seem like a very big if.

"You look sick. You need help or somethin'?" The young man wearing a brown uniform and wheeling a dolly full of packages stopped next to Avery.

Help or something. But she didn't know what. She stood just outside Dwight's building, trembling. Full. Empty. It was hard to feel which. "I'm fine. Thank you." She sent him on his way. Pedestrians streamed around her, kicking off the weekend by leaving work on time for a change, eager to hit happy hour at the top instead of the bottom. Or running out of the office for a frozen yogurt or latte to get them through completion of their last-minute project to show the boss they're team players. *What do I do now? What do I do?* She'd said what she had to say and now she was outside, alone. As usual. Why was that usual? As far as Avery could see, people raced past her. They looked like they were heading toward something. Someone. She didn't have either. And for the first time in a long time she missed both.

Avery jumped hesitantly into the teeming pedestrian sea, afraid she'd be swept away. Certain she would drown and that no one would even see her flailing. As if to prove her point, a guy with a Chihuahua on his shoulder, staring at his phone screen, stopped right in front of her without any warning. He laughed out loud, thumbed a message back, without ever noticing her presence. So she stayed close to the buildings—at that moment, the only solid things around her—convinced she could not take her empty self home to an empty house.

Avery saw a coffee shop across the street. She just needed to sit for a minute, gather herself until she could come up with a plan or at least a next step.

"What can I do you for?" The clerk had Popeye forearms, replete with an anchor tattoo. "Not much left this time of day."

Avery could see that. The nearly empty pastry display, and two lonely doughnuts under their glass dome, had zero appeal, not that she was hungry. "Tea, please." A bag and hot water looked to be a safer bet than a coffeepot that had been sitting on the warming plate who knew how long, simmering its contents to sludge. In seconds a tea bag on a saucer, a thick, white ceramic mug, and a small stainless-steel pot that might have been shiny in its early life but had long since settled into a dull but serviceable state appeared in front of her.

She dunked the bag, let the tea steep. *Dwight and Trey.* She couldn't imagine Dwight continuing a friendship with Trey, so she simply hadn't and she felt stupid. Other people's lives had gone on. Only hers didn't. Oh, she put up an excellent front and a pretty good show. No one would know the calm, collected, levelheaded Avery Lyons, who could be counted on to have the answer, the right answer, was really a mess. A mess who ran away from home at the ripe old age of twenty-two. A mess who never forgave her father, her uncle, or her cousin for sacrificing her in order to keep up appearances, keep alliances intact, and not sully the family reputation. A mess who always chose men she knew would not be any more available to her than her family had been, so she would never think to count on them in the first place. A mess who made work her life instead of a part of it. A mess who still blamed her mother for believing her father's story that her injuries resulted from a fall down the stairs because she had been out drinking and for being unable to read her mind.

"You want more hot water?" The counterman was now mopping the floor back by the kitchen. She knew it was a sign for her to kindly get out and go home or somewhere else, like a normal person on a Friday evening.

"Uhh—no. Thanks. I'll take the check." She paid and left, but didn't know what to do, where to go. She still felt as agitated as she did when she stormed into Dwight's office. Her explosion had vented built-up steam she'd kept cool and contained for decades, frozen solid and deep like a glacier, with her history, her story, documented in each level of ice. Avery shivered. She needed to call Walker to tell him the deal was off. He'd said call him anytime, but did she really need to reach him at the start of his weekend with something that could clearly wait until Monday? She thought of calling Van, but didn't.

Alicia. I'll call Alicia. She'll find a way to turn this into a celebration.

Avery took out her phone—correction, her mother's phone—and saw a message was waiting—the last thing she wanted. Another wrong number or one of her mother's friends checking to see if she was making out okay "by herself," or if she wanted to play bridge next week or have lunch or . . . *scream.* She did not want to step into her mother's life like some kind of plug-in replacement, and she didn't want people to think she required tending. *I have to get my own cell.* Then she saw Alicia's name on the missed-call list and hit the key to check voice mail. It had only taken two tries to figure out her mother's password, YREVA, because there are just some things you know.

"Hey, Av, sorry I missed you. Some days life sucks and this is one of them." *Tell me about it.* "That rat-ass ex-husband of mine went and had himself a heart attack. Miss Teen Hussy girlfriend is in the wind. Seems she took one look at him sick, pathetic, and *old* and said, 'Adios, Poppy.' And the rat still has me listed as his next of kin, the person to call in case of an emergency, *and* the one to make medical decisions . . . blah blah blah—you get the picture. So as much as I'm hating on that SOB, I'm about to board a plane to L.A., 'cause I guess even a sack of shit shouldn't have to die—oops, did I say *die*? I meant *be sick*—alone. Oh, yeah—how'd your meeting with Paperboy go? Maybe I shouldn't say it like that—sounds a little Mary Kay Letourneau freaky. An-y-way—glad you met Toni. Isn't she the greatest? I'll call you when I know more. Ciao, Chica!"

Avery just stared at the phone. *What am I supposed to do now?* Before she fully realized what she was doing, she saw the next number, pushed redial before the tears spilled over, she made a fool of herself, and she became the object of ridicule in a conversation among chittering executive assistants over cosmos and chocolate martinis. "I saw this woman standing right on Sixth Avenue, bawling her eyes out!"

➢ ➢ ➢

"I didn't expect to hear from you, ever. Much less in a couple of hours!" Jazz took the stool next to hers.

When Avery told him where she was, he suggested Del Frisco's, a couple of blocks away, and promised to be there in less than an hour. She found a seat at the bar and, following Jazz's instructions, introduced herself to Mike, the bartender, who, as she had been promised, took good care of her. She hadn't finished her glass of Barolo when Jazz arrived.

"You don't know me and you certainly don't owe me anything. I'm not even sure I've changed my mind, but you said you wanted to be friends and right now I could use one of those. Okay? So can we try out this friend thing, and if it doesn't work, no harm, no foul?" Avery's only interest was getting through the next couple of hours until she was calm and rational enough to go home.

"Deal."

"Don't worry, I will not get drunk, cry, and embarrass you in public." Avery slowly swirled her wineglass. "I just needed not to be by myself. Sounds pathetic, huh? And by the way, just for the record, whatever I do say is off-the-record."

"No notebook, no tape recorder." Jazz held up his hands, then opened his jacket. "No harm, no foul. And for the record, you don't sound pathetic. Just a drink and a little conversation between two new friends. Okay?"

Avery nodded.

Mike popped over, shook hands with Jazz. "The usual?"

"Guess you're a regular."

"Been here once or twice. But Mike and I go back a ways."

"We were both young then. Now only one of us still is." Mike headed off down the bar. Compared to Jazz's salt-and-pepper, he didn't have one gray hair.

"When I was at Rutgers, he worked in a place I'd go when I was trying to impress a girl. I needed all the help I could get since I really couldn't afford to be there, but this guy always hooked me up, made me look good."

"That's nice." She couldn't tell how long ago the good old days had been, but they certainly weren't kids. Avery wondered how it felt to share a history like that with someone, even a casual one—experiences and memories that keep you connected through time and distance and life's crap. To have a friendship you build, stories that span from one era of your lives to another. Her bridges were either short, only joining spaces that were already close, or the narrow, one-lane kind where traffic could only pass in one direction at a time. Or they were in such a state of disrepair, she didn't dare start across. That pretty much summed up all the relationships in her life. *It exactly why I'm sitting at a bar with a man I met five hours ago.*

"Hope I didn't drag you away from whatever you were doing." She noted the blazer, which wasn't part of his earlier outfit.

"Sometimes I need to be dragged away. Occupational hazard. I can get sucked into my computer."

"Looks like you had plans." He was dressier, but without being fussy or formal. The charcoal cashmere suited him.

"Oh—the jacket? This is a nice place. I was meeting a new friend. Though I'd put in a little effort. Besides, it will give Mike something to tease me about next time. He usually sees me at the end of a scruffy reporter day."

As if on cue, Mike delivered a frosty manhattan.

"My mom drank those."

"A person of discerning taste and strong character. At least that's how I described the handsome, rakish, manhattan-drinking-reporter-slash-spy main character of my cliché, unfinished, semiautobiographical novel."

"I would have taken you for more the screenplay type."

"Every reporter has to be working on one or the other. It's a job requirement."

Avery laughed. "I guess that's true. And you're right. Mom definitely had discerning taste in cocktails and other things. I'm a lightweight though. Wine's pretty much it for me."

"The drink of the civilized."

"At least according to Hemingway." Avery took another sip.

"I can't seem to impress you with my witty and urbane literary references."

Avery laughed again and resisted the urge to offer a snappy comeback so he wouldn't mistake it as flirting. She also tried to deny she was feeling better, comfortable. Because she didn't know this man. She didn't want to feel comfortable. She was still mad at Dwight.

"Thanks for the laugh. It's been kind of an extra-crappy day—at least the end of it has. The early part was fine. With the exception of me thinking I was ready for the hundred meter again. I'm going to pay for that tomorrow."

"You used to compete. There was speculation you might enter the trials for the Empire Games. Maybe even the Olympics, but . . ."

"You and your homework. I didn't have the heart of a true competitor. Still don't. I just liked to run and was good at it. And for some reason, in a totally delusional moment on my morning walk, I thought I still could. But I, of all people, should know some things that were, will never be again."

"Pretty fatalistic . . . almost bordering on nihilism."

"Okay. So you're smart and you're well read. You also moonlight as a shrink? When you're not working on the great American novel, that is?"

"Ouch." Jazz feinted, then picked up his glass. "Sorry. Not analyzing or judging. Maybe I should be quiet for a while and let you talk."

"That's not what I meant. And I'm still not sure I want to talk as much as I wanted company. This just wasn't a good time for me to be by myself. Fatalistic or not, at least I had sense enough to realize that, although I probably shouldn't have picked a total stranger to unload on, huh? Lucky you."

"Stranger, sort of. Total, no."

"By the way, has anybody ever told you that it's annoying, not to mention unfair, for you to have all this information about people and they don't have any about you?" Avery shifted on her barstool to face him, crossed her leg.

"Not really. But then the folks I've got the skinny on are just interviews for a story. They're not people I want to get to know—in my real life. So, yes, it's unfair that I know an awful lot about you and you know very little—like nothing—about me." Jazz noticed her empty glass. "Would you like another wine, or to have dinner? I don't know what your schedule is like."

"Schedule? That's pretty funny. I have no schedule. I'm a stranger in my hometown—in my own house." Avery clasped her hands on the bar, to make herself stop fidgeting with her empty glass. "I'm an only child with dead parents, and my only relative is a . . . never mind. Let's not go there. I have one friend, who I'm lucky is still willing to be my friend, because I've ignored her since we were in college. But she's a big enough person not to hold that against me. A much better person than I am because she did try to stay in touch, and I just froze her out. Warning—I'm very good at that. But I digress." She looked over at him, to see if he seemed bored by whatever it was she was saying. But his eyes were fastened on her, which almost made Avery lose her train of thought. "She's so good that I can't even be mad at her for not being here when I really, truly need her. How can I be? She went to L.A. to take care of her *ex*-husband, who just had a heart attack, because he doesn't have anybody else. How's that for a remarkable human being?"

"Guy Harvey's wife? I knew she was in your class at Breton, but not that you two were still—"

"There you go, knowing stuff again. It's so wrong. Yes, I would like another glass of wine." Avery pushed her empty glass aside. "And I think dinner might be a good idea too. Or I may have to eat my words about embarrassing you in public." Avery turned around to see that the restaurant had filled and the bar was now three deep. "If we can get a table."

"No problem."

"It's rush hour in here. The place is jammed."

"We already have a reservation." Jazz smiled. "Mike thinks of everything."

"Uh-huh. Why do I think Mike had very little to do with this?" Avery got up. "Be right back." Avery headed upstairs to the ladies' room, not because she needed to use it, but because she needed a time-out. The new arrivals had primped before they'd left their offices, and they hadn't reached the tipping-point third cocktail, which inevitably necessitated a trip to the restroom, so fortunately she was alone.

Avery washed her hands, splashed water on her face, then stopped to look at herself in the mirror, a rare occurrence after her morning routine. She kept her hair, makeup, and clothing choices simple enough that they could be tended throughout the day without her actually having to look again. A quick hand or comb through hair she kept relaxed and bobbed to chin length, because she could keep it in order herself, which, depending on where she was assigned, was necessary. The language of black hair is definitely not universal. Bronzer-blush and earth-toned lipstick got her through most days. For special occasions she would whip out the mascara and sometimes a bit of cover-up for the circles that would appear after too many official late nights without enough late mornings to balance them. Her wardrobe pieces—suits, skirts, slacks, and sweaters in navy, tan, gray, and of course black—mixed well with each other, required little thought or planning, and were perfect for travel. She would sometimes see colleagues in pink or floral or stripes, and even though she thought they looked nice, Avery would be confounded by the impracticality of their outfits. They also reminded her of her mother.

Avery stared at her face, ran her fingers through her hair. *Not bad.* Not beautiful or glamorous, but not bad. Forty had come and gone, and whatever it was supposed to bring, it hadn't left her looking much different from how she did ten years ago. Her wheat-colored skin hadn't grown blotchy or freckled like her mother's had by the time she reached her early forties. Avery was still without crow's-feet or brow furrows. Forty was the new what? She saw the magazine covers, but was never lured in by those articles. What for? Thirty, forty, fifty—they were whatever they were. She didn't have enough interest or vanity to expend energy waging an unwinnable war against time. Avery leaned in closer, reapplied her lightly tinted lip gloss, took a step back, straightened her slim, gray skirt, adjusted the matching twin set. What she saw in the mirror was undoubtedly her, but a faded version. Like when the printer is running out of toner—the words are there, faint and hard to make out, but there nonetheless, and in that moment she realized that while "not bad" was certainly acceptable, she had allowed herself to be totally unremarkable.

How can anybody else see me when most of the time I don't even see me? When was the last time I wore a color? She accepted that black and neutral colors were the standard uniform of New York's sophisticated urban career-club members. *I used to wear colors all the time.* She remembered the yellow cotton skirt and lavender top she had on the last time, the only time, she'd seen Trey Gordon. She had thrown the outfit away. After that night, color slowly washed out of her world.

"You are having a very interesting life." Not "you are an interesting person." Not "I think you're attractive." Not . . . Not what? What did I want him to say?

The door flew open and two young women in platform spikes, butt-hugging pencil skirts—one red, one electric blue—and almost identical ruffled blouses burst into the ladies' room. They plopped enormous leather handbags, decorated with enough spurs and bits and chains to set off any decent metal detector, on the counter, removed makeup bags the size of Avery's entire purse, and retouched faces that already looked well painted, all the while arguing about whether the New York Giant who had just bought them drinks was still married.

Unable to imagine her faded reflection caught between the Technicolor twins, Avery ended her self-examination and left.

Jazz waited at the bottom of the stairs. "Table's ready."

"Tell me something," Avery said once they were seated. "Why did you say I was having an interesting life?"

"Because I think you are."

"Okay. But why didn't you say *I* was interesting?"

"Because I think 'interesting' as a description for a person is what people say when they're not sure what they think about someone and don't want to commit one way or the other. It's a cop-out. And it doesn't mean anything. Believing a person is living an interesting, intriguing—and I used that word too—life is about them making deliberate choices, or handling circumstances they don't make choices about, in a way that still yields growth and vitality. Someone who is having an interesting life is doing more than passing time. And you fall into that category."

"Well, that's certainly more of an answer than I was expecting."

"I'm in the answer business. For me, the whole point of any story I write is to give people the answer—either to the question no one else has asked, or the real answer—the truth behind what somebody has been lying about. Giving my own answers, when asked, seems only fair. So to be clear, I didn't mean to imply that I did *not* think you were interesting, quite the contrary, Avery. I just wanted you to know that my interest was genuine. Not small-talk BS you say when you can't think of anything else."

"Guess I was being a little overly sensitive."

"You said you were having a bad day—goes with the territory."

After a quick glance through the extensive menu and making a when-in-Rome decision, they both ordered steaks. New York strip for him, rib eye for her, both medium rare, with the usual accoutrements along with a bottle of the Barolo Avery had been drinking.

"So, Mr. Christmas, tell me about you." Avery tore off a piece of bread. "New Yorker? You went to Columbia J School. Or are you a Jersey boy—the Rutgers reference and your connection to the coffee-shop owner. And you said you have a son."

"And that my parents are gone. I'm Jersey born and bred, but after twenty years in New York, I granted myself dual citizenship. I'm equally at home in both places. *Christmas* is a hard name to grow up with, and when you put *Jasper* in front of it . . ." He shook his head. "Let's just say I had to develop pugilistic skills early in life." He put up his dukes. "I wasn't very good, but I learned that being willing to stand up for yourself, for what was right, counted." Jazz smiled, shrugged his shoulders.

They talked easily, Avery asking most of the questions, Jazz doing most of the answering. Their steaks arrived and Avery was glad to have some meat to put under her wine. She hadn't realized she was hungry. The conversation rolled around to marital status.

"I have one ex-wife—we were married six years, tried to make it work for the sake of our son, but parents who shouldn't be together make for a lousy home. Kids just aren't that dumb." He selected a roll.

Avery passed him the butter, hoping it wouldn't interrupt the flow.

"Thanks. She remarried and moved to Arizona when Jake was ten. At first he came to visit me for vacations, long weekends, and several weeks in the summer. But the older he got, the more his life, his friends, were out there. He hated it here. We fought. He came less often. Now I see him once a year for a few days, twice if I'm lucky."

"That must be hard."

"It was, but I got used to it. And I can't complain. His stepdad's a good guy. Jake's now a senior at the University of Arizona, Tucson, graduating in May. Wants to be a meteorologist, of all things. My son, the weatherman."

"That's great." Avery didn't know what else to say. She was always at a loss when people talked about their children. She had no parenting experiences of her own to refer to or compare, and her own rearing wasn't necessarily the best model, so she ate her meat—which was very good.

"I have three sisters—married with grown kids. One doesn't speak to me. We had a disagreement about how much money she was giving to a televangelist. He's now in jail. Yes, it was her money, as she pointed out, but I still felt like I had to at least try and protect her—even if she didn't want me to." Jazz shook his head. "She now believes, mistakenly I might add, that I was responsible for her favorite cleric's tragic downfall." He poured more wine in both of their glasses. "I love my job, but it drives me crazy. I've had an apartment in SoHo since before it was trendy. I jaywalk, but I floss, which I believe balances my disregard for the law. I cook because I like to eat. I like both dogs and cats, but have neither. I speak Spanish and a little French, but I would rely on my translations if you were lost, not if you were about to be arrested. My last vacation was a ski trip to Idaho in January, from which I returned uninjured. I'm lactose intolerant, but love ice cream and have been known to willingly suffer for my butter-pecan passion, but tonight I will show restraint. I'm not allergic to anything I know of except indifference. How's that for a start?"

Avery laughed. "That's more than I know about most people."

"Maybe you should ask more questions, 'cause this isn't much information at all."

Avery looked at the openness in his face. He wasn't being Jasper Christmas, investigative journalist. He was just being. It was a skill she hadn't developed. "Maybe. Or maybe I just need to know different people." She tapped the stem of her wineglass. "My mother was having an affair." Hearing the words aloud startled her, even though she'd said them.

"Pardon?"

"You're going to make me say it again?"

"No . . . but your mother was a widow—for a long time. If she was in a relationship, I hardly think you could call it—"

"I mean before." Though Avery hadn't brought herself to read any more of Reggie's letters to her mother, she had been back to that bundle several times. Flipped through the envelopes and found the postmarks that told her in no uncertain terms that correspondence had been regular from 1981 to 1988, stopped, then resumed again in 2002. "While my dad was still alive, while I was in college. It seems to have ended, at least the mail did, but it looks like it was back on when she . . . died. I met him. He was at Mom's funeral, but I never made a connection—not like that. It just never occurred to me that she—either of them—would do that. Don't get me wrong. The last thing my parents were was lovey-dovey. I knew that. They had separate bedrooms for as long as I can remember. I've never known two more opposite people." *Why am I telling him all this?* But the flow of words didn't stop. "My dad was so rigid, and Mom—she just floated around on her own little free-form cloud. Above it all and happy to be there. Or so I thought. I mean, there must have been some kind of attraction at the beginning. But what I saw growing up was . . . I don't know, I guess *tolerance* is as good a word as any. Which

I imagine could be said for a lot of marriages, not that I'm an expert or anything. And it's not that I'm devastated by this in some morally superior way. It just shocked me, coming out of the blue. And why am I telling you this?"

"Because you need to tell someone."

"I didn't even tell Alicia. She was there when I found the—the—evidence." Avery made air quotes around the word. "That makes it sound so much more than it is, doesn't it? But she was there and you know what I did? I slammed my finger in the drawer, I closed it so fast. I didn't want her to know. Why is that? What differences does it make? Mom is gone. Alicia wouldn't care. She certainly wouldn't judge her."

"Finding out your parents have a sex life is always a kick in the head. When I was fifteen, I actually heard mine. I couldn't look at my mother for a week." Jazz took a drink of water.

Avery rested her fork and knife on her plate. Smiled. "I have to admit I still feel—I don't know—weird, about my mother and *Reggie*, but this is nice. Having a real conversation, about real things. Thank you."

"Hey, a little wine, a little food, and getting to know a new friend. No harm, no foul, no rules, no penalties. And by the way, I'm enjoying it too." He bowed his head in mock gallantry. "So thank you for dragging me out."

Dinner was leisurely. Conversation waxed and waned, and while it remained lively, it also grew lighter, less personal. They meandered away from families and indiscretions and touched on travel, bosses, the new president, weather, and New York—because whether you love it or hate it, the city is a never-ending source of stuff to talk about. Even during a couple of lulls, there was no rush to fill the spaces. No tripping over each other's words in fearful anticipation that silence, even if only to take a breath, was to be avoided at all costs. They had a slight tussle over the check, Avery insisting it should be her treat since she invited him out. Jazz reminded her he wasn't that kind of guy. "I was raised to hold doors and chairs for women, and to pay for dinner."

"But I'm now a woman of independent means. Or so they tell me."

"All the more reason I should pay. I wouldn't want you to think I was only interested in you for your money."

She laughed. He paid.

The crowd at the bar had thinned, so they stopped to say good-night to Mike, who convinced them to have a nightcap—on him. They'd had enough to drink, but to keep Mike happy, they ordered espressos, doubles, and listened as he filled them in on what happened with the Giant and the Technicolor twins. "Business as usual for him. Glad I wasn't subpoenaed in the divorce. But, hey, far as I'm concerned, your bartender is like your lawyer and your doctor. Subject to professional privilege!"

At nearly two o'clock in the morning, they headed back out to the now deserted avenue. The temperature was doing that spring thing—rising overnight—and the air felt almost balmy. Definitely warmer than it had in the month Avery had been home. They stood in the plaza in front of the restaurant having their first awkward moment of the night. Awkward moments after dinner with men she barely knew were so far from Avery's experience, she had absolutely no idea what to do. But she did know she didn't want to go home. She'd never minded living alone, she wasn't fearful—even in countries where maybe she should have been—but tonight, she just wasn't ready to be only with herself or to try to find a corner of the house that didn't remind her of the place she didn't want to be.

I wonder what his place is like. She was appalled that she even had the thought. *I didn't mean it like that. What did I mean?* Avery was debating with herself, in her own head, and then she realized however it turned out, she would never win the argument.

"Can I get you a taxi?" Jazz asked.

Saved. "I think I'd like to walk a bit."

"Mind company? It's late, and, yes, I'm being sexist this time."

"Glad you volunteered—I didn't have the nerve to ask. Seeing as we're such new friends and all." Avery smiled and turned right. *Why am I so damn happy?*

"I'm pretty sure you know you're heading away from home, but . . . ?"

"I haven't been gone that long. Yes, I know home is that-away." She pointed her thumb in the opposite direction.

"And you don't want to go there. Got it. No problem." They walked several blocks, played a few more rounds of *This Is Your Life* as they went.

"Okay. I have to ask," Avery said, because this she did have to ask. They had wandered south and west and were now in the midst of the madness that is Times Square—at any hour of the day or night. "It's a Friday night, you're unmarried, employed, good-looking, and—I'm taking your word on this—a *decent* guy. From what I hear tell, that's a pretty rare combination and definitely a hot commodity. So why on earth would you be available to spend your evening babysitting somebody you hardly know, when I'm sure you could have your pick of women—or men if that's your preference?" She was pretty sure it wasn't, but she put it out there anyway.

Jazz grinned. "Thanks for the compliments. And I guess I'm stuck now since I told you I was in the answer business, huh? First—no, I'm not gay. No issues with folks who are, I just don't happen to be one of them. Second—yes, I meet a lot of people—women people. And some of them, plenty of them, make themselves *extremely* available, but I can't say that works real well for me." He stopped, looked at her. "Now don't get me wrong, I'm not *that* old-fashioned, and despite my home training, and not letting you pay for dinner, and not wanting you to walk alone at this hour, I'm really not a chauvinist Neanderthal, 'me hunt,' 'you hunted' "—he pounded his chest—"kinda guy. But my ego also isn't so huge that I think all these women are after me because I'm so wonderful. It feels like they want to trade—they'll give me pretty much whatever I ask for, immediately, in exchange for the *potential* of a *future* relationship." Jazz started walking again. "And that makes me believe that the same thing happened with the guy who was before me. And will happen with the one who's after. Which means that it's not about me. It's not about them. It's about desperation. And desperate women—desperate people in general—scare me. Their motives might be real and honest—good even. But I don't want to make a deal like that, Avery. I've interviewed enough desperate folks, heard them explain why they did what they did—rob a store, embezzle from their company, kidnap their own kid, kill someone, whatever. And how it made sense at the time. It seemed like the only way to get what they so *desperately* needed or thought they had to have. That end-justifies-the-means thinking that ultimately leads to some kind of sad, regrettable action—it just doesn't work for me, in any area of my life. Now I'm not saying that all the women I meet are like that, but enough of them have been. So I'm pretty careful."

"Boy, that makes me really glad I didn't say what was on my mind when we left the restaurant."

"What would that have been?"

"I was going to say—" *I wonder what your place is like.* "Never mind. It was silly." *Ridiculous is more like it.*

"Okay. Keep in mind, silly's not always a bad thing." Jazz smiled. "Did you know they're going to close off this whole area to cars—turn it into a pedestrian mall? At least that's the mayor's plan. I've been talking with a few cabbies and some guys who've been maneuvering delivery trucks around here for a long time. I can tell you they are not happy. We'll see how it goes, but I may have another story brewing about what trickle-down progress means in the city."

"Always looking out for the underdog?"

"The big dogs have a voice. They have money and power and lawyers. They don't need me. Like I said, I'm about answers. And sometimes, if nobody else does it, I have to ask the question too. The hard ones the big dogs don't want to hear. But a small paper like the *New York Spectator*—the mission statement is right on the front page: 'Your eyes. Your ears. Your voice.' It gives me the freedom to keep whistling until I find the frequency that annoys them enough that they hear me and have to respond. Yep. I love my job, but it drives me crazy."

"Funny—I don't know if I love my job or not. I have a career I've done well in. But Alicia asked me this morning what made me happy, and I didn't have an answer. Which only bothered me a little then, but after a few hours with you, I'm really bummed out about my lack of purpose and passion." Avery gave him a smart-ass grin. "Thank you."

"Aw, come on. I'm not that righteous. Really. I can be just as self-serving and shortsighted as the next person." He chuckled. "I have an idea . . . you said your schedule was open, right?" She nodded. "Okay. You trust me?"

"I guess so." She looked him in the eyes. "Somehow, I get the feeling you would tell me if I shouldn't."

"Good." He grabbed her hand and pulled her toward the curb. "Taxi!"

FOURTEEN

A new day always dawns

"Where are we going?" Avery fastened her seat belt as Jazz eased the car into traffic. The taxi had dropped them in front of a garage on Varick Street, where the attendant greeted Jazz by name, then disappeared, returning with a black Saab.

"My favorite place to go when I'm trying to figure something out. It's always where I end up when I need to see things in a different light." He merged right, into the lanes for the Holland Tunnel. "Relax, I'm a good driver and I've made this trip a thousand times." He removed a pair of glasses from the visor, put them on. "Had laser surgery several years ago, but still need a little help with night driving."

"Okay." Yes, Avery did realize it might be foolish to head across state lines for parts unknown with a man she knew little about. She'd watched enough *Crimetime, Crooks R-Us, 72 Hours: Still a Mystery* investigative reports, with melodramatic reenactments of the mysterious circumstances surrounding the murders, mutilations, kidnappings, or deceptions of college girls, mommies, ex-wives, or brides, perpetrated by some man. Usually one the woman knew—or thought she did. *Then I should be safe with this one. I don't know jack about him.*

But for reasons she couldn't explain, she believed Jazz. Believed he was a good guy. Believed it bothered him that his sister didn't speak to him. Believed he really was happy his son had a good stepfather. Believed his dedication to his work was sincere. Avery even believed his spiel about too many too available women—mostly. But she was also cynical enough to take comfort from the fact that Mike the bartender and Rico the garage attendant knew Jazz by name. Besides, who would she call to tell where she was going? Who was there to worry about her, or her whereabouts? Avery thought about sending Alicia a text, but decided Alicia had enough to deal with at the moment without adding to her load. So she read highway signs—SECAUCUS X, GOETHALS BRIDGE . . . exhausted from the emotion of the day, her Barolo-heavy eyelids flickered—

—*Where am I?* Avery woke with a start. *Why am I moving?* Then it clicked. She was still in the car with a man named Christmas. But she was nestled in the corner, her head between the window and the headrest, and she felt calm. She felt all right. Okay.

When she and Van took car trips, which wasn't often, he drove and Avery's job was to be on alert, keep conversation going, provide a travelogue, which she would thoroughly have researched, along with directions and points of interest along the way. Which, when she thought about it, was a lot like the rest of their relationship. They both had assignments, and one of them was to keep things interesting, keep it moving. When they were apart, they collected information—obscure, unusual, clever—that they would exchange when they were together. It was a competition, a constant contest to impress. *How many of our conversations start with "Did you know . . . ?"* The information had to be worthy. You had to bring your best game. Because Avery lacked the competitive spirit, Van usually trumped whatever tidbits she had managed to dig up. When they weren't *doing* something—going to a concert, a museum, a lecture, a reception—their conversations were about what they were going to do, or what they'd done. There was no such thing as just hanging out. No lulls, no time for quiet reflection, no ease in just being together. She couldn't recall the last time she had fallen asleep before Van did, much less dozed off to the hypnotic lullaby of a car ride. *Guess I did—I do trust Jazz.*

But so far, with Jazz, she felt no pressure to perform. She closed her eyes again for another few miles, then, without fully opening them or turning her head, she stole a glance at him. His eyes were fastened on the road, left hand steering, right hand at ease on the armrest, fingers lightly on the gear-shift. *Must have driven a stick once upon a time.* So many cars overseas were manual, she had been forced to learn, and now when she drove an automatic, she too got the itch to give her right hand some work to do. The radio, on low, was tuned to an all-jazz station, no surprise there, although she guessed a guy named Jazz could just as well be into reggae or rap or opera for that matter.

Shifting her half-open gaze, Avery could see they were no longer on a major highway. The road wasn't wide enough. But nothing else was familiar—not that she knew much about New Jersey. Newark Airport, a few concerts at the Meadow-lands eons ago, a couple of suburban mall adventures with Alicia in the Chevelle, and a visit with her folks to South-ridge Academy—an all-girls boarding school near Princeton—before she decided on Breton was the sum total of her Garden State experience.

The road went from two lanes to four, then back to two again, through towns with quaint cottages and corner drugstores, and long stretches of open land. She still couldn't hazard a guess where they were heading, but maybe it was time to be awake. "Hey." She sat up. "Sorry about that. Didn't mean to fall asleep."

"Hey yourself. I'm glad you felt comfortable enough. Not much farther."

"I wasn't snoring, was I?" Van had never mentioned it, but she had no idea if she was a quiet sleeper, a buzz saw like her dad, or if she had the same wheezy whine as her mother.

"Nope. Silent running all the way."

"Good. So, are you going to let me in on our secret destination?"

"You'll be able to tell soon. Probably even now—if you open your window."

She found the switch, and the moment the glass slid down, damp, musky salt air rushed into the car. *The ocean.* Wherever she'd been in the world, that scent was the same. "It's not exactly beach season."

"Don't worry. There's a boardwalk. We're not going swimming." Jazz glanced over, gave her a playful smile.

A few minutes past four thirty he pulled into a sand-sprinkled parking space. "People argue about which is the best beach, but this is my beach, where I used to come when I was a kid, so Point Pleasant has a special place in my heart." He unfastened his seat belt. "Game?"

"Why not?" The breeze was strong, cooler than in the city. It blew her hair in her eyes, tickled her cheeks, refreshed her.

"I've got a blanket in the trunk." Jazz fished out the blue plaid bundle, led her across Ocean Avenue.

"The houses are right on the boardwalk." Avery had the urge to loop her arm through his. *Get a grip. I mean . . .*

"In that one over there they play Sinatra music all the time. It's kind of a sound track as you go by." He pointed. "It'll be easy to find a bench. Not in a couple of weeks though, even at this hour."

Despite the breeze, the ocean was calm and purred in the distance.

"Bradley Beach, Asbury Park, Wildwood, Surf City—my buddies and I used to hit 'em all in the summertime, lookin' for some hot fun."

"I bet." Avery smiled.

"We found plenty too. Most of the action is on the other end in season, stores, restaurants, bars. But I like this end exactly because it's where action is not. This was my by-myself beach."

"I've never been to the beach here, or what is it you Jersey folks say . . . *down to the shore*?"

"*Down the shore.* No *to* necessary. And to clarify, *down the shore* is the *destination*. Once you're here, it's *the beach*. Strange I know, but it is what it is."

They passed a few soon-to-be-hungover leftovers from a long Friday night of seaside revelry. But mostly the town seemed to be asleep. They continued up the boardwalk awhile until Jazz stopped, looked in all four directions. "Here good?"

"As any place." They sat on the wooden bench. "Is this the contemplation seat, where inspiration meets good vibrations?"

"If that was the case, I'd have taken it home." Jazz draped the blanket around her. "Nope. I'd cop a squat anywhere. Depends."

"On?" In front of them the first dusty pink of morning pushed back against the dark.

Jazz shrugged. "When I was a kid, my family would rent a shore house for two weeks every summer. I couldn't wait for the day to begin. So I would get up and wait for the sun. Then I'd take off on my bike, just to get away from my parents, and especially my sisters for a while." He laughed. "I don't know what was worse, being named Jasper Christmas or having three sisters who all thought they were my boss, including the one younger than me." He rested his elbows on his knees and looked out toward the water. "When I got my license, I could come here whenever I wanted, as long as I could scrounge up gas money . . . easier than it is for a kid today."

"Must have been nice—the whole family. We used to go the Vineyard, or Mom and I did. Dad would come up once or twice, but mostly it was just the two of us. She would work in the garden and I was supposed to make friends. I tried, but I wasn't very good at it, and the next summer I'd have to start all over again. Mom wanted me to keep the house, but Oak Bluffs wasn't a place where I had great memories—not like you, here."

"I'm not sure spending a summer fighting with my sisters qualifies as great, but I guess we managed to have fun." Jazz took off his glasses, slipped them in his breast pocket. "These days, my mood is mostly what brings me here . . . mostly around this time. Sometimes I only want to think. Not about anything special, but to sit here and let my mind wander, let it float away from me. Let some things go, make room for others to come in, like the tide. Other times I'm working a problem. Stuff is all in a knot, and the more I try to untangle it, the worse it gets. But the water loosens it all up. And sometimes I just need to look at the sky . . . see with my own eyes the end of one day and the start of the next. To know that everything changes. It all passes." He sat back again, clasped his hands behind his head. "But there are constants too. A new day always dawns, a new chance to do what you didn't, fix what you broke, look for what you lost, go where you haven't been, even if it's just inside yourself." Jazz looked at her. "Okay. Philosophy lecture over. I thought you might enjoy a change of perspective."

Avery peered at the clouds as they took shape on the horizon. "It's so peaceful. Beautiful." She watched as the sun and the sea met at the starting line.

"Cold?" Jazz didn't wait for her to answer, tucked the blanket more snugly around her, then let his arm rest on her shoulders.

"Thanks." Avery allowed herself to relax her head against him.

"You're welcome."

Gulls squawked and the surf splashed against the shore.

It had been such an A-to-Z day. The good, the bad, and the unthinkable. Avery felt as though she'd been sucker punched, won the race, and been short-sheeted all since the last sunrise. The disparate pieces of her life, the ones she'd so valiantly kept isolated from each other and walled off from herself, had been drifting together ever since she arrived in New York—home. Maybe before that, at a glacial pace she never noticed. But now they were colliding—like atoms smashing, like galaxies clashing in a huge, hot cosmic mash-up. And what kind of havoc would that create?

For nearly an hour they sat like that—still and silent, while night passed, the sky brightened. When the sun popped out of the ocean, it was nine minutes to six.

"That was *spectacular*." Avery said it breathlessly, the way she felt. It was a fresh, unwritten day, and she was there to welcome it.

"Still game?" Jazz had a hint of mischief in his question and his tone.

You like the flow. Go with it. "Yep." It was "What difference does it make?" on the flip tip.

On the ride to wherever, Avery stayed awake. Jazz found

a radio station that played old R&B. He told stories and pointed out places along the way that were the backdrop of his life, and she liked what she was seeing.

The sun followed them west, and by the time they turned onto a narrow road that snaked through an open field, the day was bright and clear. “Nobody from New York thinks there are real farms in Jersey. I actually heard once that King grew up on a farm . . . haven’t been able to confirm it.” The land on either side of the narrow strip of asphalt had been plowed, but the new crop hadn’t been planted.

Jazz turned into a driveway and stopped the car at the top of the hill. He parked in the gravel turn-around in front of a clapboard-and-stone colonial surrounded by evergreens, oaks, and maples. An apron of lawn sloped to a fieldstone wall at the road. Avery could see about a dozen windows, flanked by black shutters, and a slate pathway led to the front door in one direction and around the side of the house in the other. It was lovely, picturesque, and Avery was sure the people who lived there were equally pleasant. But she’d been up all night and wasn’t exactly in the head to meet Jazz’s old fishing buddy or whoever lived here. But she’d said she was game, so she would be. “I hope we haven’t come visiting too early.” It wasn’t seven o’clock yet. “But I will welcome a bathroom.”

“There are three of those, and a powder room. And as for our timing—believe me, it couldn’t be better.” Instead of ringing the bell, he put a key in the brass lock. Avery looked skeptical. “Okay. It’s mine.” She followed him inside. “Down that hall, first door on your right.” He pointed. “I’ll tell you about it when you’re—refreshed.” She headed down the hall. “When you come out, turn left—you’ll find me. And you’re welcome to look around, not that there’s much to see.”

When she finished, she poked her head into a few rooms

on the first floor, but other than an L-shaped, brown leather sofa and bookcase-size flat-screen TV in what she presumed was the living room, the place was pretty empty. Eventually she worked her way to the kitchen, where she found Jazz, jacket off, sleeves rolled, stainless-steel fridge wide-open. "I'm guessing there's another story here."

"Stories are my business." He took out a carton of eggs. "I'm thinking it's time for another meal. Anything you don't eat?"

"I don't care for food that's still moving. I've had to politely decline a lively delicacy or two on occasion. But other than that, you're good." Avery leaned against the granite-topped island. "So the house? I thought you lived in SoHo?"

"I do. This was my folks' place . . . grew up here." He took a package wrapped in white butcher paper from the freezer. "I told you my mom passed last year." He grabbed a mixing bowl from the cabinet. "My sisters are all married. They have houses and none of them were interested in this one. We tried to sell, then the bottom fell out of the housing market. I took it as a sign I should keep it."

"It's a great house, but didn't you grow up with—furniture?" Avery laughed. "Just asking!"

"Yeah. And what was here had been here for as long as I remember. I decided that if it was going to be my house, I had to make it look like me. I told the girls to come get what they wanted 'cause I was ditching the rest. Cheryl, the one who doesn't speak to me, gave the others a list." He continued to gather ingredients. "They took dishes, photos, their old bedroom furniture, stuff like that. Then I had a garage sale."

"Just got rid of it all?"

"I kept a few things, but mostly, yeah. Not that I didn't have a lot of good memories here, but I'll remember. My sisters will remember. That's enough. No mementos required."

"What did your folks do?" Avery took an orchestra seat at the island. She thought about helping. Decided she'd rather watch.

"My dad was a dean at Rutgers and he wrote a couple of textbooks—labor relations—nothing you might have stumbled across when you were looking for an airplane read. But they were well respected and sold well enough—still do as a matter of fact. And my mom was an RN. By the time I came along, she had stopped doing clinical and started a staffing agency." He put the package from the freezer in the microwave.

"You lived here your whole life? It's way different from SoHo, or Harlem."

Jazz tossed a dish towel over his shoulder. "That it is. And I love the city. But sometimes I need a break from the in-your-face pace. My neighborhood is only quiet between two and three a.m. on the third Sunday of months that contain an *r*. When I was a kid, I used to whine that nothing ever happened, but now that's what I love about it." He scooped flour from a big apothecary jar into the bowl. "And I have a real kitchen, 'cause I really do cook. It's the only room I've completed." It was a modern kitchen—black walls, what you could see of them, white cabinetry, checkerboard floor, with state-of-the-art stainless appliances. Cabinet doors and drawers opened and closed with the slightest touch. The microwave beeped and he removed the package. "Bacon. I don't eat it often, but when I do, I want the real thing. Turkey is for Thanksgiving."

"Swine is fine by me." Avery laughed. "So between your two places you've got the best of both worlds."

"Works for me. I'm here mostly on weekends, but my schedule is flexible so I'm just as likely to drive out on a Wednesday. And as long as I have E-ZPass, they let me cross the border freely."

Avery watched him measure ingredients and add them to the bowl. "I would offer to help, but I'm pretty awful in the kitchen."

"Fortunately, I'm not." Jazz took two steps down the island, leaned over, and kissed Avery. It was quick, but it was also full on the lips. "Needed to get that off my mind. Hope it was okay—and if it wasn't, I promise it won't happen again. But thinking about it was getting in the way of pancake making. I needed to take care of it so we can eat." With one hand, he cracked two eggs into a small bowl.

Avery tried to make her lips stop tingling so they could form words. "Um, nice." She hoped she was smiling, but it might have been a grimace for all she knew.

"Nice? Not exactly a rave." Jazz turned on the burner under the skillet.

"You could do it again and maybe I'll come up with a better word." *Why did I say that?* She didn't want him to think she was one of the offer-anything, do-anything babes he talked about, because she wasn't offering. *Am I?* "My mom always said there was the right word and the easy word. 'Don't be lazy, Avery.' " *Why am I babbling?* "So I guess I was being lazy and—"

Jazz cut her off with another kiss. This time there was no mistaking his intention. He held her tight and she let herself sink into him, into his mouth, into his taste. His hands massaged her back, slid down to her waist, where his fingers lingered at the place where her skirt and sweater met, slipped between them long enough to touch her skin, light enough to make her wonder if he really had or if she'd only imagined it. Then his hands worked their way up again, finally cupping her face, letting his tongue slow dance with hers.

Her arms tightened around him, her breath getting shorter. He slowly pulled back, tugged gently on her bottom lip, and left her. Wanting—

—more than she had wanted in a long, long time. Avery struggled to catch her breath and ground herself again. She cleared her throat. "That was outstanding." The memory of the nice kiss had already been supplanted by the naughty one.

"Good." Jazz peeled off strips of thick-cut slab bacon, arranged them in the hot pan. "How are you at making coffee?"

"Primo." Avery needed a task she could handle, since she wasn't sure how well she was handling herself.

"It's over there." He pointed to the electric drip. "Beans and the grinder are up in the cabinet."

She whirred; he sizzled, mixed, poured, flipped. In short order, they were sitting catty-corner at the island, polishing off a feast that beat diner fare, hands down.

"Those may be the best pancakes I ever had." Which may have been true, or maybe not. But Avery was sure that was enough. She knew she wouldn't be challenged to compare them to seventeen other pancake experiences, then deliver a more rational, considered opinion the way she would have been with Van. The pancakes were great. Period.

Jazz made a ceremonial demi-bow. "Thank you." Then he started clearing the counter. "I know this isn't going to sound right no matter how I put it, so here goes."

Avery braced for the weirdness.

"I really need a little sleep before I take you back. Just a couple of hours and I'll be fine." He put their coffee mugs and silverware in the dishwasher. "And this is not a lame ploy to get you in bed. Up all night used to happen pretty regularly. I'd work all day and write until daylight. But I'm afraid those days are history."

"Not a problem. I had a nap and I'm sleepy too." She handed him the rest of the breakfast dishes.

"I'm going to sack out on the sofa. There's one room upstairs with a bed . . . feel free. Or you can stay down here. It's a very big sofa. Sleep, turn on the TV, there are plenty of books and magazines. Whatever you want to do."

"I can manage that." They finished loading the dishwasher together. Avery felt comfortable, regular, not awkward like a stranger.

He lifted the seat of the ottoman and pulled out a huge scarlet-and-white, crocheted afghan. "One of the things I kept." He grabbed the remote, turned on the TV low. "School colors—Cheryl made this for me the year I started Rutgers."

They chatted a few minutes about the garden he was planting. His folks hadn't been into growing anything but grass and their kids. Then he drifted off. Avery flipped through a few pages of a foodie magazine, tried to focus on the television, but couldn't get into the migration patterns of wildebeests. So she slipped in next to Jazz, under the cover made by his sister who didn't speak to him, and fell asleep thinking this going-with-the-flow thing wasn't so bad.

FIFTEEN

His world was at his feet

"Dwight, the market is soft all over Manhattan, but particularly uptown." The room was wood-paneled, with shelves of thick legal tomes, just like a movie-set law office. "To be frank, Harlem was getting the spillover. Buyers priced out of the Upper West Side, TriBeCa—"

"You don't think I know that?" Dwight barked at his attorney. "Don't give me a real estate tutorial, Stan." When Dwight had started assembling the pieces for Dixon Plaza, all lights were green and you could flip an apartment in the city in six months and make a serious profit.

"So you know I'm right when I'm telling you there's a surplus of luxury condos in the Harlem market." Stanley Spielvogel was tall, with a small voice that tended to make him sound hesitant, but what he lacked in volume he made up for in persistence. "Valuations have dropped. The offer you have on the table for 111th Street is already thirty percent above current market value. Easy. From a fiscal standpoint, it doesn't make sense to up the—"

"I don't care. All right? She's family." Which sounded better to him than whining about Avery having him at checkmate without that building. He hadn't even told his father about the recent developments. It was King Jr. who was on the ropes, and he wasn't going down without a fight. Whether the numbers made sense in the short run, or he had to look longer term, Dwight could not walk away from the chance to make his mark on the Manhattan skyline.

The last forty-eight hours may as well have been 120 days, or the rest of his life. That's what was on the line. Until she'd barged into his office, Dwight had really almost forgotten the connection between his cousin and the long-term councilman. It was ancient history. At this point they had each become somebody else.

Dwight had gone from spineless frat boy to high-level wheeler-dealer with financing from foreign countries to back his maneuvers. He had passed through the public-service sector, long enough to make connections, learn that's not where the money is made, be voted out of office. And to learn how to apply campaign funds where they would do the most good.

After Trey flunked out of Harvard Law, he spent time as a club bouncer and a construction worker. That's when Chester III emerged, ambitious, connected, and determined to use the family name to his advantage wherever and whenever possible. He graduated from a less prestigious though well-respected law school and embarked on a career in doing "the people's business." Chester III married an earnest and righteous helpmate who fit the image he needed to project and set about his reinvention. He worked tirelessly for the community, including waging a successful campaign for Dwight's old Council seat, with Dixon support. Dwight found it hard to swallow his transformation into a solid citizen, but Trey still owed him, so Dwight decided, rightly so, that Trey could be useful.

Dwight wasn't sure whom Avery had become, other than middle-aged and angry. He didn't know what it would take to make her go away, but the only thing he had to throw at the problem was money.

Don't let that little girl fuck up all I've done.

He rarely found inspiration in King's words, but it had become Dwight's rallying cry.

"I can move forward with your new offer, but I have to advise you—"

"Of course you do. I'm not holding you responsible. This is my decision. And I need you to act with all deliberate speed."

Because Dwight truly had no time to kill.

"And you're not going to want to hear this." Stan leaned back in his ergonomically correct desk chair, the only modern touch in the traditional decor. He took off his glasses, cleaned them with the tail of his tie. "You might want to consider the wisdom of acquiring 111th Street at all and scaling back the scope—"

"Out of the question." Dwight wasn't willing to shrink the project. Grace had already told him that wasn't an option she was willing to consider.

Dwight cleared out, headed back to his office, trying to only sweat the big stuff, but still worried about that nagging little story on the low-level vice bust. That's how he thought of it. He had to or his head would explode. Besides, he never used his real name. Or a credit card like some idiots. It was still a small story in the New York tabloids, probably wouldn't even have made the headlines except it was lewd and crude and titillating. "Call Me Madam" was the latest headline. Five apartments in the West Nineteenth Street building had been raided. One was the office, the others were described as "dungeons of love."

Even in the Dixon offices there were jokes around the coffeemaker. Madeline was too through. "I wish somebody *would* pay me to put a hurtin' on them. I'd be good at it." The more his employees laughed, the more Dwight pulled back, retreated to his office. They didn't understand. They couldn't. And no one needed to know his secret. But he had plenty to concentrate on. Like what he could offer besides money to encourage Avery to change her mind and sell the building.

But in the meantime, Dwight decided Dixon Plaza needed to look like it was moving forward, making progress. For him that meant the site needed to come alive. It had been dormant, an eyesore, a punch line, for years.

Dwight would go by his site, sometimes at daybreak, when the block was quiet and the birds chattered, and he'd look up at the rendering standing tall above the sidewalk shed. Grace might have been about the deal, the math, the hard-and-fast numbers, but what Dwight appreciated about her father was the showmanship. On the nineteenth hole of their golf outing, Vance Kidder, who sipped a soda, heavy on the Coke syrup, a scoop of chocolate ice cream, extra cherries, and two straws, leaned in and told him, "Whatever it costs, make it fun. Make them believe the good time starts when you walk through the doors . . . before there are doors. People already have a place to live. Give them entertainment. Give them enchantment. Make them buy your dream. And your dream becomes theirs."

And right now, dreaming was better than what Dwight had to walk around in.

Mitch was the first step. Dwight needed to get him moving again. "Listen, I'm ready to get back to work. How soon can we get up to speed on the demo of building two." Dwight felt the excitement of his plans as he spoke.

"I'll need to schedule a crew, notify the Department of Buildings of a start date."

"Excellent." At least something was working smoothly.

"I'll get somebody on it today."

"Let me know as soon as you have a date. We're going to create a little excitement."

Dwight wanted to make the teardown a happening. It couldn't have the drama of a dynamite collapse, like those old Vegas casinos in the middle of the desert. This was Manhattan. They had to preserve the building next door. But it had to be an event. There hadn't been a clear-cut Dixon celebration in such a long time. It would make him feel good. He really needed to feel good.

Next, Dwight was on the phone with his PR firm, percolating about the event they would plan around resuming demolition.

"We could have a band, like from a high school in the area. Do they still have those? And we could hand out hot dogs, like it's a picnic."

Dwight spent the rest of the afternoon calling the designers, suppliers, members of the Dixon Plaza team, whipping up their enthusiasm. And his own. He'd let battle fatigue set in. Let the accident, the funeral, bring him down. It was sad, no question. But he'd been running in place. It was time to move forward. To make this project work he had to get out in front and lead and stay far enough ahead not to get trampled. Cobb Rowan was not available—typical. Dwight decided it would be best to talk to the architect on a full night's sleep.

But it didn't help.

The good news for the day: Mistress-gate was not mentioned in the papers.

The first whiff of smoke that morning came from a reporter, calling to verify that Rowan and The Dixon Group had parted ways over creative differences. Dwight was stupefied. The reporter offered to fax the press release, but before it arrived, a messenger showed up with a letter from the architect. Dwight ripped it open, and as he read, the words started melting on the page. "It has become painfully apparent to me that we no longer share the guiding vision for the Dixon Plaza project. I once believed that jointly we would conceive and give rise to a complex that would soar. Sadly, it seems The Dixon Group aim is far more pedestrian." Dwight could hear Cobb's annoying sneer as he read. "Therefore, it is with sadness and regret that I tender my resignation from this endeavor."

Dwight balled up the page and bounced it off the wall. In less than a hundred pretentious words he had been dismissed. And Dwight was on fire. "Get him on the line."

But Rowan would not be got. His office said he was unavailable.

"The son of a bitch has been available for the last five years. He's been available to bill me." Dwight smoldered through the office. "He can't do this."

Except after Dwight spoke to Stan, it seemed that he could, that his contract came with clauses that specifically allowed for his resignation over creative differences. The Dixon Group had been fired with no warning or recourse.

Dwight was sure he knew the arsonist. "Did you put Rowan up to this?" He barked into the phone.

After a prolonged interval of dead air, Grace hung up.

Dwight was still ranting when she called him back.

"You won't believe this. Someone sounding a lot like you just called my office" Grace paused for effect. "And this person had the colossal gall to accuse me basically of sabotage."

Dwight seethed as he listened.

"I hung up on him, because I knew you would never be so stupid as to threaten me."

"You are trying to undermine—"

"If that's what I wanted, how hard would I have to try? Really."

Dwight's head was in the vise and she turned the screws.

"I'm going now. Sounds like you've got a lot on your plate."

When Madeline buzzed to tell him Baily, their publicist, was waiting on the line, Dwight was still squeezing the receiver.

Then it became all about controlling the spin.

For the rest of the day Dwight ranted, called Rowan egotistical, arrogant, self-serving and all of the unholy names he could think of, but was advised it would not be to The Dixon Group's advantage to start a spitting contest over this in the press since Rowan would be working with Kidder and they had more spit. Bailey's press release spoke about the challenging collaboration and the need for The Dixon Group to explore other options. Like it had been their idea all along. Like they'd shaken hands and wished each other Godspeed.

Before Dwight did anything else, he phoned Mitch. Get somebody to CPN to paint over the rendering. "I want the damn thing obliterated. Today if possible."

Mitch hadn't heard about Rowan's defection, so Dwight filled him in.

"Are we putting the demo on hold?"

As mad as Dwight was, he could have gone over there with a sledgehammer and given them a good head start. "No. We're moving forward." Dwight was not going to let Cobb or Grace or Avery stop him from seeing this through to the end.

The rest of the day Dwight spent pacing, yakking into the speakerphone, painting a bright new picture. Usually if he told the same story ad infinitum, he would start to believe it. But with each retelling it got harder to repeat Cobb's name in a civil tone, to call him a unique talent, and to say the split was amicable, as if anything called that ever is.

Christmas on four, Madeline's voice came over the intercom.

Dwight had been expecting it. Deep breath. "Jasper Christmas, I'm sure you know we've been going through some changes around here, but ultimately it is for the good of all involved."

The interview went surprisingly well. Christmas verified the whos and whats of the day's developments, wanted to know if The Dixon Group had another architect waiting in the wings.

"There are several who impressed me during the initial search. I'm sure we will be revisiting them. We are looking to move forward with this in a timely fashion. The demolition site is like a missing tooth in the smile of the park."

"Do you see changes in the direction of the project, based on the fluctuating economic landscape?"

This is too easy. Dwight was glad for questions he could field without going through contortions. "We remain committed to bringing a level of modern residential and retail elegance to this very special setting."

"You were granted Council approval based on your pledge to add an additional four thousand square feet of public space to the project, is that correct?"

Dwight wasn't thrilled with this new line of questioning. "Yes. We are eager to encourage an open exchange between the citizens of New York and the residents of Dixon Plaza." Dwight knew that was bull. The people paying high six figures and up would want a mammoth wall and armed guards surrounding their little slice of Manhattan tranquillity, but that was the game he was required to play. The new architect would make it look good on paper, and building security would take care of the rest.

"And will this additional space come from the existing footprint, or from an additional acquisition?"

Dwight paused to consider his choice of words. "We are

currently in negotiations with a seller. I'd like to leave it at that."

"Last question. One of the properties adjacent to your 110th Street holdings was deeded to your late aunt, Forestina Braithwaite. Would this be the building you're referring to?"

There was no good answer and Dwight knew it. He'd told Grace he had already bought the lot. After last week's blowup, if Avery read anything about negotiations for the building, he had no idea what she'd do.

Before Dwight could answer, Jasper added, "In the interest of full disclosure, I had dinner with Mrs. Braithwaite's daughter, Avery, last week. It was strictly social and off-the-record."

Dwight accidentally bit his tongue. "Mr. Christmas, I won't have you using my family to gain confidential access to sensitive family affairs."

"Mr. Dixon, you can rest assured we didn't talk about your family's property or business affairs, but am I to understand that the deal you're working on concerns the 111th Street apartment building formerly owned by your aunt?"

"We're done here, Mr. Christmas." There were 8 million people in New York, and those were only the officially counted ones. Dwight felt as if the ones he knew kept colliding in ways that felt about as inviting as a noose.

Madeline came on the intercom as soon as Dwight hung up. "King is here, Mr. Dixon."

Shit, piss, and corruption. Nothing like his father to add thunder and lightning to a deluge. He'd been feeling well enough for outings in his contraption, so by the time Dwight stood up, King had wheeled himself in the door, sporting a red warm-up suit with black stripes.

"What kind of asinine—"

"He quit. End of story. I'm taking care of it." For a moment Dwight wasn't sure King would stop his buggy before he ran it into the desk.

"If you took care of it, you'd still have an architect."

"If that's what you came here to tell me, you can go home." Dwight sank back in his seat.

"This thing is coming apart at the seams, Junior—like a cheap suit. You standing there zipping up your fly, but your whole ass is hanging out."

"I can do this. All right!" Dwight pounded his fist on the desk and his phone jumped. "I got slapped in the face with this Rowan business as soon as I came in, but I got people on it and I handled it. I got Mitch getting ready to demo the other building—"

"And you don't have plans or anybody to draw 'em. And do you have 111th Street?"

It seemed to be the question of the day. "We're negotiating."

"Then you ain't got doodley-squat and you're about to knock down the one building you got left and do what? Make it a football field? How 'bout a dog run?" King squeezed the throttle of his chair like maybe it was Dwight's neck.

"Get off my case, old man!" Dwight felt backed into a barbed-wire corner. I got us this far. I'll get us to the finish line.

King looked over at Dwight a moment. Then he shook his head. "If I had the chances you did—"

"I'm sick of you beating me with that." Dwight's growl came from an ancient place. "I don't need it. So if that's all you're offering . . . keep it." You could hear Dwight panting in the silence. As if he were about to spring.

King twisted his lips, somewhere between a smirk and a pout. "Blugh!" He grunted, then bowed from the waist up, turned on his big wheels, and left without another word.

By the time Dwight emerged from his office, most of the

staff had gone and he was drained. He stepped into the reception area, and there it was, the Dixon Plaza model, floating on its high-class Plexiglas pedestal, all spectacle and promise. It made him furious.

And the fury propelled him to send it crashing down. The pieces sounded hollow as they skittered across the floor, landed on top of his shoes. His world was at his feet.

But Dwight had survived the day. It was almost a relief to go home, where Renee chattered about the mundane dailiness of their lives. She hadn't heard about Cobb Rowan, which meant the whole city didn't have an opinion about it, or him, yet. He'd tell her tomorrow. Dominique played him "The Jellyroll Rag." It was too slow, and steady, not bouncy. But she'd just learned it.

His shower was blistering—he had so much pent up, and no valve to release it. So he dabbled at sex—routine, lips, breasts, pubis. Not even completely out of his underwear and done by the eleven-o'clock news.

At six minutes after the hour Renee lay with her head in the crook of his arm, absentmindedly tracing circles on his chest with her finger, as video of the five women, now collectively know as the Chelsea Mistresses, came on the screen. It was like all of the blood in Dwight's body had been boiled and raced through his veins. He couldn't speak, couldn't move or react to the horror of seeing Debbie Patton, aka Delilah, wearing sneakers and heather gray sweats, the hood pulled up to hide her face, but he knew the hair. She ducked into a waiting Jeep with no comment. The report said client lists were found on the computer that was seized.

They'd found chains, riding crops, leather masks. Renee turned over, backed her butt into his hip, snuggled into her pillow. "What kind of people go to women like that?"

SIXTEEN

It's difficult to write out in words
what has been written on your heart

"I don't care what he's offering now. I don't want to sell." Avery paced between her father's study and the sunroom. "I know you think I should take it. . . . Yes, it's a substantial increase. How much more money do I need?" She plopped down in her dad's wooden swivel chair. "All right, that wasn't a good question, but you know what I mean." Avery scanned the ledgers on the shelf above the desk. "You don't have to give him a reason. Just say I changed my mind. And I understand The Dixon Group won't stay on as property management. Which is fine with me." She removed the four books labeled 111TH STREET. "All I can say is my reasons are personal." Avery opened a ledger at random. "Thanks, Walker. I know this is a pain." She returned the phone to its cradle.

Avery knew Dwight would go ballistic, but he had to be

expecting it, didn't he? *Or did he think if he gave me a few days, I'd cool down, see the dollar signs, and let him and his buddy work their show?* She spent a lot of time considering if her decision was stopping progress. If she alone would singlehandedly halt growth and commerce in Harlem. So she had looked up all she could find online about Dixon Plaza and discovered Jazz wasn't the only reporter writing on the subject. Maybe he was the most passionate, but he was not alone in his interest. The truth was, change was coming, had been for years. It was inevitable and unstoppable, and if Dwight had gotten this far without the 111th Street property, he'd find another way to make Dixon Plaza happen, since it looked as if that's what he'd been doing. No, her angry fire wasn't raging anymore, but she wasn't going to give him what he wanted just because he said he had to have it. For a change, Avery would do what suited her.

Alicia had been apoplectic when Avery told her about Dwight and "Chester." "I'll get the next plane and come and kick his ass right now if you want me to. Hey! I have a better idea. You make a lot of interesting connections out here. I know people who *know* people who could take care of them—if you get my drift. Hell, I know people who *are* the people." Avery decided Alicia was only half-kidding and convinced her she would handle the situation—no mysterious disappearances or broken kneecaps required. Although, the image of Dwight whimpering while someone threatened to take away his bow ties and lock him in a room full of pigeons tickled her. *Would serve him right.* Alicia was due back tomorrow, and Avery was sure she'd have much more to say on the subject of Dwight.

But the person Avery wanted to talk to was Jazz. Although she hadn't seen him since their whirlwind dinner till dawn and beyond, they had spoken on the phone several times. Despite how she felt about Dwight, when she talked to Jazz, Avery found herself straddling the line between what was personal and his profession. It wasn't that she didn't believe he would honor the off-the-record agreement, because she was certain he would. He had shared a lot about himself, and she knew she hadn't been quite as forthcoming, but Avery just wasn't sure she was ready to be that open, with anyone. Although when she least expected it, their kitchen kiss would sneak up, flash through her mind—and her body—leaving her wanting a repeat at the least, and wondering what more would be like. She hardly knew Jasper Christmas, but she did find herself hoping it was him every time the phone rang. Then she told herself she was being silly. That she didn't miss him. How could she?

Avery flipped through the ledger. Her father's hand was so neat, so precise. Written in the small spaces between lines, the words looked almost as if they had been typeset. As she scanned a page, a star next to one entry caught her eye. *3C—Watkins, Boyd and Elizabeth, 4 children—husband/cancer, 3 months rent forgiven—charge back personal.* Then she saw *5K—Johnson, Janice, 2 children, new baby/crib—charge back personal.* She found several entries in each of the books where her father had given tenants a break, bought them groceries, given them flu shots or a physical, had their phone turned back on. This had all been either charged back to his draw or paid directly out of his own pocket. *Dad?* She knew her parents made donations to lots of charitable causes and organizations. But to discover that her father had given things to people just because they needed it and he had it to give, knocked the wind out of Avery. She sank back in the chair, holding the ledger and thinking about her father, the man she didn't know. *Wonder if Mom knew?*

It had been raining when she got up, so Avery hadn't taken her morning constitutional, but once the drops stopped, she felt the urge to go by "her" building. She replaced the books, went downstairs, put on her sneakers, grabbed her windbreaker, her cell phone—her mother's had officially been retired—and headed out the door.

A half hour later, she stopped by the lamppost across the street from her property, pretended to stretch her hamstrings. But this time watching felt different.

She had seen the tenants before, coming and going about their business. Who they were and what their lives were like day-to-day had only been idle speculation—like watching a movie with the sound off. You guess what's going on, but you're probably going to miss important details. After finding her father's notes, the tenants had became more than anonymous occupants she guessed about. They were people with families and lives to manage. Of course she knew the people Doc B had helped were long gone—at least most of them, but they had been replaced by others, most of whom worked hard, tried to do the right thing, and from time to time ran into the same kinds of problems everybody does—the kind where you need help or at the very least understanding. Even though the one time in her life she'd needed help and understanding, she didn't get it from the place she expected, Avery still knew she was in the lucky percentile. *Maybe some people can only do what they can do—give what they can. It might not be what you need, but it's all they've got.* She walked to the corner, bought a bottle of water from the deli, headed back in the direction of the building.

Avery slowed her pace, watched a young man come down the block, suit coat draped over his shoulder, hooked on his thumb. He stop to chat with three boys who looked to be between ten and twelve. They sat on the stoop of the building next door to hers, passing a basketball among them. After a few minutes of lively conversation, tie guy snatched the ball, dribbled twice, set it spinning on his index finger, and shot it back to them. They exchanged high fives. "Later," he called as he took out his key, walked up the three steps, and entered Avery's building.

On the way home, Avery ran into the senior couple she had seen coming out of the building before, arm in arm like the last time. The mister smiled, nodded. Avery wondered how long his hair had been white. They could have been the grandparents she never knew. "Afternoon," the missus said, and smiled.

"Afternoon." *Where would they go? Do they know they were going to lose their home?* "See you soon." She didn't know what that meant exactly. *Maybe I'll have a tenants' meeting before I go back to Wellington. Introduce the new management company.* It wasn't just stubborn spite that kept her from selling. This decision had to be *for* something, not just against Dwight. That felt more right.

Before she got to the corner, she felt the phone vibrate, took it out of her pocket, hoping. She'd only given her new number to her job, Van of course, Alicia, Walker, and—Jazz. She smiled when she saw the LED.

Within minutes she was on the phone with Alicia. "Are you coming back soon? I need your help."

➢ ➢ ➢

"I was looking for not too fancy, but definitely dressy." Avery stood in the dressing room in her bra and panties, surrounded by the next round of contenders. After Jazz's call, Avery went into panic mode. Yes, she would love to go to the National Journalists' Dinner with him. *What am I going to wear?* was screeching in her head. Fortunately Alicia was coming in on the red-eye. Avery knew she'd be more than happy to help remedy Avery's paucity of proper party attire. "He said it's black tie, which means that—"

"Trust me. I got it, Av." Alicia scanned the dressing room.

"I'm just saying that because you used to shop here doesn't mean it's the only place. How many black dresses did you pick out?" Alicia had gotten off the plane, dumped her bags with her doorman, and met Avery at the store. She called from the cab, the street, and the elevator, warning Avery not to buy anything until she arrived.

"I thought a little black dress was always a fashion 'do.' " They were a staple of Avery's work-formal wardrobe.

"Maybe for somebody else. Maybe even for you, another time. But all I've seen on you since you got here is 'color me drab.' And I'm betting Paperboy would like a little pizzazz." Alicia rifled through the dress selection Avery had gathered. "Whoa, a blue one. Try this." She handed Avery a royal blue silk.

"You're going to have to remember not to call him that when you meet him. *If* you meet him. I mean, we're not—never mind." Avery unzipped the sheath.

"Now tell me again why he asked you at the last minute?"

"He wasn't planning to go, passes every year. But he said he thought he might enjoy it if I went with him." Avery pulled the dress over her head to cover her grin.

"Uh-huh. And what's the rest of his last-minute sob story?"

"It's not a sob story." Avery poked her arms through the sleeves.

"Right. And this event is in Philadelphia? Is there a hotel involved?"

"It's at a hotel, Alicia. And he booked two rooms. So there." Avery turned around.

"You look like Margaret Thatcher. Next." Alicia waved Avery on. "Two rooms? Is that a good thing? Do you like him? Do *you* want two rooms?"

Avery looked at herself in the three-way. *Doesn't look that bad. It would be perfect for an embassy dinner . . . never mind*—which she guessed was exactly the reason Alicia gave it thumbs-down. "I'm not answering that."

"So you *are* interested in doing the do!"

"Not necessarily. It just means I'm not going to answer you." Avery held up a rose-patterned floral. "This is so unlike me, I thought I'd try it."

"Save the no-comment routine for Paperboy. Taking the Fifth is a dead giveaway, meaning 'I like him but I want to make sure he likes me back.' "

"Is not!"

"Is, is is!" Alicia did her happy dance.

"You're worse than when we were in high school. Besides . . ." Avery couldn't hide the smile anymore. "He already said he likes me."

"Ah! You didn't tell me that! What else are you keeping secret? I know you've already *slept* together." Alicia paused, winked, then picked up where she'd left off. "And if all you *really* did was sleep, then seems to me the next step is just a technicality." Avery had given her the Cliff's Notes version of her unexpected dinner and Jersey excursion with Jazz. Alicia probed for more details, but Avery assured her there were none.

"*Sleep* is all we did. Why did I even tell you that?" Avery zipped up the dress, looked at herself in the mirror. "Don't say it."

"What? That you look like grandma's sofa cushion?" Alicia unzipped her. "Take it off and let's get out of here."

They breezed through Bendel's, where Alicia scored two shirts and some grapefruit bath gel. Avery got a pair of sunglasses Alicia insisted she have, then they moved on. "I've never even been in Barneys," Avery protested when they approached the corner.

"Then it's about time. I still have a place in my heart for Seventeenth Street, but this will do fine." Alicia sailed past the doorman, Avery trailing behind her. "Come on, time's a-wasting. What about your hair? It's so middle-of-the-road, middle-aged . . ."

"I was thinking of shaving it off."

"That would show off your eyes."

"It'll be fine."

"Fine is a texture. But one thing at a time, Av." Alicia pushed the elevator button. "We'll start on five and work our way down."

Avery had to admit she was more than a little giddy. *When was the last time shopping made me feel happy?* "You didn't say this was a marathon. I just want a pretty dress." She had more than her share of dress-up occasions, but she was always on duty—appropriate was preferable to outstanding. Once in a while she *brought* a date—an escort really. She had not *been* the date. There was nothing official for her about tomorrow. All she had to do was show up, try to look nice, and have fun. The trip was only overnight. He was coming from Miami, where he was on a story. She would meet him at the hotel. The dinner might even be painfully boring. So often they were, but she felt like a schoolgirl getting ready for the prom. They would take the train back to New York the next day.

Alicia hijacked a sales associate, flashed her Black Card, asked the confounded young woman to ready a dressing room. They wanted the personal-shopping experience, sans the shopper—Alicia had that part covered. The clerk, dressed in a tight black dress with short, puffy sleeves, pushed her chartreuse eyeglasses back up her long nose, introduced herself as Leah, then followed dutifully as Alicia cut a swath through the store like a woman on a mission, because she was. Avery mostly stayed out of the way and let her friend rummage through the racks. Alicia held up outfits, felt fabric, collecting, dismissing, oohing, groaning, grinning, and handing over her bounty to Leah, who would periodically disappear, unload her cargo, and return for the next phase of shop till you drop.

In ninety minutes they covered four floors, seven departments, including shoes, and were ensconced in a dressing room the size of many Manhattan studio apartments. Alicia dismissed Leah—told her she'd buzz if they needed her. Six dresses in, Alicia said, "That's it. You don't have to try on another thing!"

Alicia was so decisive Avery was almost hesitant to look. The dress was definitely not one she would have selected if you'd given her all day. It was lemon yellow and strapless, a color she had retired and a style she had never considered. "I can't wear this. I look like Big Bird."

"Don't be ridiculous. It's a much richer color than Big Bird!" Alicia cracked up. "I was going to suggest a boa, but seeing your antifeather stance, I'll let it go." She saw Avery's panicked look. "Kidding. But the dress is flawless. And sooooo you! A you, you left stranded by the side of the road, but . . ."

"I don't have a strapless bra."

"We're in a store, Av. It'll give Leah something to do."

"It's so—yellow."

"Yeah, and? Not everyone can wear that color, but with your skin . . ."

"But it's so . . . I don't know . . . 'look at me.' I don't need that. What's wrong with this one?" Avery held up a mauve jersey dress with illusion sleeves.

"Bo-ring. Much too matronly for you. My bad. I should never have allowed it in here." Alicia took it from Avery and dropped it in a heap on the floor. "It will fade into the crowd and take you with it. Besides, yellow used to be your favorite color. Is there some rule that diplomats have to be dull? Give yourself a break, girl."

Avery ran her hand past her waist, down the front of the dress. The bodice fit snugly—so well in fact she couldn't tell she wasn't wearing a bra. The skirt flared just above the hipline. The look was deceptively simple—no shimmer, no lace, no sequins, just an elegant silk faille that had body without bulk and let the color do its job. "I don't know." Avery reached under her arm, fishing for the price tag.

"If you look at that tag, I'll . . . I'll call Paperboy and tell him you like him!"

Avery stopped looking and smiled. "You know, I think you would."

"At least you know me that well." Alicia searched the stack of shoe boxes. "It might cost more than you would usually spend, but this is going to be a special evening."

"I don't know. It could be a—"

"Hush." Alicia handed Avery a box. "Put these on." Avery slipped into swirly yellow-and-white peau-de-soie slingbacks with a kitten heel she actually found walkable. "It will be a long night, and I'm guessing there won't be a limo waiting. Not that walking is what you'll be doing afterwards . . ."

"Li!"

"An-y-way, you look smashing. Simple, special, the dress says it all." Alicia put her hands on her hips, stood back to admire her handiwork. "Yep. It works. And this is what you need if you really want to complete the outfit—it might be cool at night. It comes in black too, but I'm not feeling the bumblebee look." She pulled a pearly white, silk satin trench coat from a hanger and draped it around Avery's shoulders. "Uh-huh. I am so good at this." She pulled Avery's hair away from her face. "Just make a low pony—like here, then pin it under, like this. It's not fussy or fancy—clean, uncluttered, sophisticated. No big jewelry either—matter of fact, I've got the perfect earrings for you. Yellow, big-ass diamond studs—second-anniversary gift from sly Guy. I think I've worn them maybe three times. I'm a dangle, not a stud, girl, but he didn't seem to know that." Alicia sounded almost sad. But she recovered quickly. "Let's pay for this stuff so we can go eat. You are going to get the outfit, aren't you? Because if you tell me I spent my whole morning, starving and sleep-deprived, finding a fab-u-lous outfit for your shindig and you are going to ignore my efforts, and my singular taste, I'm going to—"

"I've been threatened enough for one day. I'll buy it. All. Okay?"

Leaving Leah with the packages, they headed for a restaurant to get Alicia fed.

"Let me get this right. You're not selling the building to Dwight out of what—a sudden do-goody benevolence?" Alicia bit into a spinach-and-goat-cheese ravioli.

"Sounds sappy when you put it like that. But I guess that's the gist of it. He can do what he wants with his property. And maybe I'm late here, but I do care about the people they'd put on the street." Avery told Alicia about her father's secret generosity. "Never thought of him as anybody's angel, but that's what it looks like. It's like the way Jazz is with Cheryl, the sister who doesn't speak to him. He just loves her like he always did. And I can tell it would make him happy if she came around, but if she doesn't, he'll keep caring anyway."

"You lost me somewhere in there, but I guess I get it." Alicia wiped her mouth, put down her fork. "Slipping Paperboy into your explanation, huh? Nice touch."

"Would you call him by his name."

"Touchy, aren't we?" Alicia smiled. "On the nitty-gritty side, you're going to handle all of this from the other end of the world?"

"I'll find another management company. People do it all the time." *Don't they?* "Besides"—Avery hesitated, knowing her next statement would draw fire—"I've been thinking about extending my leave."

Alicia kept chewing, let Avery's revelation hang out there a moment, get some air, before she batted it around. "Would that be because of 111th Street or *Jazz*?"

"Neither." Avery saw Alicia eyeing her over the next forkful. "I'll get building reports whether I'm here, Wellington, or

Kathmandu." Avery speared a grape tomato from her salad. "And I had a good time with him last week. I think tomorrow will be lovely too, but no sane person turns her life upside down on the basis of what? Two pleasant evenings? And I am quite sane, thank you."

"Too sane, if you ask me . . . which you didn't. Okay. So why then?"

"Because I'm not sure what good it did, staying away all this time." Avery hadn't admitted that to herself until now. "Maybe I need to slay the dragon right here."

"Just jump right into the middle of what's on the plate, huh? No games, no more eating around the edges and waiting for the magic word?"

"Maybe. But it's not even like I made a decision. I said I was *thinking* about it."

"You keep thinking. You can ask Toni about management companies. And this is a great reason for me to call Ty Washington. I can ask who runs his buildings. I've been wanting to reach out. I knew him through Guy, but I need to work on my own NYC connections."

They finished eating, and Alicia took the check. "I got this. And then I'm in the wind. Got to pick up a new computer." She handed over her credit card. "I left mine at the house—Guy's house. Remembered it the minute I got on the plane. He won't be out of the nursing facility for another week, and I cannot go that long without the Internet." Alicia signed the receipt. "I'm totally addicted to the Sims. I have a boutique there and—"

"The virtual online thing?"

Alicia nodded. "Yep. Tell you about it another time. But I have customers waiting."

"Look, Mom had a laptop. It looks pretty new. You're welcome to it until you can get yours. I've got one, since they haven't made me turn it in. Yet."

"You sure?" Alicia grabbed her shopping bags. She'd added two pairs of shoes she could find no reason to resist.

"It's not exactly an even swap, but I get loaner diamonds, and you get a loaner PC."

"Deal."

When they got back, Avery brought the laptop from the sunroom and put it on the kitchen table, in front of Alicia. "Here's the cord. I didn't see a case, but I can't imagine Mom traveling with it. Of course you could have knocked me over with a Bluetooth ray when I found it in the first place. Turn it on before you go to make sure the thing works."

"Now she tells me." Alicia opened the lid, pushed the button. "By the way, I've got a hookup if you want to get your hair done in Philadelphia. I know I said you could—"

"I've got it covered. Stop. I'll just warn him to remember his sunglasses." Avery sat next to her.

The computer sang its start-up tune and the idyllic tropical desktop came to life. "Looks like your mom had some stuff open. It's asking if you want to save it—maybe you should take a look? I'll use the loo."

Avery slid the computer in front of her. It was a reminder to purchase tickets for something called a Spring Fling—cocktails, dinner, dancing, charity auction, location, date, time. *That would have been this weekend.*

Avery thought about her mother shopping for a new outfit—how much Forestina loved getting dolled up. Yet another thing they didn't share. Looking nice was fine, but Avery didn't get pleasure from the ritual of getting ready. Her mom seemed to enjoy it as much as the event she was preparing for. *But I used to love watching her*—choosing her accessories, humming softly under her breath, usually a tune from an old Broadway musical. *And I did have fun today.*

A wave of sadness washed over Avery as she closed the document. That's when she saw the list of recently opened files. There, lined up one after the other—"Avery-Today," "Avery 2," "Avery"—wondered what they could have been for.

My darling daughter, the first one began. Then went on with typical newsy tidbits.

Next paragraph: *Where to begin? It's difficult to write out in words what has been written on your heart.*

It stopped abruptly. Avery heard the words in her mother's voice. They gave her a chill.

The next one started with a cozier greeting:

> *Hi Honey,*
>
> *Surprise, I got myself a computer! My goodness, the internet is a fascinating place. So much to see and learn! Who knows? I may just get to like this box. But the real reason I bought it was you. I know you tune out half of my silly chatter. I don't mind. But I had a lot of time to myself on the flight home from Paris, and so much I promised myself I was going to say while we were together, except I didn't. It occurred to me when I got home that I should write this down, and that you might hear it better if the letter was typed in sharp, precise letters instead of written in my fussy old Palmer longhand. So please, please don't take this as a criticism of any kind, because it is not. This was just the best way I could think of to give you the distance you seem to need.*

It ended there. *She knew I kept my distance. . . .*

"Are we good to go?" Alicia came in, rubbing lotion on her hands.

"Um, give me a sec. I need to print this."

"You look different. What just changed?"

"I found a letter . . . letters Mom was writing me."

"Then you've got reading to do." Alicia picked up her purse.

"No, but—"

"I was kinda hankering for a red laptop anyway. Red with pink stripes. That would be fierce. They should let me design them."

"I'm sorry. I dragged you out of your way."

"No need. I told you, you never know what you're going to dig up. Now, as for tomorrow, you know you have to call me, text me, before, during, or after you have some Philadelphia Freedom."

"You are so wrong." Avery wrapped her arms around Alicia. They sank into a hug that was interrupted a long time ago, deepened by the lives they'd led in the years since then. She kissed Alicia's cheek. "I'm glad we—"

"Me too. I been missing you, kiddo." Alicia pulled back, looked at Avery a second. "Okay. I'm outta here before we get all sloppy."

Avery went upstairs and hung her outfit on her mother's closet door, set the shoes on the floor beneath it. The color made her smile, like sunshine and daisies. She puttered for a long time before she hopped up in her mother's bed with the laptop, to read what seemed to be the final draft.

Avery Dearest—the first paragraph read the same as the previous letter, but this one continued:

> *I've felt for a long time that something isn't right, hasn't been right between us. Or at least I think it's between us. I once thought it might be your father, but I was sure you would have come to me—if not before he passed, certainly after. He's been gone a long time. But even now, for reasons I don't fully understand, you have not been willing or able to share the source of your unhappiness with me.*

I don't know if it's something I did, or didn't do? Said or didn't say? Did I betray a confidence? Ignore a need? Forget to acknowledge an occasion that was more important to you than I realized? You went away to college one young woman and returned another. And I guess to be more accurate, you never really returned. You stayed "away," Avery. Even from your cousin, Dwight, and neither of you has ever said why.

I have asked myself these questions a million and one times. I have asked you—maybe not as directly as I could have or probed as deeply as I needed to. But you have always been quick to assure me that all is "fine" even when it was evident it was not. There have been times when we tripped over a moment—times when our guards were temporarily off duty and I thought you might open up, but somehow those moments slipped through our hands.

But you are an adult. There are boundaries I have to respect, even though you will always be my child.

We are so very different, yet we are also, in ways you cannot see yet, so very much alike. I know what it's like to carry around resentment and disappointment. It weighs you down. It probably won't break you. It didn't break me, and Lord knows it tried. I know you come from sturdy stock—I'm a lot tougher than you think, Avery. But the load wears on you, in places you might not even notice. No one else will either. You get good at shifting the burden from one shoulder to the other, and there are even times when you might put it in a basket and carry it on your head like our far away sisters do, but there is no real relief. And the longer you carry it, the less you notice. It starts to feel like it's a part of you, because that's what it has become, and I'm afraid that's when damage becomes irreversible.

As a child I watched the seeds of unhappiness take root in my sister, and grow until joy was a stranger to her, as was love. It took a long time for me to learn that would never change. And I'm sure you know that although we both loved him, your father was a challenging man, in many ways like my sister. I didn't realize it when I married him. Maybe I thought I could be happy enough for the both of us, but it doesn't work that way.

But now I have found my peace. My joy. That's a story I'll share with you another time. But I want the same for you. I can finally accept that I will likely not be the person with whom you share your burden, whatever it is. But please find someone, a person you trust. Van maybe? Surely you have a friend who fits that bill. I don't want you to carry your load until you're old and tired. I still look at you as young, Avery, and I know how many birthdays you've had. Trust me, one day you will look back on this age as young too because there can be so much more.

I love you. I have always loved you. I will always love you. So I want you to let it go while you can, move toward the place where you might find . . .

It took Avery a long time to finish. She'd stop, reread, rethink, review, recompose herself. Try to remember what it had been like that Sunday, when her mother came home. Why Avery expected her to know she wasn't drunk. That there was no falling down stairs, even though her father said it with such authority. She felt her mother was supposed to know she wouldn't do that, and for so long her mother seemed able to read Avery's thoughts and feelings that she expected her to be able to do it then. When she failed, that one important time, Avery painted her with the same broad strokes she applied to the others. *I should have told her.*

Avery sank back into the pillows. Wondered what place her mother wanted her to find, but couldn't find the word. Wished she had sent the letter before it was perfect. *Nothing ever is.*

That evening Avery felt fragile, but not breakable—buoyant, relieved, sad, and grateful.

She allowed the flutter of excitement to accompany her as she packed an overnight bag. She'd leave the yellow dress until the next day. Looking at it made her happy.

➢ ➢ ➢

"You'll have to meet Alicia—so she can stop driving me crazy." Avery laughed. Alicia had called three times during the ninety-minute train ride from New York to Philadelphia and twice again before Avery went down to meet Jazz in the hotel lobby.

"Look forward to it." Jazz waved to someone he knew as he steered Avery through the ballroom, toward the exit. "You came all the way down here to have dinner with a bunch of people I hardly know, the least I can do is meet your best friend." He nodded at a passing colleague, accepted her congratulations. "I hope it wasn't too boring."

"Not at all. I had fun. Who knew reporters could be so—entertaining? And you should have told me you were getting an award." She had actually had a great time. Instead of long-winded, dull speeches like the dinners she usually attended, this one had been more like a high school variety show—skits, songs, jokes, all irreverent takes on issues currently in the headlines. Avery couldn't remember when she had laughed harder. She had been totally surprised when Jazz was announced as the winner of the organization's award for "hard target" reporting. He had smiled at her sheepishly, then gone up to the stage to receive the Golden Arrow.

"I'll make sure it's not a last-minute invitation next time—give you plenty of notice since it'll take a little bit more to get here from New Zealand than from New York!" He smiled in spite of himself. "And you can even wear the same dress. I know women don't do that, but you look so spectacular tonight, I'd be happy for a replay."

Next time. Avery beamed. And the dress was officially a hit. Despite her reservations, the look on Jazz's face when she'd stepped off the elevator had dispelled her concerns. "Wow! You look like the goddess of spring" is what he said.

Guests from the banquet spilled out of the ballroom, streamed through the huge domed lobby. "Would you like a nightcap?"

"How about a stroll? I haven't been to Philly since a class trip when I was thirteen."

"Sounds like a plan."

"I can feel the breeze every time someone goes out—think I'll run up to the room and grab my coat. Come on, you can leave your ahhh—your arrow, and get it when we come back."

Avery retrieved her coat from the closet in her room, and Jazz, who had deposited his award on the desk, waited by the door.

"Let's go." Avery slipped into the trench and grabbed her bag from the foot of the bed.

"You wouldn't let me do this last time." Jazz reached out, lifted her collar, which had gotten stuck inside the coat.

His hands brushed her neck, and the warmth from his fingers ignited a fire that surged through her. All of a sudden, Avery realized she didn't want a walk. She didn't want a talk. She didn't want a nightcap. She wanted Jazz. She lifted her head, looked at him, her eyes telling him everything she wanted to say. And he knew. Jazz pulled her to him, she let her arms slip under his, the heat between them sealing their intention. They didn't need words so their mouths sought another expression. The kiss was hot and sweet, at the same time both the burn and the balm.

Seconds later, his tux, her yellow dress, were in a heap on the floor, and any questions or doubts they might have had, faded in the half-light coming through the window from the street nine stories below. For a brief moment fervor and desire yielded to caution before their bodies met, new to the touch, but at the same time intuitively familiar. Skin on skin, touch, taste, smell, they explored. Senses and sensation, surrender, learning, teaching, leading, following, they traveled together, knowing their destination was the same. Time melted away just as their clothes had, and Avery knew she had crossed some invisible boundary. With Jazz she had not only connected to him, she had connected to herself, completed a circuit that had been broken long ago. And when they had exhausted each other, Avery knew she was different, knew she had been somewhere new.

When first light replaced half-light, Jazz stirred, waking Avery, who lay curled close, her arm across his chest. Their second shared sunrise.

"Hey, you." Jazz traced her collarbone with his index finger.

"Good morning." Avery smiled, reached for the sheet, which was tangled around them, then Jazz leaned in and nuzzled her neck. His beard, fuzzy and soft, tickled her skin, sent a warm flush tingling through her. She could feel her body respond—it felt good, really good, and she could also tell he was a man with a plan, but she didn't want him to think she had thrown herself at him with a plan of her own. Avery rolled away—putting space between them for the first time since they had come together. "Listen, Jazz, I want you to know that—"

"What, you're not the kind of girl who sleeps with a man on the second date?"

"That isn't exactly what I was going to say." Avery raised herself on her elbow, tugged the sheet higher. "But I don't want you to think that I think this—our sleeping together—is a big deal. It happened. We're grown-ups. It doesn't mean I have some kind of crazy future plan about you and me."

He looked at her, furrowed his brow, feigning seriousness. "So you had your way with me on a whim? And now you're ready to toss me aside and go back to New Zealand and your tattooed Maori boyfriend, without a second thought?" Jazz clutched his hands to his bare chest.

Avery cracked up. "Funny, ha-ha. I just don't want you to have the wrong idea and—"

"First my kiss was 'nice,' and now, 'it happened'? I'm crushed." He sat up. "I'm only half joking, Avery. I realize we don't really know each other, and there are no guarantees. What happened with your mother probably makes that clearer than anything I could say about tomorrows not being promised. But I'm kind of at the point in my life where I'm looking for some tomorrows—which I've figured out means making some 'todays.' "

"Jazz, I'm not—"

"I know. You're only here temporarily. Pursuing this in the first place was probably extremely foolish. But like you said, I'm a grown-up. I knew what I was doing. So, I'm not asking you for anything—no commitment, no promises."

Avery sat up, the sheet tucked under her arms. "So much has changed for me, in such a short time. . . . I thought I had my life figured out, but I don't know what I want anymore. Doesn't seem the best way to start . . ."

"I understand." He reached out, took her hand. "I'm willing to take this for whatever it is. I believe there's a reason our paths have come together. Notice I did not say *crossed.* I may be wrong, but I don't think that reason is Dixon Plaza, and I don't think this is the end." Jazz brushed a lock of her hair behind her ear. "I'm not pressuring you for some kind of definitive answer. But I couldn't let you think this 'just happened,' and that it doesn't mean anything to me." Jazz leaned over, kissed Avery. "Because it does."

SEVENTEEN

... that far into now

"Back her up there. We have a cave-in and my ass is the one in a sling, swinging from a sour-apple tree." Rain tattooed the windshield of Mitch's SUV, and hot air fogged the windows.

"Nobody will blame you in the long run." Dwight had called him first thing that morning to arrange one of their parking-lot powwows before he went to the office.

"Are you nuts? Suppose somebody gets killed? Suppose the whole damn building falls down?"

Dwight wanted to shake Avery till she made some sense, but he knew she needed more incentive than that. He'd already offered her more money than was sane. The night before while he lay awake next to a peacefully sleeping Renee, Dwight had plenty to keep his mind churning. He kept the days busy, but the nights were long and quiet, with nothing to distract him from the what-ifs that gnawed at him. Like what client names did police find as they continued digging up dirt on the mistresses of Nineteenth Street. That story was like a bad rash—just when it seemed to clear, it would flare up again. Dwight agonized, trying to come up with a speedy plan to acquire the last little piece of ground standing between him and his destiny. That's when he hit on the plan to accidentally on purpose damage Avery's building to encourage her to unload it, go back wherever in the world she had been, and stay out of his business. "We need to give her a reason to sell." Made perfect sense at 3 a.m.

"I can't take that chance."

"Damn it, I took my chances with you."

"And you got your money's worth. I'm not sticking my neck out any further to save your cheap ass."

Dwight had stayed in perpetual motion, trying to run around the avalanche that picked up momentum with Avery's "no sale," because he had to keep climbing the mountain. He had already seen two architects about replacing Cobb Rowan and had meetings scheduled with more. The demolition of building two on 110th Street was set for the next week, complete with hundreds of balloons, clowns on stilts, and a marching band. Press releases had gone out. He was all ready to proceed, except for the big dead end that was getting closer and closer while the days melted away.

Dwight's phone went off. He yanked it from his pocket, checked the number. Madeline. "I'll be there in . . . *What?* How bad? . . . Call Stan and Baily. I'll be there as soon as I can." He squeezed his head between his hands, like he was trying to keep it from exploding. "It's one of your damn kitchen cabinets at Hudson Common . . . fell on some kid!"

"Your people signed off on it." Mitch's voice took on a steely edge. "They're not my cabinets. They're yours."

That knocked what air was left out of Dwight. The two

men glared at each other across the small space. "Just get me back to the terminal."

Dwight wanted to catch a train in the opposite direction. Buy an Amtrak ticket and head for parts unknown, but he hopped the next thing smoking back to NY Penn Station.

The office was buzzing when he got there. Madeline met him at the door, followed Dwight to his office. "I'm forwarding the calls to Baily. You're supposed to call him as soon as you get in."

"The kid?"

"Don't know yet, but it sounded bad. He was putting his cereal bowl in the sink and the cabinet just gave way . . . full of dishes." Madeline shuddered. "Eric is already over there."

Dwight paced in his carpeted cage, trying to get the vibration inside him to stop, like he needed one more distraction. No doubt about it, this could be a PR storm—a lot of noise and show, and hopefully it would blow over without any real destruction. *I can take it.* He and Baily worked on a statement, a culpa without the mea because under no circumstances were they going to imply The Dixon Group was to blame, and got Stan's okay for immediate release.

Except by the noon news, everyone else blamed them. Lightning had found a target. Dwight closed himself in the conference room with the TV, amazed at how quickly the stations got news crews to the apartment, where the cameras did slow pans of the mangled cabinet and the shards of broken dishes covering the floor, followed by comments from neighbors about the friendly, happy child. And Pastor Phil didn't wait for a publicist to okay his remarks. They shot out of his mouth as soon as a mike was in range.

"This tragedy did not have to happen. It was not an isolated incident. Management has been told on numerous occasions. What we have here is a systematic pattern of neglect and disregard on the part of The Dixon Group."

Dwight wanted to dump the set out the window. Whatever favor he had curried with the volatile minister had obviously reached its expiration date.

Next came file footage of the Dixon Plaza site and the standard summary of the project delays. With its painted-over sign, and the sidewalk shed covered in graffiti and pasted-on posters, nothing hinted at the gleaming future. For the first time it looked to Dwight like any other broken-down wreck in the city. He shut the TV off before they finished and felt the eyes of his employees follow him back to his office.

An hour later Eric phoned in, suggesting they advise the tenants in both buildings to remove items from all upper cabinets until they could be inspected.

"I'd say a third of them are not secure. Maybe half. I suggested it in my report—"

"Just get it done, Eric!"

Madeline came over the intercom. "King is on two."

"Tell him I'll call him back." Talking to King was like shaking up a beehive. You know you're gonna get stung. The only question was how badly. Not what Dwight needed to help him stay calm and think straight.

"He won't hang up."

"Then let him sit there." Dwight would pay for it. So be it, but he couldn't worry about that now.

The rest of the day the office was bombarded in tsunami waves that intensified as the evening news approached. Now and again Dwight would look at the phone. Line two stayed lit for hours.

Dwight put in a call to Grace. He wanted to tell her first-hand what he was doing to manage the situation. It went immediately to voice mail. Each time the phone rang, he hoped it was her, but she had not called back by the time he left for the day, early. Dwight had always enjoyed coming into his office, but today he needed a change of scenery. At least those were things he could change.

Dwight had Madeline call him a car. He couldn't have all those people on the street seeing him. Not that home was the place he wanted to go, but what choice was there? His oasis had dried up and turned to burning sand.

The news was on the radio when he slumped in the backseat. The driver pulled out into traffic.

"That's something, about that poor kid. He's in a coma—"

"You're not being paid to talk." Dwight didn't know if the remark was specific, or if it was just the driver's opening line for the day, because who wouldn't feel sorry for the kid? "Just drive."

Renee was all over him as soon as he walked through the door. "It's just awful, Dwight . . . that little boy. He has such a sweet little smile. Did you see him?"

"Shut up, Renee! Do you think you can manage that?"

Dwight didn't look at her—headed straight back to the kitchen for vodka and ice cubes. He even passed Dominique, who'd headed downstairs when she heard the door open, stopped midway at her father's outburst. He knew the look his daughter would have on her face, but he couldn't fix that at the moment.

The boy's sweet smile, his devastated mother—Dwight didn't want to know about any of it. He did not want to think of them as real people. That would be overwhelming—no time for that. He had to find a way to stay strong all on his own because it felt as if the world had conspired to break him. And right at that moment, he wanted to be left alone.

➢ ➢ ➢

Avery had followed the story all day, on TV, on the radio. At first because she tried to imagine what she would feel like if it happened to one of her tenants—awful. The poor mother, a young woman with her hair braided in a spiral around her head and reddened eyes, could barely speak. Not until Avery heard Pastor Phil did she realize it was Dwight's building. She kept waiting to hear his side, for him to show up at the hospital, or back at the apartment building, even at his office, but so far he'd stayed out of sight. The statement read by some spokesman had as much compassion as a credit-card-user agreement—a mere formality because you have to say something.

Then she saw him—Councilman Chester Gordon, standing among his Hudson Common constituents. At first Avery saw his lips moving but couldn't comprehend what he was saying. He was real, not a bogeyman she'd made up. The phone rang before the story was over—Alicia. Avery could imagine her friend organizing the march on City Hall to turn Trey out. But she couldn't talk to Alicia that second or to anybody else. She wanted to sit with herself, just be. For so long that night had not been about Trey. It was about her and Dwight and betrayal. But there he was, defending his decision to vote for Dixon Plaza, but vowing to get to the bottom of any improprieties that had occurred during the building of Hudson Common, expressing wishes for the recovery of Marlon Cumberbatch, the seven-year-old, who was still in critical condition.

Avery turned off the set. Where did she think Trey would be all these years later? Drug-addicted? Jailed? Cleaning windshields with a dirty rag for hustled quarters on Houston Street? She'd never imagined him that far into now. *What am I supposed to do?*

Upstairs, downstairs, the house was too small to contain the feelings Avery couldn't define. Sweats and sneakers on, she went outside. Rachel and Louis, her neighbors across the street, were just getting home with their baby boy and groceries, and Avery went over to compliment the flower boxes they'd planted over the weekend. The pink and yellow petunias, the draping ivy—"They make me smile when I see them." So did baby Zachary, wiggling and gurgling in his stroller.

Avery already felt better outside. She took in a deep breath of the fresh air as she gradually increased her pace and the length of her stride. People around her filtered home from work, or school, carrying dry cleaning, or books. Avery found herself hooking a left on Adam Clayton Powell and realized she wasn't walking away from the house. She was walking toward a place she'd been meaning to check out for quite a while.

"You're Miss Tina's daughter, right?" The teen's hair was pulled back tightly into a ponytail that erupted in wiry waves. She popped out of the door at the center just as Avery reached for the handle.

"Yes. I am." Avery smiled, surprised to be ID'd.

"I'm Shareese." She turned back around, looped her arm through Avery's, and led her inside. "I'ma take you to Jill. She's our counselor."

Avery had only meant to stop by, see what the place looked like, since Ladies First had meant so much to her mother, but as Shareese proudly marched Avery around, both showing her off and showing off all that was going on, her appearance became an event. They had become a party of four by the time they found Jill, helping out with homework in the computer lab. Avery remembered her from the wake.

"Glad you stopped in." Jill welcomed her warmly.

"I should have called."

"No need. We're just happy to have you here."

Shareese let Avery go, reluctantly. "Hope you come back."

Avery stumbled for an answer. "Me. Too . . . I mean, I'll see." *No promises you can't keep.*

Jill took Avery to peek in the auditorium, where a poetry rehearsal was in progress. "It's scaled down from when this used to be a theater, but it's a good-size performance space. The kids learn how the lighting, scenery, all of that works. There's recording equipment upstairs."

"Very impressive."

"The board is great. I don't know how Mr. Washington does it. He gets people to give up their time, their money, whatever they've got. But our Miss Tina is just irreplaceable. She was truly our first lady of Ladies First."

A month ago that would have made Avery sad, but now she was glad to know her mom had found such a wonderful fit for her talent and enthusiasm. Avery learned there was Gentlemen Foremost as well, where the boys learned some old-school ways from men in the community.

On her way out, she noticed the separate bank of elevators that went up to the apartments. Outside she could see where the original redbrick building met the new, sleeker construction. *They compliment each other.*

Avery was looking forward to the opportunity to actually talk to this Ty Washington at Alicia's upcoming I'm-back-in-New-York, old-friends/new-friends soiree. Avery had gone back and forth about whether she should go solo or invite Jazz, which Alicia championed big-time, because she had yet to meet him. Did Avery want to meet new people on her own, or as a "pair." Was that what they even were? Questions she hadn't wrestled with in quite some time. Ultimately the decision was made for her when Jazz had to return to Florida for a couple of days.

On the walk home, Avery wondered what she was really going to do—with herself. Her official leave time was dwindling, and as the days went by, it was harder to imagine packing her suitcase, turning over the keys to the house, and flying back to the other side of the world. She'd relaxed into a routine, finally removed her clothes from the middle of the floor and put them in the spare closet. Even though at times she felt as though she were in the middle of an elaborate game of life swap—and that someone in New Zealand was giving her briefings and writing policy papers—it was working okay. *Maybe better than my real life works.* But she didn't know where that thought would lead, so she stopped having it.

➢ ➢ ➢

The three-story, white-limestone building with Moorish arches appeared to hover on a cloud of blue light like an urban mirage, and although it was not as big as most of its neighbors, Lush dominated the block. Avery didn't know how she had missed it on her uptown explorations—zigged when she could have zagged, made a right instead of a left—but she had definitely never seen it. She would have remembered. Just when Avery thought she was getting the hang of twenty-first-century Harlem, it would surprise her again. *Leave it to Alicia.*

Avery's postwalk, ten-minute power nap had turned into a full-fledged REM-sleep snooze, so she was late when she walked through the towering, etched-glass flamingo doors. She was greeted by a stunning young woman with cobalt-and-silver fingernails who stood behind a glass oval, wedged between ten-foot bronze nudes. "Welcome to Lush."

"Thank you. The Harvey party."

Avery was directed to the elevator, instead of the bustling restaurant on the main floor, just past the reception area. When the doors opened on the third floor, Avery realized she had entered a sanctuary not only a world away from the restaurant downstairs, but also the world outside. She was met by an impeccably tailored man she guessed to be in his early seventies, who led her through the quietly elegant ebony, ivory, and gold room, past the bar—a half-moon of brass and leather—past clusters of lacquered tables, surrounded by black and white calfskin chairs, most filled with stylish patrons who were surviving the economic roller coaster or still capable of talking the talk. Avery recognized a network news anchor, who was balder than she thought, a popular-magazine editor holding court at a table for six among others who looked familiar but weren't as easy for her to identify. Her escort deposited her at the entrance to a private dining salon.

Alicia pounced as soon as Avery came in. "I know you were screening your calls, and you're late." She smiled as she whispered in Avery's ear, "Love you anyway. All you have to do is say the word and Chester Gordon is dog meat, him and Dwight both—canned by-products I'll be happy to serve to the hounds, in big old shiny silver bowl. Slurp slurp. But that's later. Come on, now I want you to meet . . ."

Alicia whirled Avery through her dining dozen with lightning-fast introductions, only half of which Avery remembered. Jorge, Alicia's brother, looked much the same as the last time Avery had seen him, which was forever ago. She'd never met his curly-haired wife, Greta. There was a shoe designer Avery thought was called Koki, and his boyfriend, an off-off-Broadway director, whose name Avery definitely missed. There was Dr. Henry Jeffrey or Jeffrey Henry—she wasn't sure—but he was a plastic surgeon who owned a condo Alicia had looked at but decided not to buy. There was the author of yet another ten-steps-to-total-fulfillment self-help book. And finally, "uptown's dynamic duo, Ty Washington and Regina Foster."

They shook hands all around. "Good to see you again, under better circumstances." Ty slipped his arm around Regina's waist. "I had such respect for your mother."

Regina agreed. "I hear you live overseas, that must be exciting. I travel a lot for my business, and Ty and I have been to every continent except Antarctica, which he says he wants to tackle—he can bring me back a T-shirt and a picture of a penguin, thank you very much—but I've never lived anywhere but the States.

"It can be exciting, but mostly—" Avery was interrupted by Alicia's asking everyone to sit.

Avery was not surprised to find her assigned seat between the music mogul and the doctor at the big round table. Alicia was directly opposite. The group was large and diverse enough to spark a party atmosphere but at the same time intimate enough to allow for a real exchange. Conversation heated and cooled, and laughter ruled the evening. Avery found Ty fascinating—he was obviously a successful businessman who had had a vision for himself, his company, and a plan to bring it to reality in the early stages of the music revolution—when the beat changed and you didn't have to be a name label to get your artists heard. His industry was changing again and he was already adapting, exploring new technology and taking his company, Big Bang, in new directions in addition to giving back a full measure to the community. Avery also liked his "ace," as Ty called Regina, whom he had met when they were in college. They were not married, but had been together almost twenty years.

"I think her dad's finally convinced I'm sticking around." Ty chuckled as the waiter put a glass filled with a murky brownish concoction in front of him. "But her dad's mellowed a lot since he retired and started baking for Regina."

"The coffee places." Avery finally made the connection. "I had a meeting with Jasper Christmas—he was telling me how he grew up with her brothers."

"Oh, yeah—I like Jazz, though he probably isn't one of your favorite people right now." Ty shook his head. "He's really giving your cousin a hard time."

"Dwight and I aren't close," Avery offered.

"Ah, I see. Well, being honest, I can't say he's been one of my favorite people. Long story from a long time ago. But I give him props for his plan for 110th Street. I'd like to see more economic integration, but that's my thing. I wish him the best. Hope he can pull it off. Should bring a capital infusion we can use up here."

And will I be part of the reason if he can't? "Yes, well—" Avery was rescued from either having to defend or sympathize with Dwight's predicament by Alicia's tinkling her glass to get attention so she could thank everybody for coming. "And who's giving the next party?"

The next morning, Toni called a little after ten with building-management info. Avery had planned to ask Ty, but didn't. After he brought up Dwight, she wasn't sure she wanted to talk bricks and mortar with him. Toni also wanted to know if Avery had made a decision about listing the house. "We can make such a splash. It's a super house and it hasn't been on the market since pay phones cost a dime."

"I'm still making up my mind." Avery knew she couldn't hold all the pieces. She had to start letting some of them go, but she cut the conversation short when she got the beep for an incoming call and saw it was Jazz. "Hey." Her voice was light and breathy, not one among her repertoire she had often used.

"There's a story breaking now. I didn't want it to catch you by surprise."

Jazz sounded more serious than she'd gotten used to. "About what?" Avery leaned against the kitchen counter.

"It's about your cousin."

"Did the little boy die?" He was still critical the last she heard, but that had been early in the morning.

"No. He's holding his own."

"Oh, thank God." Avery nestled the phone on her shoulder. "Then I can wait and get the news the regular way."

"You really want to hear this, Avery."

EIGHTEEN

. . . none of his private parts were private anymore

Still in his clothes, Dwight had fallen into vodka-induced sleep in the lounge in his study. Renee had tried to rouse him, until he chewed her head off. He woke with a start at 2:12 a.m., hauled himself up to the bedroom, dropped his clothes in a heap, and lay down, but sleep did not come when his head hit the pillow. Or the hour after that—or after that.

By morning he felt like hot-hammered hell, wanted to call in, play hooky, but he knew he needed to be at the office, so he dragged himself there.

Pastor Phil and Councilman Gordon had been high on Dwight's nocturnal agenda—how they'd turned on him soon as they got the chance. But Dwight hadn't had his say. So he called Baily first thing. Said he wanted to work on his own statement. "I am the face of The Dixon Group. I should be the one out there."

"You're putting yourself in a vulnerable position. I don't advise it."

"They need to see I'm not hiding. Hopefully the kid will be out of ICU soon. I'll find a way to make it up to his parents."

"Make it up? What do you mean 'make it up'? Have you talked to your lawyer about this?"

Dwight didn't know what he meant, and he knew Stan would advise him to keep his mouth shut, but he needed to speak out. That's what leaders did.

So all morning Dwight sat at his computer pecking out what he wanted to say to the city. He monitored the Hudson Common situation by phone. With Crawford's assistance, and a security detail, Eric began getting the cabinets emptied and inspected. They were making progress. By midday Dwight had a draft of what he wanted to say, shot it to Baily for comments so he could get it into the news flow. But Dwight was dragging, had to rev himself up for the rest of the day. He couldn't inspire confidence looking and feeling the way he did. Coffee had only made his sleepiness agitated. He thought about the gym, worried he might be harassed. *What are you hiding from?*

While he was trudging uphill on the treadmill, or heaving seventy, eighty, or a hundred pounds on the Nautilus machines, Dwight saw no finger-pointing from other exercisers, but he felt some sideways glances. A few years back, male or female, he would have assumed he was being cruised—he liked that unrequited longing and admiration. Except now he was sure these looks were not about sex. His picture had been splashed all over the news—guilty before there was a charge. He'd checked in about the boy before he left the office—no better, no worse—couldn't help wishing the kid's bowl of Honey O's had lasted longer.

After the workout, he pulled on his trunks and took to the

pool. Dwight had to wait for a lane, but once he slipped into the cool water, stroking hand over hand, he found his rhythm. That's what he needed. He kept building momentum just to run into roadblocks, detours. If people would just get out of his way, he could show them.

Refreshed and revived, Dwight shaved, dressed, grabbed a baby-spinach-and-blueberry smoothie from the juice bar, decided not to check his phone—bad news would still be bad in ten minutes—and talked himself up while he walked back to the office. He saw the news van as soon as he rounded the corner and was glad he'd gone for a workout. He was surprised Baily had gotten them over so soon. And that he didn't want to revise Dwight's statement. He always had some nitpicking to do. *Good. It'll make tonight's news.*

Dwight saw the newswoman and the cameraman hop out. They could go up to the office so he could get his copy to read. Stomach in, chest out, Dwight strode confidently—

—into the quicksand. "Mr. Dixon. Your name was leaked from Mistress Delilah's client list. Care to comment?"

The workout rush drained from Dwight, replaced by temporary system failure. He couldn't move, couldn't talk. A loud roar raced in his ears, and the world moved in slow motion. Dwight was prepared to talk about the boy in the coma, but not about the Mistress Delilah. *This isn't happening.*

But the reporter was still there, and her expression was so pleasant as she held the mike in his face, like she could have been saying "Happy birthday," or "Congratulations," instead of "Are you a client of Mistress Delilah's?"

By then the word had begun to filter out among the people who'd gathered. Dwight heard their exclamations—"For real?" "Oh, snap!" Then there was laughing. And he could not find a single word, not *yes, no,* or *go away.* Couldn't find a convenient lie when he needed one. The reporter and the camera were between him and the door to his building and he had to get there. So he started walking. It felt like he was staggering, but he kept moving, hand in front of the lens until he could grasp the door handle with just enough strength left to pull.

The security guard, the people he passed every day, coming in from lunch, now they knew his secret and he wanted to shrink, escape through the floor, out of existence. He could not take this.

But the nightmare was just beginning.

"Are you sick?" Madeline looked startled when she saw him.

How does she mean that? Does she know? "Hold my calls." Dwight's voice sounded foreign to his own ears.

"People keep calling here asking about you and that skeevy place on Nineteenth Street. I've been telling them they have the wrong number and hanging up, but—" She paused, leaving room for a handy-dandy explanation, but none came. "And Baily said call right away. It's—urgent. What is going on?"

Dwight closed the door. He knew it was urgent and he knew he was going to need help, but he couldn't talk yet. Not about this. No one was supposed to know. Ever.

Hand on the phone, he thought about all those who would know—King, Grace, Renee, Dominique, Mitch, Madeline, all the tenants in all of his buildings. What would they think of him? What would they say? How would he face any of them again? That's when the first tear hit the glass, then another, and then he was sobbing, shoulders shaking, uncontrollably.

The door flew open. Madeline looked alarmed. "Mr. Dixon—"

"Get out!" She could not see this, but she already had. *You're a disgrace.* And Dwight cried until he couldn't anymore, could not even escape that room without making the phone call.

Each digit was torture, but he punched all ten, waited for the answer.

"Dwight, I—"

"Baily, I'm dead."

➢ ➢ ➢

The knock at the back of the house surprised Avery, but as soon as she peeked out, she unbolted and yanked open the door.

"I didn't know where else to go." Renee's voice shook as she stood there, a lime green backpack and her purse on her shoulder, a bulging black garbage bag in each hand.

"I tried to reach you as soon as I heard. Give me this." Avery grabbed for a bag, led her inside. Even in bad situations Renee managed to look resilient, but this time she seemed beat down, crushed. When Jazz called to warn her, Avery's mind went immediately to Renee and Dominique, could not imagine how this would come down on them.

"I was picking up groceries when I heard about . . . I left the cart in the aisle and came home, stopped answering the phone." Renee's eyes were red, puffy, panicked, and her face appeared swollen, the skin stretched thin like an overripe plum. She looked around her at the bags on the kitchen floor. "I didn't know what Dominique and I would need, so I grabbed a bunch of stuff." Tears ran down her face. "It's probably all wrong. I'm sorry."

Avery wrapped her arms around Renee. "Don't worry about that now. Whatever you need, we'll get it. It'll still be there." The animosity Avery held toward Dwight was not enough to keep her from feeling how much Renee needed help now and being glad she was there to give it.

It took Renee a moment to pull herself together again. "I hate to ask you for anything else. You're already being so kind . . ."

"Just tell me what you need, Renee."

"Could you . . . could you go get Dominique?" Renee looked so sad. "There are reporters all up and down the block. They can't get to her in school, but they'll follow me."

"Of course. That's what family does. And I know you and Dominique were family to my mom, and so you are to me." The last time the idea of banding together for the good of the family had been put into practice, Avery became the sacrificial lamb. But this time she understood what the sentiment really meant.

Renee shook her head. "I want her out of there before the other kids get wind. With cell phones and computers they might know already, but I need to protect her as long as I can. At least until I can talk to her." Tears welled up, spilled over. "What am I going to say? How do I explain when I don't understand myself?"

"I—I don't . . ." Then Avery realized Renee didn't really want an answer. The question was one she was asking herself. "I'll go now."

"I'll let them know you're coming, and I'll give you the code word."

"Pardon?"

"The school won't release a child to a nonparent without a security word. Things aren't like they used to be. They don't trust anybody anymore."

Seems they have good reason. Whatever Dwight had done to her, Avery could never have wished this kind of scandal on him, or the humiliation on his family. "I'm so sorry, Renee. And I want you to know you two can stay here as long as you want."

No one bothered Avery when she left the house, and although she hadn't been back to Breton since she graduated, once she walked through the big red doors, she remembered the layout as if it were yesterday and not more than two decades since she'd been there. But instead of being able to turn left and head to the main office, she was stopped at a massive oak desk by a woman who, while dressed innocuously enough in a dove gray pants suit, allowed her open jacket to make it clear to visitors that she was much more than a friendly greeter posted to welcome you to the school. Avery showed ID, signed in, and was met by Ms. McGann, an assistant to the head of the Lower School, who said Dominique was in accountability class.

"Interesting," Avery replied. "I guess it's never too early to learn to keep good records." She thought about her father.

"Accountability," the young woman repeated as she walked Avery to the office. "Not accounting. It was citizenship back when you were a student here, Ms. Lyons. We've updated the curriculum to include a strong emphasis on morality, philosophy, honor, and decency in addition to the core social studies."

So they knew she was an alumna. *Renee probably told them.* "Sounds very progressive, but pretty heavy for fourth-graders."

"Young people today live in a complex world, and independent decision-making occurs much earlier. We want to help prepare them to weigh their choices in a reflective, responsible way."

To Avery, it sounded like a lot for a ten-year-old.

"You can have a seat. Diqui will be here shortly."

Diqui? Ponytail bouncing, she burst through the door, full of questions. "Where's Mom? Did something bad happen, like with Auntie Tina?"

Avery assured Dominique her parents were well, but something unexpected had come up. They exchanged the secret word, which Ms. McGann verified, and they were on their way.

"So tell me about Diqui." Avery turned to her young charge once they settled into the taxi heading uptown.

Dominique looked at Avery, then out the window and back again. "I wanted a nickname. All my friends have them. But Daddy made this whole bo-ring speech about nicknames being stupid and stuff like that. But at school they call me Diqui and I like it." Dominique folded her arms across her chest, and in that moment, for the first time, Avery could see Dwight. Not just in his daughter's long, lean legs and arms, but in the defiant tilt of Diqui's head, the determined set of her jaw.

"I have a friend from Breton who still calls me Av. I call her LiLi. I think it's pretty cool, Diqui."

For the remainder of the ride Avery asked questions about things she remembered from her days at Breton. Dominique laughed at the outdated recollections and gave Avery the scoop on how it was in the twenty-first century. "No—that's where the robotics lab is." "No—our report cards get e-mailed." Although Avery managed to keep Dominique talking and distracted, out of the cab, up the alley, and through the garage, she couldn't imagine what Renee was going to say. How would she explain what Dominique was sure to hear on the six-o'clock news.

"How come we're going to Auntie Tina—I'm sorry—I mean, your house?"

"It's okay. It will always be Auntie Tina's house, and I think that's a wonderful way for you to remember her. But your mom is here, and this is where she wanted me to bring you." Avery unlocked the kitchen door.

They found Renee in the living room, and Avery hugged Dominique and left the two of them alone. The explanation would be difficult enough without an audience, no matter how well-intentioned.

Two hours later, Renee found Avery in the sunroom reading e-mail. "She doesn't really understand." Renee plopped down in the slipper chair. "She cried some. I told her we would be okay. Then I made her a sandwich. Hope you don't mind, but Aunt Tina kept PB and J here just for Dominique. Now she's asleep on the couch in the study."

"You could have given her my old bedroom." The one place Avery hadn't made peace with, but she remembered Dominique talking about the trophies.

Renee folded her arms, held on to herself. "What if they have the wrong person and it's not true?" She looked at Avery, but there was no hope in her eyes.

"I suppose that's possible."

"Wishful thinking." Renee, her eyes brimming over, dropped her face into her hands and sobbed.

➢ ➢ ➢

Dwight hid in his office until Baily arrived, dismissed Dwight's staff for the day. Then it was just the two of them, and Baily became all about logistics.

"There's a back way out of here that leads through a building on the side street. I'll have a car pick you up there. I can book you into a hotel."

"I have to go home."

"You're a sitting duck."

"My wife and daughter . . ."

"I'll get them too. You need to make sure they're on board."

But there was no answer from Renee on either the home line or her cell, so the first stop would be home. Baily's take-charge attitude helped Dwight calm down, at least enough to realize there was nowhere to go except through it.

The publicist rode uptown with Dwight, went over the drill. "You're making no statement at this time. If anything needs to be said, I'll say it. Try to look normal. They can smell fear. Just get in your house and stay there." Once in the car, Dwight didn't look at the driver. There were no pleasantries, no news on the radio.

The cluster of press outside his house was unsettling, but none of his private parts were private anymore. The distance from the car to the house was short, but he was crowded, jostled, hounded, in a dizzying spin.

Door finally closed, the house seemed startlingly quiet. "Renee!" Dwight searched the rooms, eager to see her calm, comforting presence, dreading the look in her eyes. But the house was empty and Dwight had never felt more alone. The note taped to the parlor mantel read, *At Avery's. Use the back door.*

Renee didn't look at him when she let him in. She turned and walked toward the parlor. He trailed behind.

"Where's Dominique?"

"You obviously weren't concerned about her well-being before. Why worry now?" Renee sat on the couch and glared as if it hurt her eyes to see him. "She's here. She's safe."

Dwight stood across from her, arms awkwardly at his sides. It felt like miles between them. "I don't know how . . ."

"Is it true?" Arms crossed, legs entwined, Renee waited for an answer.

"I didn't mean for this to happen." Dwight looked for compassion in her reddened eyes, but what he saw was harsh and cold.

"For what to happen? For you to get caught?"

"It doesn't have anything to do with you." And for Dwight it didn't. Not until now.

"So it is true?"

It would have been easier if she had hit him. That he could take. "I love you, Renee. You and Dominique."

"Sure you do. That's why you won't make love to me unless I beg you. But you pay somebody called Mistress Delilah? Mistress?! Does she beat you? Never mind. I don't want to know. But obviously, whatever it is must do something for you, Dwight. Something I don't do."

"I didn't mean to hurt you." Dwight dropped his head.

"They said you've been going to her for years. Years!" Renee threw up her hands, got up. "And you got in our bed, and I let you touch me. I wanted you to touch me. How long, Dwight? Two years? Five? Ten?"

More like twenty. But not with Delilah. She was the third mistress to put him through his paces. He remembered the ad—small, discreet, simply worded—probably overlooked by most. He could almost feel the weight of the glossy magazine in his hand, both relished and loathed the tingle as he punched out the number that first time. And at this moment, he hated himself for it.

"I'll make it up to you. I swear." Dwight moved to come closer.

"Don't."

He stopped. "I have to make a statement tomorrow. I need you with me."

"No." Renee shook her head, her whole body, like a spasm. "Not even if you let me hit you." She got up to leave.

"Please, Renee."

"Don't beg. It's a really unbecoming habit. And you know what, Dwight? You're right. This doesn't have anything to do with me."

NINETEEN

That's it. It's over. Finito. The end

"Does that have to be on?" Dwight already had images of himself over the last two days seared in his brain.

"Why not? It's the news, Junior. You're on before the president, the mayor—"

"Stop. All right." It was more a plea than a command. "Just stop." These were not scenes he needed to see repeated in forty-two-inch hi-def flat-screen. Dwight was officially spent, empty, taking refuge in his father's apartment. The security was better. The co-op board was not pleased.

But King had the remote and he wasn't ready to change the channel. Which meant Dwight sat through yet another rehash of the one-ring media circus that had become his life, because he didn't have the energy to leave the room.

After video of the escape through the gauntlet and into his front door came excerpts from his press conference of the following morning, where he became both ringmaster and clown. He had tried to keep the proceedings dignified, read the statement he had prepared about Marlon Cumberbatch, who was still in intensive care. Dwight expressed his deep concern about the boy and his family, the measures he had already taken to address the complaints of Hudson Common residents, and his determination to get to the bottom of the problems at the complex. He read it slowly, making himself look out at the sea of reporters, the largest crowd he'd drawn since the initial announcement of Dixon Plaza. But nothing about the morning was triumphant, and this time there were no staff, no collaborators, no family. Dwight stood there alone but for his public relations contingent guarding his flanks and his image, such as it was.

Baily had reminded him to hold his head up. "Look concerned, not guilty." But it was hard gazing out at the assembled reporters with their notebooks and bared fangs. As soon as he came to the last syllable of his prepared remarks, they pounced, but the hot topic wasn't tenant safety. They clamored for details about Dwight's involvement with Mistress Delilah.

Baily had drilled him. "Don't confirm or deny. You haven't been charged with a crime and police haven't named you."

Sounds easy until you face a horde barking questions with heated breath and wild eyes. Jasper Christmas actually brought the gathering back to some semblance of decorum when he asked, "Any comment on the three-hundred-million-dollar lawsuit just filed against The Dixon Group on behalf of Marlon Cumberbatch?"

It was news to Dwight, but at least the question had some weight. Dwight's answer was the same as for the other inquiries: "No comment." Then he'd wandered out of the room because, really, what else did he have to say?

While he was handling bad news, Dwight headed to his

attorney's office, where Stan confirmed the lawsuit. "We're ready to fight this. They'll have to prove negligence, but I have to tell you, it's going to be a challenge."

Dwight understood the translation—lots of billable hours. The dollar amounts had become laughable. Even without speaking to his accountant, he knew that in terms of liquid capital, The Dixon Group was at the breaking point. "Capsized by a kitchen cabinet, is that how it goes, Stan?" And Dwight started to laugh, a kind of nervous giggle at first, which grew into an uncontrollable, tears-rolling belly laugh. Stan looked disturbed, but Dwight couldn't stop. He'd done whatever he had to do to get where they were, and now it looked as if his success or failure would come down to falling laminate-covered particleboard. What else could he do but laugh—and cry?

By the next morning's papers, Dwight had become the punch line of a citywide joke.

The headline: "Dixon and the Vixen." Dwight's photo was next to one that had surfaced of Delilah, dressed to thrill in thigh boots and a leather bustier, her signature leather crop in her hand. The photo was black-and-white, but he knew her lips were red. It awaited him with his coffee when he dragged himself up from not sleeping. Overnight his new name had become "Troubled Developer Dwight Dixon." The daily rags and the newscasts gave space to the Cumberbatch lawsuit, but the titillation of Dwight's alleged sexploits was more prominent. The development of Harlem was yet again a sideshow, left for tomorrow, upstaged by the bother and fuss surrounding Dwight's improprieties, which were ultimately foolish, but signified what? Nothing but his personal struggles and emptiness.

The torture he paid for couldn't compare to the torture he felt at being outed in the press, whether he commented or not. Then there were those around him. Dwight expected his cell to be ringing nonstop, but it had gone silent. No one had words of encouragement except the people he paid to keep him going. Nonessential staff of The Dixon Group had been given the rest of the week off, but he had no idea how he would face them again. He kept hearing Madeline's disparaging remarks at the coffeemaker, seeing her disbelief the day the story broke. How would he look at her now?

Renee had said he could see Dominique, but his daughter wasn't ready yet. Dwight didn't understand how much he loved her until then. He'd never considered how she would feel about the things her daddy did. She wasn't ever going to know, except now she did, and it seemed she was disappointed and ashamed, and he was heartsick.

Dwight couldn't imagine what Grace was making of this hoopla. Clearly she wasn't ready to share her opinion. He'd lost track of how many messages he'd left her, but she had not deigned to answer.

Then there was King, who persisted in rubbing Dwight's nose in the dirty details, but only halfheartedly. He was surprisingly laissez-faire about Dwight's predilections. "You're grown. Told you a long time ago I don't want to know what you do with who. But couldn't you cover your tracks any better than that?" It was like he didn't know what else to do besides goad Dwight until he got back on his feet and straightened out his business mess. "I gave you a profitable business. You plannin' to lay up here lookin' at me, or are you gonna go run it?"

"What difference does it make?" Dwight got up and walked toward the guest room. "Just leave me alone. Can you do that? Leave me alone." He slept on and off all day, stayed awake most of the night, watching infomercials for hair replacement and ab-ercise contraptions. He laughed for a solid half hour during the get-rich-buying-real-estate-for-no-money-down program. *You have to do more than own it to make yourself rich.* He thought of trying to find Grace in Macao. If that's where she was, she'd be on her way out to dinner. If he was lucky, she was on the other side of the world and hadn't heard about his setbacks. But lucky seemed to be somebody else's star. Besides, she seemed to have eyes and ears all over the planet. He had no idea what she was doing, with whom or where. But somehow, from the penthouse of whatever skyscraper she chose to be in on any given day, he was sure she had a bead on him.

Dwight was still awake with a fuzzy tongue and a fuzzier notion of how to piece together his world when the messenger from Baily arrived at seven thirty the next morning with a special home delivery of the *NY Spectator.* It was marked for Dwight's reading ease, as if he'd miss a story called "Does Dixon Plaza Addition Equal Uptown Housing Minus?" by none other than Jasper Christmas.

Dwight didn't wait for coffee to start his morning reading. He already knew it couldn't be good or it wouldn't have been expressed to him. Barefoot, in the rumpled pants and T-shirt he'd pulled from the pile on the floor, he perched on the spindly chair in the foyer, elbows on his knees, and scanned the piece, letting his eyes alight on key phrases, then move on when the message became too painful.

The standard history of The Dixon Group appeared, starting with King's acquisitions, which were viewed in a surprisingly positive light. He was portrayed as a buyer of real estate no one else wanted, but with a commitment to the integrity of his property, if not the rights of those who lived in it.

The piece alleged that all changed when Dwight took the helm and Manhattan property became a commodity, traded like stock, oil, or pork bellies, which gave rise to the Kidder-Dixon alliance and the Dixon Plaza project. The rendering on the page of those gleaming towers above the park taunted Dwight. They may as well have been on the moon. The article traced the slow and steady amputations that were undertaken to get the plans past various agencies and mentioned the final

Council approval, the public space to be added, the 111th Street property that had not yet been acquired. *That's it. It's over. Finito. The end.*

Dwight didn't know whom Christmas had been talking to, but whatever Dwight had tried to hide and maneuver in the name of progress was right there in ten-point Times Roman, starting with 162 building-code violations on Dixon properties in greater Harlem. *It can't be that bad. I was going to fix them.* It was such an extreme number Dwight couldn't comprehend it, and there wasn't enough money to do it all at once. It had taken so long to navigate the bureaucratic maze—longer than he could afford. He thought of Eric, and his lists and memos, but Dwight considered himself a man of vision. He'd been keeping his eyes on the prize, not the fine print.

Dwight rose slowly as he followed Christmas connecting the dots, between Dixon and Mitch at Dun-Rite Construction, which it turned out was only one of the dozen names he operated under. Mitch Branigan was involved in several major lawsuits of his own in central Florida over shoddy construction and the same defective drywall Christmas alleged was used for portions of Hudson Common.

The piece teamed Dwight with his longtime associate Councilman Gordon, highlighted their mutual back-scratching—Gordon had a history of support for luxury development in his Harlem district in general and Dixon projects in particular. Dixon returned the favor, providing thousands in campaign funds and other assistance. Funny thing was, he never really trusted Trey or liked him, but Dwight had leverage there, so he used it.

Then came the economic downturn, a concept that did not exist when Dwight peddled this project to Kidder, Theismann years ago. Real estate didn't crash in Manhattan, but Jasper documented that declining prices in Harlem, the last-in/first-out, were especially steep.

The whole time Dwight read, he felt himself sinking, going down with the ship. And it was so long since he'd been in the water, he wasn't sure if he could still swim.

At the end of the article Dwight was left standing in the overdecorated little space. He let the pages slide from his fingers. They skittered across the graphic black and white of the tile floor, and he walked off like a zombie, headed for the bar, poured a snort of vodka, neat, and knocked it back. He just wanted to be numb.

Dwight heard the wheelchair rumbling down the hall. He was convinced King could walk, he was just too lazy.

"What the hell are you doing? It's eight o'clock in the morning." King, in his robe, rolled into view. "And what is that mess?"

"The obituary, King. Read it and weep."

The article was like an open invitation to pile on, and the whole Dixon Group empire was fair game. The city came down hard on the violations in Dixon buildings, and the tabloids dubbed him the "Luxury Slumlord."

Through it all Dwight had to keep going, at least through the motions. Returning to his office was painful. The first time he saw Madeline, he wanted to melt through the floor, but she was surprisingly kind. "We all fall down. What matters is how you stand up again." He couldn't get into his office before the tears started to fall. In his whole life he had never shed so many tears as he had over the wreckage of most of what he had touched. He'd spent years acting strong, but he'd have to find more than pretense now.

It was weeks before Grace Kidder surfaced, phoned him one afternoon from the family getaway in Amagansett. "Thought I'd give you time to wallow in your unpleasantness."

"I don't have 111th Street, so the deal is off. Is that what you're calling to tell me?" Dwight was at least glad she couldn't see him, with his shaggy hair and unshaven stubble. He hadn't worn a bow tie in weeks.

"In short, yes."

"I have another proposition for you." In the moments when he'd made himself concentrate, Dwight had come up with a way to attempt to salvage much of The Dixon's Group's holdings, but it was an awful sacrifice, like cutting off a bad leg so he would have one good one to stand on.

"A proposition? Poor choice of words."

Dwight could imagine the curl of her lip, that wincing smile, and as much as he hated to admit it, he missed it. "My proposal involves selling my two, prime, Central Park lots to Kidder, Theismann." Saying it aloud was painful. So was discussing the idea with King, who'd looked as physically ill as he had in his hospital bed. But a sale would give them an infusion of capital to do necessary repairs on their other properties, including Hudson Common.

"But the climate will . . ."

Her pronouncement was as sterile and as precise as a surgeon's slice. "Uptown is over, Dwight."

"If I was going to gamble, I'd prefer Thoroughbreds. They're beautiful and I can hire someone to muck out the stalls."

A long silence expanded the space between them. "Then I guess we're done." It was not the answer he'd hoped for, but it was time for a clean break. "Good-bye, Grace." He would not have her to toy with him anymore, and hanging up felt braver than anything he'd done in a while.

➢ ➢ ➢

It took weeks for the Developer and the Dominatrix to fade from the headlines and the top-of-the-hour evening-news report. In the beginning, the prurient and the lewd details of the S&M angle dueled for column inches and coverage minutes with how greedy, reckless ambition had cost Marlon Cumberbatch the use of his legs. Then, as these things inevitably do, one day at a time, the story slipped below the fold, got tucked after the first commercial, sandwiched between a story on consumer fraud and a bank robbery. The weeklies, like the *New York Spectator* and the *Voice,* took to unveiling newer, bigger, dirtier scandals—alleged police misconduct, hospital misconduct, teacher misconduct. The torrid tale and all attendant drama surrounding the Fall of the House of Dixon slowly but surely made its way down the news food chain until it was relegated to the third page in the local-news section or "and in a follow-up to . . ." by a third-string anchor on the Saturday-morning weekly wrap-up.

For the most part, Avery watched with the dispassionate detachment of a stranger or former constituents who were just glad Dwight Dixon wasn't a part of their lives. Once Dominique and Renee left to stay with family in Atlanta, maintaining the distance between herself and Dwight got a lot easier for Avery. She had done her best to give the two as much space as they seemed to need while they were with her. She didn't press for information or try to make small talk that she knew, while meant to distract, was irrelevant and probably even annoying. Their problems were bigger than platitudes and anecdotes would cover. What they were going through was unimaginable—except situations like theirs had become so common that wives and children of disgraced public figures could probably hold a convention.

Dwight came over several times, but Renee did not leave with him and only went to her house when she knew he wouldn't be there. Renee also declined to comment, give an interview, or make a public appearance with Dwight, which made her at least look like she had sense and enough dignity left to preserve.

But ultimately she decided what was best was to get away

for a while. She made arrangements for Dominique to finish the school year with a tutor and take her final exams under a proctor's supervision.

Then in a flurry of hugs and tears, they were gone. The phone stopped ringing with reporters looking for a new slant, more dirt—whatever. Even though her guests hadn't been there long, Avery found the house without them unsettling—even more so than it already had been. Alicia came by, as did Jazz. Avery wasn't afraid or sad or lonely, but something was off. It took several days for her to realize that the rapid, though transient, population shift—rooms empty, rooms full, rooms empty again—was another reminder that life isn't static. Life moves too—all by itself. Whether you want it to or not. It's like jumping onto the moving train. You can work on strategy and planning your leap, but by the time you've got it worked out in your head, the spot you had your eye on is gone—another one is right behind it, but that one will be gone too if you don't move. Things only stay the same in your mind, so changing her mind might be the only way she would ever really go forward.

She had changed her address dozens of times, but Avery never changed, not really. She had gotten older for sure, her job description and duties had grown more complex, and she hoped her work yielded results that changed other people's lives for the better. But the truth was, everywhere she went, there she was—filling her rooms and offices with the trappings of the job, but decorating with the same stuff. Avery was convinced that each new place would be a fresh start. But each time she framed her resentments and hung them on the walls. She placed her rage on rosewood end tables. Her throw pillows were stuffed with her fury and indignation. No wonder nothing felt different. Instead of getting on the moving train, Avery had been jumping on and off an abandoned car that sat in the rail yard, wheels rusted to the track—but still expecting to end up in a new place. She also realized what she had to do to get beyond it.

Dwight.

Aside from the file photos, which now had sleazy, demeaning captions instead of the hopeful, if misdirected, praise that used to accompany them, or video of Dwight getting into a car, or leaving his lawyer's office, Avery hadn't laid eyes on him since that day in his office. When he came to talk to Renee, Avery stayed a floor away, two when she could arrange it, because she didn't want to overhear what was being said. In her own way, Avery felt sorry for Dwight. Ultimately, she decided that whatever demons had driven him to the brink, then over the edge into the secret life he was leading, had to be greater and more powerful than her own.

Deciding to go see him wasn't as obvious a conclusion.

Before she could think herself out of it, Avery left the house, locked her front door. He was close—right down the block, but so far away. Unlike her first solo walk to that house, this time no one was watching her back and no grape Popsicle reward was waiting at the other end.

She walked up the stairs and without even thinking hit the bell three short bursts—the way she used to when she was a kid. It had been their signal so Dwight would know it was her.

No answer. She pushed the bell again. He was in there. Where else would he be? Renee had told her that Dwight was social only because it served business and kept her off his case. But now, even if he had a sudden hankering for a cocktail party, invitations to wine and dine had disappeared into the ether with the first whiff of the Mistress of Nineteenth Street scandal. There was no late-night wheeling and dealing over cigars, no ball games where his presence or absence would be noticed. He had no best friend to commiserate with over a few too many brews at Londel's. Avery knew he was there. She laid on the bell again. After another minute or so, she heard shuffling, and the opening of the foyer door. The one she could hear King bellowing about closing before she or Dwight let the heat in or out—depending on the season.

But Avery was not prepared for the man who opened the door.

"Gloating from the other end of street wasn't enough?" Dwight had lost ten or maybe fifteen pounds, which on a build as slender as his was impossible to overlook. His face was drawn. Gray stubble sprouted from his chin and cheeks. What he'd lost in pounds, he had gained in years.

"That's not why I'm here. Let me in, Dwight."

He stepped back, let her pass. "If you're here to borrow a cup of sugar, I'm fresh out."

"I didn't come to borrow anything. I came to give something back."

Avery looked around. What she could see of the house was much the same as it had always been—like hers. When she was growing up, their homes, decorated by sisters, had been similar in style and feel. Whatever decor changes Renee and Dwight made over the years were minor—meant to update, freshen, not alter. There had been no clean slate here. Drapes were taupe instead of steel blue, the furniture was "new American classic" instead of "traditional American classic," and the living-room and foyer walls were no longer pale yellow, but café with extra lait. Nothing about the tasteful, gracious room would appear dated or tired to new eyes, but Avery could see the old under the new. Pentimento. And there in the middle of this elegant, polished interior stood Dwight, who looked anything but—shoulders slumped, clothes rumpled, hands loose at his sides, the right one clutching a remote control instead of his cell phone. Avery saw that despite what she thought, he hadn't really moved on either. This was still Wilhelmina and King's house. Dwight was as stuck in the past as she was, trying to surpass his father, build something bigger, all the while finding a way to keep himself tortured. His history hung around his neck like a noose.

"You don't have anything of mine—at least nothing I want." He closed the front door, wandered toward the living room.

"Maybe not. But I have to say this anyway, and you can do with it what you choose." Avery stayed in the hall, but she could hear a TV on upstairs.

"Speak your piece, Avery. I got nothing but time." Dwight leaned against the fretwork archway.

"First, you know when I decided not to sell you 111th Street, it was because of your involvement with Trey—Chester. But I've changed my mind. Not about selling. But now I have a much better reason than being mad at you. I'm not going to disrupt all those people's lives—for money I don't need? For progress that won't include them? I won't do it. And second, I'm done being mad at you, Dwight. Finished. It's over. It happened a long time ago and I've held on to it—I don't know, like it was a life raft. But I realized it was just the opposite. Holding on to the thing that's pulling you under doesn't save you. Twenty plus years and I'm still doing the same damn thing. I have to rescue myself."

"So after all this time you've decided to forgive me for—"

"This is not about forgiving, Dwight. And honestly, it's not about you either. This is about me." She took a few steps toward him. "And while my motives may be selfish, I hope you might get something out of it too. But that's up to you." Avery shrugged. "*I* have to let go of the anger and resentment I've been dragging around the globe without even knowing it."

"Thanks so much for stopping by to let me off the hook for being a punk back then. Can't tell you what a relief that is.

Whew. Don't know how I got this far without your forgiveness or nonforgiveness or whatever you want to call it." Dwight went over to the stairs, sank to the bottom step, so low his long, spindly legs angled like a grasshopper's, his hands draped loosely over his knees.

"Stop being such a baby. What you did was wrong. I know it. You know it. And nothing will ever change what's already happened. But I've decided to change how I've been handling it. And from the looks of things, I'm thinking maybe it's time you did too." Avery fought the urge to put her hands on her hips or fold her arms across her chest, so she walked across the foyer and took the place Dwight had just abandoned. "I'm not saying that's the only reason your life is so screwed up now."

"Whatever, Avery. I don't have time for analysis at the moment—money either." He tapped his knee with the remote.

"My mother knew something terrible was wrong with you—and me—she just didn't know what to do about it. She loved you and was kind to you because she knew you needed someone to do that, no matter what. She knew your father and she'd grown up with your mother. So Mom did the best she could with what she had to work with." Avery walked over, stood in front of Dwight. "She didn't know what happened between us, what happened to me, but she never stopped asking me what was wrong. And I didn't tell her because Daddy said not to? How long has he been dead? How long has your mother? And King? I don't think he's ever gonna die. Too ornery. But we can't let all that stuff keep us in this place, Dwight. Or at least I can't." She sat next to him on the step. He drew himself up tighter. "Every time I'd think I was getting a new start in a new place, it never happened. So I'd stick it out for a couple of years, then pack up and try it all over again. I haven't been on the track in ages, but I never stopped running. And it's taken me all this time to see this race doesn't have a finish line. That the farther I run is just the farther I run. Period. That's it. No trophy, no 'Atta girl.' I've given myself plenty of points for endurance, but that's not enough anymore."

"Nice metaphor, Avery. Poetic. Deep, even. You learn to talk that way in diplomat school?" Dwight got up. The remote clattered to floor. "But I'm not the runner in the family. And in case it somehow escaped you, my whole life has turned into shit." He kicked the remote aside, leaned against the railing post. "My family is gone, my company is in shambles, my reputation is shot, my personal business is public fodder, I'm the subject of party jokes, I'm being sued by every third person I know—and on top of that, I'm broke. I own a house I can barely pay the taxes on. And everything else I own, along with King and several of the country's banks, is mortgaged, leveraged to degrees I didn't realize would sink me." Dwight left Avery at the stairs and started to pace the hall. "And this is the time you decide to mosey down the block and say, 'Let's put bygones aside and be friends again'?! Are you fucking kidding?!" Dwight's voice had risen to a yell. "There is no me. I'm done. So in the grand scheme, in the ebb and flow of life as we know it on this speck in the universe—see, I can be poetic too—what does it really matter how 'we' feel?"

They eyed each other a long moment before Avery spoke. "I didn't think it mattered either. But now I know it does. That's the key. Figuring out what matters. And feelings do. That's why we have them." Avery didn't raise her voice. "I don't know if we'll ever be friends again. I'm not ready for huggy-kissy either. But I don't want us to be enemies. There isn't enough time." She smiled. He didn't. "And I'm not hauling this crap into another decade. I keep burning bridges. And I guess my toes had to be smoking for me to see that if I don't stop, I'm going to destroy the one I need to cross—the one that will take me home. I'm standing on it right now."

"What do you want *me* to do? Hand you a fire extinguisher?"

What you do is on you. I can't make you do anything. But you can't stay holed up in here forever. Or are you going to become one of those people who never leave their houses and die surrounded by fifty years' worth of pizza boxes and newspapers?" Avery got up. "I'm not going to get in your business with Renee, that's husband-wife stuff, but I will tell you that your daughter loves you and she needs you. For lots of reasons. But the main one is to do the right thing by her. You can't be the first man who lets her down. It's a really bad precedent, one she'll struggle with for a long time, maybe her whole life."

"Avery, I don't even know—" Dwight shook his head. He looked even more dazed than he did when she arrived.

"Don't say anything. Just think about what I said." She opened the door. "And I don't know if it will 'matter,' but I may have somebody who might be interested in helping you find a way out of the Central Park North mess. I had a long talk with him at a dinner a few weeks ago—a music producer who surprisingly enough was friends with Mom. He was at the funeral too, maybe you—"

"Ty Washington?" Dwight snorted. "I'm the last person he'll help. We have history and it's not good."

"Kind of a theme, isn't it? But from our conversation, whatever it was, doesn't seem like an issue with him. He wanted you to be successful because for him it's about building community. I thought it was worth a mention."

"Yeah, well, thanks."

Avery could feel it was time to go. She wasn't sure if this talk made any difference or was just more words added to the noise. But at least she wouldn't regret not having said it.

"Take care of yourself, Dwight."

EPILOGUE

. . . full to the brim of future

Eighteen months later

"Think it's okay if we show up together?" Avery wrapped a towel around herself like a sarong.

"I don't know, it may be the talk of the town. 'What Manhattan real estate mogul was seen at the groundbreaking for Harlem Plaza, Ty Washington's new uptown development with'—who was she with?" Jazz selected a tie from the rack on the closet door—pale yellow dotted with tiny red biplanes piloted by a chicken.

"*Mogul.* You're very funny. *Landlady* is more like it. Did I tell you the new laundry room is a huge hit?"

"Had to be—not having to haul your dirty duds to the neighborhood Wash-o-rama? Priceless." He wrapped, looped, and made the last pull through on the tie. "Tell you what, landlady, I can drop you on the corner. Then you can show up all by yourself." Jazz jiggled the knot, walked across the bedroom. "All you have to worry about is being on time, and with you standing there in that towel, we might be in trouble." He scooped her into his arms.

"I wouldn't necessarily call it trouble, but—" Avery wriggled away. "I'm removing temptation. And thanks for not choosing the one with the astronaut bunnies on it." She tugged the end of his tie. Jazz didn't wear them often, but from time to time it was unavoidable. So he had a collection that was quietly unusual. You had to look closely to see the bucktooth dinosaur or the little red wagons, and this small anti-establishment irreverence made him happy.

"You're welcome. I know you hate it." Jazz took his suit jacket from the hanger. "And I am going to restrain myself, not because I want to, but because it's the right thing to do."

"That's what I love about you." Avery disappeared back into the bathroom. "You're a real do-right kinda guy. And you know, I really believe Ty is too."

"Thank you, ma'am. Nice of you to say so—even if you did have to add another guy into the compliment. But can't argue with your assessment. And this is a concrete example, pun intended, of putting your money where your heart is—not his mouth because he's definitely quiet about what he does—but today warranted some noise. I'll make coffee. We can take it in the car."

"Be down in five minutes," Avery called from closet. She didn't keep many things at Jazz's house—or the place in SoHo for that matter. After all, it wasn't like they were living together. But at times, especially now with all the chaos going on at her place, it was nice to have options—without planning. But today was definitely planned, and she had brought her suit when they drove down to New Jersey on Friday.

They had spent the weekend puttering. Jazz worked in the garden awhile, clearing away the dregs of winter so it would be ready to plant in a few weeks when spring was official. They'd gone to an Amish market a few towns away and gotten steaks, which he grilled outside in the rain because he said they'd taste better. They made love instead of watching the movie they put in the DVD player—twice—and had fallen asleep in each other's arms surrounded by the Sunday papers. A perfect weekend.

This morning was sunny, bright, and full to the brim of future. It had been two years since her plane landed at JFK and she walked into a cold, rainy night and the course of her carefully crafted life changed in ways she could never have anticipated.

But from the moment she received the invitation to the groundbreaking for Harlem Plaza, Avery felt the timing was poetic, something Ty Washington could not have known when he told her he wanted to announce an intern partnership program between Ladies First/Gentleman Foremost and Big Bang Entertainment, and that it would be named for her mother. It was one of those cosmic confluences that made her smile.

Like her deciding to stay in New York.

Jazz parked the car in a no-parking zone on Frederick Douglass, slipped his press placard in the front window, and hand in hand they walked down the block.

Even before Dwight's dream of empire disintegrated and Ty stepped in, Avery had been leaning toward not returning to New Zealand. The two things had both a little and a lot do with each other. She had built a career, but not a life, and she felt she was in one of those now-or-never moments. So, after six months away, even before she called her job, she called Van, let him know about her change of plan, and ended their relationship. He was courteous, wished her well, didn't try to change her mind. Avery didn't mention Jazz. He wasn't a replacement. She felt Jazz helped her toward the happiness her mother's letter wished for her.

Avery reread her mother's unfinished letter a hundred times—with each reading she shed a few more tears, until she was done with the sadness and the sorry for what had been unsaid. Eventually she revisited the Reggie correspondence. But after the third note she felt wrong, like she was invading her mother's privacy. Yes, she was gone, but Mr. Bishop was not. So Avery called, invited him to lunch at "21" because she knew it was one of her mother's favorite restaurants, and presented him with the bundle, ribbon and all. His eyes welled, but he maintained his composure. He thanked her profusely, said he would keep them with the ones Forestina had sent him and cherish them always. When Reggie talked about Tina, Avery could feel the love, knew it was real in a way she never felt about her parents' relationship, and by the end, they had planned to lunch again.

When she really thought about it, listened to her heart and not just her head, the choice to stay wasn't difficult at all. She had friends, old and new, who welcomed her into their lives. She had enough time in with the State Department to qualify for retirement benefits when she reached the right age. She could have enough involvement with the building on 111th Street to give her a sense of purpose and responsibility, enough money to allow her time to figure out how to build that life she had been missing. She even had a place to live—albeit one currently in the throes of renovation. Avery had seriously considered Alicia's question "How would you make it you?" She thought about Jazz's need to start from scratch. Seeing Dwight living in his parents' house was the final straw. Avery met with a few architects and interior designers, looked at other row-house redos, and made up her mind. She would make the place the same on the outside, brand-new and contemporary on the inside.

"Hey!" Alicia met them at the corner. She had just come from LiLi, her soon-to-be-open boutique. "Hope you're ready for another party. Two weeks till the grand opening! It is going to be fabulous. Regina is planning it—Ty's Regina—did you know she was a party promoter back in the day? That's how they met." Alicia looped her arm through Avery's while Jazz held on to the other. "An-y-way, she has been amazing. Her ideas are just—well, wait till you see—Hollywood comes to Harlem—in the most sophisticated way of course."

Two blocks of Central Park North had been closed to traffic, and before they reached the VIP area, Alicia spotted someone she "had" to talk to and disappeared.

"Nobody like her on the planet." Avery had to shake her head and grin.

"I don't know if the planet could handle more than one."

Avery and Jazz threaded through the crowd toward the official viewing platform. Behind the stage was a billboard-size rendering of Harlem Plaza, which would integrate the existing building into a new mixed-use, two-tower structure that would house Big Bang Entertainment's headquarters, offices, and two restaurants, in addition to moderate-income housing. Harlem Plaza was not the glittering Mount Olympus, home to titans and goddesses, that Dwight had envisioned. But it was smart, sophisticated, modern, and attainable. New and old came together to make a better place where real people could live and work and play.

While Jazz spoke to a young man with a clipboard, Avery scanned the crowd.

On the heels of the scandal, King started spending months at a time in Hawaii with Barbara, and now he was in Oahu more than in New York. No one missed him. She knew Dwight wouldn't be there, but somehow it seemed he should be. The sale of the CPN property to Ty helped, and even though

Delilah-gate didn't result in any criminal charges against him, Dwight's legal bills were mounting. None of the lawsuits had gone to trial or come close to settling, so Dwight still needed money. He had put his house on the market, moved into a small apartment in one of the buildings he still owned, and taken a consulting job that put him in Atlanta for two weeks each month so he could be part of Diqui's life. Avery got most of her news from Renee, who had settled nicely into her new life and gone back to her profession as a CPA. They still hadn't divorced. Renee wasn't sure if that fence could come down. Time would tell. Avery had planned a trip to see them after Alicia's opening.

Avery and Dwight hadn't fully mended their rift and still didn't speak often. The only time in years she'd heard him sound positively gleeful was when he spoke of the collapse of Grace Kidder's Dubai deal after Dubai World gorged itself on corporate debt and choked, losing Kidder Theismann a wad of development money. "Couldn't have happened to a better bitch," was how he'd put it. It was the closest Dwight came to adding some sweet to the bitter taste Grace had left in his mouth.

"Your seats are right over there." Jazz pointed to the right of the dais. "Avery Lyons and guest. Now if you're still concerned, I can go hang out with the press. They won't be embarrassed to be seen with me."

"Stop. I was being silly this morning." Avery took his hand. "I'm very happy to be seen with you, Mr. Christmas."

Shortly after Avery and Jazz took their seats, the dignitaries and official contingent, which included Pastor Phil Ewing, Eric Wallace, formerly of the Dixon Group, who would be general contractor for the project, and various representatives of state and city government, filed onto the stage. Chester Gordon had been turned out of office. Nedra Cortes, the new councilwoman, was bright in a tropical print and greeting everyone within two feet of her. Courtesy of the special brand of magic that is the music business, one of Ty's artists took center stage, and the air filled with the sound of an orchestra playing the national anthem. Everyone stood and remained standing as "Lift Every Voice and Sing" floated across the street and over the fourth and final facet of New York's emerald, Central Park. Pastor Phil offered a prayer. Then the speeches and proclamations started.

Jazz leaned over to her. "How are you doing?"

"You know, when I got here two years ago, it felt like I was opening Pandora's box," Avery whispered to Jazz. "I couldn't handle all the stuff that poured out. So I slammed the lid shut, just like she did."

Jazz squeezed her hand. Eric stood at the podium and began his introduction of Ty.

"But I had no idea how the story ended, so I found a copy and reread it. All people remember is the mess she created because she was curious. They don't realize she opened the box again. And there was one thing left inside."

Ty took the stage, the new rendering of Harlem Plaza rising in the sunlight behind him.

"I know," Jazz leaned over and kissed Avery.

"Hope."

Dear Reader,

Place in a novel is geographical, but it's also emotional—a feeling you get that reminds you of home, a vacation, a longing, a cherished memory—or a forgotten one. The setting may have an irresistible lure that calls us back—the excitement of New York, the romance of Paris, the mystery of New Orleans. Or maybe, like for Avery, the pull is about unfinished business . . .

Harlem has made appearances, brief or lengthy, in *Tryin' to Sleep in the Bed You Made, Better Than I Know Myself,* and *Gotta Keep on Tryin'*. Neither of us lives there, though Donna's mom told many stories of growing up on 143rd Street and Seventh Avenue—now Adam Clayton Powell Jr. Boulevard—and Virginia's first New York digs were the 5D shared by Carmen, Jewell, and Regina, the young women of *Better Than I Know Myself,* on 110th, now called Central Park North, where we located Dixon Plaza.

Harlem is definitely physical and emotional. It is steeped in history, legend, culture, and magic. It is a state of mind that also occupies a prime location adjacent to some of the priciest real estate on the planet. How do you value that—in dollars, or is there an intangible worth that is even higher? Who gets to make that determination? Given today's real estate roller coaster, we felt it was a perfect place to explore the conflict.

Those fifty or so blocks south of the Bronx and north of Central Park, have their own vibrant life force. And like all things that are alive, it has to change and adapt, while retaining its essence and uniqueness, in order to survive. Evolution is not fast or easy, but Harlem is a survivor. It called us and we answered, not with what is intended to be the definitive, Uptown tale. We would never be so presumptuous as to try and lay claim on a place that declared it's freedom to define itself, make it's own rules, and sing it's own song, decades before we ever set fingers to keyboard. The Uptown of our saga is one of countless thousands—past, present and future.

By now you know we also brought back some characters from the past whose business was not done—at least according to you. The misters Dixon were deliciously full of story still to be told, and in need of a good whupping, so we were happy to resurrect them. We are aware we didn't leave Dwight dead or in jail—which may not be enough to satisfy those of you who are still mad at the way he treated Jewell, but sometimes the best punishment, and the best lesson, is having to sleep in the bed you made.

Thanks for still caring, and going where we go. We hope you enjoyed your visit. We know we did.

Sending you a heartfelt, double-hug!

Virginia Donna

deberryandgrant@gmail.com
http://deberryandgrant.com
http://facebook.com/deberryandgrant
http://twitter.com/deberryandgrant
http://twomindsfull.blogspot.com
http://myspace.com/twomindsfull

DeBerry & Grant
PO Box 5224
Kendall Park, NJ 08824

P.S. We enjoy meeting you so please check our website for our travel schedule, and updates on movie news.

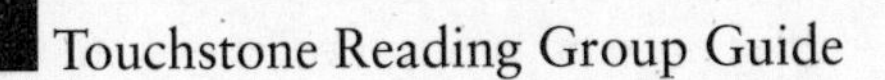

Touchstone Reading Group Guide

UPTOWN

Bestselling authors Virginia DeBerry and Donna Grant are back with a tale of scandal, sex, ambition, betrayal, greed, and politics. Set in the high-power, high-stakes world of Manhattan real estate, *Uptown* delves into the complex lives of a wealthy and aristocratic African-American family in Harlem. In the center of the story are Avery Lyons and Dwight Dixon, first cousins who grew up as close as brother and sister, but whose relationship was irreparably damaged by the devastating aftermath of one terrible night. When they must finally face each other after years of silence, family bonds are stretched to the breaking point.

For Discussion

1. We first meet Dwight in the prologue as he is announcing the construction of Dixon Plaza at a high-profile press conference. Dwight has to face a large crowd of protesters. Before you knew how he behaved after the incident at Brown, did you sympathize with Dwight? How did your perspective change after you read about the incident at Brown?
2. In descriptions of Avery, it becomes evident that she has issues with closeness. Her job keeps her moving before she can get attached to any person or place. When she first sees her mother in the hospital room, Avery "handle[d] the scene as a movie—a spectacle she could observe from a safe distance, no interaction, please." With her formerly close friend, Avery admits she "had pushed Alicia away from her life—and had done a pretty good job of keeping her out there." However, Avery does not think of

herself as alone: "she was a solo, not a solitary. It was a choice. She could add other voices or companion travelers any time she chose." Do you think Avery was really alone? Why is she so uncomfortable with close relationships?

3. Dwight seems to prefer fantasy to real life. He wishes for a "magic BlackBerry—one without a dozen snarling messages from King, and insipid reminders from his wife to stop for flowers . . . or another condescending bulletin from Grace Kidder . . ." When preparing for a public appearance, he puts on a silk tie, "the last step in donning his armor." When confronted with the many safety problems with the Dixon buildings, he "couldn't have this problem," as if it could be wished away. Finally, he has a private fantasy life with Miss Delilah. Do you think Dwight can separate fantasy from reality? Does his fantasy life help or hinder him?
4. Soon after Avery lands in New York, she thinks she is "over the wishbone after Thanksgiving dinner, faded Polaroids, click your heels together, no place like home feeling . . . she'd just as soon reside elsewhere." When she actually reenters her childhood home for the first time in years, she thinks, "this was the box and she felt like Pandora." What is Avery's idea of home? Does it change over the course of the book? How does Jazz influence her idea of home?
5. Avery has a strong aversion to the airplane food coming to New York. A fruit run led to the accident that killed Forestina and injured King; when Avery first enters the hospital, she is met with the lingering "smell of canned string beans and cold gravy." Are negative connotations of food tied into negative connotations of home for Avery? How are these reactions to food different from the meals she later shares with Jazz?
6. Both Dwight and Avery address the notion of survival. As Dwight traveled to the hospital, "he let the cold air brace him for whatever the hospital would bring. Not exactly Navy Seal training, but survival was survival, and Dwight worked with what he had." Avery's take on survival seems more about blocking things out, or creating a sense of distance: "usually Avery

could press on through distraction, boredom, temptation and pain. Suck it up and drive on—her father taught her that when she was a little girl—and reinforced it regularly." Are there similarities in the ways Avery and Dwight try to "survive" their situations in the book? Differences?

7. Avery never tells her mother what happened that fateful night at Brown. Do you think, by the end of the story, she accepts what happened?
8. What personality traits does Dwight share with his father, King? Does Dwight aspire to be like him, or to be different? Does he expect to be more successful than King?
9. In contemplating Avery's relationship with her parents, "as a kid she used to look for similarities to connect her to these two people who made her, but she came up empty." Avery is not particularly close to either parent and she ultimately learns something shocking about each: her seemingly cold and ultra-strict father regularly helped his tenants, and her mother had an affair starting well before her husband's death. How did these discoveries affect her memories of each parent? Does she share any qualities with her parents?
10. Dwight visits Miss Delilah to be humiliated in order to become stronger and better able to handle his life. As described in the book, "Dwight could feel himself growing stronger with every insult she hurled." Why else might Dwight seek out her verbal abuse? Dwight experiences humiliation from his father and other situations in his life—why does he only get pleasure from Miss Delilah? Later, when Renee finds the marks on Dwight's chest, he first asks himself, "how did I forget?" He then asks, "why did I forget?" Did Dwight *want* to get caught?
11. Avery ultimately accepts the fact that forgiving Dwight is the only way she can get beyond her past, which has been like a prison for her for years. Did her confrontation achieve that for Avery? What, if anything, did it achieve for Dwight?
12. What do you see in Avery's future? What do you see in Dwight's?

A Conversation with Virginia DeBerry & Donna Grant

***Uptown* is a departure for you both: many of your other novels have a much lighter tone and are centered around one or two strong female characters and their relationships. Why and how did you decide to take this new direction? Was the experience of writing *Uptown* significantly different than your previous works?**

We enjoy stretching ourselves in our writing—working a new muscle group. For example, *What Doesn't Kill You,* our last novel, was our first attempt at writing in first person. We had a ball and will undoubtedly do it again—hopefully with Tee. Readers got her, and she has much more to say. And just as with Tee's economic woes, we wanted to be ripped-from-the-headlines current. The real estate bubble—mortgages, foreclosures, speculation, bankrupt developers—has been all over the news and affects lots of us, and Harlem properties were hot. When we were hatching a story about secrets, wounds, and a family real estate business rooted in Harlem, we realized we had already created the Dixons for *Better Than I Know Myself* and that their moment was now. So this time the men came first, definitely unusual for us.

The cold, manipulative Dwight and the overbearing King made a strong impression with readers and they were juicy for us to write. Dwight needed a foil—a female character with Dixon family history. We had already introduced Aunt Forestina when we met Dwight and King. That gave us the opportunity to bring her daughter, Avery, into the picture. Once we came up with Avery and her self-imposed isolation from her family, we knew she had to have a friend to bring her out, someone she could talk to, someone who knew her before she withdrew. That's when Alicia appeared, just when we needed her.

We wrote *Uptown* pretty much the way we always do. Whether it's the doll business in *Gotta Keep on Tryin'* or the cosmetics business in *WDKY,* we always research our background subject. In the case of *Uptown*, that was Manhattan real estate development—not an area we knew much about.

Then we develop our characters. Both Avery and Dwight have deeply layered personalities. What you see on the outside is not who they really are, and we needed to create each buried level in the way it might have occurred naturally, then place the next on top—so we could then have the characters reverse the process as they maneuvered through the story which took place in a few months, but really covered many years of family history.

Once the pieces are in place, we get down to the real nitty gritty, telling the story.

How do you think your fans will react to this departure?

As always, we hope our readers enjoy *Uptown* and that the story keeps them needing to turn the pages to find out what happens next. Our male characters have always gotten a lot of attention—either because people want to know if they're real and have an available brother, like Marcus and Ron (we hope Jazz has joined that crew), or because they can't stand them and want to see them get what they've got coming, like Dwight and Ramsey. The rest is about coming along for the ride. We do our best to craft a good story, with compelling characters. In the end we hope readers feel satisfied and get something they can carry with them.

You have written as a critically acclaimed and bestselling team for years. Are there any particular challenges or rewards that you face as a team, rather than writing solo? What is your writing process like?

The greatest challenge we think is that with two of us it does not, as some have assumed, mean we write twice as fast. Actually, it is the opposite. Our writing and editing process happens simultaneously which is good and bad. Good because mostly when we're done, the first draft has been redrafted so many times already, it's pretty much the finished product. Bad because it does take so much time and unlike other teams, we need to be physically in the same place—no e-mailing chapters back and forth for us. So while we are writing, we end up checking out of our personal lives for long stretches of time. Because Virginia lives alone, Donna stops being a city girl for a while and moves to her "country home" in New Jersey where our rhythm is whatever we choose for it to be. Days start and end according to a schedule that is totally of our making. We don't divide the book by chapter or character—we really do write together, side by side at one desk—check out our video at http://simonandschuster.com. And at the end of a book, we have written and re-written every single word—together.

You have a wonderful and very active website. Especially entertaining are the photos you post in the gallery, including one when you met with President Barack Obama. Can you describe that experience of meeting him?

We had the good fortune and honor to meet Barack Obama at a private reception during a fundraiser prior to his election as the 44th President of the United States of America. In person, Mr. Obama was present, sincere, funny, smart—all the qualities we had seen on TV. We've met a number of important, influential people of all stripes—actors, singers, governors, senators—and we can usually feel the "spin," tell when we are talking to the persona and not the person. But with the President, there was no posturing, no pat political clichés. We had a genuine conversation, mostly about the books we've written (he was interested as a fellow author) and our relationship with the mutual friends who had invited us to the event. We were truly taken with how relaxed he was in such a high-pressured situation. After our meeting we were both convinced that he was the real deal and more committed than ever to doing our part to help get him elected. And now that Mr. Obama has taken office, we are working to answer his call to service.

Through your website or at your many book and speaking events, do your fans ever share their own stories with you? Do any of these stories (or aspects of them) work their way into your books?

Yes, readers often share their stories and experiences with us—not only at events, but also through e-mail. Most of the things they share

are about how situations and/or circumstances we wrote about mirror similar incidents in their lives. They will often say "You wrote about my life!" "How did you know?" "You two must have been following me!" Of course we did not really write about them or their lives—we make our stories up—they are fiction—*really!* But over the years these kinds of comments have proven to us that nothing we make up is too far out of the norm for readers to connect or identify with. Most importantly these reactions remind us that most of the challenges we struggle with in our lives are universal and that we all, to some degree, feel better because of that connection, the feeling that we are not alone.

Do either of you have experiences in real estate that helped influence *Uptown*?

No, not really. The influence was more about connections to neighborhoods in New York that were changing radically. We had no real estate moguls in our families though Virginia's first New York apartment was on the 110th Street block we write about in *Uptown* and once upon a time she worked for a real estate law firm. Donna's Mom grew up in a walk-up on 143rd St and Seventh Avenue. The family maintained connections to the area even after they moved. Donna has memories of going with her mom to Miss Helen's beauty shop around the corner for a press and curl. Or making rounds uptown with Grandma. Donna would sit on a barstool sipping Coca-Cola with extra cherries while her grandmother caught up on the neighborhood news—but that is a story for another day.

What do you see happening to Avery and Dwight after the end of the story?

We did leave them both with a lot on their plates. We like to bring our characters through the mess we made of their lives and point them toward a new beginning. After that, they're on their own to take the next steps—unless you want to know more. So, if you want to know how Avery adjusts to her life back at home, how her relationship with Jazz progresses, if Dwight picks up the pieces of his life or becomes a bitter, vindictive man, let us know.

Here you brought back King and Dwight Dixon from *Better Than I Know Myself*. Do you have plans to write a sequel to *Uptown*? If not, will some of these characters show up in future stories?

We have a habit of slipping characters from one book into another. Sometimes they are mentioned by name, other times just by profession and a description. There have even been a few readers who have discovered our predilection (hope you enjoyed a glimpse of what Ty and Regina are up to)! But if we've already "invented" a doctor or photographer and need one in the book we are working on, if the timeline fits, we borrow them without hesitation. We also have a practice of giving even minor characters a pretty detailed backstory, so there is always more to them than is revealed in the book where they first make an appearance (Alicia certainly has more stories to tell). *Gotta Keep on Tryin'* is our only sequel and *Uptown* is our first experience spinning characters off—though we have thought about it as a possibility for several other characters. We're not saying yes or no—we just have to wait and see how *Uptown* does—how readers like it before we contemplate a sequel. But if we need a diplomat turned real estate queen, an investigative reporter, an owner of a fancy uptown boutique, or even a dominatrix—who knows?!

What would you most like readers to take away from this story?

Well, there are a few things. Virginia's grandmother had a saying—"There's more room out than in." She meant that if an event or situation is gnawing at you, changing who you are and how you live your life, you need to find a way to get it out, talk about it, cry about it, whatever it takes. Avery's life was altered by keeping a painful secret. So was Dwight's and ultimately the pain he inflicts on himself costs him. Alicia, on the other hand, is pretty much the opposite. She says what she feels, deals with the consequences, and goes on without the burden of the misunderstandings and anger caused by not revealing the truth.

We are also in a time when success is often measure purely in terms of money. Whomever has the most wins, no matter what they did to get it—cheat, lie, or put others in danger. Is that really what we feel makes someone successful? Is it okay to turn whole neighborhoods and people's lives upside-down to turn a profit? Does ownership grant you the right to do what you want? We wanted to raise the questions and give folks a chance to think about how they feel.

What are you working on now?

We've been checking out the headlines again. This time we're doing research on a subject that effects about two thirds of Americans, and it's a subject we know *lots* about from personal experience. We'll keep you posted.

Enhance Your Book Club

1. Check out the authors' website, www.DeBerryandGrant.com. Sign their guestbook as a group and tell them about your book club discussion! Keep tabs on what the authors are up to on their blog, www.TwoMindsFull.blogspot.com.
2. Learn more about the complex and rich history of Harlem using an online search engine or searching your local library. Use an online mapping program, such as GoogleEarth, to locate the area where Dixon Plaza was planned.
3. Bring a bottle of Barolo to your discussion to share with the group—it helped get the conversation flowing with Avery and Jazz!
4. *Uptown* brings back two characters from the earlier novel *Better Than I Know Myself*. Read this book to get a better background on these fascinating characters. Also, check out other DeBerry and Grant books like *Gotta Keep on Tryin'*, *Tryin' to Sleep in the Bed You Made,* and *What Doesn't Kill You.* Visit www.SimonandSchuster.com for more information.

MORE FROM
VIRGINIA DEBERRY
AND
DONNA GRANT!
From the bestselling authors of Tryin' to Sleep in the Bed You Made
Gotta Keep on Tryin'
~ A Novel ~
VIRGINIA DEBERRY DONNA GRANT
From the bestselling authors of Gotta Keep on Tryin'
What Doesn't Kill You
A Novel
VIRGINIA DEBERRY DONNA GRANT
TOUCHSTONE
A Division of Simon & Schuster
A CBS COMPANY
AVAILABLE WHEREVER BOOKS ARE SOLD OR AT
WWW.SIMONANDSCHUSTER.COM